The Burnt District

Ellen Gray Massey

Hard Shell Word Factory

Dedicated to the memory of my brother,
Vernon Gray 1917-1975

© 2001, Ellen Gray Massey

ISBN: 0-7599-0143-0
Trade Paperback
Published May 2001

Ebook ISBN: 1-58200-653-9
Published February 2001

Hard Shell Word Factory
PO Box 161
Amherst Jct. WI 54407
books@hardshell.com
http://www.hardshell.com
Cover art © 2001, Mary Z. Wolf

Introduction
General Order No. 11

Headquarters District of the Border
Kansas City, Mo., August 25, 1863

FIRST—All persons living in Cass, Jackson and Bates Counties, Missouri, and in part of Vernon [north of the Osage River]...are hereby ordered to remove from their present places of residence within fifteen days from the date hereof.

Those who, within that time, establish their loyalty to the satisfaction of the commanding officer of the military station nearest their present place of residence, will receive from him certificates stating the fact of their loyalty... All who receive such certificate will be permitted to remove to any military station in this district, or to any part of the State of Kansas, except the counties on the eastern borders of the State. All others shall remove out of this district. Officers commanding companies and detachments serving in the counties named will see that this paragraph is promptly obeyed.

Second—All grain and hay in the field, or under shelter, in the district...after the 9th day of September next, will be taken to such stations and turned over to the proper officer there...All grain and hay found in such district not convenient to such stations will be destroyed.

By order of Brigadier-General Ewing:
H. Hannahs, Adjutant.

Although Missouri as a border state was divided in its sympathies about the slavery issue, it did not secede from the Union. However, because the Bushwhacker/Jayhawker raids on the Missouri-Kansas border when Kansas was seeking statehood were continuing during the Civil War, the Union Army officials stationed in Missouri considered every citizen an enemy even though the state sent almost three times more soldiers to the Union Army than to the Confederate forces. Within the district designated by this Order, property was confiscated without restitution, the whole area was burned, and regardless of their loyalties, all persons who did not leave in the proscribed fifteen days were treated as prisoners of war. Prairie fires scorched the land, so that it became known as the Burnt District.

Though the characters in this novel are fictional, happenings similar to these experienced by the Rockfort and Kerrigan families occurred from 1856 to 1864 in northern Vernon County.

Chapter 1

"MAMA, MAMA!" Leah called frantically.

Hannah quickly pushed the pan of bread back into the oven and motioning Dolly to watch it, hurried from the hot, yeasty-smelling kitchen. She grabbed the door frame to keep her balance as the cat dashed out between her feet. Hastily, she tucked a loose strand of hair back under the heavy braids circling her head. Before she made two strides onto the porch, the long brown strand fell down partially covering her worried face.

Because Hannah's eleven-year-old daughter was looking back over her shoulder as she flew up the porch steps two at a time, she collided with her mother. Breathless and sweaty from her run, her long brown pigtails under her sunbonnet bouncing against her back and shoulders, Leah grabbed her mother's arm and pointed back the way she had come. Her little dog who had been sleeping on the porch, jumped up, yipping excitedly. The calico cat meowed once and disappeared under the house.

"Quiet, Poco," Hannah ordered. The wiry dog ignored her as he raced back and forth in front of them, his high-pitched bark broadcasting their presence. Leah picked him up in her arms caressing and hushing him. With the sudden attention, he wiggled in delight and thumped his skinny tail against her side.

"What is it, Leah?" Hannah asked.

For answer Leah again pointed north up the grassy trail through the waist-high prairie grasses.

Hannah heard the beat of marching men before she spied the blue-coated leader cresting the rise in the prairie. He was holding back his spirited bay horse to avoid out-distancing the men who followed him.

"Put Poco in the cellar," Hannah said. Though struck with panic, she kept an unflappable demeanor.

Leah nodded and pried open the slanted wooden door that led under the house just to the right of the porch. "Please, Poco," she said, patting his head, "be quiet."

In the moment Hannah stood watching, there appeared over the mound within half a mile of her, an infantry company, flanked by at least a dozen men on horseback.

Hannah gasped. Too late to hide or flee. The leader spotted her and signaled the horsemen to spread out and surround the buildings. With so many soldiers, protecting the house was impossible.

Though her mind was working rapidly to find a way out of this threat, Hannah called calmly over her shoulder to her two younger daughters, "Dolly, Mazie, come here quick." She turned her head for her voice to carry into the house, but she did not lose sight of the intruders—the short leader sitting his horse as if he were Napoleon, the irregular ranks behind him, or the cavalrymen who were already trotting into position around her.

Silently the little girls flew to their mother just as Leah returned.

"Who are they?" Leah whispered, though the soldiers were still too far away to hear her.

Hannah waited until they were close enough for her to be sure of their identity. "Some of the Second Kansas Volunteers and some infantry. Probably from Fort Scott." Her voice was composed as if soldiers marched over her land daily, yet each word sounded like a death knell.

"You said they wouldn't..."

The sound of the wind through the grasses was blocked out by the rhythmic beat of the horses and foot soldiers. The normal noises of insects and meadow birds were replaced by the creak of saddle leather and an occasional snort of a horse.

Hannah put her arm over Leah's shoulder and drew her closer. "I didn't think they would come this far south. Too close to the river. They're probably just patrolling the Kansas border for bushwhackers."

Hannah's calming words didn't fool any of them. They knew that the soldiers were not here in this western Missouri region to seek out the Confederate guerrillas who might be hiding between their frequent raids against the Union forces in Kansas. Even the youngest child could see that the soldiers' movements and expressions were not protective, but cautious, guarded, and hostile toward them. They were the targets of this raid. Poco's lunges against the cellar door and his muffled barks increased their anxiety.

Leah voiced the fear in all of them. "It's that Order Number Eleven, isn't it?"

Her sisters grabbed their mother's skirt and half hid behind her. They were old enough to understand what that was. They had read the military announcements prominently posted at every crossroads.

"Will they take us away?" the youngest asked.

"I don't know, Mazie," her mother said. She clenched her teeth to hold back a sob. Two of the mounted soldiers rode past the house. They held their rifles ready as they slowly entered the barnyard. One constantly eyed the woman and girls on the porch as the other surveyed the area for hidden snipers.

"And will they burn our house like they did all those in Nevada City and in Bates County?" The middle girl was watching the flanking riders that had galloped wide around the homestead buildings and were now closing in. They stopped in a semi-circle facing the house to await the arrival of the captain and marching men. Behind them and to one side was a soldier who seemed to be too tall for his good-sized horse. He didn't participate in the movements of the other men. Probably the scout, Hannah guessed, but something different about him made her notice him. Though his face was stoic and impassive, when their eyes met, she read compassion there.

All of the rigid Kansan faces wore identical expressions of blank minds ready to carry out any order. Beside the scout, only one seemed human—the young officer who pulled his sorrel to a stop just to the left of the porch, his rifle still sheathed. When Dolly peeked at him from behind her mother's skirt, his face broke into a half smile which he quickly removed when his captain drew near.

"I don't know, Dolly, whether they will burn us out or what they will do," Hannah said, knowing that the girls' fears were probably correct. She unconsciously pushed the hair back from her face. As soon as she moved, it fell back over her eye. "Stay by me and don't say anything." She looked her daughters in the eyes. Leah and Mazie nodded.

"Dolly?" The child was still watching the cavalryman whose face was now an impenetrable mask as he awaited his superior. Following her daughter's eyes, Hannah glanced at the young lieutenant.

"Dolly?" she asked again. Dolly's long golden curls bobbed as she nodded. "All right now, girls, whatever happens, stay together." Hannah glanced again at the young officer, but saw no change in his expression.

Leah, the oldest, took a hand of each sister. Their mother stepped in front of them, crossed her arms, and waited. Her stance was mannish and self-assured, though the strand of hair dangling over her right eye, her flour-smeared apron, and the three girls clinging to her, revealed her weakness. No one would see that under her floor-length skirt, that her knees were weak enough to buckle. Hannah held them rigid.

Lord, Hannah thought as she stood exposed and vulnerable. How could I have let this happen? She should never have relaxed her vigil. Why did she not anticipate and prepare for this raid as she had all the others? The image of her boat in the river and her shack hidden in the timber crossed her mind. Too late now. She should have realized the danger when the last of her neighbors left. But she heard that the soldiers had left neighboring Bates County after moving out its remaining citizens. The bushwhackers were out of the county, the Confederate Army was too far away in the south and east to worry them, and, so she thought, the Union patrols sent to enforce Order No. 11 were on their way back to headquarters in Independence. She had felt safe for the first time in months.

Safe? Her frightened daughters and Poco's renewed barking echoed her own dread. This well-equipped and organized unit invading her ranch was the worst threat they ever faced. She didn't know how she could take any more. The Lord was asking too much of her.

As the captain approached, she let her shoulders slump so that she appeared shorter.

Urging his horse to the raw, sawed off edge of the wooden porch, the captain reined his bay in the middle of Leah's marigold bed. The spirited stallion pranced and stomped in place, his iron-shod hooves crushing some flowers, while those still standing radiated their gold in the hot sun of the mid-September afternoon. Leah moaned, but said nothing.

"Your ranch is in the Federal Military District of the Border," the captain shouted. "No one is allowed here." Though speaking to Hannah, he looked at his mounted men to see if they had found anyone else.

When the young lieutenant, his mask intact, shook his head, the

captain turned to Hannah. "Did you hear me, woman? I said no one."
When she said nothing, he stated as if reading a military directive. "I have
orders to remove all persons living in the counties of Jackson, Cass, and
Bates and in Vernon County north of the Osage River."

He let that loaded information sink in, grimacing in satisfaction
when he saw Hannah trembling slightly and heard the quickly stifled
gasps of the two smaller girls. "You have heard of General Thomas
Ewing's General Order Number Eleven?"

Hannah forced her body to stop trembling and for the first time
looked boldly at the officer. His broad-brimmed military hat pulled low
over his forehead had hidden his upper face. He raised his head enough
that the sun highlighted his pale blue, blood-shot eyes. When she caught
the full view of his face to see the fanatic expression in his eyes, she
managed to stifle a scream of recognition but couldn't control her feet.
She took a faltering step backward, bumping into Leah. Hannah now
expected the worst. She knew this man, but so far, he did not recognize
her. Allowing her strand of hair to remain over her eye, she pulled onto
her head her sunbonnet which had been hanging by its strings down her
back.

When Hannah did not answer, the captain continued his statement.
"Within fifteen days of its decree—it's been nineteen days now—
everyone," he paused briefly, "everyone living within those counties must
leave. Those who prove their loyalty to the Union can go to a military
station to await the end of the conflict. Those who do not leave within that
time, will be moved to the nearest military facility."

While delivering this speech, he signaled his lieutenant to begin the
search. The officer reined his horse around the spirea bush to a nearby
sergeant, gave some orders, and returned to his post by the porch, pulling
up just short of trampling Hannah's herb bed of comfrey, golden seal, and
catnip. The mounted men rode the perimeters of the barn lot and over the
roadless grassland toward the mouth of the creek at the river. The
infantrymen entered the house and out buildings.

Ignoring the steps, several soldiers tramped through the marigolds as
they jumped onto the porch. Even though the little girls were hanging on
to their mother's long skirt, they were jostled roughly when the men
pushed behind them to enter the door. The thuds of their boots in the
house renewed Poco's barking.

"Can't you speak, woman?" the captain shouted, his eyes like blue
flint, his lips so thin they were hardly visible.

"Yes, I can," Hannah said. She straightened to her full five feet eight
inches and took a deep breath which emphasized even more her robust
figure. The deep brim of the sunbonnet shadowed her face. "You have no
right to move us from our land. My husband is in the Union Army, the
Eighth Missouri State Militia."

The captain sneered at her as he wiped the perspiration from his face.

Fighting hard to keep control of her fears, Hannah continued. "His
name is Paul Rockfort. We own this ranch. We have always been strong
supporters of the Union and have never participated in the Confederate

forces or given aid to the bushwhackers."

The captain sent a stream of tobacco into the marigolds, its amber color staining the gold blossoms. "Likely story. That's what they all say. Everyone hereabouts is the enemy. Slave-owning snakes, border ruffians, that's what all you Missouri trash are. Need to rid the earth of the likes of you."

"We have never owned sl..."

"Silence, woman," he roared, his eyes flashing fire.

Mazie sobbed audibly. Dolly pulled her mother's full skirt around her to hide. Behind her mother, hidden from the captain's enraged face, she kept her eyes on the lieutenant. He glanced at her briefly with no change in his expression and then back to his captain.

"You are north of the Osage River," the captain stated, daring anyone to contradict him, "so you must leave." When no one moved, he roared, "NOW!"

Hannah and the girls jumped. Mazie's sobs continued. Poco's growls, barks, and thumping against the cellar door increased. Moderating his voice, the captain said, "And even if I believed you, the Order plainly says," he resumed his rote-reading voice, "everyone, regardless of their innocence or guilt in aiding the guerrillas." He turned to his lieutenant. "Knowles, take five cavalrymen and escort this woman bushwhacker right now to Captain Cardwell's encampment."

"Sir," the lieutenant said, looking at the little girls' bare feet, "could I allow her to gather up some things to take with her?"

The captain glared at his officer and then said as if granting a great concession, "Fifteen minutes." He reined his bay back to the center of the yard, jerked him around to face the porch again and bellowed, "And get rid of that damn dog."

"Mama," Leah whimpered.

"Come, girls," Hannah said, herding them into the house quickly to shield them. She knew she could not save the little dog. Though she tried to distract the girls, she couldn't shut out the rough voices of the men, Poco's growl as he lunged out the opened cellar door, the shot from a rifle, or the dog's surprised yelp and subsequent silence. The three girls looked at their mother in stunned disbelief. In past months they had witnessed the stealing of their stock and beloved horses, but no one had yet harmed their pets.

"Puss," Mazie cried, looking around frantically and pulling away from her mother to find the cat.

Holding her tightly and putting her finger to her lips, Hannah said, "She's safe. You know how she hates strangers. She hid under the house. They won't find her."

Puss was probably safe for now. What if they burned the house with her trapped under it? No time to think of that or to mourn poor little Poco. Fifteen minutes was all Hannah had to collect what she needed. Killing the dog was only a sample of what this captain was capable of. Given the provocation, he would just as readily kill one of her children. Of that she was certain.

She had not forgotten that face. She knew from experience that their survival depended on doing as he asked and, most important, keeping away from him as much as possible. They had no alternative. So far he did not recognize her. And praise God, he himself would not personally escort them. She took another quick look at the young lieutenant. His military expression softened as he dismounted.

"Quick, girls." She wiped the tears from Dolly's and Mazie's faces with her apron tail and pushed them into the kitchen to get their minds off their dog. "Go get the satchels, and Leah, fetch that basket from the back porch."

When the girls were out of sight, Hannah leaned against the wall to control her trembling. She wiped away her own tears with the back of her sleeve. The aroma of bread baking brought another sob when she remembered how Paul enjoyed her fresh loaves. Even if he was still alive, she could never bake for him again in the kitchen he built. She knew the captain was just waiting for them to leave to burn the house as he had done all others buildings in the area.

She pulled the bread from the oven, surprised that it was just nicely brown and not burnt. Though the time had seemed long, she realized it had been merely minutes since she last checked on her baking before the soldiers arrived. No way to hide it from the soldiers with its yeasty aroma filling the house.

THE LIEUTENANT entered the kitchen. This is just like home, he thought, visualizing his own mother back in Virginia.

"Are you hungry?" The woman asked him.

Eagerly he broke open the bread to let the steam escape. Tossing it from hand to hand until it cooled enough to eat, he watched the woman. She pulled back the cloth on the table that was spread over the fried chicken and mashed potatoes left from dinner. He gulped down half of the loaf as he hadn't eaten all day. He pretended he didn't see her stash a loaf into each of her bags and begin to collect the things she and the girls would need.

Lieutenant Knowles hated this assignment. This spunky woman didn't look like a Bushwhacker. He believed her story. She was simply trying to survive. Actually he admired her. He had joined the army to free the slaves, not imprison women and little girls.

He grabbed a drumstick and pictured the middle girl, the golden-haired girl with the bouncy curls and big eyes who had completely captivated him. But he knew his duty. The woman disobeyed Order No. 11 and he must obey his superior's orders even if he didn't approve of his methods. In the meanwhile, he would enjoy this delicious food.

WHEN HANNAH and the girls gathered in the loft that was the girls' bedroom, Hannah spoke quietly as she encircled them with her arms. "No time for me to explain how I know," she said, but before she could continue, she had to pause to control her voice. "I know that captain out there is an evil man. The worst we've seen. So we won't cross him."

"Is he the devil?" Mazie asked, her eyes big and full of fear.

"No, sugar, but he's a bad one, so that's why you must do as I say so he won't be mad at us."

All three girls agreed.

"Good. Now as quickly as you can, put on two sets of clothes, just your everyday stuff. Pack your winter underwear and coats in these bags. And put on your winter boots." Dolly looked at her as if she had lost her mind.

Leah understood. "That means we won't be back until winter?"

Hannah didn't answer her. "Just do what I said," she whispered and pointed to the lieutenant below to warn them to speak quietly. While supposedly guarding them, he was more interested in his food and what the men outside were doing than overseeing women packing.

Hannah quickly pulled out the few garments she wanted them to take, favoring sturdy clothes. Downstairs in her bedroom she filled her satchel with some of her husband's work clothes and his heavy coat. With tears in her eyes, she ran her hand over the coarse fabric that used to keep him warm. Was he warm now? Or cold in an unmarked grave someplace.

No time for those thoughts. She pawed through a chest until she found three old knitted stocking caps and an old shapeless felt hat, which she added to her bag. In the basket she packed scissors, thimble, needles, and thread. She searched through her scrap bag and removed some brown and black remnants. She slipped on one of her husband's brogans that still showed the shape of his foot and the inside of the left shoe that showed where he toed in slightly. Not a bad fit if she wore a pair of his heavy socks over her stockings. She must take them with her.

Sneaking a look at the lieutenant who was still engrossed in his meal, she slipped her Smith & Wesson revolver and some ammunition into one shoe. After wrapping the brogans with a blouse, she put them into the basket. On top of these she laid a plain butternut-colored wool dress, the fullest petticoat she had, and one pair of cotton drawers.

As she had instructed the girls, she put on two skirts, leaving behind her Sunday dress. "Time to be practical," she told the girls who joined her. "And it's going to be cold soon." She grabbed her husband's cuff links he wore when they married and her mother's ornamental brooch. Since the lieutenant still wasn't watching her, she put her marriage license, the deed to the ranch, and what money she still had in the pocket of her inside skirt. Last she grabbed her doctoring bag and sack of herbs.

"Time enough," the captain's voice roared. During all this time he had remained seated on his bay, shouting orders.

"Come, girls," Hannah urged as she double checked that her medical supplies were hidden with clothing. When Dolly tarried, Hannah dragged her roughly after her. She had to be stern and keep her own fears hidden for the children's sakes. She could not show any weakness. Halfway to the door, Mazie pulled away to get her doll. Her mother took the doll from her hands, laid it on the table, and shook her head. Hannah knew the captain would shoot them given any provocation. They must go quickly and quietly so that he wouldn't look at her too closely. No matter what they did or said, the buildings were lost. She steeled herself to do whatever she had to do to save her family. Right now that meant leaving quickly without any resistance.

They hurried outside and down the porch steps. Dolly and Mazie were weeping quietly, while Leah was fighting back her tears. But when she saw Poco's dead body sprawled in her ruined flowers, she gave a deep moan and started toward him.

Controlling her own emotions, Hannah held her back, cocking her head toward the captain and shaking it in warning. Then she hugged each daughter and whispered, "Poco died trying to protect us and our home. We'll be back. And, Leah, we'll plant more flowers to be blooming when Papa comes home. Be brave for him."

Though Hannah herself didn't know how or when they would get back, or even if their father was still alive, her assurance quieted the girls. Mentioning their father's name always helped. They would do anything for him.

Two years now since they had heard from him. The girls had more faith than Hannah did. Though she believed that Paul was killed, the girls wouldn't consider any doubts, even though little Mazie could barely remember him.

With their bags on the grass around them, Hannah and her daughters huddled together in the shade of the young maple tree by the porch. The three cavalrymen who were sent to scout out the outlying fields and woods returned.

"Well," the captain demanded.

"Nothin', sir. Just prairie grass. No more cattle. Only one field of corn, but it ain't ripe enough to pick. I ordered the men to cut some for our horses and destroy the rest."

"Good," the captain said. "Any other buildings or signs of hideouts?"

Hannah caught her breath.

"No sir. We went plum to the river. Didn't see nothin'."

Leah grabbed her mother's hand. Hannah patted it reassuringly and shook her head to warn her.

"Want us to cross the river and take a look?" the cavalryman asked.

Hannah tensed.

"What's over there?" the captain asked.

"Just more timber far as I could tell. Looks mighty swampy and wild to me."

The captain glanced toward the lone, tall soldier Hannah suspected was the scout. He had stayed back, still separated from the others. He held himself very erect and nodded confirmation.

"Any ford or evidence that anyone's crossed there recently?" the captain asked.

"No, sir. Banks are too steep. No crossing we could see."

Again the captain glanced at the tall soldier. "Didn't see any, sir," he said in a soft voice unlike the other soldiers.

"What about a boat?"

Leah moaned. Hannah frowned at her to be quiet.

"We did find an old boat sunk into the mud," the cavalryman said. "It's useless. Probably got a big hole in its bottom."

The captain turned abruptly to Hannah, startling her. "What's over there, woman?"

"Where?" Hannah asked innocently.

"'Cross the river. What's on that side?"

"Mostly timber."

"Look at me when you answer me, woman!"

"There's just timber and beyond that open prairie." Hannah looked straight up into his eyes. She was standing so that the brim of her bonnet cast a shadow over her face as he looked down at her from his horse.

"Any cattle?" his bay, impatient at so much inactivity, began prancing again so that the captain's attention was diverted to controlling the stallion.

"No. Bushwhackers stole them, that is what Sterling Price and his Confederate Army didn't steal two years ago in 1861."

The captain sneered at her and said to the soldier. "Likely story."

The cavalryman said, "We didn't see any recent evidence of cattle except that one cow in the barn lot."

"Very well. Get on with loading what you have found."

"Yes, sir." The soldier saluted.

"Captain," Hannah couldn't help saying, though she knew she was going against her own resolve not to draw any more attention to herself, "I understand that Order Number Eleven specifies that the military is to make a report of the hay and grain taken and report the names of loyal owners and how much is taken from them. I would like a copy of your list."

The captain jerked around in the saddle toward Hannah, his face as red in the afternoon sunlight as she had seen it years before in the firelight. The red in his eyes obscured the blue iris. "Silence! You are my prisoner!" he shouted.

Hannah made an involuntary step back expecting to see him pull out his revolver as he had done seven years ago when she heard him say these same words. Instead, he neck-reined his stallion, forcing the horse's nose right up into her face. She had to step back against the house to avoid the stallion's head. The spray from his snorts covered her dress. "Whatever I find on enemy lands is mine. Spoils of war."

Having forced her to retreat, he started to thrust his hand into his jacket, like Napoleon. Instead, he removed his hat and ran his hand through his thinning hair. Wiping his brow, he carefully replaced his hat, cocking it to its former angle. "Since you seem to know so much, you should know that the Order said that the ninth of September, 1863, was the deadline for loyal people to leave." He grimaced at her as he announced, "Today is the twelfth."

He then turned his horse away from the house so that he could better survey the farmstead. He watched his men carry out the household goods and fork the hay from the barn loft. Squinting, he nodded with satisfaction as he saw how efficiently they were carrying out his orders.

"Lieutenant Knowles."

"Here, sir."

"Are you ready to take this female Bushwhacker to join the other civilian prisoners of war?"

"Yes, sir."

"Good." He rubbed his hands together in pleasure of an assignment well done. "This is the very last place. I'll finish up here and report back to Fort Scott tonight where I'll send word to General Ewing in Kansas City that Order Number Eleven has been carried out. In the District of the Border there is not a building left standing. Not a living soul and no farm animals." While the lieutenant waited at attention, the captain stood up in his stirrups to get a better view. He looked from Poco's body, to the cow and calf his men were corralling, and then into the defiant eyes of the eldest daughter of the tall woman.

Settling back into the saddle with a pleased grunt, he continued, "I won't need the infantry anymore. The cavalry can more swiftly, police the area to watch for outlaws and keep people from coming back. Tomorrow we'll cut back across to rejoin the rest of the cavalry."

He smiled when he looked at the men preparing to burn the barn. "Did you know that people are calling this area the Burnt District?" he said with great satisfaction of a job superbly done.

"Yes sir, I have heard the term."

"Good name. It will keep people out for a long time." His tight lips turned up slightly at the corners as he paused. Then resuming his air of command, he ordered, "Meet me at the post in Fort Scott when you deliver these last prisoners."

The lieutenant saluted. "Yes, sir."

Not waiting for the lieutenant to order her to leave, Hannah snatched a satchel in one hand, the basket in the other, and marched up the trail. The girls each carrying bags followed, three brown-clad figures almost hidden in the tall blue-green grasses undulating in the wind. Caught by surprise, the lieutenant scrambled for his horse, gave the cavalrymen assigned to him some hurried orders as he mounted, and galloped up the trail to get in front of Hannah. The men rode behind him to catch up. When they tried to take the girls' bags, Mazie and Leah hung on to theirs.

"Madam," the lieutenant said kindly, touching the brim of his hat. "let us carry your things. I give you my word, I'll return them to you undisturbed." He already had Dolly's bags which he was tying behind him on his saddle.

Hannah motioned to the girls to let the men take the bags. Freed of their loads, the two smaller girls each grabbed one of their mother's hands. Leah, her head held high like her mother's, followed closely behind.

Dolly yanked on her mother's arm. When Hannah leaned over, the child looked toward the officer and whispered, "He won't hurt us."

"I know, honey. Keep quiet now until we get as far away from that captain as we can. All right?"

Dolly nodded, as did the other girls.

Humped over, her hair hanging in her face and hot from the extra layer of clothing, Hannah pulled the girls along as fast as they could go. They had to run to keep up with their mother's long strides. When they reached the crest of the rise in the prairie and started down the back side of the mound, from which point they could no longer see their house, Hannah intended to march on. Leah turned to take a final look. Dolly and Mazie both stopped, jerking their hands from their mother's grip.

"Don't look back, girls," Hannah said gently although it was already too late. The three girls were facing the homestead. Hannah didn't need to turn around to know what was happening there. Though this was the first time she had been forced from her home, it wasn't the first time it had been raided.

Back at her barn the soldiers were trying to corral the hogs. One Kansan led Bessie away while her calf leaped behind her in fright. Smoke oozed out of the open barn door. At the house the soldiers were carrying out the family's belongings that were of any value and loading them into her wagon. Two cavalry horses were hitched to the wagon, for bushwhackers had taken Hannah's last horse months ago.

She blamed herself. The pause allowed her to catch her breath. "I should have known." Though she had heard stories of what was happening in Bates and Cass counties north of her, she didn't believe them, just as she had thought Order No. 11 held no danger for her. The Order barely included Vernon County. Only that portion "north of the Osage River," it stated. True their house was north of the river, but they owned land on both sides.

She had dismissed the stories of burnings and families being evacuated as exaggerations of Confederate sympathizers in war time. The Union forces would not harm their own people. Missouri did not secede from the Union. Many thousands of Missouri men, including Paul, were serving in its army, almost three times more than those serving in the Confederate Army.

She now knew that the stories were true. The terrible injustice overwhelmed her. This after surviving all the other threats! In spite of her preparations and plans, here she was surprised, captured, and led off to a military station as if she were the enemy. Even poor Bessie was finally caught, the only cow wily enough to escape the other raids.

Her despair was more than being caught and led off as a prisoner. Over the past years she had survived her real enemies—Jayhawkers, Confederates, and Bushwhackers. They had merely stolen from her. Now this. Her own side was forcefully moving her as they destroyed everything she and Paul had built in their fifteen years of marriage. What little she had saved during the two years of guerrilla activities since he left was gone.

Though her mind told her not to look back, her heart let her take a last look at her home. But instead of hearing the voices of the soldiers as they piled the furniture in the wagon, the hiss and pop of the blaze now coming from the barn, or the frightened squeals of the hogs, she heard in her mind sounds of moans and gunfire from a night seven years earlier when she was doctoring a sick neighbor. She heard the sobs of the sick woman in bed, the voice of the husband, who in his nightshirt was inviting strangers into his house during a storm. And she heard the voice of this same haughty captain who just now ordered the ruin of her home. She heard him yell to his host the exact words he just shouted at her, "You are my prisoner." Then in her mind she heard the blast of his gun.

Hannah understood then why this horror was happening. It was because she had once again crossed the path of Carl Murdock, a former Redleg Jayhawker and abolitionist. Running her tongue over the gap in her front teeth, she knew very well her danger. For now he was even more dangerous; he was a captain in the Union Army with a well-equipped and experienced cavalry at his command. And he had absolute power over this border district.

But in spite of the danger, the loss of their few remaining belongings, and being forced off her land, Hannah was not defeated. Her momentary despair lifted as she remembered that some of her precautions were still protecting them. Believing the boat useless, the soldiers did not cross the river. The captain failed to recognize her. And he put them under the command of a lieutenant who seemed sympathetic.

Not one to dwell on regrets, from the first moment on the porch when she realized her error, she had been working on a plan.

"Don't cry, girls," she said, pushing her hair back into her bonnet. The tears on their faces mingled with their perspiration. "We'll soon come back home again."

"So Papa can find us?" Dolly asked.

"Yes. We'll get it ready for him."

"And Puss will be there?" Mazie asked.

"Yes, sugar, Puss will be there waiting for us."

Chapter 2

HANNAH HOPED Puss was safe. Lord, how she hoped. Silly to worry about a cat when there was so much more at stake, but she couldn't help it. Over the years Puss had become a symbol of their survival. That was a silly notion, too. But Hannah saw many comparisons between the resourceful cat and herself. Puss and she had both learned to keep out of sight of any questionable people. They knew how to live off the land and find shelter wherever they could. And most important of all, they both had the same goal—to protect their babies.

Each in her own way helped the other. Hannah gave Puss a bowl of milk at each morning and night milking. She and the girls petted her, allowing her free access to soft pillows and a special spot by the fire during cold weather.

In return, Puss presented them with dead mice and an occasional snake. Once, when there had been no meat in the house for a week, she dragged in a fat squirrel almost as big as she. She deposited her gift at Hannah's feet and then gave herself a bath in front of the fire. The family feasted on squirrel and dumplings that night. But Puss's greatest gift was her presence—independent, self-assured, calming, and loving.

Puss's escaping the soldiers and remaining home gave Hannah hope that she and her daughters could also. When they returned, Puss would be there.

Hannah turned away from her house and resumed her march. Bending forward at the hips, with her head thrust out in determination, she did not look back. After a few steps down the slope she could no longer see the buildings. Knowing that view would never be the same—was already different with the barn in flames—she concentrated on what she was seeing on either side. This view would not change. Not Jawhawkers, marauding armies, or Bushwhackers could permanently alter the land. In turn they had burned it and tramped over it. Two years ago the army commissioned some Jawhawkers to winter a huge herd of longhorn cattle on it, almost denuding the grass. But the land always revived. The blue asters and golden rod were blooming again. Even in the past hour after this most recent cavalry detail tromped a flattened path through it, the grass was recovering. Bent toward the buildings, as if telling her she was headed in the wrong direction, the tall, seed-heavy heads bounced in the wind as they were already righting themselves.

As the group reached the north boundary of her land at the main road to Fort Scott, they passed under the ranch sign Paul had so optimistically painted a few years earlier. "Prairie Wood Ranch," she read the faded words aloud as she looked back. This was their amazing prairie acres and their even more wonderful woods in the creek and river bottoms. Such a valuable combination! And she was forced to leave it. She put her hand on her skirt over the hidden pocket. Yes, she could feel the stiffness of the folded deed. She and the girls would return.

She noticed that Mazie and Dolly were panting and stumbling from the strains of the last hour and their mother's rapid pace. "Mama," Mazie said. Hannah looked at her thin, puckered face and realized that she was practically dragging both girls along. This was no way to protect her children. Feeling less threatened now that they were out of sight of the captain, she slowed to a more comfortable normal pace. She straightened up from her hip-bending position and squared her shoulders to her normal posture. Like the grass, she could revive.

The lieutenant dismounted, lifted Dolly into his saddle, and set Mazie behind her. Leah declined the offer of one of his men's mounts. Leading his sorrel just in front of Hannah, the lieutenant adjusted his gait to hers. Hannah gave no acknowledgment. For now she was a prisoner, a non-entity with no rights, no voice, and therefore had no reason to exhibit human courtesy.

Her children safe for the moment, Hannah could give her memory full sway to replay what just happened. She allowed herself to feel.

She had difficulty stopping a sob in her throat when she thought of poor Poco, but she let his memory stay. Now she could mourn him. Poor little harmless fellow. He hadn't been with them long, a half-grown pup that showed up a few weeks ago, undoubtedly left behind by a displaced family. Though loyal and lovable, he was not as entrenched in the family as Puss. The cat was truly one of them, Puss and Mazie being born during the same stormy night.

Hannah's step faltered when she remembered that their births were also tied to her previous experience with this cavalry captain from Kansas. Both Hannah and Mazie came close to ending their lives before Mazie ever had a chance to live. Hannah's body quivered visibly enough that Leah grabbed her hand.

"You all right, Mama?" she whispered.

Hannah patted Leah's hand and nodded. Running her tongue past the gap in her teeth, she resolved that this captain would never again harm her family. The fact that she was his prisoner and he would be stationed in the area for some time made no difference in her resolve. Somehow she would defeat him. She would not let him destroy her family as he did the neighboring Newman family years ago. Not this Carl Murdock, former Kansan Redleg, now Captain Murdock of the United States Cavalry. Captain? His true title should be Assassin.

But at the moment she was helpless. She must wait to set her plan in motion. She needed time to make some clothes and time to figure out the best opportunity and means to escape. In the meanwhile she might as well let the old memories surface. Perhaps they would seal her resolve and remind her what to expect.

AT HOME a late December afternoon almost seven years before in 1856 while the two little girls were napping, she was relaxing after clearing up the dinner dishes. Eight months pregnant, she was tired from her daily chores and care of four-year-old Leah and two-year-old Dolly. While Paul was outside filling the hay racks in anticipation of the coming storm, she dropped into the rocker by the fireplace. With a sigh of contentment, she started to pick up her sewing basket when Old Puss (she called every female cat Puss) jumped into her leg, circled to find the most comfortable spot in her shortened lap, and began purring. As Hannah fondled her, her practiced fingers reminded her that the cat would soon have her babies.

Hannah was startled from her dozing by a loud knocking on the door. "Miz Rockfort. Miz Rockfort." She recognized the voice of Sally, her neighbor's slave. Old Puss disappeared.

"Goodness, Sally," she said as she opened the door just as Paul entered the kitchen. Paul reached Hannah's side and pulled Sally inside out of the wind.

"What in tarnation are you doing out in this weather?" he said. Sally's faded red shawl was sprinkled with snow.

"Miz Rockfort, ma'am, oh lordy, Miz Gracie's bad sick. Mister Philip wants to know if you'd come see about her."

"Tell me how she's sick."

As Sally described the symptoms, Hannah pulled on her boots and coat while Paul lifted her medical bag off the mantel. He didn't need to be told that his wife might not be back until morning. He kissed her goodby and watched her follow Sally into the storm.

The young couple was used to Hannah's being called away at all hours. Her skill as a healer and midwife was much needed. The extra money her doctoring brought in helped pay the mortgage on their ranch. Not being able to afford a hired girl, and morally opposed to slavery, Paul assumed the double load of ranch and housework when she was away. He checked on the sleeping children, and since there was no outside work to do during the storm, relaxed in his wife's rocker after seeing her off.

Hannah and Sally soon covered the distance to the Newman place. Greatly relieved when he spied them through the window, Philip Newman opened the door for them, mumbling his thanks. Hannah quickly assessed Gracie's condition as the fever that was plaguing the area.

"She's not bad," Hannah assured Philip. "I'll give her something to bring down her temperature." She gave the feverish woman a tea made of wild quinine and sat down beside her to bathe her head and body with cold, wet cloths.

As the storm outside increased, Hannah moved Gracie onto a cot nearer the fire. She didn't want her to chill, now that her fever was abating. While Hannah was busy with the sick woman, Philip and his young son ate the supper Sally prepared for them and went to bed. Hannah made a pallet for herself in the fireplace corner to be handy if needed. Everyone in the Newman family was soon asleep except Sally who was finishing up in the kitchen.

Suddenly there was loud banging on the door. "Hello the house," a man's deep voice called out. "We want to stay all night. We can't cross the river and it's too cold to camp."

Philip jumped out of bed. Barefooted and in his night shirt, he grabbed his six shooter that was in a scabbard hanging on the wall. To keep the pistol from accidentally discharging, he always kept a string looped over the hammer. In his hurry and because of the poor light from the fireplace and the one candle in the kitchen, he couldn't remove the cord that was tangled with the cylinder.

"Please let us in, neighbor," the man outside kept pleading over the barking of the dogs. He spoke in the soothing voice of a preacher pleading with sinners to repent. "It's too cold to turn away a fellow Christian on a night like this. God will bless you."

Philip looked out the window but could see only dark forms in the swirling snow. "I guess they are all right," he said.

"No, don't let them in," Hannah warned. The usual frontier hospitality had been suspended during the recent border troubles over whether Kansas would be a slave or free state. Kansan guerrillas, called Redlegs from the red morocco leggings they wore, often used slavery as an excuse to raid Missouri border areas.

"No, Pa," the boy said, going to him and pulling him back.

"They're all right, Bud. The man's a preacher." Philip patted the boy on the head and handed him the useless gun. When Bud saw that the cord was all tangled so that the cylinder wouldn't revolve, he gave it to his mother. She slid it under her quilt.

Philip padded to the door, threw back the wooden bar, and after quieting the dogs, called out, "Come in friends."

Abruptly pushing Philip aside and spewing snow over the wooden floor, three of the men stomped in. Two men went directly to the fire. They sat down and spread out their hands to the blaze. The light showed their red leggings. Philip stepped quickly between them and his wife's cot, too late recognizing his danger.

The third man remained standing. He stationed himself in the center of the room, his short legs apart, his thumbs hooked over his gun belt. Without saying anything he looked over the room, at the boy, the sick woman, and Hannah. Hannah unconsciously moved back into the shadows when she met his leering eyes and saw his thin lips turned up in a slight sneer. Scanning the room, he raised his eyebrows and cocked his head in satisfaction when he spotted the slave woman's frightened face. Last of all he glared at Philip. The old man's hands were by his side.

The short man drew his pistol, cocked it as he pointed it at Philip, and with his first words announced in sanctimonious assurance of his righteousness, "You are my prisoner."

Sally screamed and fell over a chair as she tried to reach the back door. The boy ran out the front door onto the porch where some men caught him. Trapped in the fireplace corner by the two men warming by the fire and the gun-holding intruder, Hannah crouched behind a wooden bench. A single pistol shot reverberated from the walls. The stench of the fired gun filled the room.

"I am gone," Philip gasped to his wife. He fell beside her cot on the hearth stones.

Gracie leaned over the edge of the cot and put her hand on her husband's face. He was sprawled on the floor, his eyes open and his lips slightly parted from his last words. In shock, Gracie looked at the leader who was waving his gun around. She stifled a cry by pulling the quilt over her head.

"Get the slave girl," the leader ordered. His self-assured expression now showed satisfaction. Sally shrieked as the two men by the fire grabbed her. Dishes broke and pans clanked on the floor as she struggled. Quickly the two men pinned her arms behind her and dragged her screaming from the kitchen.

"Get your coat, girl. You're now free—free of the sin of this place and forever free from the curse of slavery," the man preached, pushing her roughly out the door. The men outside held on to her as she kicked and screamed.

"Shut her up!" the leader yelled. When she continued to scream, he stalked to the door, pointed his gun at her, and blared, "Shut up or I'll shoot you, too."

Immediately Sally's shrieks became sobbing moans.

The leader searched through Philip's britches that were hanging on a chair by the bed and took several gold pieces from the pockets. In disgust at not finding more, he spit a stream of tobacco juice onto the clean floor. The spittle made a dark brown, wet circle on the wood which was scrubbed almost white with lye.

"See what else you can find," he said. He pulled Gracie from the bed and ordered her to show him the things he wanted—money, jewelry, provisions, and good clothing. With his gun always pointed at her, he pushed her from dresser to chest and to other possible hiding places.

Though he ransacked the house, he did not find any more money. The men outside rounded up two yoke of oxen, two horses, and eleven mules.

Finished with Gracie, the leader pulled Hannah out from her dark corner and jerked her bag from her. When he dumped out its contents to find only medical supplies and herbs, his face mottled with anger. "A witch doctor, eh?" He shook her. Then he noticed that she was far in her pregnancy. He grunted in disgust and pushed her away from him.

"You must be one of John Brown's men." Hannah said. She was young and inexperienced with religious fanatics. Although she had heard about John Brown and his abolitionist cohorts who were terrorizing the Missouri border counties from their base in Kansas, this was her first encounter. She hadn't yet learned to curb her tongue when in the power of such men.

"Yes," he said proudly, speaking slowly with self-righteous importance. "We're doing the Lord's work to rid the country of the scourge of slavery." His pallid blue eyes seemed to ignite as he turned toward the firelight.

"And murder and robbing and kidnaping are part of His work?" Hannah knew she shouldn't goad him, but her anger and horror at his blatant shooting of her defenseless neighbor overcame her sense of danger. "Or are there other names for these acts when they are done by a preacher of the gospel?"

Stunned into inaction by her gall in addressing him, the abolitionist stared at her as she raised to her full height. She almost towered over him as she continued, "You're not liberating this woman. Kidnaping is what you're doing. You think you're so righteous taking this poor slave woman. You should know as well as anyone that we are only two miles from the border. If she wanted to, she could have run away anytime in the years she's been with the Newmans."

The man glared at Hannah, his fanaticism and greed turning to rage. "The law is wrong and these people have no right to their wealth."

"And evil men like you can judge. You can kill and rob because you have more guns?" Hannah could not stop her anger at his blatant greed and disregard of human life and civilized law.

With fury in his pale eyes, the man pointed his pistol at her just as he had done at Philip.

"Go ahead, God's messenger," Hannah taunted without thinking of the consequences. "Go on. Kill a pregnant woman and her unborn child just as you did that unarmed old man in his night shirt. See how God likes that." Hannah faced him defiantly, looking boldly into his eyes.

The man cocked his pistol and held it steady for a few seconds. Then, instead of shooting it, he swung the gun at her, striking her hard across her mouth with the muzzle. Hannah heard a crack as it hit her teeth. She fell back against the hearth, choking on blood and the tooth knocked out by his blow.

The man spun around and marched out the door. On the porch he shouted orders. With their booty, including Sally, the men disappeared into the snowy night.

Gracie, Bud, and Hannah were alone with the fallen Philip. Mother and son were locked in each other's arms weeping. Hannah pulled herself up and stumbled into a chair. She snatched off her apron and pressed it to her mouth to stop the bleeding. Her head throbbed from its knock against the stones when she fell. Her knees were skinned and her back ached. Her jaw and mouth began to pain as the initial numbness disappeared. She steeled herself against the nausea and faintness that she always experienced after a painful injury.

As she assessed her injuries, her first thought was relief that she was alive. And the baby? She ran her hand over her abdomen. The baby stirred. Her bump on the head would soon disappear. Her mouth would heal. She tentatively explored the inside of her mouth with her tongue. A lower incisor was gone. No time for regrets. Better a tooth than what she might have lost.

"I'm all right," she said to Gracie, though the act of speaking caused more bleeding. But her next thought was of Philip. Maybe he was still alive. Careful not to hurt her knees, and slowly so that she wouldn't lose her equilibrium from the dizziness, she knelt beside him. The bullet had entered his chest. There was no heartbeat. At Gracie's anguished look, Hannah shook her head. She could do nothing for him. Gracie and her son were unhurt. Time now to see about herself.

She gathered up the medical supplies spilled on the floor and found some salve. "We better get some help." She spoke carefully trying not to move her battered lips.

When she stood up, a much greater pain seared through her body, causing her to double over as she grabbed the chair for support. She knew what that pain meant. Maybe she wasn't as fortunate as she thought. Perhaps the tooth wasn't all she would lose. Her fall brought on premature labor.

When the pain passed, she knew she must get home. Wrapped in the misery of her own loss as she knelt beside her dead husband, Gracie didn't notice Hannah's paleness nor pain. Her son, his eyes filled with fury more like a man's than a boy's, was hanging on to her as she cried over and over, "Oh Buddy, Buddy! What're we gonna do?"

"I must get help," Hannah repeated.

Gracie nodded agreement, assuming Hannah meant getting someone to help her. But first Hannah had to get home to Paul. He would know what to do. Together he and she could bring this child into the world as they had done twice before. Gracie and Bud were in no danger now. Morning would be soon enough to send them some aid. Always helping others and putting their needs first, Hannah knew that this time she must think of herself and the baby. Paul would take over. She merely had to get to him.

Home was only a mile away, downhill off the mound and across the prairie. She could make it. The storm seemed to have abated. She was dressed for winter weather, and the familiar trail was well marked. Even at night in the snow, she could find her way.

She put on her coat and almost made it out the door with her bag before another pain struck. Too close together, she thought. Not a good sign. Not much time. But forcing herself to hide from Gracie how severe the contraction was, Hannah pointed to her bloody mouth as the cause of her pain. "I'll get some help," she repeated as she closed the door.

The icy air slashed across her mouth, causing her to reel from the sharp pain. She wrapped her scarf around her lower face. Only her eyes showed. Holding to the rough stair rail, she carefully descended the slippery steps that were packed with hardened snow from the outlaws' boots. Safely on the ground, she turned in a different direction from the path the men had taken.

"Only a mile." She was hardly out of the Newmans' yard when another pain pierced through her. Hannah had helped in the delivery of too many babies not to know how quickly her baby was coming. When the contraction subsided, she hurried on, counting her steps to keep her mind off her pain.

"One, two, three."

After the next constriction, she stopped counting. It didn't help. Two more came and subsided before she glimpsed the light from her window. With the great need to get home, she pushed aside her dizziness.

"Paul," she called out. Too far away, she knew, though the wind had stopped and the night was silent.

She no longer felt her throbbing mouth with this more urgent movement in her body. She longed to lie down, but knew she must keep on and somehow hold back her urges to push. "Paul," she screamed his name as another contraction started.

Warm light spilled out the opened door as Paul stood in it. "Paul," Hannah called again. This time she held on to a sapling to keep erect. The baby was coming. She could feel its head between her legs.

Paul reached her just in time to prevent her from falling. "The baby is coming," Hannah said. He swung her up in his arms and ran into the house. She was safe now with Paul.

In spite of the imminent birth of her baby and the lightheadedness that was overcoming her, when Paul carried her through the front room to their bedroom, she saw Old Puss stretched out on some rags near the fire with three tiny kittens suckling her. One of them was calico.

"MAMA," Mazie said. While holding on to Dolly's waist as she sat in the lieutenant's saddle, the little girl turned to speak to her mother walking behind them. "I have to pee."

Now, seven years later, her daughter demanded her attention. "Amazing," Paul had said when the baby appeared within minutes of his laying Hannah on the bed. "You and the baby are truly amazing." He had kissed her cheek and held his fingers above her swollen and disfigured mouth. "Amazing," he repeated. His wavy blond hair caught the glint of light from the lantern as he shook his head in awe.

"Yes," Hannah had said. "Little Amazing Rockfort."

And so she was named, though shortened to Mazie.

"I've got to pee real bad," Mazie said.

This was a problem Hannah wasn't prepared for. Four females on the open prairie with these men.

She needn't have worried. The lieutenant stopped his horse, lifted Mazie down and pointed to some brush along a draw a short distance to their right. His men immediately stopped.

"Me, too," Dolly said.

"We can rest now," the lieutenant said. "Ladies first," he said bowing slightly and sweeping his arm out to point the way.

Holding Mazie's and Dolly's hands, with Leah close behind, Hannah waded through the grass to the brush that was about two hundred yards away. When she looked back she saw that the men had all dismounted and with their backs to them, were taking advantage of the pause right there in the road.

As the girls squatted down behind the bushes, Leah said, "We can run away now."

Hannah had the same thought. They might get far enough away to hide and perhaps sneak back to the shack.

Then she shook her head. "Not now. With their horses they would soon catch us and then things would be worse. And our bags are still with the horses." Most important, she didn't have her medicines.

"What's going to happen to us?" Leah asked.

"These soldiers are taking us to a military encampment where other people like us are held."

"And then what?" Leah asked. "Will they let us come back home?"

"Not for a long time, I'm afraid."

Leah was watching the soldiers. "They aren't paying any attention to us. We could crawl in the grass to that rise up there and get away."

Hannah had already dismissed that possibility. She and Leah might make it, but not Mazie and Dolly. They were already so tired they could hardly walk.

"No, Leah, we couldn't. If we try something like that, that lieutenant may not treat us as well."

"He's nice," Dolly said.

"He's all right. And if we cooperate with him, we might be able later to use his liking us when we have a better chance of getting away. C'mon, girls, we better get back." She brushed the errant strand of hair out of her face.

When they were almost back to the soldiers, Hannah said to Leah without the other girls hearing her. "Good thinking, Leah. I've been working on a plan, and you have just shown me how to do a part of it I couldn't figure out."

"What?" Leah asked with excitement.

"Later." Hannah cocked her head toward the lieutenant who met them and put the little girls back on his horse.

As she walked farther and farther from her home, Hannah began to wonder if she had made a mistake in not trying Leah's suggestion. They might have gotten away. She could have carried Mazie on her back piggyback style as she often used to do. She knew the country, knew where every ditch and depression was. If they reached the creek, they could easily lose themselves in the swampy and wooded lowlands, and then follow it to the river and to their shack.

They should have tried. They wouldn't be any worse off. What of her grand resolve to outdo this Carl Murdock? But even she was beginning to tire. She had made the right decision. They might have been shot or beaten. She was going to protect what she still had, not risk it. Later when everything was ready, then she'd get the girls back home.

Though she had been lagging behind some, she quickened her pace to her usual stride. The sooner they got to this encampment place, the sooner she could begin her preparations.

THE LIEUTENANT watched the plucky woman who marched so steadily with her head high. God, how he hated this assignment! The little blonde girl impressed him the minute she glanced at him with her blue eyes that were much too mature for such a small child. What a shame! He could not imagine what was going through the mind of the mother. He pictured his own mother back in Wisconsin and his two younger sisters. What would they think now of their brave brother who marched away to help abolish slavery?

His only comfort was that they would never know about Order No.

11 or about Captain Carl Murdock, Kansan Abolitionist who enslaves little girls.

Chapter 3

TWO WEEKS later, lying on a cot near the tent opening, Hannah waited for it to be light enough to finish her sewing. As usual, she was awake long before any of the other women or children, but this morning her mounting anxiety and the first cold spell of the season awakened her even earlier than usual.

Carefully feeling her way around the girls huddled together under the thin blanket the army issued them, she pulled out from the bags their winter coats to spread over them. Her bags were still packed, all lined up under her bed. Though the other women in the tent had spread their few belongings out in an effort to make it look more homelike, she was always packed and ready to leave at a moment's notice. Today was the day. Her hands shook slightly from nervousness until she forced them quiet. No time for emotions. She couldn't afford the luxury of feeling. Not until they were home again.

Moving cautiously not to awaken anyone, she dressed more guardedly than usual, deliberately choosing each garment. Just as she did when they left Prairie Wood Ranch, she dressed in double outfits and secreted her papers and money in a special pocket she recently sewed into her chemise. She pulled out of a bag her husband's brogans and eased out the pistol. She held it a moment not sure what to do with it. Too bulky to hide in her clothes. Someone would notice it. Also risky to leave it in the bag without the protection of the brogans that she planned to wear today.

She decided the safest plan was to leave it in the bag, for she didn't need the gun in this phase of her plan. She thrust it down into the toe of a stocking, put that stocking inside its mate, and rolled its long legs around the gun. Then she put the bundle between the folds of a petticoat and returned the package to the bottom of the stoutest bag.

As soon as it was light enough, she pulled out a roll of brown material and her sewing supplies. She needed to finish this garment before anyone stirred. She would continue organizing the bags later. Pulling back the tent flap enough to let in more light, she began sewing. Periodically she peered out the opening and scanned the sleepers in her tent to see if anyone was awake.

The mother of the family next to her coughed a couple of times, but otherwise it was quiet. She worried about Beulah's cough. Her dosage of hickory bark tea helped some, but she wished she could do more.

As Hannah worked, she heard the usual morning sounds, guards chattering as they began their morning duties, the cook clanging his heavy pots, and the horses snorting contentedly as they ate their grain. When the guard poked his head into the tent to wake them and take his morning count, Hannah pushed the garment and her sewing supplies under her blanket and pretended to be just getting up.

After the soldier moved to the next tent, and while her tent mates were busy getting dressed, Hannah handed Leah the garment she had been working on. "Put it on," she whispered.

Leah's eyes widened in excitement. "Today?" she asked.

"Yes. Everything's ready now." Hannah pointed to the packed bags and the girls' dresses laid out on her cot. She opened one bag a crack to reveal right on top two other brown garments similar to the one she handed Leah, only smaller.

Leah held up the skirt of the petticoat she slept in and quickly pulled on the brown trousers her mother gave her. Next she took off her petticoat to put on the boy's shirt Hannah had fashioned from her extra blouse. Leah then put her petticoat back on, worked her stockings up over the trouser legs and anchored them with a garter above her knee. Last she slipped on her dress. Though Leah rubbed her hands over her body to feel the extra layer of clothes, she looked the same. The trousers didn't show.

She and Hannah helped Dolly and Mazie dress the same—boys' clothes under their dresses and petticoats. The smaller girls stared in amazement at the trousers and shirts that seemed magically to appear in their bags. "Don't let on," Leah whispered to her sisters, "Don't even let Beulah or her children know." Since coming to the encampment and finding their neighbors from home already here, Hannah had helped them out as much as she could.

"How'll we pee with these britches on?" Mazie asked in her normal piping voice. Her pantalettes had an overlapping, open crotch so that girls and women didn't need to remove any garment.

"Hush, Mazie." Leah glanced at the Kerrigan family next to them in the tent. Busy with their own morning duties, Beulah and her children paid no attention to Mazie. "You have to pull them down," Leah whispered. "I'll show you later."

"Is this your new plan?" Dolly asked Hannah. She giggled as she pulled on the trousers. As long as she and Mazie could remember, their mother was devising one scheme after another to ensure their safety. At the ranch they often hid or sometimes play-acted a role when strangers came. But they had never dressed their part. Since they had been at this camp, they knew she was working on a plan for them to escape, although neither she nor Leah had mentioned it to them.

"Yes, girls, but don't say anything about the boys clothes," Hannah warned them, cocking her head toward the Kerrigans. While she and Leah helped the younger girls dress, she told them what they were to do, as if directing them in their part in a play. "I have an aunt and uncle in Independence. Their names are Rhodie and Bill McGill. We are going to stay with them. Do you understand that this is our way to get out of the camp?" When they nodded, she continued, "You know that Captain Cardwell has allowed other people to leave if they can prove they have loyal Union relatives out of the border district that they can go to?"

The girls nodded. Their mother did not have to tell them that this aunt and uncle didn't exist. Hannah had them repeat the names until she was sure they remembered.

"What about these boy clothes?" Dolly couldn't help touching the strange wool trousers cloaking her legs.

"We'll need them later. For now, just pretend you aren't wearing them." She pulled up her own skirt to show them that she too was wearing male clothing. They recognized their father's work jeans and brogans. She put her finger to her lips as she pointed to the others in the tent. "Just remember we want to go to our... our what?" Hannah prompted them.

"Go see Aunt Rhodie," Dolly sang, and then laughed.

"And Uncle Bill," Mazie said just as the call for breakfast came from the cook shack.

Hannah had two reasons for choosing this particular day to escape. This morning she finished an essential part of her plan—making the boys' clothing for each daughter out of the garments and material she had brought from her home. But the main reason she picked today was because Lieutenant Knowles was back in camp. Dolly had seen him yesterday and told her he was leaving the next day for Independence.

"Mama," Dolly asked as they were walking to the mess shack, "You won't get the lieutenant in trouble, will you?"

"I'll try not to."

After the captain in charge of the camp had eaten, Hannah and her daughters asked permission to see him. Everything was working their way. Lieutenant Knowles was at his headquarters. While waiting for permission to enter they heard the two men talking.

"...a confession that we can't handle two, three hundred Bushwhackers and Redlegs," Cardwell said, "to move out twenty thousand people."

"But they burned the town of Lawrence. Had to do something."

"A tooth for a tooth, and eye for an eye, eh?"

"Something like that."

"But these poor women, children, and old men here are the ones that suffer." Captain Cardwell paused. "And the Bushwhackers still continue, I hear."

"Yes, sir. Now that all of the residents are out of the region, Captain Murdock is busy going after Bushwhackers. It seems they are more active than before we depopulated the border."

"Well, I hope he's successful."

Hannah was granted permission to enter. She presented a sad picture of a lone woman standing stooped before the captain with her three small girls clinging to her. The lieutenant touched the brim of his hat in recognition. The smallest one was sobbing. The middle one that unnerved him so looked at him with her grownup eyes.

"Some of Captain Murdock's dangerous guerrillas?" Cardwell asked Knowles in a mocking tone. The lieutenant shrugged his shoulders and grinned. He had wondered how the family was managing since he dumped them here a fortnight ago. The woman's first words showed him he didn't have to worry about her.

"Captain Cardwell, sir," Hannah said after introducing herself, her hand on Dolly's shoulder, "my daughter told me that Lieutenant Knowles is on his way to Independence today. I have an aunt and uncle there who are willing to take us in. My uncle is a broker and supplies hay and other supplies to General Ewing. May we be permitted to leave and accompany the lieutenant?"

From her quiet observations since arriving in camp, Hannah had learned the problems Captain Cardwell faced. Supplies were as low as the morale of the soldiers. His primitive post was suddenly turned into a temporary detention camp for homeless civilians. He had more people than provisions.

Though General Thomas Ewing at Kansas City should have anticipated the effect of his Order No. 11, neither he nor his officers in the field were prepared for the resistance. Nor did he foresee the zeal with which Captain Murdock would scourge the district. The crowning blow to the residents was putting Carl Murdock in charge of enforcing the Order. He was the hated Redleg agitator of many raids on Missouri citizens years before the war started. The noted journalist and artist George Caleb Bingham had tried to stop Ewing. The word around camp was that Bingham said to the general, "If you persist in executing that order, I will make you infamous with pen and brush as far as I am able."

Captain Cardwell was one of General Ewing's officers who had to deal with the results. Winter was coming. There was already sickness among his men and the civilians. Hannah hoped, in view of these conditions and her observation of Cardwell, that he would be willing to let them leave, maybe even glad to have fewer people to feed.

"What is the name of this uncle?" Captain Cardwell asked. His voice was brusque. One of his men just reported two more sick prisoners.

"Uncle Bill and Aunt Rhodie McGill," Mazie said, proud that she had remembered. Then she puckered up her face ready to cry when Captain Cardwell looked disapprovingly at her.

"I was speaking to your mother, girl," he said and then shook his head at Hannah as if commiserating with her about children's behavior.

Leah put her arm around Mazie and spoke some comforting words to her to keep her from crying. Dolly watched the lieutenant.

"You are here, ma'am, at this military post because you disobeyed Order Number Eleven." He let her think about her actions for a few seconds before he asked more kindly, "Why didn't you go as directed to this Bill McGill when the Order first went into effect?"

"I couldn't believe that it applied to loyal families of Union soldiers," she answered meekly, unconsciously pushing her hair back under the braids circling her head. "And we had no horses or mules to take us there." Though gruff and enjoying his power, this captain was not a Carl Murdock. He was doing his duty in a difficult and unpleasant assignment. She believed he would be reasonable. "My husband is serving in the Eighth Missouri State Militia, but I don't know where he is as I haven't heard from him for two years."

Dolly ducked her head down so that her blue eyes looked up through her bangs at the lieutenant. Her golden curls hung loosely over her shoulders, not pulled back in tight brown braids like her sisters' hair.

When the lieutenant looked at her, she beamed, her round face lighting up.

The lieutenant spoke for the first time. "If you'll allow me to speak, Captain Cardwell, sir." When Cardwell nodded, he continued, "I believe that the lady is telling the truth."

"You brought her in, didn't you?"

"Yes, sir, about two weeks ago. From the Osage River near the Kansas border."

"Almost out of the military zone, isn't it?"

"Yes, sir. Much of her place was not in the zone."

Captain Cardwell studied Hannah as he stroked his gray beard. "Cause you any trouble?"

"Not a bit, sir. She came willingly."

The captain looked at some lists on his table. "She's given me no trouble, either." He paused again. "McGill, you say?" he asked Hannah. She nodded. He pondered for a minute. "I think I know some McGills in Independence."

"Yes, sir. There are several families there," Hannah said with no change in her expression.

"Hummm. Yes, I believe there are." Then he asked Knowles, "Would you be willing to let her accompany you?"

"Yes, sir, I would."

Dolly grabbed her mother's hand and squeezed it. Mazie's tearful face broke into a smile.

Captain Cardwell turned abruptly to his aide. "Inform the cook that Lieutenant Knowles will need provisions for four more people—this woman and her three daughters." The aide saluted and left. Cardwell then asked Hannah, "Can these children walk that far?"

"Oh yes, sir." The girls all nodded vigorously.

"May I suggest, sir," Knowles said, "that they might ride the confiscated horses we brought in yesterday. In that way they won't slow us down."

Dolly's grasp on her mother's hand tightened. She was right about the lieutenant.

"Good thinking, lieutenant. After you leave these women at the McGill house, then you can deliver the horses to Captain Murdock. He always needs more mounts. See to it."

"Yes sir." Knowles saluted, clicked his heels together, and spun around. Before he left he winked at Dolly.

Captain Cardwell turned to Hannah, "Get your belongings and report back here at nine sharp."

Leah and Dolly pulled their mother out of the building and ran with her all the way to their tent. They didn't need to say anything. They all knew that Part One of the plan was successful. Whatever happened next, they were leaving this dismal post. And, with a stroke of good fortune, they were leaving in the care of Lieutenant Knowles. Hannah had to keep a tight hold on her resolve not to show any feelings. Her girls' glee was contagious. They'd were free again! Well, almost.

Back in their tent, Hannah quickly repacked the bags to organize the clothing and other things for more efficient use. She put the most essential items in her own bag. This time in order to give more space, she instructed the girls to wear their winter coats, though the coats would soon be too warm for the mild late September day. After they had packed everything they brought, she glanced at the ragged, Kerrigan children watching them. Without hesitation she pulled out one dress of each girl and gave them to the children. She took out one of her dresses and handed it to the children's mother. "Here, Beulah, if you take up the hem, I think this will fit you."

"Bless you," Beulah said, clasping the dress to her chest. She, her children, and father-in-law were brought to the camp with only the summer clothes they were wearing when the soldiers routed them from their home. For a moment Hannah wondered if she could include them in her plan, but that was impossible. None of them could escape if she tried. She must concentrate on saving her own children. She consoled herself on seeing the Kerrigans' pleasure with the warm clothes. Maybe later she could....

"Mama," Dolly said, her face pouting, "we don't have any other dress but what we're wearing."

"Yes, honey, I know. One's enough. The bags are too heavy for us to carry, and when we get to Aunt Rhodie's we can get nicer ones."

"Beside," Leah said, "we don't need many clothes for the trip and Beulah's girls don't have any."

Hannah lifted each bag to check its weight. Then she pulled out her one pair of shoes. "I'll get more later," she said. "Here, Beulah, can you use these?" She pulled her skirt up to her ankles and held up one foot. "These old brogans are better for the trip." When Beulah caught a glimpse of the denim trousers underneath Hannah's skirt, she clamped her hand to her mouth. Hannah shook her head to warn Beulah not to say anything.

While Beulah and her children were busy putting on their clothes, Hannah gathered her girls around her to explain Part Two of her plan—the escape from the lieutenant and his detail. When she was sure that they each understood exactly the part she was to play, she hugged them, telling them how wonderful they were.

Though the Rockforts were anxious to be gone, their parting from the Kerrigans was tearful. Already acquainted from being neighbors at home, their sharing the same experiences and being tent mates cemented the friendship of the two women and their children. "Good luck," Beulah said to Hannah. Then she held her short body erect in a mannish fashion to show that she understood part of Hannah's plan. "I hope it works." She pointed to Hannah's skirt, but both women knew she was referring to the trousers underneath.

"I'll see you again," Hannah whispered. "Maybe..." She didn't dare give Beulah any hope until she herself was free.

The Kerrigan boy ran to Leah and tugged on her arm. "Who'll tell me stories when I can't get to sleep?" His face was puckered up ready to cry.

"You all remember them, Archie," Leah said. "You and your sisters just take turns telling them." She looked back to see Beulah comforting the little boy, her two daughters in their new dresses standing on either side. The forlorn group waved until the Rockforts were out of sight behind the cook shack.

Halfway to headquarters, one of the lieutenant's men met Hannah. He took Dolly's and Mazie's bags before leading them to the corral where the rest of his detail were waiting with the extra horses. He tied the two bags together with a rope and hung them over a pack horse's neck in front of the rest of the soldiers' gear. When he started to take the other bags, Hannah and Leah shook their heads. "Stuff we need," Hannah said. "You know, women stuff." The soldier backed off.

"I could get only two horses for you," Lieutenant Knowles said. He seemed embarrassed that the saddles were not side saddles. "You'll have to ride astride."

"That's all right. We're used to that," Hannah said. "On the ranch it was safer and easier. We used to do that all the time before our horses were stolen." She put her foot into the stirrup and swung easily into the saddle of her mare, being careful to keep her skirt down to cover her trousers. Knowles lifted Mazie behind her as Leah climbed into the saddle of the second horse. Dolly straddled the horse on the blanket behind Leah's saddle. Hannah caught her breath when she saw the cuff of Dolly's trousers. Her skirt blew up when she swung her leg over. None of the men noticed it. Facing forward, the four cavalrymen were mounted in formation awaiting the lieutenant's command.

Everything ready, Knowles mounted his sorrel and trotted him to the head of the detail. He led the way out of camp at a walk. Behind him on the dusty road were two soldiers riding side by side followed by Hannah's and Leah's horses with their double loads. Bringing up the rear were the remaining two cavalrymen, each leading a pack horse. As soon as the group cleared the cluster of temporary buildings and tents clinging to the prairie, the lieutenant changed the pace to a gentle lope. Neither Hannah nor her girls complained of the dust that swirled around them and caused them to sneeze, for they were free of the camp and were waiting for just the right time and place for Hannah to put into action Plan Two.

Since the military post was on the eastern edge of the depopulated military district, they did not see anyone as they rode northwest. Not a house or barn was left intact, only blackened chimneys now labeled "Murdock's Tombstones." Already honeysuckle vines were covering the ruins where only slugs and lizards now lived. Zigzag lines of broken-down rail fences, and an occasional grouping of marigolds or zinnias that survived in the yard of a burned home swayed in the wind, sad testimony of a once flourishing region. It was truly a burnt district. But where the prairie grass had been burned, new green was already beginning to show through the charred ground.

In areas that had escaped the fire, the grasses waved luxuriously over the rolling land. Hannah's practiced eye picked out familiar medicinal flowering forbes among the grasses—yarrow to stop bleeding, blazing star for snake bite, and sensitive plant whose seeds were her standby laxative.

In the low places and along the creeks she spotted boneset that made a tea that helped broken bones to mend.

This was the land she loved, living, giving, and healing. Just like her land at Prairie Wood. But that was not surprising. By Hannah's calculations the military camp was about fifty miles from her home. She often glanced southwest as if she could see it over the rolling land. Only now they were traveling northwest in a steady seven-mile-an-hour gait.

After about two hours, Hannah searched the surroundings with greater care. Since they were far enough from the camp to avoid alerting the soldiers stationed there, she didn't want to travel much farther north. As they crossed a wooded and soggy area of a draw and started up the slope, she found the place she was looking for. "All right, Mazie," she whispered, putting her hand lightly on the child behind her. "We're ready."

Mazie started wiggling back and forth. "Be still, Mazie," Hannah ordered loudly enough that the lieutenant in front of her could hear her. "Quit your squirming."

"I got to pee," Mazie piped in her loud voice.

"Not now, sugar. The lieutenant can't stop."

Mazie didn't say anything, but kept wiggling. Knowles slowed the horses' pace to a walk as they climbed the slight slope to the top of the rise. To their left was a thicket of cedar saplings. "Now," Hannah whispered.

"Mama," Mazie almost cried as she rocked back and forth behind her mother on the mare. Then in an even louder high-pitched voice she said, "I feel sick. I've got to go!"

When the lieutenant turned back in his saddle to look, Hannah held out her hands in an expression of apology, as if asking what could she do.

He held up his hand for the detail to halt and trotted back to Hannah. "Time for a rest, anyway," he said, giving his boyish smile. Everyone knew the routine from their earlier trip. Hannah and the girls dismounted. Mazie and Dolly ran ahead to the cedar thicket as Hannah and Leah followed more slowly. Hannah carried her bag.

Ten minutes later Leah returned alone. Mimicking her mother's stoic expression, she held tight to the excitement within her. Her family's escape now depended on her. She watched the men closely. The lieutenant looked toward the thicket. He smiled when he saw Hannah's sunbonnet and butternut-colored dress through the shield of thick branches.

"Mazie's sort of sick," Leah said. "Mama said to tell you they'll be back directly."

Lieutenant Knowles frowned at the delay. He pulled out his watch fob, glanced up at the sun high in the sky, and ordered his men to stop for a meal. They tied the horses to some scrubby bushes along the roadside where they could graze. The men then hunkered down in the abandoned road to eat. None of them paid any attention to Leah. She sat on the ground beside her horse to eat her meal. Without the men noticing, she put some food in her satchel that was tied to the saddle horn of the horse she and Dolly rode. Then she waited quietly. Her heart beating extra fast didn't make any outward sign to warn the men how nervous she was.

After almost half an hour, the lieutenant's patience gave out. "What's taking them so long?" he asked no one in particular. He seemed to have forgotten that Leah was there. "We can't wait any longer. Jenkins, go tell Mrs. Rockfort to come back." When the soldier was half way to the cedar thicket, Knowles changed his mind. "Jenkins, wait. I'll go." While Jenkins waited, the lieutenant waded through the grass toward Hannah, whose dress and bonnet showed that she was still standing in the same spot among the trees.

The three other men watched the lieutenant, their backs to Leah. This was her opportunity. Darting behind the soldiers' horses, she stepped from one horse to the next. With trembling fingers, she quickly untyied all five of the men's mounts as well as one pack horse. When she reached the second pack horse, she glanced back to see that the men were still engrossed in the lieutenant's movements. Before untying the pack horse, she pulled her sisters' bags from his neck. Tossing the bags over her mother's mare, and holding tight to the mare's reins, she jumped on her own horse. She didn't take time to see if she was detected, but jabbed her heels hard in the horse's flanks. He bolted forward right into the middle of the other horses.

Just as Leah spurred her horse, Lieutenant Knowles yelled an urgent order from the grove. "Jenkins, get down here." Wrapped around a cedar tree was Hannah's butternut-colored dress he had been watching for more than thirty minutes. Her sunbonnet was perched on its top like a Christmas star. No Hannah. No little girls. Only the impassive faces of the sunflowers, nodding and keeping time to the sudden barrage of hoof beats from nine horses galloping out of sight across the prairie.

Chapter 4

WHEN HANNAH had left the soldiers, she didn't run toward the cedar grove as Dolly and Mazie did, though she wanted to. Clutching her bag to her chest, she put out her hand to Leah to warn her not to seem too eager. They walked in a normal pace to the thicket which already hid the smaller girls from sight.

As soon as she joined them, Mazie grabbed her hand, her eyes excited as she glanced back at the soldiers. "How'd I do? Did I do everything right?"

"You were perfect, sugar."

Leah tried to drag her mother farther into the thicket out of sight, but she said, "No, Leah, I need to be where the lieutenant can see me. That will keep him satisfied."

"What are we going to do now?" Dolly asked. She thought she should be told more of the plans. Now that they were this far away from the men, she didn't know what her mother planned next. "And why are we wearing boys' clothes under our dresses? I'm hot in this coat."

Even Leah didn't know the next plans. "What do you want me to do next, Mama?" she asked.

"I'll tell you girls everything now. This is the first part of Plan Three, our escape from the soldiers so we can go home. Now listen closely and make sure you understand everything because we don't have much time."

Since Leah had the most important job, Hannah went over carefully step by step what she was to do when she returned to the soldiers. Then she explained what she, Dolly, and Mazie were to do, and pointed to where Leah should meet them. To be sure that Leah understood how to get there, Hannah picked up a stick and drew a crude map in the bare ground under one of the cedar saplings. She pointed out the various landmarks, first southeast to where the creek wound through the grass. It was easy to see where it went because the trees bordered it. Then she pointed out the only other trees within their view—a clump of cottonwoods in the distance that she felt sure was a burned home site. "We'll wait for you there. Do you understand?"

Leah studied the map, looked again at the creek, the cottonwood trees, and back to the soldiers. She nodded. "I can do it, Mama." Then she hugged her mother.

Though Hannah didn't watch Leah amble slowly back to the soldiers, the younger girls did. As always they were excited about what they planned to do, but this time as their sister walked away from them, their expressions of enthusiasm were tinged with anxiety. It was the first time in their years of eluding Bushwhackers that they had been separated. This time the success of Hannah's strategy depended on Leah acting alone. "Will we ever see Leah again?" Mazie asked, tears in her eyes ready to spill down her cheeks.

"Of course, sugar, in about an hour. Don't worry about her. The lieutenant is a nice man. Think about what we must do before she rejoins us."

Assured by their mother's confident tone, the girls peeled off their dresses and petticoats down to their shirts and trousers and crammed them into their mother's bag. Seeing each other dressed so differently made them giggle. While Hannah was watching to see that the soldiers were preoccupied with their meal instead of looking their way, she stepped out of her own dress and slipped it over a cedar tree that was just her height. Dolly giggled even more as her mother tied her bonnet to the slender tip of the tree. To help make the bonnet look more realistic, Mazie gathered some dried grass to stuff in it.

"You're too fat at the bottom," Dolly snickered as she spread the butternut-colored shirt out over the sticky, lower branches of the tree.

"The other trees hide the bottom of the skirt," Hannah said. "The soldiers can see only the top part." She studied the effect and decided it would do.

She then debated what to do with her petticoat. There was no more room in the stuffed bag that could barely close with the girls' dresses. She didn't want to leave it behind as she knew they would later need every piece of material or clothing they could salvage. Dolly's comment about being fat gave her an idea. She pulled up her husband's shirt she'd put on under her dress that morning and wrapped the petticoat around her chest and shoulders, tucking the ends in the folds. When she put the shirt back on, the bulk disguised her figure and made the shirt fit her better over the shoulders. Pulling out the old felt hat from her bag, she shaped it the best she could and adjusted it on her head, forcing her heavy bun of hair inside the sweat band.

"How do I look?" She twirled around to show the girls.

Mazie said, "Like a man."

Dolly giggled again. "You really do, Mama. No one would take you for a woman."

"Good. Now, girls, let's finish transforming you two. Put on these stocking caps with your hair hidden." Mazie pulled her cap down almost to her eyes.

The two girls in the homemade britches and shirts and with no hair showing could pass for boys.

"All right, boys," Hannah said grinning at them. "This is good enough for now. We must leave."

She pointed the direction they needed to go—down the slope to the draw or creek. Since the cedars were on the crest of the slope and were between them and the soldiers, they had only a few yards they had to crawl on hands and knees through the tall grass before the slope would hide them from the soldiers' sight. Hannah crawled after the girls, dragging her bag. "Hurry. Keep your heads down and don't make any noise," she cautioned, keeping a tremor from her voice though her legs shook.

Just before she crawled under the slope out of view of the men, she raised her head cautiously above the grass to look back. Leah was sitting cross-legged on the ground by her horse. The men were all eating and chatting among themselves. The lieutenant was the only one still standing. He glanced her way, or rather, he looked at her dress on the tree. He peered at the position of the sun to judge the time, and then hunched down to give his attention to his food. Seeing him unperturbed calmed Hannah.

"Now," Hannah whispered.

The girls stood up and ran as fast as they could to the creek. Hannah overtook them before they reached the thick line of bushes and trees. "Follow me," she said as she crossed the narrow and shallow, sluggish stream of olive-brown water. She jumped easily across the water and turned back to urge the girls. Unable to jump it, Mazie sloshed across, getting her boots wet. No matter, the day was so warm that their coats were uncomfortable. "Come on, Dolly," she urged.

Dolly waded through. A few inches before she reached dry ground she screamed. Hannah grabbed the trembling child and clamped her hand over her mouth before she could scream again. She said crossly, "Dolly, hush. What's the matter with you?" She followed Dolly's eyes to see the head of a snake swimming away from them.

"It's a cottonmouth," Dolly gasped when her mother let her go.

"Did it bite you?" Hannah tore at the child's trousers to see if there was any evidence. Worry about the soldiers hearing the scream was minor compared to this.

"I don't know. I felt it against my leg."

"Where?"

Dolly pointed to her right leg just above the top of her boot.

Hannah took off Dolly's boot and stocking and pushed up the loose legs of her trousers. She didn't see any marks on the child's smooth, white skin.

"Does it hurt anywhere?"

"No. It just felt like a limber stick floated against my leg. Then I looked and saw the snake."

Hannah slumped down in relief. "You're lucky the snake didn't strike you."

"Could the lieutenant hear my scream?" Dolly said hurriedly putting her boot and stockings back on.

Hannah listened. "I don't hear anything from them. They're probably still eating. Even if they heard you, they probably just thought you and Mazie were playing. Come on. We're got to hurry to make up for the time lost here."

Now that they were on the side of the slope hidden from the soldiers, Hannah maintained a steady pace following the southerly flowing creek. The girls ran single file behind her.

The ground was firm, but the pathless way was irregular and difficult because of the thick growth and numerous marshy patches. She tromped down the grasses and small bushes for the girls to pass more easily and helped them leap over the muddy spots. She didn't worry that she was making a broad trail. If things went well, Leah would scatter the soldiers' horses. By the time the soldiers rounded up their mounts and tracked her, she hoped they would be several miles away. That is, if all parts of Plan Three worked.

When they had gone about a mile, Hannah slowed down. Dolly was right on her heels, but Mazie, several rods behind, was clamping her lips together to keep from crying.

"Mama," Dolly tugged on her sleeve to get her to slow down. "Mazie can't keep up."

Hannah stopped. She listened for any sounds from the direction of the soldiers. Did they suspect anything yet? She tried to estimate how much time had passed since Leah returned to them. How long would the lieutenant wait for Hannah and the girls to return before he investigated the cedar thicket to see what was holding them up? Luckily the men are eating their lunch, so that should give her some time—maybe twenty minutes. She figured it had already been at least fifteen minutes. The men hadn't discovered she was gone yet, nor had Leah scattered the horses, for she wasn't too far away to hear the men when they shouted.

Still no sound. She needed to get farther away as quickly as possible.

Little Mazie plodding behind her looked like a sharecropper's boy. Her trousers, covered with stick-me-tights, were already stained at the knees. With boots muddied and cap askew, she bore no resemblance to her little girl, except for the same screwed up face that was trying not to cry.

She looked at her other daughter. "You all right, Dolly?"

The transformation of pretty Dolly was even greater. Without her golden ringlets framing her smudged face, she, like Mazie, looked like an unwashed urchin. Only the one curl that escaped from her cap and danced on her shoulder spoiled that picture.

"I'm all right," Dolly said. She kept looking back. She hardly knew how to behave without Leah with her.

Hannah poked the errant curl back into her cap. Giving Dolly her bag to carry, Hannah stooped down for Mazie to climb on piggyback style. "Just a little farther," Hannah said. "Mazie, you're up high now. Keep a lookout for Leah." She pointed to the open prairie east of them. "She'll come in from that direction." When Mazie looked back the way they had come, the obvious direction to watch for her sister, Hannah said, "Remember, Leah will circle around to fool the soldiers into thinking she went in the other direction?" Mazie nodded. She remembered. "Now, when you see her or hear anything, don't call out to her. Just tell me. And watch back the way we've come to see if the soldiers are following."

Mazie nodded. Her mother didn't need to tell her to look. She had been watching ever since they left.

"You're our lookout now. Dolly and I are depending on you."

Time seemed to stand still as Hannah hurried on as fast as she could with her load. She stopped once to get her bearings, and then turned east at right angles from the creek toward the house place she had seem from the cedar thicket. On the lower ground where she was, she couldn't see it over the slight rise in the prairie. She trusted that her sense of direction was correct, and leaving the protection of the brush along the creek with the wind at her back, walked up the grass-covered slope which she hoped hid the rendezvous spot from the soldiers.

This was a calculated risk. In the open as she was, the soldiers might spot her, and if they had even one horse, they could easily overtake them. She had to depend on Leah routing all the horses.

"Keep looking behind, Mazie," she said. Both she and Dolly were too busy running through the waist-high grass, avoiding the sharp blades and numerous briars to be able to look behind.

Hannah and Dolly didn't need Mazie to make them aware of a shout, though they were too far away to distinguish whose voice it was. Probably the lieutenant's. Immediately they heard other shouts.

Hannah and Dolly both crouched in the grass. By leaning over, the girls were not visible in the grass waving in the wind, but Hannah was too tall. She had to get down on her hands and knees as they moved toward the house site. Hannah stopped to catch her breath and to see if she could observe anything. Nothing. Even the cedar thicket was hidden behind the contours of the earth and the tall grass. Obviously, if she couldn't see the soldiers, they couldn't see her. She stood up and stumbled on carrying Mazie on her back.

Hannah reasoned that even if the lieutenant had a horse and started searching for them, he would continue following the creek bed. After all, the creek was going in the direction of their home, which she was sure he would assume was her destination. And Knowles knew exactly where her home was. By now he would know that the aunt and uncle in Independence were a ploy to get out of camp.

After laying the broad trail along the creek, she had suddenly veered off east away from her ranch. Her objective was to get over the next rise out of sight of the creek. Only a quarter of a mile to go. She had picked a route through some bushes to head east. With the footprints of just the two of them, going single file over the solid prairie soil, she doubted he would pick up their trail, but would continue southwesterly along the creek. Even if he did pick up their trail, he might think she was headed east to Cedar County and give up the search.

More muted shouts caused her to drop to the ground again. Still nobody in sight. "C'mon, girls," she said, taking the bag from Dolly and hoping that Mazie was rested enough to run again, "get up over that slope as fast as you can. Go." She pushed them ahead of her as they ran. Halfway there, the feathered bodies of three or four prairie chickens suddenly flew up in front of Dolly, squawking in fright. She added her scream to the birds' screeches before she recognized what they were. Coming upon them was unexpected. Since the fires, the native fowl had left the open areas for the protection of the draws and creeks.

Hannah and both girls immediately dropped to the ground. Dolly's anguished face turned to her mother. She had her hand over her mouth as if trying to retrieve the shriek. "I didn't see them," she said, "and I couldn't help screaming."

Trembling herself from the sudden encounter, Hannah nodded her understanding. She raised her head enough to look behind them. Still nobody. Unless one of the men was trailing them on foot, she doubted Dolly's scream would carry beyond the creek they just left. Hannah waved to Dolly to continue. Humped over, they ran up the slope the remaining few yards to the house site.

They were too far away now to hear the men shouting to one another as they were trying to catch the horses. Hannah and the girls reached the clump of trees at the burned site. All that was standing of the house was the chimney. The barn and all outbuildings were gone; only some scorched boards, blackened ashes, and piled rocks showed where once several big buildings stood. There wasn't even anything left solid enough to hide them from view across the grassland.

Panting from their run and still shaking, the three stood behind one of the large cottonwood trees. Hannah put an arm around each child to comfort and reassure her. "The men didn't hear or see us," she consoled them, hoping it was true.

Mazie was the first to look around her. She spotted a mashed and soggy body of a stuffed baby doll sprawled by what was once the porch of the house—just like little Poco's body when she last saw him. Dolly pointed to the limb above where dangled just out of their reach the cut end of the rope from a child's swing. Seeing at close range the evidence of children in the desolation they had traveled through brought into focus their own loss. Mazie voiced what they were all fearing, "Does home look like this?"

Though they had ridden by ruined houses, they hadn't been actually inside the yard of one. It struck all three of them for the first time what they might find when they did return home. Hannah last view her place was the barn already in flames.

She answered honestly, "I don't know."

"Every houses we've seen is burned down," Dolly said. "Ours probably is, too."

Before Mazie could pucker up to cry, Hannah said, "But we don't know. Remember Murdock was in a hurry to leave."

Seeing how her words upset Mazie, Dolly said, "But the soldiers couldn't find our shack, could they?"

"No, I'm sure they didn't. You both know that when we do get back home, that's where we'll have to stay, don't you?"

They both nodded. That was all right with them. They'd already spent many days there hiding from outlaws since their father left. "We'll be home, anyway, even if the house is gone. Papa will find us, won't he, Mama?" Dolly said.

"Yes, he'll find us because we'll be home. No one has the right to move us off our own land."

Since the girls were comforted with talk of their father, Hannah planned what to do until Leah came. "Mazie, you sit down here." She took her to the tallest cottonwood that had some bushes around it. "Keep hidden behind this trunk, but look and listen to let me know if you see or hear anything." The spot overlooked a broad expanse, though the creek they had just left was not visible.

She and Dolly looked for a cellar or another place they could hide if needed. Finding nothing, they sat down behind a remnant of the rail fence around the barn lot that the fire had missed. In the angle of the rails were some sumac bushes, whose leaves were already bright red. Ignoring the threat of poison ivy, chiggers, beggar's lice, briars, and possibly another snake, they crouched down out of sight. Even with her worry about Leah and her fear for the success of her escape plan, Hannah was aware of how comfortable Paul's clothing was. She and the girls had been able to run more easily among the briars and were less tired than if they had needed to deal with full skirts.

Now came the hardest part of her plan—sitting and waiting, not knowing what was happening with the soldiers and with Leah. Was she able to rout the horses and get away herself? If she didn't get away, then she and the little girls would go back. They would all stay together no matter what.

She remembered when she was outlining to Leah what to do that Leah had said, "Mama, you and the girls go on without me even if I don't get away with the horses. All the lieutenant will do is take me back to the camp. I would be with Beulah until you figure out how to get me."

"No, I won't leave you. We'll stay together and think of another plan," Hannah had told her.

Leah tried to convince her mother. "You could get me when you come back to get Beulah and her family. You said you were going to do that."

"Yes, and I mean to try," Hannah said, "but first I have to get us home, all of us."

Sitting in the warm noontime of late September with the billowing grass and the noises of insects and birds around her, Hannah vowed again that she wouldn't leave without Leah. Now that she was forced into inactivity, she worried that she had given the child too much responsibility. Leah was only eleven! She should be playing with her dolls rather than stampeding horses and hiding from soldiers.

Too dangerous! What was she thinking? Hannah started to get up to return to the soldiers when Dolly put her hand on her mother's arm. "Don't, Mama. Leah can do it and we're going to make it. It's too soon for her to be here."

Hannah crouched back down. When had her children become so adult? She could answer that. They'd never had a normal childhood. She determined if they did reach home that she would see to it that they had time for play. In the back of her mind she knew that probably wouldn't be possible because of the continued danger they would face there, even more than during the past two years because in addition to the usual dangers from outlaws, there was now Captain Carl Murdock to avoid. But she would try to let them be girls before they were women.

The waiting was demoralizing. She was usually patient. One time she and the girls had hidden quietly under some boards beside the barn for over two hours while Bushwhackers searched their buildings for any loot they could carry away. But then all three girls were with her. Dolly was right. It was too soon. Leah could not be here this quickly even if everything went smoothly.

Hannah reviewed what Leah was to do. After untying all the army horses, she was to mount her horse and, leading Hannah's, scatter the men's mounts and the pack horses. From hearing the shouts of the soldiers, Hannah figured that she had succeeded in doing that.

Next she was to gallop up the road the way they had been traveling for a distance before veering off north. The idea was to mislead the soldiers. When she was out of sight over the slope, she was to cut back east and then south to meet them at the copse of cottonwoods. That way she would come to the meeting site from the east, the opposite direction Hannah and the little girls had come from.

Did Leah have enough sense of direction to do that? "She could easily lose her way in this trackless grassland." Hannah didn't realize she said this aloud.

"No, she won't," Dolly said. "It isn't trackless. She'll know when she crosses the creek to turn south. Then when she gets back to the trail we came on, she'll know she's going right. When she gets on the higher places she can see these cottonwood trees. Even Mazie could do it."

Hannah doubted that, but again Dolly was right. Of course Leah would find them. She'd lived all her life on the prairie. "Little prairie dogs" she often said of her children who were attuned to all its moods, its delights, and its dangers. Now when they got home and lived in the shack in the woods by the river, they'd be "little river rats."

Picturing them in boys clothing tramping around the river took her mind off Leah. She relaxed her tense shoulders. Instead of holding herself rigid, she should be taking advantage of this rest. She needed to conserve her strength, for they had much to do when Leah joined them. Plan Four had to be worked out.

Chapter 5

TEN MINUTES later Dolly tried to get her mother's attention. When Hannah didn't respond, she touched her. "Mama," she said softly. "Mama, I hear horses coming."

Instantly Hannah was on her feet. She motioned to Mazie, who was still sitting on the ground by her cottonwood tree, to stay put. She also heard the dulled thuds of horses on the heavy sod. "Sounds like two horses," she breathed to Dolly.

"Leah?" Dolly's worried face broke into a smile.

As if saying her name conjured her up, Leah appeared over the rise, riding one horse and leading another. Hannah and the two girls ran to her, grabbing her horses, and pulling her from the saddle as they hugged her. Up until this point she had carried out her instructions with no outward sign, relying on the adrenaline of excitement. Her hands were steady. She had untied and scattered the soldiers' horses, mounted, and escaped pursuit to find her mother and sisters right on target. But as soon as Dolly grabbed her foot from the stirrup and she slid off her horse into her mother's arms, she began trembling so much that she could hardly stand. The perspiration under her winter coat suddenly turned cold and she couldn't stop her sobs.

"Were you scared?" Dolly asked. She didn't remember her brave sister ever showing fear before.

"Did the soldiers shoot at you?" Mazie asked. "Are they right behind you?"

"No, no," she said, controlling herself. "The last I saw of them they were all running after the horses. I don't think they even saw which way I went."

"Did you..."

Hannah stopped the questions. "Not now, girls. Later. She'll tell us all about it later. Right now we've got to get as far away as possible." The waiting was finally over! Then she noticed that the girls' bags the soldier had put on a pack horse were slung over her mare. "You even got all our bags!"

"I know you said not to risk getting them, but it wasn't hard. The soldiers didn't pay any attention to me, and I couldn't leave them." Even as she was talking, Leah was pulling off her dress and petticoat down to her boy's clothing underneath. Dolly had a stocking cap ready to replace her sunbonnet and hide her pigtails. Mazie stuffed the clothes into one of the bags thrown over the mare she and her mother rode.

While waiting for Leah to come, Hannah changed her plans from heading straight home. She was sure the lieutenant would track them. Seeing the trail leading southwest would lead him back to Prairie Wood. Her new plan was to ride east into the hills of Cedar County, which was out of the restricted zone of Order No. 11. There she would test their new status as males and trade the two army mounts for some other horses before heading home.

She explained her plan to her daughters while they mounted up as before, only this time Dolly sat in the saddle with Leah behind her. Leah was still too shaky to take control of the horse. "We'll ride across the prairie fast until the horses need to rest," she told Dolly. "Stay right with me."

The grass had been burned on the eastern side of the house site. With nothing to deter them, and every draw and depression visible through the short new grass, they loped their horses for forty minutes before Hannah pulled up by another burned-out home place. Here a shed had escaped the fire. Dolly and Leah watered the horses from the well while Mazie looked unsuccessfully for a few handfuls of corn or hay to feed them.

"Dolly and Mazie, take the horses behind the shed and hold them while they graze on this patch of grass. Leah, come with me."

Hannah took her catch-all bag and entered the shed. Taking out her sewing scissors, she handed them to Leah. "Now, cut off my hair." She took off her felt hat, and quickly undoing her bun, braided her hair into two long braids. With rag strips she fastened the ends which almost reached her waist.

"Mama!" Leah didn't move. She left her mouth open as she stood with the opened scissors in her hand.

"Do it," Hannah ordered, "or I'll have to."

"But Papa loves your beautiful long hair."

"I know, my only claim to being pretty. But it has to go." When Leah still didn't move, Hannah grabbed the scissors, and holding one braid in her left hand, she cut it off close to her head. The braid was so thick she had to almost saw it off. When it was free of her head, she handed it to Leah, carefully holding the loose cut ends to keep them together. "Tie this end with a piece of rag so the braid won't come undone." Then she cut off the second braid.

"But Mama?" Leah stared in horror at the stubby ends on her mother's neck.

"Just do it, dear. Right now we can't pass for men and boys with long hair." She took the two heavy braids, and wrapping them securely in a piece of calico from her bag, she carefully positioned the package in one corner. She handed the scissors back to Leah and turned her back to her. "Now trim the ends up in the back so that it looks kind of like Lieutenant Knowles' hair."

The damage already done, Leah willingly clipped and shaped the raw ends of her mother's brown hair. Satisfied that it looked passable, she brushed the loose hairs from Hannah's shoulders.

"Now your turn," Hannah said.

In all her life Leah had never had her hair cut, except trimming the ends occasionally. But without complaining, she pulled off her stocking cap and turned her back to Hannah. "A little hair's not important compared to being home, is it?" she said bravely, though tears trickled from her tightly-closed eyes as Hannah held one braid in her hand ready to cut it off.

Hannah hugged her. "No. It's just hair. It'll grow back." Hannah quickly snipped off Leah's pigtails and packed them away with hers.

While Hannah was shaping the back of her head, Leah asked, "What are you saving the braids for? We can't put them back on." In spite of the sadness of losing her hair, Leah laughed.

"Oh, but we can. That's why I'm saving them so carefully. We can sew them to our bonnets when we need to be women again."

Leah grinned her understanding. Depending on which was safer at the time, they could switch from male to female by changing clothes and head coverings.

"Now go hold Dolly's horse and send her in."

"She won't like it."

"I know." Hannah had given up long ago braiding Dolly's long curls as she did the other girls. The child was proud of her beautiful, long hair that curled in long golden ringlets down her back. She would not let it be braided. Hannah dreaded having to cut it, but she knew no other way. Even in the short time since Dolly had worn the stocking cap to try to hide her hair, the stubborn curls insisted on poking out around the edges in unboy-like fashion. And as she told Leah, the hair would grow back.

Surprisingly, Dolly didn't object. Big tears rolled down her round cheeks as Hannah first braided her hair to keep it in two neat strands and then clipped off the braids close to her head.

Mazie's only objection when it was her turn was that Papa wouldn't recognize them when he came home. "He'll know his little Amazing girl no matter what she does to her hair. He'll know," Hannah assured her. Mazie smiled in anticipation of that day and stood still while Hannah clipped her hair in a boyish style. Afterwards she shook her head. "It's so light," she said. "I feel like I could fly!"

Ready to ride again, Hannah lifted Mazie behind her saddle and mounted herself. She couldn't believe how much easier it was to get on a horse now that she didn't have to worry about the long, full shirts and petticoats that always hampered her movements. Like Mazie, she felt unencumbered and light, ready for any physical effort.

"Dolly and Leah, we'll ride as far as we can, maybe until dark. Is that all right? Can you do it?"

Both girls nodded eagerly.

After her rest, Leah took the reins. Dolly was again riding behind her sister. As the two horses side by side loped easily over the hard, level ground completely out of range of the soldiers, the girls chatted. "Mama, shouldn't we use boys' names?" Dolly asked. "If we use our real names, people will know we aren't boys."

"Yeah," Leah laughed. "Who ever heard of a boy called Dolly?"

"You're right. What name do you want?"

"Bob," Dolly said immediately.

"Fine, Bob. And Leah?" Hannah asked.

"I can be just plain Lee," Leah said. "It's part of my name anyway."

"Good. Now Mazie." They all thought for a few seconds as they walked their horses across a rough area. "Max is pretty close. We'll probably remember to use the boys' names easier if they are close to the real names." They all agreed that Mazie would be Max.

"What about you, Mama?" Mazie asked.

"I'll be Hank. We also need a different last name. We can't use Rockfort. Maybe we better make it completely different, like Smith or Jones."

"Too common," Leah said.

"Yes. If anyone suspected us, they'd know that wasn't our real name." They all thought of names that would suit. "It should be a common name, one that wouldn't attract much notice. What about Johnston?"

That suited everyone. The girls practiced their own names and calling their sisters their new names.

"Now so we won't have to think about it when other people are with us," Hannah said, "let's use our new names all the time when we are dressed as boys. Beginning now. How about it Max? Bob? And Lee Johnston?"

"Yes..." Leah started to say Mama, but stopped. "What will we call you, Mama?"

"Father. It'd be hard for you to say, 'Papa.'"

"Father sounds too uppity," Dolly said.

"Yes, it does." Hannah said.

"What about Pa?" Leah suggested.

"Good boy, Lee," Hannah laughed. "I'm Pa now." Hannah's shoulders were more relaxed now. The worried strain she'd worn since they were taken from home was replaced with one of determination.

They had to camp for the night before they reached the county line out of the military zone. Since they hadn't met anyone all day, Hannah thought it would be safe to travel an easier east-west road rather than across the open prairie. This far east a few of the homesteads they passed had not been burned, but all were vacant and vandalized. Windows were broken and, just as their own marigold bed, flowers and gardens were flattened. Fences were pulled down and cornfields trampled down or burned. Through the open door of one house they passed, Hannah saw that someone had stabled horses in the living room.

Hannah debated whether she should spend the night in one of the houses, but decided against it. If the lieutenant chased them, a house would be the first place he would search. When she saw a partially-destroyed barn beside a burned down house, she decided this would be suitable.

They ate the food Leah had taken from the soldiers. The girls were surprised when Hannah brought out some dry bread and jerky she had stashed from their meals at the detention camp. That with water from the well made their evening meal. They staked out the horses to graze before putting them up in a barn stall for the night. Huddled together in some old hay in the corner of the loft, Hannah and her girls slept.

Except for the Bushwhackers, the only men not in one army or the other in all Missouri were very young or old, or were wounded soldiers returned from the army. The next morning to avoid questions and suspicions, now that she was a military-aged man, Hannah wrapped her left arm in a sling and put a bandage around her head under her hat before they continued traveling east.

Safely out of the military zone, and into the woods of the western edge of the Ozark hills, they stopped at a crossroads store. The little settlement of three or four occupied houses seemed like a city after the loneliness and desolation of the military zone. The weathered-oak, gray store front with its faded sign seemed to welcome them. A real greeting came from an old man warming himself in the sun on a bench on the store porch—the first person they had seen since escaping from the soldiers.

"Howdy, fellers," he said as Hannah and Leah tied up their horses. He noticed that they had some luggage and came from the west. "Been run off'n yer place?"

"Yes," Hannah said. Though she had an alto voice, she pitched her voice a bit lower.

"Seen some action, too, I reckon," he said pointing to her arm in a sling.

"Yeah, Eighth Missouri State Militia. Hank Johnston's the name."

"And they even run you out?"

"Yeah. Everyone no matter."

"Dadblamed shame," the old man said shaking his head. "Lots of folks come through here not knowin' where to go." He eyed the children and then asked Hannah, "And yer wife?"

"Dead."

The old man made a clicking noise of sympathy and moved his chaw of tobacco to his other cheek. "Where'ya from?"

Hannah had decided they should tell as few lies as they could. All they needed to disguise was their names, the name of their ranch, and the fact that they escaped from the soldiers. "From northwestern Vernon County. Our ranch is on the Osage River."

"You've come a fer piece." He leaned over and spit a stream of tobacco juice over the edge of the wooden porch onto the dirt road.

"Yes, we have. The boys and I need some supplies."

"Soldiers didn't let you take much, I see." He studied the horses and the four bags hanging from the saddles.

"And they burned our barn," Mazie said.

Before she would talk too much to this friendly man, Hannah ushered the girls into the store. She had basically the same conversation with the storekeeper and his wife. Hannah bought the supplies she needed, mostly food, a water canteen, and four blankets. Even with their coats spread over them the night before, they were chilled in the early autumn coolness.

"Hello, little boy," the storekeeper's wife said to Mazie. "What's your name?"

"Max Johnston," she said readily. "And I'm six years old and soon be seven."

"Can you introduce me to your brothers?"

Full of her importance, Mazie took Dolly's hand. "This here is Bob and Lee is the biggest."

"I'm sorry you had to leave your home," the storekeeper's wife said. "Were you able to bring any of your toys?"

Remembering her doll, Mazie's face started to pucker. "No, I wanted to get my..."

Leah interrupted before Mazie would reveal that they were girls by telling about her doll she had to leave. "Pa wouldn't let Max get his toy animals he made for him." She pushed Mazie toward her mother and gave her a stern look while shaking her head.

"Here, little Max," the woman said, handing her a toy horse. "Maybe this will help."

"Thank you," Mazie said after Leah poked her.

"It ain't right what's happenin' to all you folks," the storekeeper said. "Did you know that some of the women and children are held in army posts just like prisoners?" Hannah shook her head in amazement. "There's one jest west of here a piece. Lucky you missed that. Being a veteran and all, I guess they let you leave."

"Yes, I left before the soldiers came." Hannah had noticed that he had some horses in a corral behind the store. Before he would wonder what she had been doing during the three weeks since the deadline of the Order, she changed the subject. "My horses are worn out, carrying double and all. I wondered if you would trade them for some fresh ones. The boys and I want to get to Jefferson City where I have relatives. Mine are good horses, but I don't think they will last."

It took them thirty minutes to finalize the trade. They made an even switch, though Hannah knew the fresh horses were not as good as the ones Captain Cardwell let them ride. But the trade was worth it. If she ever met up with the lieutenant or any of his men, they would immediately know the horses even if they didn't recognize Hannah in her male disguise. She planned now to head straight to Prairie Wood Ranch. They had passed the test. Everyone at the store believed them to be what they said they were. She thought that they could even fool the lieutenant, but not if they rode the same horses. She struck the deal.

Before they left, the storekeeper gave each child a stick of candy and Hannah a plug of tobacco. Dolly stifled a snicker at the picture of her mother chewing and spitting like the old man on the porch. Hannah thanked the merchant and stuck the tobacco in her pocket. It might not hurt to have the smell of tobacco on her, she thought.

Mounted on their fresh horses, they continued following the road east until they came to the first one heading south. From then on Hannah traveled the roads that went south and west. She rode boldly, feeling safe from detection. And since she was now a man, she took her revolver from her bag and stuck it in her belt. A man, especially a wounded veteran, would carry a gun in this country. When the gun poked her in the stomach and her ribs as she rode, she decided she would buy a holster at the next store they came to.

She couldn't believe how well their escape had gone. All her plans from Plan One to Plan Four had gone like clockwork. The final one, Plan Five, would be the easiest. Simply get home, assess the situation there, and prepare to spend the winter in the shack on the river. Reviewing in her mind the map of the region, she believed that she would reach home tomorrow. She tossed her head, whose lightness without her heavy bun still seemed strange. She unbuttoned her coat since the day was warming up, and looked around her at the wooded area they were traveling through. The fresh horses had lots of pep. She dug her heels in her gelding's side and brought him to a steady lope. Beside her in the road, Leah slapped her mare with the ends of her reins to keep up.

"Say, boys, let's go home, what'd'ya say?" Hannah asked.

Sitting behind her on the gelding, Mazie hugged her mother. Both Leah and Dolly nodded. Dolly pulled off her stocking cap and waved it in the air. Her short hair that curled up into tiny curls hugged her head. The mid-morning sun streaking through the tall oak and hickory trees bordering the road shone on her hair, forming a halo around her. The child looked so pretty Hannah wondered how anyone could mistake her for a boy.

Then Dolly whooped loudly, pulled her cap back down over her head clear to her eyebrows. Holding her seat behind the saddle with her knees, she swayed with the swing of the horse as if she were part of him. "Pa and brothers, let's make tracks," she said. She jammed her heels into the mare's flanks, making her jump ahead of the gelding. Leah laughed and let her gallop full speed down the road.

Hannah changed her mind. Dolly not only looked like a boy, but she could act like one, too. She smiled with real pleasure for the first time since seeing Captain Murdock ride up the trail at Prairie Wood. They were together and would soon be home. Never again would she let down her guard and allow anyone to capture her. Her smile was one of satisfaction that she was no longer alone with all the responsibilities. The girls had proven themselves capable and inventive.

She almost looked forward to the charade they would have to play. Though she shivered slightly when she thought of Murdock, she was confident they could fool him if their paths crossed again. Wouldn't that be something? To get the better of that Redleg bandit. That would be worth the risk of confronting him.

But there was no mistaking her foremost wish to be home. Even if all the buildings were burned, it was still home. The land was there, and the girls were with her. With her knowledge of plants and animals, they would survive. She patted the revolver in her belt.

"Hold on tight, Max," she said. When she felt Mazie's arms tighten around her waist, she spurred her gelding to a gallop and soon caught up to Leah and Dolly who were disappearing around a bend in the road.

Chapter 6

IT WAS too cloudy to see the sun that was high in the sky the next day when the Rockforts rode boldly up the trail to their house. Their winter coats were comfortable in the chilly, damp air.

Because their attention was focused straight ahead through the tall grass, none of them noticed that it was about to rain as they crested the rise where they had paused over two weeks ago to catch the last glimpse of their ranch buildings. Hannah believed the patches of unburned prairie was a good sign. With anxious glances at their mother, Leah and Dolly pulled their mare ahead of her gelding.

"Careful, girls," Hannah warned them unnecessarily. A few miles back they had seen Captain Murdock's detail coming toward them in time to gallop across the prairie and hide behind a swell in the ground. They were lucky that time. Even with their new disguises, she didn't want to face him again. After the soldiers had loped by, she returned to the road.

As soon as they had turned into their lane from the main road, Hannah had walked her horse slowly as she looked for recent tracks or other evidence that anyone had been there since they were taken prisoners sixteen days ago. At the entrance, they were forced to detour around her husband's arched sign for Prairie Wood Ranch, because it was lying in the trail. Raw axe marks showed where a soldier had chopped through the poles holding it up, but she saw no evidence that anyone had come this way recently. The motionless grasses were standing upright in the humid calm of the dreary late September day. The rains had washed away the hoof marks of the shod cavalry horses, the heavy boot prints of the marching men, and the narrow tracks from the iron rims of the loaded wagon which carried away their best furnishings and clothing. She let the girls ride ahead, but called out, "Get off before you get to the crest of the mound."

They waved back. Hannah wanted to make sure no one was at the building site before riding in. They dismounted, tied their horse to a bush and hidden by the tall grasses, walked to the top of the rise to get their first glimpse. Hannah and Mazie were right behind them. Prepared for the total devastation they had seen everywhere, they held their breaths, at first not believing what they saw. Although the barn and all outbuildings were burned, the house still stood, solid, inviting, and safe, its white clapboard siding a beacon in the gray day. It seemed so natural that the little girls stood up to run home.

But looking more closely, they noticed smoke-blackened stains around the opened front room windows that looked like the house had been crying tears and when wiping them off, smeared its face with the soot from the seared barn lot. The spirea bushes in the yard drooped and the leaves of the young maple by the porch that should have been in full fall color were dull and lifeless. Some pieces of furniture were still in the yard. From their distance they could not discern the damage.

The girls began talking excitedly. "Hush, girls," Hannah said, putting her finger to her lips. "Listen."

The scene seemed peaceful and unoccupied. The only sound was a meadow lark that called. Though Hannah always loved the bird's cheerful call, this time it sounded mournful and lonesome. Seeing no one there, she said softly, "Dolly, come with me. Leah, you and Mazie stay here with the horses while we look around. Come when I wave."

Hannah and Dolly cut through the grass rather than use the lane. Hannah bent over to keep out of sight, though her husband's long brown coat and felt hat blended in with the dried grass so that she was well camouflaged. When they reached the burned stretch around the buildings, she motioned Dolly to stay still while she circled the area. It was deathly quiet.

Concluding that they were alone, she waved to Dolly to join her. She stepped over a pile of rubble. Immediately from under the carelessly stacked boards came a frightened, high-pitched squawk. A mottled-gray body brushed against her outstretched arm and flew up in her face. Even as she was controlling her panic, she knew it was a hen. If she had taken one more step she would have trod on the hen's nest of three brown eggs.

Hearing the hen, Dolly ran delightedly to her mother and hugged her. "Mama, the old dominicker. They didn't get her!" Then Dolly scrambled around trying to catch the still squawking hen that darted through the barnyard. "We've got to take her with us," Dolly said, thinking of their little dog, Poco. She didn't think she could stand the death of another of their animals. She sometimes woke in the night screaming from nightmares reliving the moment when the soldier shot Poco. When she and her mother first approached the house she had looked first toward the cellar door where little Poco's dead body lay when she last saw him. There was no trace of him. Reared on the prairies, she knew the ways of nature. Coyotes, or vultures probably carried him off.

Hannah laid her hand on Dolly's arm. "No, not now. The hen is safe here."

"But if the soldiers come back and find her, they'll wring her neck and eat her."

"She got away once. She probably will again. I wouldn't have seen her if I hadn't almost stepped on her. She was hidden good. If we take her to the shack, she might show herself to the men and they would know there's someone around and come looking for us. Here at the house, even if they do find her, they will realize she escaped from them the first time. They won't think anything about a hen being here, but back in the woods? No. She'll just have to risk staying here."

Reluctantly Dolly agreed. From past experience they knew how hard it was to catch the old wily hen. Already the hen had disappeared.

Hannah was as happy about finding the hen as Dolly was. Something had survived the raid and fire. If one hen got away, maybe there were more. Later she would look. But for now there was more urgent business.

Knowing for sure they were alone now, as the noise the hen made probably carried to the two girls almost half a mile away, Hannah walked boldly to the house. Together she and Dolly stepped on the porch, trying not to see the ruined marigolds and Hannah's mashed herbs. They peeped inside the door that was standing open.

The serene exterior of the house belied the mess inside and the smell of smoke still hanging in the air. The living room walls and floor at the front were badly scorched. Near the door the rag carpet was burned. There were spotty holes in the center of the room where sparks must have lit, but the fire did not harm the rug along the back wall. The curtains, jerked off the windows onto the floor were half burned. It looked as if a soldier had thrown a lighted torch through the door. The fire it ignited in the rag carpet and curtains burned for a time in the front part of the room, but for some reason didn't spread any farther. Puzzled why the fire fizzled out in spite of all the flammable material around it, Hannah studied the room. Then she noticed that the patchwork quilt she kept draped over her old davenport to hide the worn places was folded in half and then clumsily wadded into a roll. Scorch marks on one end indicated it had been used to extinguish the flames.

"Dolly, someone put out the fire after it was set! He used this quilt to beat it out." She saw no other explanation why the partially burned curtains were pulled down and why the fire which burned for a time, enough to spew smoke out the windows and stain the white paint outside, did not spread throughout the wooden house. For the first time in months, she felt that they weren't alone. One of the soldiers had secretly helped her.

She tried to visualize the men to figure out which one he was, but except for the lieutenant and Captain Murdock, she could bring up no other individual face. The rest seemed to wear identical masks. Although she rarely doubted her ability to do what had to be done, she felt certain now that she and the girls would survive this war with her triple dose of luck—an unknown ally in Captain Murdock's cavalry, the unburned house, and the old dominicker hen.

But when she looked in the other rooms, her elation was short-lived. Though not vandalized, the house had been ransacked. Books, pots, utensils, clothing, bedding, everything not valued by the soldiers had been thrown on the floor, broken, torn, or tromped on. Some wild animal, probably an opossum, had made a nest. There were tracks and droppings from other small animals and birds that had come into the opened doors and windows.

Feeling it was safe, Hannah waved to Leah to come. She and Mazie each climbed on a horse and galloped to them. Like Dolly had done, they each glanced first to the ground in front of the cellar door to see if Poco's body was still there.

"We'll take only a few minutes to look around and take what we can, but we better get to the shack right away." Hannah didn't need to say that for they already knew they would live in their log hide-out. "Leah, you and Mazie get all of Papa's clothes that are left. Dolly, see if there's any bedding, and I'll check in the kitchen and cellar for anything we can take now."

Some of their old clothes were still there, though pulled out and scattered over the floor. Anything of value was gone, but Hannah saw with satisfaction that there was still some old bedding and kitchen utensils. They could make do with them.

When the girls had gathered up what they could take with them on this trip, Hannah and Leah carried inside a table, three straight chairs, a dresser, and their old dish safe that the soldiers left in the yard. Evidently there wasn't room for them in the wagon.

The mist thickened. Their coats were damp before they moved all the furnishings inside. Hannah didn't want to take the time, or to risk building a fire as the smoke might alert someone that they were back. She removed her wet coat and Leah's coat and, tearing the patchwork quilt in two, used it to protect them until they could get to the shack.

"Can't we stay here tonight?" Mazie asked. She looked longingly at her old bedstead that was still in her room, though the featherbed was gone and the straw matting was pulled off and slit open with the straw strewn over the floor.

"No, we better not. Let's first go to the shack and fix a place to hide the horses. Then we'll come back to make a thorough search and get what we can."

She closed the windows and door. Wrapping her half of the seared quilt around her like a shawl, she took the reins of her horse that was loaded now with bundles wrapped in old blankets and sheets and started walking through the burned barnyard on the path to the river.

"Mama!" Mazie shouted. She was behind her mother, but ran back toward the house before Hannah could stop her.

Then the others heard what caused Mazie to run back. "Meow." Then a brief pause and another piteous, "Meow."

"Puss?" Dolly's eyes lit up as she caught up with her sister. Mazie was on her hands and knees at a small opening in the rock foundation of the house. From behind it came a series of heart-rendering meows.

"Here, kitty. Here Puss," Mazie called. She stretched out on her stomach on the wet ground, her tear-streaked, but happy face pressed against the four-inch hole in the piled limestone rocks of the foundation. "C'mon, kitty." Mazie was talking non-stop to lure the cat out. Mazie stuck her arm in the hole as far as she could reach. Puss stayed just out of her grasp. Though the cat came close to the hole, meowing all the time, she wouldn't come out.

The girls were jumping around and all calling and talking at once. "We're scaring her," Hannah said. She knelt down to peer through the rocks. In the gloom under the house she could make out their pet by her white and yellow markings. "She's all right, not hurt or anything. Let's leave her alone for now. We'll come back and get her later."

None of the girls would listen to that advice. This was their Puss that they believed killed like poor little Poco. She was one of the family. Ignoring her mother, Dolly ran around to the back where she knew there was a space large enough for her to crawl under the house. She had hidden there before. She pulled out a few rocks and crawled in. Guided by Mazie's voice, she crawled on her stomach in the semi-darkness toward Puss. "Here, Puss, here Puss," she kept calling. Since Dolly was under the house, apparently Puss thought she was safer than Mazie because the cat ran up to her readily. Dolly hugged her tight, her tears falling. "I got her, I got her!" she called. Puss immediately began purring.

The others ran to the back hole to greet Puss when Dolly brought her out. Though anxious to get out of the rain which was still light, Hannah was as delighted as the girls. When Dolly handed Puss to Mazie, the child looked up at her mother and said, "You said Puss would be waiting for us, and she was."

"Yes, sugar, she's been waiting for us." Hannah remembered the first time she saw Puss. When she first escaped Carl Murdock's wrath at the neighbor's house seven years ago Puss was a brand new kitten nursing her mother.

"And now Papa can find us, too, can't he?" Mazie was convinced that her mother knew everything.

Hannah looked at Mazie. Her stocking cap was barely on her short-cropped head and her boys' clothing were mud-stained and wet. Mazie's expression demanded an affirmative answer. Knowing what survivalists cats are, she had really believed her promise of Puss being here was very possible. But the child's father? Though Hannah's realistic mind had convinced her time and again that he would not come home—two years is such a long time during a war with no news—down deep, like her daughters, she still hoped. When she analyzed her recent actions, she realized that hope was what made her stay after Order No. 11 and what had brought her back home. It would have been so much easier and safer to leave the county as everyone else did until the odious Order was revoked. But on the chance that Paul would be alive and come for them, she had to be here. Being anywhere else was unthinkable.

"Yes, Mazie, Papa can find us now," she said. And she meant it. The other girls hugged Mazie and Puss. "Now, hurry. Let's get to the shack out of this rain."

Mazie put Puss inside her coat. The cat snuggled down against her thin chest, purring loudly and working her claws in and out in ecstacy.

They found their shack untouched. Its log walls blending among the protective trees escaped the soldiers' notice. The provisions they'd stored for emergencies were still there. Hannah's first task was to build a fire in the fireplace from the hidden pile of wood. She had collected white oak wood because it burned clean without much smoke that would broadcast their position. The girls carried in all their bags and the bundles from the house. It didn't take long for the fire to take the chill and dampness from the one room and heat the water in the kettle. The girls took off their wet clothes and drank hot mugs of sassafras tea.

The rain was coming down steadily. Though the wind had risen on the prairie, down in the river's swampy and wooded bottom, they could not feel it. Soon the girls were no longer trembling from the chill, their cheeks becoming rosy with the warmth of the fire and the tea. Puss stretched out in the warmest place contentedly washing herself with her red tongue and white-tipped paws. Hannah put on Paul's oiled leather coat he used in winter and went outside to see about the horses.

Unsaddling them, she led them through the pathless brush and trees along the steep river bank for about a quarter of a mile. When she came to a barrier of brush and fallen branches that looked natural, she smiled in satisfaction. The corral was still here even though she hadn't used it for over a year since the army stole her last horses. Even then they didn't take the horses from this hidden place, but caught her working them in the field. So far no one had discovered this paddock.

She pulled back some limbs and led the two horses inside. There she removed their bridles and turned them loose. Since she hadn't been here for several months, she walked the perimeter of the rather large paddock. It would hold the horses for now, she decided, but she would need to do some repair on it later. She crossed the area, happy that the open glade was lush with grass. Before she returned to the shack, she walked to the draw that cut through the grasses and trees to spill into the river. Everyplace else along this side of the river, the ground fell abruptly down to the river eight to twelve feet below. But by following the easy slope of the draw that cut through the mud banks, the horses could reach the river for water.

Hannah looked it over carefully. This was the escape route from the shack and the only access across the river for several miles in either direction. She doubted that even Captain Murdock's scout knew of this ford. She saw nothing to alarm her. She could discern no hoof prints either on this side or across the river where the heavily wooded bank sloped gradually upward.

Rain dripped from the brim of her hat, some of it finding its way inside the collar of Paul's coat. She patted the horses who had followed her to the water. After a long drink from the river, the two horses settled down to graze. As she looked over the improvised paddock with scattered brown tree trunks and the drying grasses, she thought of still another piece of luck. Instead of being gray, white, or spotted as were many of the common mustangs in the area, the mare and gelding she had traded for were bays. Their dark coloring blended into the foliage.

Satisfied that the horses were secure, Hannah headed back to the shack, planning what she needed to do. She'd need to go to a town for necessary supplies. Since the little county seat town of Nevada City had been burned last spring and was still almost deserted, she'd have to cross the Kansas border to Fort Scott. That town and military station was actually closer than Nevada City, but going there would be dangerous because she risked running into Captain Murdock, Lieutenant Knowles, or some of the other soldiers that might recognize her. The only alternative was traveling much farther to neighboring counties, east to El Dorado Springs or south to Lamar. No, the extra travel and time expended to reach these other towns would be just as risky. And, she reasoned, with the success so far with her male disguise, she should have no difficulty in Fort

Scott.

That decided, she thought through the immediate tasks facing her. First, double-check the security of the shack during the winter when the protective leaves would be gone, return to the house for other things they could use and repair the damage there, sew some more boys' clothing for the girls, gather more wood, resupply her herb bag... The list seemed endless.

But these tasks weren't difficult. She had become accustomed in the past two years to this type of work and actually looked forward to the challenge. From this time on, her labors were reinforcing their ability to stay on their own place so that when the war was over and Paul returned, they would be able to resume building their family's future on the ranch.

She stopped in her tracks. For the first time in many months she was planning when Paul returned, not if. Surely their good fortune in getting back home meant that God intended them to all be together again. As always when she surveyed her land, either the marvelous open prairie, or even this boggy woodland along the river, she never failed to become overwhelmed with a sense of pride and ownership. She felt large enough to embrace the entire thousand acres. It was her land to cherish. Hers to sustain her family.

The rain was easing up. From behind her as she hurried back to her children, the sky was brightening. Tomorrow will be a good day. Another good omen in this day of happy surprises.

But she couldn't be content with only her own escape and good fortune. On her trip to her ranch she had seen the Kerrigan place, like many others they passed, with every building burnt to the ground, and acres of prairie land scorched. Her neighbors were still prisoners at the camp and maybe sick. And like Hannah, Beulah was labeled as a lady bushwhacker because she had to be forcefully removed from her home instead of obeying the mandates of Order No. 11. The Kerrigan case was even worse than hers, for Beulah's husband was serving somewhere in the South in General Sterling Price's Confederate Army.

In Hannah's view both sides in this war were equally ruthless, each committing unspeakable acts which they justified. A war for abolishing slavery. A war to preserve states' rights. Both were good causes, but evil men latched on to them as justification to commit murder and mayhem in the name of God. She saw both evil and good on both sides. What was evil was not one side or the other, but the war itself. Slavery was wrong, no question, but fighting a war, destroying property, and enslaving others like herself and the Kerrigans was not the way to solve it.

Or even if the war was restricted to the opposing armies, then only the men who wanted to fight would be involved. But from her experience she believed that some of the greatest suffering was by those not wearing uniforms. The people at home, the women, children, and old men, like Beulah's father-in-law, and, she'd never forget, the young men, like Paul, who were taken from their homes to serve against their will. Then perhaps worse of all, whole families including babies and little children abducted and ruined by the whim of a general in Kansas City who commissioned a fanatic captain to war against civilians rather than against Bushwhackers and Rebels.

As she thought of the suffering she had witnessed at the detention camp, she knew she could not be content with her own escape. She had to do something. Though she couldn't free everyone there, she could at least honor her promise to Leah to get Beulah's family from the camp before the weather turned cold. From Beulah's past history of lung problems, Hannah knew she could not survive a winter there. Since she automatically knew how to do the chores to prepare her own family for the winter, she turned her thought to how she could free the Kerrigans.

Shivering slightly as more rain water ran off her hat brim into her collar and down her back, she pulled her coat closer, and taking big strides, returned to the shack. Only the squirrels saw her long legs cover the ground, and no one but the birds heard her boots squishing with each step she took in the oozy ground. The wildlife would instinctively known that she was female, but had there been any human eyes watching her, they would not have suspected. Not only her clothing, but her bearing and the determination in her walk indicated that this assurance was from the head of a family.

Chapter 7

A WEEK later on a beautiful, warm early October day, Hannah rode openly into Captain Cardwell's military encampment on the eastern edge of the Burnt District. At Dolly's suggestion, in addition to wearing Paul's clothes and having her hair cut like a man, she wore a false mustache Dolly bought in Fort Scott. Hannah had practiced with it at home for hours to see if it would stay fastened tightly. Though it bothered her when she talked or wrinkled up her upper lip, she soon learned to ignore it except for running her forefinger over it occasionally. Leah thought that gesture made her seem more like a man. Most of the men she knew who had face hair often stroked it with pride in their masculinity just as women often ran their hands over their long hair.

No one they had met on the road, or in Fort Scott when they made a brief visit there for necessary supplies, ever doubted that Hannah was a man. She was as tall as many men and always held herself erect and proud. Her self-respecting stance was probably the main reason Carl Murdock had assaulted her those years ago at the Newman farm. He expected women to be more subservient in their bearing, especially with guns pointed at them. Nor had anyone doubted that the girls were not the boys they pretended to be. But so far, none of the people she met had known her or seen her before. Now just a week after requesting leave to go to Independence, approaching Captain Cardwell in the closeness of his office was a gamble. The mustache might be the added touch she needed to pull it off.

Hannah had worked though all the details of her plan, practicing it with the girls and getting their input. She believed it would work, if, and it was a big if, Captain Cardwell or his aides didn't recognize her.

"He saw you only that one short time, Mama, uh, Pa, and remember you had on your bonnet that shaded your face," Leah said.

"Yes," Dolly said, "and he was talking to my lieutenant most of the time."

"He hardly looked at you at all," Leah agreed.

"But he may have heard that we escaped from Lieutenant Knowles and be suspicious when he gets a request for another family to leave. So we must be careful."

"He wouldn't expect us to come back here," Leah said.

Hannah laughed. "No, he wouldn't. If I were in his place, I'd think this was the last place Hannah Rockfort would come to."

The camp wasn't where she should be. Several times on the trip up to the camp she asked herself why she was endangering her family again. They were safely away. Why risk it? As she drew nearer, she experienced again the fear and hopelessness she felt when they were first brought here. Then she remembered the dominicker hen and Puss and the unknown soldier who put out the fire that saved her house. Beulah had none of those advantages. In contrast, she had watched her home burn. She had no escape shack to return to. And not in good health herself, in addition to her children, Beulah was burdened with an old and frail father-in-law. With no relatives, Hannah was her one hope. Of all her neighbors from before the war, the Kerrigans were the only ones whose whereabouts Hannah knew. She had been there at the birth of all three of her children and helped Beulah doctor their childhood illnesses. Beulah's husband used to trade work with Paul.

With renewed resolve, Hannah continued her mission.

"Dolly and Mazie, whoops, Bob and Max, you remember what you are to do?"

"Yes, Pa, we know." They still giggled when they said, "Pa," though Leah and Hannah cautioned them about that.

"Where will Beulah go when we get her out?" Leah asked.

"I don't know. She'll have to decide that, she and her father-in-law. Our job is to get her safely away." Though Hannah had thought only of Beulah all this time and her three little children, a pre-school boy and two girls, she knew that she had to include Beulah's old father-in-law in her plans. At the camp they hadn't seen much of Virgil as he was quartered in the men's tent across the camp and ate in a different shift. Even Beulah rarely had any contact with him, though her little boy often visited him.

It was mess time when Hannah and her girls dressed as boys rode into the camp on their two horses. When she presented her request to the sentry to see the officer in charge, she was told to wait. The captain was eating his dinner. Though acting annoyed, Hannah was glad for this interval. She hunched down, man-like, concealed behind her horse by the main path beside the cook shack.

Dolly was the first to spot Beulah and her children leaving the mess shack. She poked her mother and pointed. "Now?" she asked. Hannah nodded. Dolly then whispered to Mazie, "Remember what you're to do?" Mazie nodded and chased Dolly up the path. The Kerrigan children, a few rods ahead of their mother, turned to watch when these boys they didn't know ran past them. Dolly collided into Beulah, almost knocking her down.

Mazie grabbed Dolly and said, "I caught you, Bob, I caught you. Now you're It." Then she ran back to Hannah.

"I fell. It's not fair," Dolly called after her as she forced a folded paper into Beulah's hand and immediately ran after Mazie.

Startled, Beulah glanced at the paper in her hand and then at the strange boys. Dolly and Mazie continued playing tag close to Hannah, with Leah joining in. Beulah didn't at first see Hannah, and Dolly and Mazie had brushed by her so quickly she hadn't looked at them. She took a quick glance around to see if anyone was watching her before she opened the paper. There in Hannah's writing were the words, "Your crippled brother is here to take you to Clinton. Send word to Virgil." It was signed, "Hank Johnston."

Beulah glanced up to look for the boy that had slipped her the note just as Hannah stepped from behind her horse. Beulah met Hannah's eyes, recognizing her in spite of her disguise. Hannah, shook her head slightly and retreated behind the horse. Dolly, again chased by Mazie, ran to Beulah. As the two "boys" were tagging each other in front of Beulah, Dolly said, "Beulah, it's us, the Rockforts. Just go on back to the tent. We've come to get you."

Beulah clutched her children who were still eying the new boys. "Quick, now, get back to the tent," was all she told them in way of explanation. The Kerrigans hurried around the corner of the cook shack to their tent.

No one noticed the exchange of words except the sentry on duty, but he showed no signs of concern as he watched the children playing. Waiting patiently beside the gelding, Hannah/Johnston corralled the "boys" who sat cross-legged on the ground beside her. The sentry turned his attention to four soldiers returning to camp.

"Good job," Hannah whispered to Dolly and Mazie when they returned to her. This was one time she hoped that Captain Cardwell would have a leisurely meal, for she wanted to give Beulah enough time to prepare her family for the reunion with their "uncle." In a few minutes she saw Beulah's little boy running toward the men's tent.

But the captain was in a hurry. The Kerrigan boy had barely reached his grandfather's tent before Cardwell sent an aide to say that he would see Mr. Johnston. Hannah, using a stick to avoid putting her whole weight on her lame left foot, limped toward the headquarters tent. Her children followed behind. When she was admitted into the captain's presence, in her assumed deep voice, Hannah told the children to stay outside and to mind their p's and q's. Obediently they sat down on the ground to wait, Leah in the middle holding each sister by the hand.

Hannah stood in the room leaning on her stick for several minutes before Captain Cardwell looked up from some papers he was studying.

"Johnston, I believe it is. I hear you want to see me," he said, still without looking up.

"Yes, Captain Cardwell. I have learned that my sister and her family are here."

"And her name?"

"Beulah Kerrigan with three children and her father-in-law, Virgil Kerrigan."

Cardwell shuffled through his papers to find those names. "Picked up at their house in northern Vernon County September 8 for not obeying Order Number Eleven," he read. "Head of family in Price's army. Suspected bushwhacker activity." He looked at Hannah for the first time. With his eyes boring into her, she straightened up. He studied her erect bearing, noticed the stick and her rancher's clothing. "Who are you and what do you want of me?"

"I am Hank Johnston from near Clinton. I just got word that my sister was here. I've come to take her and her family back home with me."

"What about this bushwhacker business?" Although Captain Carl Murdock had labeled every family he had sent in as Bushwhackers,

Cardwell didn't take that charge too seriously when it referred to women and old men.

"I know nothing about that, Captain. It's true that her husband is with the Rebels, but so are many other men in Missouri." She assumed the most masculine pose she could master and deepening her voice still more continued, "But being an outlaw? How could she do anything with three little young'uns and an enfeebled father-in-law to care for?"

The captain studied Hannah as if thinking about her reply. "It says here that she didn't obey the Order but had to be forcefully evicted."

"She had no way of leaving. The armies and Bushwhackers had already taken her team and wagon and all the money she had," Hannah said looking boldly into his eyes.

"Why didn't you go get her then and save all this trouble?"

"I knew nothing of it. I was in the East when the Order was given. I've just returned and learned of her imprisonment."

The captain flinched when Hannah used the word 'imprisonment.' "This is hardly a prison," he said.

"What else would you call it? I know it was none of your doing. You're only obeying your orders, but these women and children you hold here can't leave without official permission, can they?"

"No. And I must hold under guard those who haven't registered their loyalty and the ones labeled as assisting the Bushwhackers," Cardwell explained. "'Detention' is the word I use to refer to their condition. Your sister is under detention."

"Why? Did anyone see her on a raid into Kansas or catch her sheltering any Bushwhackers?"

The captain read again what was on the Kerrigans' record. He shook his head. "Only that they did not leave the specified counties as ordered, and since they aren't registered, they must be detained."

"And how could they register their loyalty when it meant a trip to General Ewing's headquarters in Kansas City?" Hannah asked this in a non-accusing manner. Her purpose was not to rile the captain but encourage him to see the injustice of Beulah's imprisonment and thus give his permission for her family to leave.

"I'm not authorized to release anyone without orders." The captain studied Hannah intently for a few seconds. "If you could get an official order of loyalty."

"It's a long trip to Kansas City. I hoped that you could give that to me."

"I might be able to vouch for her." The captain studied Hannah and reread Murdock's report of Beulah's capture.

Hannah believed that he would agree to release the Kerrigans. She gave a satisfied smile that revealed her missing lower tooth just as he looked up.

"Have we met before?" The captain had a quizzical expression as if trying to place her.

"No, sir, I believe not."

"Perhaps not." Captain Cardwell stroked his neat gray beard and dropped his eyes to his papers. "Mr. Johnston, do you have the means to take Mrs. Kerrigan and her family all the way back to Clinton with you?"

"I have only two horses. I had to bring my boys along with me. No one to leave them with 'cause their ma died of the fever last winter. But they are strong and used to walking, even the littl'un. My sister and her father-in-law can ride the horses with the two smallest children."

Cardwell looked at Hannah's left foot that she was favoring by putting most of her weight on her other foot.

"Oh, I can walk. Though I've been crippled most of my life, I can walk. Have to on the farm. Yes, sir, I have the means to take them back. If necessary, I'll buy a couple more horses." When the captain didn't say anything, Hannah added, "Perhaps you have an extra horse or two I could buy?"

"No. We haven't any extra horses." Cardwell frowned. "I lost two horses just last week." He didn't explain, though Hannah suspected he was referring to the ones she stole when she escaped from Lieutenant Knowles. She wondered how much the captain knew about her escape and hoped that neither he nor the lieutenant got into trouble because of her.

"If it's agreeable with you, sir," Hannah said after a suitable pause when he continued silent, "I'd like to see my sister and help her get her things packed. We need to get as far along the road as we can today before it gets dark."

While waiting for the captain to see her, Hannah had overheard the sentry talking to the returned soldiers that in the last week two of his prisoners and one soldier had died of the fever. She held her breath for a nod of his head that could reduce his charges by five people, even if their Confederate connection was obvious. Hannah banked that he would think it better to let them leave than risk their dying on him. Since Captain Cardwell didn't have the authority to let the Kerrigans leave, he studied Hannah to assess the strange man before him who had no official standing or papers that would allow the woman's release.

"What do you do in Clinton?"

"Not in the town. I have a farm west of town." Hannah waited a few more seconds. When he said nothing more, she added, "There are plenty of people in Jeff City that can vouch for me."

Cardwell was studying Hannah very carefully. He seemed especially interested in her eyes. She removed her hat, showing her cropped hair, and running her fingers through her hair as she had seen many men do, put her hat back on, arranging it carefully to the proper mannish angle.

"You look familiar. Are you sure we haven't met?" Cardwell asked.

"I don't believe so, sir," Hannah's heart skipped, but steeling herself she continued, "but you may have seen me around the capitol. I'm often there."

"Doing what?"

"I sell hay sometimes to the army. And in season some fruits and vegetables."

Cardwell continued to study her. Then he shrugged and said, "Probably so. I was stationed there for a few weeks before being ordered here to assist in the evacuation." When he said the last word, he frowned as if he disapproved.

A sergeant entered and stood at attention waiting for the captain to recognize him. "Yes, sergeant, what is it?"

"Two more children sick in the women's tent, sir."

Captain Cardwell supported his bent head with his left hand, his elbow on his desk. His face was pained. "Hell, not more children?"

"I'm afraid so, sir. Girls, this time. They are vomiting and are feverish."

The captain stood up and glanced again at Hannah. "Mr. uh... Johnston, isn't it?"

Hannah nodded.

"Mr. Johnston, go with Sergeant Holmes here. He'll take you to your sister. Get your family out of camp as quickly as you can before they too get sick."

"Thank you, sir. I will. Right away."

After checking his lists, the captain wrote five names on a piece of paper and standing up, handed it to the sergeant. "Give Johnston here all the help you can."

"Yes, sir."

As Captain Cardwell stepped out the door he saw the Rockfort children outside the building. "Your sons?" he asked Hannah.

"Yes, Max, Bob, and Lee."

The children stood up politely and smiled at him as their names were called.

"Hello, boys." Then he turned back to Hannah, "Johnston, have you and your boys had any dinner?"

"No, but we have some jerky in our saddlebags."

"You boys like ham and beans?" When they all nodded eagerly, the captain said, "Sergeant, while the Kerrigans are getting ready, take these boys and their father to dinner. Maybe the cook can spare them a piece of that pie he made for me."

"Yes, sir," Sergeant Holmes saluted. "Mr. Johnston, this way."

The sergeant took them first to the women's tent. Beulah and her two daughters were waiting for them. The boy hadn't returned yet. As soon as Hannah entered the tent, Beulah rushed into her arms, hugging her and saying over and over, "Brother, brother."

Leah ran to the girls, hugging both of them at once and whispering, "I'm Leah, but pretend I'm Lee Johnston, your cousin from Clinton. And Bob and Max," she said indicating Dolly and Mazie.

The girls nodded. Their mother had already told them what Hannah's note said.

Since they were sure that the other women in the tent would recognize them if they looked closely, Hannah and the girls averted their faces. Hannah pulled her hat down as far as she could and the girls kept their backs to the others.

"Ma'am," the sergeant said to Beulah, "I'll take your brother to the men's tent to get Virgil Kerrigan. Get your things and be ready to leave when we come back."

Beulah nodded, smiles lighting up her round face. Even in all the excitement and play acting, Hannah noticed that Beulah wasn't coughing. She had worried that her cough of last week would be worse, or she would be too sick to travel. Apparently she had recovered. Glad to get out of the tent and from under the searching eyes of the other women, she and Dolly followed Sergeant Holmes to the men's tent. She would not be recognized there as readily as in the women's tent for she hadn't had too much contact with any of the men. Beulah's boy was sitting on his grandfather's lap when they arrived.

Hannah held out her hand to the gray-headed man, "Good to see you again, Virgil," she said.

"Good to see you, too, Hank," Virgil said in a weak, thin voice. Realizing that he still had the note in his trembling hand, he quickly stuck it into his pocket.

"Get your things, Kerrigan," the sergeant said. "This is your lucky day. Mr. Johnston, here has come for you. You, Mrs. Kerrigan, and the children can leave right away."

While the men were talking, Dolly hugged the little boy. Just as Leah had done with his sisters, Dolly whispered to him who she was. "C'mon, Archie, let's get back to your mother and get your things. Remember I'm Bob and my sisters are Lee and Max." Holding him by his hand the two children ran back to the women's tent.

"I'll be right with you, Hank," Virgil said. "Go on back to Beulah."

When Hannah returned to the women's tent, the sergeant was standing at the opening ready to take her and her children to the cook shack. As she left the tent, she had to force herself not to look at the other pitiful women who were watching Beulah pack her few belongings. Nor did she dare notice the two feverish children coughing in the back of the tent. She couldn't help everyone. This time her priority was to get Beulah's family out.

"Here, Mary," Beulah said to the mother of the sick children, "you take our army blankets, and give them young'uns a tea made of this here hickory bark." She gave her what was left in the package Hannah had given her before she left a week ago. "It'll help them as it did me."

One of the older girls had been staring at the newcomers. She came up to Leah and looked at her closely. Then she studied Dolly and Mazie. "I know who you are," she said.

With a stricken expression to Beulah, Leah turned her back and pulled Mazie and Dolly with her out of the tent.

"No, you don't," Beulah said, pushing the girl back farther into the tent where the sergeant wouldn't hear them. "They are my nephews. You couldn't know them."

"No, they aren't," the girl insisted. "They are the girls that left last week, only they're dressed like boys. I know."

Beulah waved her hand to Leah to take the sergeant out of earshot. Then she turned back to the girl. "You are right, but don't give them away. This is the only way any of us can get out of this camp. If you tell, none of us can ever leave."

"I want to go, too," the girl insisted.

"We can't take any more this time. The captain would just hold all of us here."

When the girl hesitated, Beulah handed her Leah's dress Hannah had given to her oldest daughter the week before. "Here, keep this dress to remember us by. You'll soon get out, I'm sure."

The girl grabbed the dress and held it to her chest. Then she ran back to her cot to put it on.

Chapter 8

JUST AS Hannah was strapping the Kerrigans' belongings to her two horses, Sergeant Holmes approached leading three extra saddled horses.

"Mr. Johnston," he said, "the captain asked me to accompany you and your sister's family until you make camp tonight. He thought that might help you get to Clinton quicker."

"That's very thoughtful of him."

"Yes, sir. He feels bad about all this," the sergeant waved his hand to indicate the civilian tents. "We all do. We didn't join up to fight women and children."

"I'm sure you are just doing your duty."

"He also sent some food for your supper."

"We appreciate everything," Hannah said. "I'd like to thank your captain." She started to go toward headquarters.

"No need, Mr. Johnston. Captain said to leave right away."

Hannah had mixed feelings about the captain's bounty. Having the extra horses meant that they could get much farther since none of them would have to walk. But the sergeant's presence meant continued danger. She feared one of the children might unintentionally reveal their charade. Also she would have to accompany the Kerrigans much farther than she intended. But in spite of these concerns, the captain's help revived her optimism and faith in people. For many months she single-handedly had coped and survived using defensive actions against outlaws and men from both armies. Now in addition to the unknown soldier who put out the fire in her house and friendly Lieutenant Knowles, there was Captain Cardwell and this sympathetic sergeant. With such men in the country, there was hope for a decent life after the war.

With fresh horses, the group made good time over the prairie and soon reached the Ozarks. They rode only a few miles into the hills until Hannah found a place to camp beside a spring under a bluff overhang. Though the sun was still shining above the western hills and they could have traveled farther, Hannah pulled up. "My sons and I have had a long day," she told the sergeant, "and my sister is not well. We'll camp here. Then you still have some daylight to get back to camp."

"I'm prepared to stay the night," he said.

That Hannah did not want. Grateful for his assistance, she wanted him gone. She was worn out warding off conversation and actions that might cause Sergeant Holmes to suspect they were not who they claimed to be. She noticed that Leah and Dolly, who had ridden their horse close to the Kerrigan children for the same reason, were showing signs of stress.

"You've done so much already," Hannah said. "We can manage just fine now. You will be needed back at the camp." When the sergeant started to help them set up camp, both Hannah and Virgil urged him to leave. With hugs from the children and handshakes from Hannah and Virgil, Sergeant Holmes reluctantly mounted, and leading the three army horses, retraced his steps.

The two families watched him until he was hidden by the trees. After he was out of sight, they could still hear the horses' hooves striking against the rocks in the trail. Even when they could no longer hear him, they stood silent for several minutes. Then Hannah let out a deep sigh. The children from both families ran to her. Beulah hugged Virgil. They all started talking at once, letting out the questions and emotions they had held in check all afternoon with the sergeant among them.

"Oh, Hannah," Beulah cried, pressing Hannah to her ample breast, "you're an angel."

"A saint," Virgil agreed, "to risk ever'thing fer us."

"You look like a man. I didn't know you," Archie said running up to her.

"That's good. Neither did the soldiers." She picked him up in her arms. He ran his finger over her upper lip. "How did you grow that mustache?" Screwing up her face in exaggeration of the pain caused by pulling it off, Hannah handed the fake mustache to him. His eyes grew big as everyone laughed at him.

"That's the first laugh I've had since we left home," Virgil said. His smile showed several teeth missing in his mouth that was almost covered by his untrimmed mustache and gray beard.

With the crushing weight of imprisonment from them, and in the freedom of their private and secluded camp, everyone became a bit giddy. The children forgot how weary they were as they jumped, danced, and otherwise expressed their release. The adults sat on rocks or on the soft, dry ground under the overhang. Their energy spent, the children joined the adults, all sitting in a tight, intimate circle while Hannah, interrupted a few times by Dolly who added details, told her story and how she planned to wait out the war at her shack. When everyone's curiosity was satisfied, while it was still light, they ate the food Captain Cardwell had provided and prepared pallets for beds from the colorful leaves fallen from the dogwoods, maples, and pawpaws that grew along the bluff.

As Archie and his sisters lay back contentedly on the soft bed and cuddled under their blanket, he said, "Ma, I never slept on a red and yellow bed before."

"Remember it, sonny," Virgil said. "You'll never sleep on a better one." He sighed as he looked around in the dimming light. He saw his happy family, the trees, bluffs, and sky where for the past month he had seen only suffering old men and young boys, canvas tents, and armed soldiers. He no longer looked old, but invigorated. He had been given back his life and family. The man of the family once more, he smiled.

"You'll want to get back home right away, won't you?" Beulah asked Hannah.

"Yes." Hannah had worried that she might have to stay longer to help them. But she had noticed the determination returning to Virgil's face, and the confidence in Beulah's actions that she'd never seen before.

She knew they could manage by themselves now.

"We have lots to do before winter," Hannah said. Beulah and Virgil were exchanging glances. "You're free now. Where do you want to go?"

"Well, we can't go back home like you did. Everything's burnt. We ain't got no shack or no woods," Beulah said. She glanced at Virgil who nodded for her to continue. "So, Clinton is as good a place as any and not too far from home if we ever can go back."

"That way if word would get back to Captain Cardwell where we are, he'd be in the clear," Virgil said. "Besides, I got a cousin that used to live there. I reckon he still does."

"And we'd be away from that murdering Murdock," Beulah said with a shutter.

"I've been a-listenin' to the soldiers' talk," Virgil said. "It 'pears to be quiet in Clinton now with no action since General Price was run out of the state. At least not like on the border. There ain't much bushwhackin' goin' on east of here."

"Virgil might get a job or I probably can get some house work. I know a couple of families there," Beulah said.

"That's good," Hannah said, "can you walk that far?"

"We'll have to," Virgil said. "I figure it's fifty miles. We'll head that-a-way, just stay on the main road like the sergeant said. If somethin' turns up afore we get there, we might stop."

Hannah wished that she could bring them home with her. It didn't matter a bit to her that Paul was fighting in an army against Beulah's husband. Had she the means, she would have taken them in. But she knew five more people to provide for would be beyond her.

The next morning the two families parted with vows to reunite as soon as Order No. 11 was lifted or the war was over and everyone could be neighbors again. Before they left, Leah gave each one a cardinal flower from the patch she found growing along the stream. The spot of brilliant red brightened up their drab clothing, giving a festive air.

Hannah watched as Beulah and the children walked east along the narrow road. Virgil put his hand on the shoulder of his oldest granddaughter for support as he stepped along sprightly, not bowed over as she used to see him shuffling around the detention camp. "I'm all right," he called back to Hannah. "Don't mind me. I jest need to hold on to someone to steady myself. I walked to prison with Murdock pushin' us. Now I'm a-walkin' to freedom." He grinned. "I understand now what it's like to be a slave and then be freed." He put his hand to his hat brim where the flower was and then flicked it out in a simulated salute.

"We'll not be too far apart, just the next county over." Hannah wanted to assure them that she would see them again, but she merely waved, her eyes stinging with tears.

Hannah waited until they were completely out of sight before she spurred her gelding around. "Let's go home," she paused and winking her eye at Dolly added, "Boys, let's go home."

"Yea!" Leah exclaimed, reining her mare to the front as they backtracked along the road they had traveled yesterday for a few miles to hit the southwestern trail home through the prairie.

The danger was minimal until they reached the burnt district. They had used their male persona so many times that it was now almost normal. As before, the prairie was deserted. They didn't meet anyone all that day.

The next day when they were only five miles from their turn off to Prairie Wood Ranch, for the first time the Rockforts let themselves relax from the constant strain of the past four days. Everyone was in high spirits. The girls were happily chatting among themselves. It being Dolly's turn to sit in the saddle, she was playfully jostling Leah behind her. She would race the mare forward, then turn around to watch her mother and Mazie catch up. As soon as their horse's nose almost touched her mare, she whirled around and sped ahead. The girls played a game to see who could spot the most landmarks they could recognize.

Though they were still too far away to see it, they knew that their house was not far. They were anticipating eating something besides dried meat. At home Hannah or Leah would catch a bass for supper. They would cook the potatoes and turnips that were hidden in a dirt mound by the shack. The success of their liberation party, as Leah called their rescue of the Kerrigans, had made them careless.

"When Johnny comes marching home again, hurrah, hurrah," Dolly sang the new song she heard when they had visited Fort Scott.

"We'll give him a hearty welcome then, hurrah, hurrah!" Leah joined her.

"The men will cheer, the boys will shout, the ladies they will all turn out," Mazie always liked to join when it got to the ladies turning out.

"And we'll all feel gay when Johnny comes marching home!" Even Hannah added her voice at the end, singing it in as low a voice as she could manage.

Suddenly she was worried. "Quiet, girls," she snapped at them. Dolly stopped in the middle of a word of the second verse. The children searched the rolling prairie, but saw nothing but stretches of burnt grass now almost covered with new green. They heard nothing.

"What is it?" Leah asked.

"Come ride beside me," Hannah said after a quick glance showed her that there was no cover closer than a mile and no tall grasses to hide in where they were. "I think there are horses coming toward us."

Leah slid off the rump of her horse and put her ear to the ground. She nodded.

"How many?" Hannah asked.

"Several."

"Get back on. We can't outrun them. We'll just have to play it out."

"Where're we going this time?" Leah asked. Dolly scooted out of the saddle for her sister to take the reins. With trouble, she preferred Leah's cool head and hands on the reins.

"We're cutting across here to Fort Scott." She just finished explaining her plan when a group of horsemen rode toward them over the rise. Hannah's heart skipped a beat. The men were soldiers, and the leader looked like....

"That's Captain Murdock!" Leah whispered, dread in her voice.

Mazie started to cry. "Be brave, Max. Try not to cry. See, we aren't supposed to know him or be afraid of him."

"It's all ruined," Dolly said also on the verge of tears.

"No!" Hannah spoke sternly. "No, Bob, it is not. We can get through this. Remember Captain Cardwell didn't recognize us."

"But he's a nice man."

"We can do it. Just let me handle it and don't say anything unless asked. Act like boys. I'll try to keep my horse between him and you."

While they were talking, she kept her gelding in a steady walk. She positioned Leah to her right slightly behind her. "Is my mustache straight?" She felt it with her fingers and pressed it tightly against her upper lip. Then she ran her hand over the bulge in the right saddlebag to see if the revolver was still there. She quickly pulled it out and tossed it, holster and all, as far as she could into a clump of tall grass that escaped the fire. "Watch where it lands," she said. "Is it hidden?"

"Yes," Leah said. "I can't see it."

At Dolly's questioning look, Hannah explained. "He's looking for outlaws, so it'll be better to be unarmed. That'll fit with our story. Besides, he'd take it away if he found it."

Hannah pulled up to let the soldiers pass. As soon as Murdock spotted them, he motioned for three soldiers to spread out from the road and station themselves one behind and one on each side of her. With the remaining four men still approaching them from the road, Hannah was blocked in. However, she made no effort to escape, but sat quietly on her gelding, her hat pulled low over her forehead and Paul's long, brown coat hiding her upper body. The trousers covering her legs didn't quite reach her brogans, showing a strip of knitted sock.

"You are my prisoner," Captain Murdock bellowed as soon as he drew up in front of her.

In spite of her tight hold on herself, Hannah cringed. That phrase again. She felt the same fear she experienced years before just before he killed her neighbor. Then she controlled herself. She must deal with this evil that the war had dredged up and nurtured. So obsessed was he with his power, he could think of nothing but total domination.

"I beg your pardon!" Hannah said pretending ignorance.

"I said you are my prisoner because you are on restricted military land."

"Oh, I didn't know. I thought I was south of the area. I purposely came this far south to avoid it." Hannah had looked at the other men to see if Lieutenant Knowles was there. He was not. She didn't recognize any of the other soldiers from their raid on her house, but she wouldn't know any of them again anyway. They were all a blur in her mind. This time was the same. They sat their horses like statues, emotionless and ready to obey any command. Only one of them that was hanging back had any individual characteristics. He was very tall.

"This seemed to be the most direct route," she said.

"There are notices posted."

"I didn't see them. I'm sorry. If you'll be kind enough to tell us the way, we'll get out as quick as we can."

"Who are you and what'cha doing here?"

"Hank Johnston recently from Clinton. I am on my way to Kansas. I hoped to reach Fort Scott for the night. Can you tell me how much farther it is? We've been traveling for several days already and the boys are tired and hungry."

Mazie couldn't hold back her tears any longer. She began crying, muffling her sobs in the back of Hannah's coat.

"Git down off yer hosses. You are sinners, all of you," Murdock ordered. His pale eyes looked ghostly as he glared at her. "Search for any weapons, corporal. Probably a Bushwhacker."

When Hannah was on the ground, limping with her left foot, she opened her coat to show she was not armed. She kept a tight hold on herself not to retort to this so-called preacher calling them sinners.

"No gun. Nothing but some camping stuff and dried jerky. He's sure traveling light," said the corporal. "Pardon my saying so, Captain, but I don't figure a Bushwhacker to travel with a passel o' young'uns."

Murdock ignored the corporal. "How do you expect to get very far on this?" he asked Hannah, indicating the sorry piece of jerky.

"I don't. I'm gonna get more supplies in Fort Scott. That's why we took this short cut to get there tonight. I was told there's nothing in Nevada City."

Standing at attention for further orders, the corporal seemed satisfied that Hannah's story was true, but the captain continued to frown, his bloodshot eyes darting from Hannah to the children. Leaning over from his seat on his horse, he tried to grab Mazie, but she ducked behind her mother and wrapped one of the split tails of Hannah's long coat around her. Instead he took Dolly by the arm, lifted her up, and set her on the neck of his horse in front of his saddle. With his face inches from hers, he pulled off her stocking cap and messed her short curls that were hugging her head. Then he asked with a sneer, "What's yer name, pretty boy?"

"B-B-Bob." She like Mazie couldn't keep back the tears that rolled down her cheek, though she looked steadily back at him.

"Well, at least you got a man's name," he said in disgust as he pushed her off. She fell down, sprawled in the road at his horse's feet. Though the stallion was prancing a bit, he didn't step on Dolly.

Leah ran to Dolly and pulling her back away from the horse, stood defiantly staring back at Murdock. He glared at her as if he would strike her, then changed his mind. Grunting, he turned to Hannah, "Well, feller, it seems you have one real boy, at least."

He studied Hannah, each child, and their horses for a few seconds. "To Fort Scott, huh?"

"Yes."

"Corporal, take off these miserable saddles. We'll take the horses and use them in the Lord's work." Then to Hannah he said, "Stay out of the military zone or next time I'll take this pretty boy." He spit tobacco juice onto the road, just missing Hannah. He spurred his stallion and galloped off.

Two soldiers stayed behind. One helped the corporal strip the horses. They quickly remounted and leading Hannah's horses, followed the detail. The soldier in the rear, a very tall, dark-headed man, paused for a few seconds before whirling his horse around to catch up with the others.

Hannah stood in the road, her children around her and her saddles and bags at her feet. Her two horses were quickly disappearing from sight with their captors. Mazie was still clinging to her crying softly. Both Dolly and Leah grabbed her hands and looked at her. Everyone knew how narrowly they escaped. The loss of the horses was small compared to what might have occurred. And Hannah herself had stolen the horses, or at least taken the horses that they used to trade for these. But they were so close to home. Once again Hannah resolved never to let herself be lulled into a feeling of safety as long as Carl Murdock was in the country.

"We've got to go on to Fort Scott," she said. She was angry.

"What?"

"To Fort Scott," she said. "If we don't show up there, Murdock'll learn of it and come looking."

"But he's heading away from Kansas."

"He'll be back. Now here's the plan. Leah, you go fetch the gun and use it if you have to." Hannah was thankful that their father had insisted that the girls learn how to care for and use guns. "And then you and Mazie hide the saddles and the heavy stuff you can't carry. I think it's safe for you two to go on to the shack, since Murdock is heading north. He's probably patrolling the area and won't come back for several hours. Dolly, you and I will go to Fort Scott, show ourselves in a store or two, and try to get some horses to replace those."

"But, you said we wouldn't split up?" Leah said.

"Dolly and I can go faster alone. And I don't think there's much danger. We'll come back, tomorrow at latest."

"But our horses. We could go into their camp tonight and steal them back," Leah said.

"Probably, but then Murdock would be after us for sure. He would know we did it. We'll have to get more horses, or do without."

"I want to go with you," Leah said. "I'm oldest."

"You'll do as I say," Hannah said crossly, her anger at Murdock aggravated by Leah's objections. Then seeing the hurt expression on Leah's face, she controlled herself, remembering that it was Murdock who was the enemy, not this determined young girl who was suddenly thrust into the responsibility of life and death. "That is why you have to go home, Leah." She put her arm over her shoulder and squeezed her. "You can take care of Mazie and see to things there. And in case something happens to detain me, you can carry on. I can count on your good sense." She then stared into Leah's eyes willing her to obey. "Agreed."

"Yes."

"Good girl. Now hustle." When Leah and Mazie ran to the tall grass to find the gun, Hannah said, "C'mon, Dolly. I need at least one of you to show up in Fort Scott with me. Let's get going."

Hannah walked as rapidly as she felt that Dolly could keep up with her down the main road, past the fallen-down sign of their ranch toward the border town of Fort Scott, a former frontier military fort. Now with the Civil War and border troubles, the town was once again used as a military headquarters and supply depot. It was bustling with hundreds of wagons, mules, horses, and men.

Hannah's euphoria from freeing the Kerrigans was gone. Dolly stumbled behind her, her face as gloomy as Hannah's. Instead of feeling glad that they escaped so easily, Hannah saw only the loss of the horses. How could she keep her girls optimistic when she was so down herself? Each time she came into contact with this Carl Murdock, her world went to pieces. To her he epitomized the worst in human nature. It was men like him that perpetuated the idea of war. He gloried in it and infected others.

As he rode away from them this time, arrogant and cocky, he seemed to swell with new energy created from his power—his absolute power. Even his men swaggered in his wake. His every whim was law in this area that had had no law for months. Of course, Murdock loved the war. Here he was lord and master of four large counties. He burned the grass, destroyed the buildings, imprisoned people that did not flee ahead of him, and now was preying on any individual who was unfortunate enough to cross his path. All this was nothing but banditry in the name of honor and glory in a war of brother against brother, family against family. She sighed. It seemed that every age had a Murdock that decent people had to defeat before all of humanity was infected.

Hannah did not regret helping the Kerrigans, though the thought occurred to her that if she hadn't, she would be safe home with her horses in their paddock. She wouldn't have to scold her daughters, and she wouldn't have to make this extra trip to Fort Scott.

She shook her head to drive out those thoughts and pulled her hat more to her left side to shade it from the bright October sun. "We're not put on this earth to minister only to ourselves," she said out loud.

"I know, Mama," Dolly said. "Leah and Mazie will be all right, and we'll get back home. You'll see."

When Hannah turned to look at her daughter, Dolly's dirty, tear-streaked face smiled encouragingly at her. Hannah didn't believe that anything on this earth could be any more beautiful.

Chapter 9

AS HANNAH crossed the state line into Kansas, she wondered why this last encounter had depressed her so. She should be elated that she and the girls so easily fooled Murdock. The loss of the horses and this trip to Fort Scott measured as only nuisance in comparison to other difficulties she had weathered. The murder of a neighbor, the theft of her stock and household goods, the ruin of her crops, and burning of her barn all had made her even more determined to prevail. And, the hardest of all, the day Paul was abducted, she didn't lose heart. Her anger and sense of injustice had fueled her. Her children needed her. Paul needed her. For the sake of their home, she had to keep on.

But there was only so much she could take. She couldn't do it anymore. She looked at Dolly trotting beside her trying to keep up without complaining. The child's pretty face was screwed into a frown of determination as she wiped off tears. Hannah slowed down and put her hand on her middle daughter's shoulder. Dolly moved closer, took her hand and smiled through her tears.

"We'll be all right, Mama," she said. "You'll fix it as you always do."

Hannah caught a sob in her throat. Her children needed her. Prairie Wood Ranch depends on her. Now more than ever Paul needed her. She must do more than just hold everything together and wait for him. She had to find him.

With new resolve Hannah said, "Yes, Dolly, we'll be all right. Now I have you girls to help. We're all partners."

This little set-back, and that was all it was, with Murdock was another test for Hank Johnston. She and the girls passed again with excellent marks. Now was the time for her to take the initiative. Hannah Rockfort had many restraints on her, first as a woman, and then as a fugitive with suspected Bushwhacker dealings. Hank, on the other hand, a man from outside the Burnt District, would have access to places a woman couldn't enter. Since she was heading to a town that had a military post, she'd try again to get the army to trace Paul. If he was alive, he was either a prisoner or very ill. Otherwise he would have found some means to let her know.

He was not dead. Impossible. She would know. From now on, just being there when he came home wasn't enough. She needed to make sure he did come home. "Dolly, when we get to Fort Scott, I'm going to ask the officials again to try to find Papa."

"It won't do any good. They won't do anything just like before," Dolly said.

"Maybe, but this time I'm a man asking for my cousin. Also, now except for the outlaw problem, the military in Missouri hasn't been as busy since General Price was chased back into Arkansas. I'll try."

"But won't that be dangerous, walking right into the post?"

"Yes." Hannah grinned. "But we're getting pretty good with our acting. We can carry it off. Papa must be in trouble. He needs us now more than we need him."

His needing them was a new idea. In the time since he had left, she and the children thought only of how much they needed him. But because they were forced to, they had survived without him. Now they had to find him.

With a plan of action already forming in her mind, she was anxious to get to the town. They would go first to the military headquarters on the edge of town, ask to see the commanding officer, and request an official investigation or report on Paul. Nearing town, she simulated her limp so that no one would question why a healthy young man was not in uniform.

With Paul much on her mind, she recalled the blackest day in her family, when all their plans fell to pieces.

IN EARLY September of 1861, almost exactly two years before Carl Murdock marched her and the girls to the detention camp, she and Leah were preparing dinner at the ranch. Leah was setting the table as Hannah dumped raw, sliced potatoes into the skillet of hot grease from which she had just removed the fried chicken. Out of the window she saw that Paul had returned with a wagon load of corn fodder and was unloading it at the barn.

Mazie and Dolly, then four and seven, were playing around him. Puss, who had been stalking mice, gave up with all the activity around her and jumped onto the load. Paul laughed at her, picked her up to set her on the ground, but held her in his arms for a few seconds running his hand over her snow-white back and fingering the patches of yellow and black around her head.

"I don't know who is the most help," he said, "this ornery calico cat or you girls." Placing Puss on the ground, he tapped each child playfully on her back before forking off another bundle of corn stalks. The blue-gray, white, and black speckled dominicker hen and her motley following of chicks were busy picking up the grains of corn that shattered from the ears.

Watching him out her window, Hannah wondered why Paul stopped unloading and quickly drove the wagon behind the barn. In a few seconds she knew why. Over the crackling of the grease in her skillet and Leah's constant chatter, she heard some horses approaching. Telling Leah to remove the five place settings she had just put down and to stir the potatoes, she ran to the front porch.

"Morning, ma'am," said a familiar-looking soldier wearing a simulation of a Confederate uniform. "Yer man about?"

"He's out working on the ranch somewhere."

Paul had refused to join the local Vernon County Battalion which had strong southern sympathies, even though its main purpose was to defend the county. He hoped he could lie low and avoid the conflict that was erupting around them. He and Hannah didn't believe that war would solve anything. As the fighting progressed and news from the Battle of Wilson's Creek a hundred and twenty miles southeast came to them, and even after the scrimmages in the county and around Fort Scott, he still believed he could stay neutral. None of the issues concerned him.

But both realized that he could not straddle the fence much longer. He'd have to take sides. But which one? They didn't believe in slavery, but had many good friends and neighbors who were adamant about the southern cause. Hannah's experience with Carl Murdock a few years ago and the more recent examples of some fanatic abolitionists from Kansas soured them for the Union cause. Paul had no loyalties to either side. Hannah and he had discussed moving west, where a few of their friends went to avoid the war. That was no solution; it was merely running away from all they were working for.

Both sets of parents had pioneered this area, coming before the Osages were moved out of the county in 1825. In this country that was barely beyond pioneer status, they were second generation settlers, their children third generation. This was their land. They did not want to start over again in the West—arid country with not half the advantages Prairie Wood Ranch had. So they had stayed even though they knew it would be difficult.

But military activity was escalating all around them, including them whether they wanted it or not. The men on Hannah's porch were a detachment of soldiers on their way north toward Lexington. General Sterling Price planned to wrest Missouri from the Union grip when he would confront the main force of their army at this town on the Missouri River east of Kansas City. These men were at the Rockfort home scouring the country for assistance. Since Price believed that all Missourians were for secession, he felt they owed him their able-bodied men, their horses and mules, and any supplies that his army needed. He took what he wanted. As did the Union Army when they marched through, for the Union commanders, like Murdock, viewed all Missourians as enemies. The produce of the land was spoils of war.

The soldiers pushed their way into the house. "I'm just putting dinner on the table, would you and your men like some?" Hannah asked. "Come on in. My daughter is just finishing the potatoes. I'll fix some more."

The men sat around the table and soon ate up all the food. Each man stuffed his pockets with the left-over cornbread and emptied the bowl of apples on the table into their knapsacks. "Mighty tasty, ma'am," the leader said, picking his teeth with his knife. Since the men didn't all wear uniforms and those that did weren't marked with any insignia, she didn't know what his rank was.

"Thank you, lieutenant," she said, guessing a higher rank to flatter him. She glanced quickly toward the barn. No sign of Paul.

"Corporal, ma'am," he said, touching his hand to the bill of his cap. "You don't recognize me, do you?" Without waiting for her answer, he said, "I'm Bud Newman. You know, you was at our house when Pa got murdered?" The fury that she remembered several years before in the young boy still raged in his eyes.

"Of course. I thought you were familiar, but no, I didn't recognize you now that you've grown up. You moved away."

"Yeah, lost our farm. Ma couldn't stay no more."

"Did you ever hear anything about Sally, your slave that Murdock stole?"

Newman's face hardened. The pinpoints of hate returned to his brown eyes. "They murdered her, too, only later... after they..." He controlled himself. "She was like a second ma to me, or a big sister. So much fer them lofty Yankee ideas. Sally was happy with us."

"All Yankees aren't like Murdock. Most really wanted to help the slaves."

Newman's look showed he didn't believe her. "Like they helped me and Ma and Sally? Quick as they started recruitin', I joined up to fight the Yankees. Since I growed up in this county, General Price sent me a-scoutin' fer more men and hosses." He swelled up with his importance that was fueled with his anger. "I knowed about yer place, sort of hidden back here, and yer crossin' down by the draw not many knows about, and I come to git yer man to join us."

After finishing eating, the armed men with him looked around. Hannah knew they were planning more than talk to persuade Paul. "Where's he at?" Newman asked, not as polite as formerly.

"I don't know. He left this morning and said he might be gone all day."

Newman's manner showed he was beginning to suspect something. "Why ain't yer man already signed up? Maybe he's a-cozyin' up with the Yankees?"

"He's just wanting to get the crops in first."

Newman looked steadily at her and then at Leah who was busy pretending to wash dishes to avoid attracting his attention. "You have more young'uns than this'un. One was borned the night you left our place, I recall."

"Yes, I do. Two more girls. They're out playing somewhere. Leah, run out and tell them to come in. I was just fixing to call them in to dinner when you men came. I'll cook up some more for them."

This was the excuse Leah needed to run to the barn and tell her father who the men were and what they wanted. She soon returned to the house holding each sister by the hand. Hannah shook her head at them when Newman wasn't looking to warn then not to tell where their father was, though she knew he had already instructed them what to do.

"Where's yer pa at?" Newman asked Dolly.

"Don't know."

"Would you like to rest awhile, Bud, before you ride out again?" Hannah asked politely.

"No," he said brusquely. Now that he'd gotten his meal, he was anxious to get on his way. He strutted through the front room. "We come after Rockfort. Reckon we best look fer him."

Just then Paul drove his wagon load of fodder by the house as if just coming in from the field. He pulled up beside the soldiers' horses tied to the fence. The men, Hannah, and the girls came out on the porch.

"Howdy," Paul said, still sitting on the spring seat of the wagon, his old felt hat pulled down almost hiding his blond hair. He looked more closely at the men. "You're young Newman, right?"

"Yes, Corporal Newman of the former First Missouri Brigade, now regular Army of the Confederacy under the command of Major-General Price." He stood tall and proud as he spouted off his allegiances.

"Good to see you, Newman. We hadn't heard anything from you since you moved away a few years back. How's your mother?"

"Tolerable."

"Give her our regards." Paul was pleasant, treating him as he would any visitor. "Wait a spell 'til I take care of the horses, and I'll join you for dinner. I'm sure my wife has enough."

"Already et." Experienced in scouring the country for men, Newman rebuffed with suspicion their overtures of friendship. He gave a curt nod to his men and cocked his head toward Paul. Two of them jumped off the porch and stood one on either side of Paul's wagon.

"Good," Paul said, ignoring the hostile attitude of the men. He shook the reins for the team to start. Then he paused, "Say, Newman, it's lucky you came by just now. I hear Price's planning some big doings up north. Going to get the Federals out of the state for good. I've been meaning to join up—wanted to get the corn in first—but since you're here, if it's all right with you, I'll just go with you now."

"Good idea," Hannah forced herself to say pleasantly. "Don't worry about the corn, Paul, I can finish it." They both knew that Bud was prepared to abduct Paul by force if necessary. His going as a volunteer would make his tour in the army easier.

"Fine," Paul said and clicked to his team.

"Not so goddamned fast," Newman said. The two soldiers jumped in front and grabbed the horses' reins. "Leave the wagon be. Jest git yer things, Rockfort, saddle one o' them hosses and let's go."

"Sure, I didn't know there was any hurry." Paul jumped down from the wagon and hurried into the house. He shot a quick glance at Hannah.

When she started to follow him inside, Newman stepped between them in the doorway. "You saddle his hoss." One of the men was already tying the other horse to his saddle.

"Get Papa some dinner to take," Hannah called to Leah. The soldiers had already unhitched the horses. Hannah led Paul's favorite, Black Laddie, to the barn to saddle and bridle him, one of the men at her side. She watered Laddie, gave him a couple of ears of corn, and rubbed him down. When she led him back to the house, Paul was waiting, his rifle slung across his back by its strap and his extra clothes rolled up in a blanket to tie behind his saddle. He had changed into his better trousers, put on a jacket and his good hat.

He hugged each of his daughters and then Hannah. Paul's acting didn't allay Newman's suspicions for he never left Paul's side. Neither

Paul nor Hannah could think of what they could say to each other. They dared not exchange any messages. To continue the act of Paul's wanting to go, they said only the things people would say in those circumstances.

"Take care of yourself."

"Take good care of Laddie," Dolly said.

"I will."

"I'll see to everything here until you get back," Hannah said.

"I'll write you where I am." He kissed her and each of the girls before mounting Laddie.

Then the men were gone in a swirl of dust up the trail and out of sight over the rise. Hannah plopped down on the porch step with the girls clinging to her. "Papa will soon be back," she said to them and to assure herself. Everyone believed the war would soon be over. Hannah had to believe it with Paul suddenly gone. And this business with Bud Newman was only an unpleasant interruption in their work. She could handle the crops and stock until he returned in a few weeks, even with no horses.

Several days later when Price's army withdrew back through the county after his victory at the Battle at Lexington, some of the neighbor men who had also been conscripted stopped by their homes for a brief visit. But not Paul. The unsettled state of who was in control of Missouri made communication precarious. Three months passed before she heard from him, the only message she ever received. On one of her trips to Fort Scott, she got a note saying that he had jumped camp near Lexington and joined the Union Army. "When I was forced to choose," he wrote, "I knew I couldn't fight on the Southern side. Now I'm a fugitive from their army, so I cannot return home until Price is pushed far into Arkansas. I hope this will not jeopardize you with our mostly Confederate neighbors. I know that is what you would have done."

Yes, she would have done the same. Though he was still in an army, she felt better knowing that he was working to maintain the union. She expected another letter during the next six months and especially when the Confederate Army was no longer a threat in Missouri because of their defeat at Pea Ridge, Arkansas, in March 1862. She had assumed he was in that Union offensive. Again she was disappointed, but she remembered the last sentence in his one letter. "I'm afraid the war will last much longer than we thought."

IN THE ensuing months up to this time when she was limping into Fort Scott with Dolly, there had been no further word from Paul. Though she had often asked at the command post, and she questioned every Federal soldier she met, she learned nothing of his whereabouts.

When she and Dolly reached town, they went immediately to the post headquarters. Given audience with the major, she limped in, gave his hand a firm handshake and once again asked for information about Paul, only this time posing as Paul's cousin from Clinton, newly come to town. She was listened to respectively. The major wrote down the information and promised to see what he could do.

"Mr. Johnston, you must realize that it will be some time, as it takes two days for a dispatch to get in or out. Come back in a month. I'll see what I can do."

Already her disguise as a man was paying off. As a woman, she was never listened to so attentively.

The soldiers made over Dolly, boxing playfully with her. They shook Hannah's hand, slapped her on her back, offered her a cigar, and invited her to one of the numerous saloons in town for a drink. She begged off this time because she had much business to transact before night. Then she and Dolly walked down the main street from the post to a livery stable to try to buy some horses.

They made an appearance in several stores, buying only a few supplies in the general store, mainly shoes for Dolly as hers were almost worn out from her walking. Hannah didn't have enough money with her to buy a horse, but she shopped around for one in order to record that there was a Hank Johnston in town. Just before the sun set, she was coming out of an eating place when she saw Carl Murdock and his detail ride by. She quickly ducked back into the building. Her precaution wasn't necessary for Murdock and most of his weary men looked straight ahead, their horses lathered from their long ride. They all wore grim expressions, the captain most of all. Hannah's two horses were not with them.

After they passed, she adjusted her few purchases into bundles and strapped the largest one on her back, a smaller one on Dolly's back.

"Did you see that tall soldier," Dolly asked.

"No, I didn't notice him. All I wanted to do was keep out of Murdock's sight."

"Well, that tall soldier looked right at me."

Hannah gasped and grabbed Dolly's hand as if to flee with her.

"But it's all right. He smiled at me and sort of cocked his head like..."

"Like what?"

"I don't know. He's nice. Like Lieutenant Knowles and Captain Cardwell and that sergeant that went with us out of the detention camp."

Hannah relaxed. Dolly's assessment of people had never failed. She seemed to be able to spot the finest qualities of people even in dangerous situations.

"It was like," Dolly continued, "he was letting me know he's a friend. That he really wasn't with that bad Captain Murdock."

"I think you're imagining too much. But his actions do seem friendly. I don't want to face Murdock again, that's why I ducked back in the door, but I do want him to know that Hank Johnston came to town as he said he would."

"Well, if he asked the tall soldier, he would know we came," Dolly said.

"Yes, he would." Then taking the child's hand, Hannah said, "C'mon, Bob, let's go home."

They walked out of town on a different road from the one they came in on—one that she knew would reach her home from the south side of the river. She wanted to get out of town at least a couple of miles to a spot she sometimes used to camp after a long day in town. This was the country she grew up in. She knew all the contours of the prairie, every creek, every grove of woods, every mound, and every building.

On the Kansas side of the border the buildings were undamaged, populated with people living normal lives in their homes free from looters. Hogs and chickens scurried about the barnyards. Girls played with their dolls around the front porches and boys tumbled on the ground with their dogs. The lush, unburned prairie held herds of cattle. National politics and human greed had erected an artificial border that caused such a difference in the few miles separating her ranch from Kansas. Had her and Paul's parents settled just five miles farther west, she wouldn't be a fugitive on foot returning secretly to her home which was stripped of all their possessions.

As she walked, she forced out of her mind the envy she felt toward the Kansan farmers she passed. She mustn't think about them. Instead she counted again the good things in her life. To her list she now added the tall soldier.

Hannah and Dolly found the secluded spot to stop for the night. They slept for a few hours, and even in the dark of pre-dawn, they made their way home. Though they couldn't find a horse they could afford, the trip to Fort Scott was successful. Carl Murdock's suspicions would be allayed about the business of the stranger he met on the Fort Scott road. Hopefully, he would not investigate further.

Chapter 10

A WEEK later Leah was fishing in the river while Hannah and the other girls were nearby picking up pecans and black walnuts. Dolly wandered down the river bank farther to a tall walnut tree she saw. She crawled through some briars to a moss-covered, partially open glen under the huge trees. The sun streamed through the colorful leaves that were precariously holding on to the branches or those that had given up the effort and were floating lazily to the ground. Spots of yellow light danced on the soft velvety mat underneath. Dolly picked up an orange, mitten-shaped sassafras leaf that was among the half-split pecan hulls that were strewn over the ground.

As she reached out to admire another leaf, this one shaped like a three-fingered glove, her hand touched a recent pile of horse manure. She jerked it back with repugnance and rubbed away the clinging particles on the moss. Her initial reaction was disgust. Then she became alarmed because the manure was still warm. Forgetting her pail of nuts, she ran quietly back to her mother.

Hannah looked up, knowing something was wrong. "Mama, there's been a horse here."

"Yes, dear," Hannah relaxed, "our horses." She wondered, however why their sign would be down river. Their paddock was upstream.

"No, I mean today. I saw fresh manure."

"How fresh?" Hannah gave a back-handed waved toward Mazie. The child knew that meant to warn Leah and be ready to hide in the thick brush.

"It's still warm."

Leah quickly gathered her pole and line and the stringer of fish she'd already caught. She and Mazie joined their mother.

"Come," Hannah whispered. They left the fairly open grove of pecan trees where they were picking the nuts to hide in the brush along the river bank.

"Listen."

They were quiet for several minutes without hearing anything. Then from downstream they heard a horse give a contented snort followed by a crackling as of a large animal stepping on dried leaves or twigs. As they held their breaths, they heard another horse whinny softly.

"They aren't being ridden," Hannah said after listening attentively a few more minutes. "They seem to be grazing. I'd say two of them."

"Maybe someone staked them out," Leah said.

Hannah nodded. "Stay here while I go see." Keeping to the brush and behind the trees, she reached the glen and saw the pile of manure Dolly found. Though she didn't see the horses or any men, she heard another contented snort. She eased her way closer, alert for men on foot.

Had any riders dismounted, they would not have let their mounts wander free. The sounds from these horses indicated they were not tied up. Suddenly, she heard a squeal as if one of the horses was frightened from something, followed by the racket of animals retreating through the reedy and swampy area beyond the glen.

She remained quiet, listening for any other movement or sound. She half expected to hear male voices shouting, or feet trampling through the timber in pursuit of the horses. But there was nothing but the dying echo of the animals. Reassured that she was alone, she skirted the area looking for human signs. All she found were the usual tracks of rabbits, raccoons, and, she was pleased to note, a mink. Even in her present potentially dangerous position, she made a note to set one of her traps here.

She returned to the children. "Just two loose horses," she said with no more concern in her voice than if the animals had been deer.

"Did you see them?" Dolly asked.

"No. But there was more than one. Probably two or three."

"Where did they come from?" Leah asked. "And why come here?" Her mother's assumed assurance didn't fool her.

"Probably some that got away."

Leah didn't believe that. She shook her head. "The soldiers or the Bushwhackers would have gone after them and caught them." They all knew how scarce horses were in the region since the armies had taken all they could find. The lack of horses was the reason Murdock had taken their last two even though they were not up to army standards.

"On the open prairie, yes, they could easily find them. But not in these woods."

"The horses are like us, aren't they, Mama?" Mazie said. "And like Puss. We've safe in the woods where the bad men won't find us."

Hannah hugged Mazie and kissed her on her forehead to reassure her and, turning toward Leah, shook her head slightly to warn her not to alarm her sister.

"They are safer in the woods," Hannah said honestly. She didn't want to give the girls a false sense of security, but neither did she want them to live in constant fear. Maintaining that healthy balance was difficult. "But Mazie, sugar, the bad men can come here to the woods just like we do, but they don't understand the land or know about it, so usually they skirt around us."

"Yeah," Dolly said, sticking out her soaked boots for the others to see, "they don't like to get their feet wet."

They walked the bank to see if there were any prints to show if the horses had swum the river. They couldn't tell as there were prints around a draw where they had drunk. "Looks like they've been here a few days."

Though Hannah didn't let on to the girls, she felt vulnerable. Somehow her defenses had been breached. The horses belonged to someone who might track them here. "We better get back to the shack."

The next few days went by with no unusual happenings. There were no more signs of the horses. Apparently they left their ranch. Coyotes howled, but that was a nightly occurrence. High overhead the honk of geese flying south was a welcome sound since the grassland and forest birds were gone. Each night was cooler than the one before, though the balmy October weather continued. Hannah and the girls cut and piled wood in various hideouts around the shack. They also cut wood for the main house. They repaired and cleaned up much of the fire damage to the front room.

Like monkeys, the girls climbed the apple trees to pick the red jonathan apples. They gleaned every potato, beet, and turnip they could find from their garden and stored them and the apples in ground pits in different places around the house and the shack. Hannah was especially glad she had planted plenty of parsnips, for they could be left in the ground and would continue to grow some all winter.

They set homemade, wooden rabbit gums in the woods and on the prairie and then turned their attention to placing steel traps in the river. Though the pelts of the animals were not yet at their winter best, they could be traded for supplies. The meat from the catch she cut into strips and dried in the sun. Hannah shot two deer and salted the meat.

For her medicine bag, Hannah scoured the area for bark, roots, and other plants available in the autumn. Most of her herbs she gathered in the spring. A pleasant surprise was finding a bee tree. Her head well protected with netting, she smoked the bees to make them inactive, cut down the tree, and collected the honey.

Then whenever she had a spare minute, or while she was resting, she mended the children's trousers that were showing wear from constant use, and she sewed another pair for each of them from cast-offs from Paul's clothes that the soldiers did not take.

When they were clearing off the garden in preparation for spring plowing, or they manually dragged off the trash left from the burned out-buildings, they grumbled about the loss of their horses.

"Why don't we try to find those stray horses ourselves," Leah wondered, holding out her blistered hands.

Hannah had the same thoughts. She had tried to track them from the swampy area where she last heard them, but when the tracks reached the open prairie, they disappeared. She never saw any other evidence of their presence.

She was disappointed she couldn't find them, but in a way, as the days went by with no sign of them, or any pursuing men, she felt safer. Although she did not let down her constant vigilance, she didn't jump at every sound of nature.

"Just keep looking," Hannah told Leah. "We may find them later when it snows and we can track them easier."

She always scanned the horizon for the horses as she tramped over her acres to check on the progress of the new grass on the burned areas. She saw deer a couple of times. Not being able to tell from the distance whether they were deer or horses, she crept up on them to be disappointed again.

Though there were no horses, she was encouraged to note that the scorched earth effect was rapidly disappearing with the luxurious new fall growth. Burning was good for the prairie—kept the trees out—but burning late in the season often left it open for erosion. The ground was nicely covered for the coming winter season ready for the rapid spring growth. She had no cattle to flourish on the grasses, nor hope of any for next spring. But there was always the year after that to plan for.

Hannah worried about the girls' lack of education. Even before Order No. 11 depopulated the region, there had been no organized schools for two years. She had salvaged a few books from the house. During daylight hours she had no time to teach them, but Leah took over the job of giving Mazie reading lessons. At night the family was usually too tired to study. A few times Hannah read them a story or helped the older girls with arithmetic problems after she draped a quilt over the one window.

Even though they had no neighbors within miles, she wouldn't risk anyone seeing her light. From the main house, even with the leaves fallen from the trees, their shack was still hidden by the tree trunks and the lay of the land. The view from the river presented a different problem. Men sometimes canoed the river, fishing, trapping, or using it for transportation. In the daytime, even though the shack was near by, it blended into the trees so that casual passers by wouldn't notice it. But at night a light in the shack would be a beacon announcing their presence.

"No one's on the river at night," Leah said.

Hannah didn't take any chances. The river was not included in the restricted zone. Men often hunted and did some types of fishing at night, especially gigging.

In spite of her precautions and constant wariness, they couldn't erase all evidence of their presence. At noon a week after they heard the stray horses, they were all seated at the rough table in the shack eating their dinner. Puss sat upright on the hearth waiting the leftovers she knew she would soon get. Suddenly, Dolly, who was facing the door, gave a surprised grunt and dropped her piece of cornbread on her lap. Her mouth open as if to cry out in alarm, she stared toward the door. Her hand flew to her face and she started to rise, but instead, she sat back and smiled. The others quickly turned to see what she was staring at.

Standing in the room, completely blocking the door and slightly bent over to avoid bumping his head on the exposed rafters of the ceiling, was the tallest soldier any of them had ever seen. He was smiling, his black eyebrows raised as if excusing his startling entry. He held out his hands to show that he came in friendship.

With a yowl, Puss darted behind the stack of wood by the fireplace. Hannah stumbled to her feet, covering her bare upper lip with her hand. Mazie squealed and Leah gasped back a scream as she, too, stood up. The thought that flew through Hannah's mind was dismay that even her hidden haven was not safe.

"He's the soldier I told you about in Fort Scott," Dolly said in her normal voice. "The one that winked at me." Her smile welcomed the stranger.

"Don't be alarmed, ma'am," the middle-aged soldier said in a cultured, educated voice quite different from that of the local men and the enlisted soldiers they'd met. He removed his hat to reveal ink-black, straight hair cut short in the latest military fashion. There was just a touch of gray above his ears. His black eyes and musical voice held them all motionless.

"I'm Hank Johnston," Hannah said defensively, her knees giving way when he said, "ma'am." Her disguise was useless. She dropped her hand from her mouth.

"Yes, I know. I'm pleased to meet you in person. Please sit back down and let me explain my presence."

"He's all right, Pa," Dolly emphasized the "Pa," still keeping up the charade. She went to Hannah and pulled her back into her chair. Since there were no other chairs, Dolly sat on the edge of the bed and pointed to her bench for the soldier to sit down.

"Thank you," the soldier smiled at Dolly, his even teeth showing white in his sun-browned face. There was something different about this man, sort of exotic, though none of them could say what it was. He was dressed in a Union Army uniform, but his movements were more fluid or natural than the military stance of most soldiers. He carried his long body with the grace of an antelope. And his speech resembled that of the eastern professor they had heard in more peaceful times at a revival meeting in Nevada City. It had none of the drawl of the local people or those who came to Missouri from the South.

"I am Walking Owl of the Osage Nation," he said. "At the present I am assigned to the Union Army stationed at Fort Scott. I am used mainly as a scout. As such I sometimes accompany Captain Murdock."

"Now I remember you," Hannah said. "You were the scout when Murdock came here and took us off, weren't you?" She remembered the soldier who seemed to stay aloof from the others.

"Yes," he said sadly.

"Then you must be the one that put out the fire in the main house?"

"Yes. I could do nothing about the barn, for it was too far gone. The captain was in a hurry to leave, so he threw the torch in the door as everyone in the detail rode off. Except me. I stayed back to put out the fire. As a scout, I often didn't ride with the others, so no one paid any attention to me. After that, I cut across the river back to the fort." He paused at their surprise that he knew of their ford.

"I remember Murdock asking you if there was any ford and you said..." Hannah started to say.

"I said, 'No ford that we could see.'" He grinned. "We didn't see it, but I know all this county. I've trapped all along the river since childhood. But don't worry, the army doesn't know of it."

"You know who we are, don't you?" Dolly asked.

"You are Dolly Rockfort, alias Bob Johnston." The Osage smiled when the others showed amazement.

"Tell us how you found out," Hannah said.

Walking Owl unbuttoned his jacket and took a drink from the cup Leah set before him. "Sassafras tea," he said and smiled.

Puss ventured from behind the stack of wood. Mazie picked her up.

Before the Osage continued, he stroked the cat's head. Puss began purring and settled in Mazie's lap. "My reason for being sent to Fort Scott was to scout for the army as they tried to control the Bushwhacker activity along the border. I'm familiar with all of this area as well as Kansas and Oklahoma. I knew where they holed up in Oklahoma and who took them into their houses around here. If anyone had asked me, we could have wiped out most of the outlaws. But then General Ewing gave his Order Number Eleven. So, instead of scouting for outlaws, I was leading Captain Murdock to peaceful ranchers and settlers, like you, who didn't obey the Order. He robbed them, sometimes killing them, and sent them to holding camps." The Osage's voice was sad.

"When we reached your ranch, I'd had enough. The captain was cruel beyond reason. He made no lists of confiscated hay or grain as required so that loyal residents could get compensation for their losses. He took everything for himself, listing everyone as enemies and outlaws. I saw him shoot old men and mistreat the women he captured. You were very fortunate that he didn't lead you to the encampment himself but put Lieutenant Knowles in charge."

"Yes," Hannah said. "We know that. In the camp I heard of what Murdock did to some other people. Did you believe what I said when he questioned me?"

"I knew you were telling the truth about your husband. I know about your families from years ago. And you are located right on the border of the military zone specified by the Order. You had every right to stay here. So when the captain left with his unit, I stayed back and put out your fire. I could do that much."

"But you've done more." Hannah made this a statement, not a question.

"Your little girls and your feistiness—if you don't mind my saying it—was what convinced me to stop being an observer. I figured that you were planning to escape."

"How'd you know that?" Leah asked.

"Your mother didn't act like all the other women we routed out—crying, begging, and worried about their possessions." He turned to Hannah. "You acted as if you'd planned it all out. You took unusual things with you, and you let the lieutenant remove you too willingly. Knowles didn't notice, but I did—your wearing your husband's great coat even though it was hot, and having the girls wear their winter boots, but pack only one extra dress."

"You were very observant."

"Yes, ma'am. That's my training. I'm the grandson of the great Osage chief, Pawhuska." He paused a moment as his audience showed their respect toward the chief they had heard so much about. When Hannah's parents came to the area the Osages still lived in their village east of them. "I noticed how your family has cared for the land—how you have not changed or abused it. I saw your herb garden with many prairie and woods plants from this region, and how the first thing you gathered up to take with you was your bag full of medicines."

"My mother taught me about plants and how they can heal. She brought some plants with her from Illinois, but she learned about the native plants from the Osage women."

Walking Owl nodded. "I did what I could to prevent the captain from upsetting still more the order of your life."

"We are grateful. And you recognized us when you ran into us again last week on the road even though we were dressed as men?"

Walking Owl grinned. "The captain swallowed your story, as did every man in that detail—most were the same who burned your place, but then they were too intent on destruction to pay much attention to you and the girls. I knew the moment we met you on the road that you weren't men and boys."

"How could you tell?" Leah asked.

"Several things. You girls, especially, didn't move like boys. Though your mother looked and acted like a man, I noticed that she wasn't tanned enough. If you notice, the faces of farmers are almost leathery sun tanned up to their eyebrows. Their forehead is white from being always protected by their hats. Her face was the same shade all over. And the way she dismounted and even walking with that limp... that's a good touch," he said to Hannah, "... even that movement I recognized was a feminine walk. And you girls, especially Dolly. The back of her neck was very white, showing that it had been protected from the sun. Nothing a boy would wear would cover the neck. It had to be long hair that had recently been cut."

Dolly put her hand to the back of her head to feel the still unfamiliar touch of shingled hair. "You never let on," she said.

"No. But I was afraid Captain Murdock would guess when he picked on you, Dolly," Walking Owl said.

"I was too," Hannah said. "I ran into him several years ago when he killed our neighbor. I know what he is capable of. That is one reason I left without any fuss. I didn't dare make him angry." She ran her tongue over the gap in her teeth as if to remind herself how fortunate she was to lose only a tooth.

"Dolly, you did well," Walking Owl said. "Keeping the captain's attention and that of his men on you, the least masculine-looking of any, prevented him from noticing the other clues I saw. I knew then that you were not males or the people you claimed to be. I suspected you were the Rockforts being so close to your place. And the right number of people, just wrong sex. But when we got back to town later that night, and I saw only Dolly and you, Mrs. Rockfort, without the other two children, I guessed your plan. At the fort I learned that this same Hank Johnston was searching for Paul Rockfort. Then I knew."

He paused as if speaking this much was not usual with him. "That was a brave move," he said to Hannah with admiration. "If Murdock had any brains other than greed, he might have figured it out."

"I decided that I was not going to be Murdock's victim anymore," Hannah said. "To allay any suspicion he might have that I wasn't Hank Johnston as I claimed to be out on the road, I needed to prove it by going to Fort Scott. He believed I was a man, so while there I used my male status to search for my husband and reclaim my family's right to live here."

"Still, it was a very risky move with men like Captain Murdock roaming the area."

From his manner, Hannah believed that he had something more to tell them. She noticed that he didn't volunteer any information. When he answered a question, he didn't elaborate until urged. "I don't believe you came here to tell us about what you did for us," Hannah said. She knew she was right when his black eyes showed admiration for her ability to understand him. "Why did you come here now?"

"I came to tell you that I liberated your horses." He grinned at his use of words.

Dolly gasped. "The horses we heard?" she asked her mother.

"So you've seen them?" the Osage asked.

"No. Only their sign and we heard them. Downstream here about a quarter."

"How did you 'liberate' them?" Leah asked.

The Osage was eating the meal that Dolly set in front of him. As he took a bite of river bass and washed it down with the hot sassafras tea, he explained. "After we rode off with your horses away from you there in the road, we traveled north about ten miles. The captain didn't find anyone else, and bored with nothing more to exploit, he headed back to the fort. I told him of a trail north of your road, so that he wouldn't go by your place and take a notion to ride up to your house. We stopped to water the horses at a crossing on Duncan Creek." He paused.

"Yes, I know the place," Hannah said. "People don't use that road for the crossing is poor."

Walking Owl nodded. "The bank there is steep, but passable with care. I loosened your horses' lead ropes, not enough for anyone to notice, but enough that they could get free if they tried. When we crossed the creek and started to climb the high bank on the opposite side, the fellows leading your horses were the last to cross. The gelding snorted and pulled back. When he found he was free, he reared and slid back down the bank, bumping into the last man leading your mare. Men and horses, they all lost their balance and tumbled back into the creek. Your two horses high-tailed it back across the creek and out onto the prairie."

The Osage laughed at the memory. "There was a jumble of men and horses. The captain swore and ordered everyone but me to chase the runaway horses. The fallen soldiers blocked their way. Two others slid off into the creek, and their horses ran off in the opposite direction from your horses. By the time I caught up with the soldiers' horses and returned, everyone had remounted. Your horses were far away. I crossed the creek to track them. They were not in sight, and their tracks across the prairie were mingled with ours. I told the captain I didn't see them."

Leah said, "I bet you didn't really lose them, did you?"

"No, I could have caught up with them given enough time. But the captain didn't know that. He was mad. He vented his anger by cussing out the two with the lead ropes and demoted them then and there to privates. Since it was late, he gave orders to get back to the fort as quickly as possible."

"That's why he looked so mad when he rode by Dolly and me in town," Hannah said.

"Yes."

"That ford is about five miles up Duncan Creek from us," Hannah said.

"That's right."

"Then those are our horses we heard and they came home," Dolly said.

"More likely they just followed the creek to the river," Hannah said. Then to the Osage, "So you came to tell us to look for our horses."

"Yes, so you can get them back before some of the soldiers run onto them. I wouldn't put it past the captain to send out a detail to look for them. So far he hasn't, but he's ready to ride out again in a day or two."

"We'll find them," Hannah said, "now that we know they are ours."

"I came across a recent track down by your paddock. I've scouted around your place, found the corral you fixed, and your hide-a-way here. Good work." He moved his head sideways in admiration of her ingenuity. "An Osage couldn't have done better."

Hannah smiled at his compliment. "But you found us. You've been watching us!"

"Yes."

"And we didn't know. I thought I was better than that."

"You're good enough to fool the soldiers. But I'm an Osage," he said as if she needed no other explanation. He didn't offer to leave, but sat quietly after finishing his meal.

Hannah knew enough of the Osage manner from stories her parents told her when they lived neighbors to them to know that they did not brag nor ask for rewards for helping. This man hadn't come just to tell them about their horses and certainly not to receive their appreciation for what he did. His continued presence meant still another reason for visiting them.

"Walking Owl, why have you shown yourself to us now? Do you think it's not safe for us to stay here? Or did you come to warn us?"

"No, neither reason. You're well concealed here." He paused and looked at each of the girls as if trying to decide whether he should butt into their personal business. Dolly smiled at him. Mazie leaned against his leg. Leah was anxiously awaiting what he would say next. He leaned forward and spoke to Hannah. "I learned that you—or rather Hank Johnston—asked for information about your husband. As a scout and an Osage, I have more freedom of movement than the regular soldiers. I'm able at times to scout around on my own. Therefore, I thought I might help you find out what happened to your husband."

Leah ran to him just as Dolly threw her arms around his neck. Mazie dropped Puss and climbed into his lap. Leah grabbed his big left hand between her two small ones and shook it up and down.

"It seems that my offer is accepted," he said. When everyone nodded and said yes, he continued. "I'll see what I can find out. The major at the post is a good man, but he can't do much. He's tied down at headquarters with the continued Bushwhacker raids and enforcing Order Number Eleven. This is extra work on top of his regular duties as supply quartermaster and recruiting to guard the approach to Kansas should General Price come back this way. He'll send out your request, but without someone pushing it, it will take months to learn anything."

"What can you do?" Hannah asked.

"I'll ask for a leave of absence since I have completed my term of enlistment. I can go to Lexington, Jefferson City, or even St. Louis to some of the headquarters of the regional military districts of Missouri where there may be records. I can inquire in person. I have a personal interest, for your husband and I are from the same area. His parents as well as your parents knew my grandfather. They traded for mutual benefit." He looked at Hannah and grinned. "I do know some things about you, and you are not the only one who can change his identity. I can pass for a white man anytime I want."

"I never even dreamed you were an Osage until you told us," Leah said.

"You don't dress like an Indian," Dolly said.

"Or talk like one," Hannah said, "though I should have recognized you as one from your feeling for the land."

"The point is," he said, "that as a United States soldier-scout I can find your husband if he's still alive."

"He is," Leah said with great emphasis.

"We all feel that he is," Hannah said. "That is why we are risking so much to be here when he comes back."

"Fine," the Osage said. "Now I need to know all about your recent movements and who you know. And tell me everything you can about your husband, even the color of his eyes and if he's got as nice a smile as this little one." He patted Mazie who was still in his lap.

They spent the rest of the afternoon talking. Before he left, Walking Owl also gave the girls some pointers on how to hold themselves and act more like boys.

Chapter 11

THE FIRST priority was to find the horses. The rain during the night after the Osage's visit was both detrimental and helpful. Although the rain obliterated the tracks Walking Owl told them about near their paddock, the soft ground left clear imprints showing that the horses were still near.

Early the next morning, armed with rope halters and buckets with some grains of corn they scraped up from under the ashes of the corncrib, Hannah, Leah, and Dolly planned where they would search. To cover the area more quickly, they decided to split up. They mapped out three areas to comb. From the shack, Hannah and Mazie would search upstream through the woods out onto the fringe of the prairie. Dolly would go downstream to the spot where she found the first evidence of the horses, and like her mother, zig-zag through the timber tract between the river and prairie. Leah's area was the prairie. She was to walk to the higher points where she could look over many open acres. They agreed that at noon, if unsuccessful, each was to return to the shack.

"What if I find them?" Dolly asked. "I might not be able to catch them both by myself."

"We need some way to let the others know," Hannah said. This was the first time they had needed to find a means to communicate. Until this search when they left the shack, they had stayed together. But outweighing her wish to keep the family near at all times was the need to find the horses quickly. Walking Owl had said that Murdock was due for another routine patrol through the area in a few days.

"We better not yell or call out," Hannah said.

They discussed some options, discarding banging on trees, which would scare the horses, or simply coming back to tell the others, for in the meantime the horses might disappear again.

"Why not use coyote calls?" Leah suggested.

"Yes, that's it."

For their own amusement the girls had been imitating the coyotes' barks, howls, and yippings. They had become quite successful, even fooling their mother a couple of times when she thought that the animals were right outside the shack. Mazie was proficient in imitating the high-pitched voices of the pups, her simulated barks and yips getting louder and higher and ending with a long flat howl. This indigenous sound heard frequently in the woods and on the prairie wouldn't arouse suspicion should any riders be close enough to hear it.

Hannah and the girls agreed on a sort of code. If any of them located the horses, not just their sign, but actually spotted the horses, she was to let the others know by giving a series of calls, wait until she counted slowly to ten, and then repeat the calls. Just in case the others didn't hear her, or they needed to hear the sound again to help locate her position, she was to wait several minutes and repeat the signal until the others joined her.

Leah and Dolly were eager to get started. Adding this verbal code system to their already perfected acting skills was exciting. Leah grabbed her bucket and halters and started up the path toward the main house to the prairie acres she was to search. Watching her hurry away, Hannah had misgivings about sending her out into the open lands alone.

"Wait, Leah," she called. "Maybe, just in case, we should work out a warning signal."

"Yeah," Dolly said, always ready for any dramatics, "one for a bear's got me or I'm drowning in the river." She pantomimed floundering in the river and feebly calling help.

In spite of her apprehension, Hannah laughed. "No, the coyote call would cover that because it means the rest of us are to come at once. What we might need, though, is one that warns the others to stay away because of some threat, like if you spot some riders."

"Oh," Dolly said suddenly sobered.

That danger was an ever-present possibility. They tried to think of some other animal sound they could use. Birds were always good, but many of the birds had already left for the winter.

"Quail," Hannah said. "Quail stay year around."

"And they live in the woods and in the grass," Leah said.

They experimented imitating the bob white whistle. "Sounds like Mr. Bob White has a sore throat," Dolly laughed at her mother's attempt. Once again Mazie gave the best imitation. Though none of them were very good, they decided to use it if needed.

"What if a real bob white calls?" Mazie said. "How will we know?"

"Because it will sound like a bob white," Dolly laughed.

"Good thought, Mazie. We need to give the call so the others will recognize that it is us." She thought for a few seconds. "Let's give it two times right together, wait like with the coyote calls until you count to ten, and do it again two times." She demonstrated, this time her whistle sounding more authentic. "Bob-bob-whiiii-te! Bob-bob-whiiii-te!" This time the call sounded almost real when she held the "white" and ended on a higher cut off note at the end.

"All right, Mama," Leah said. She waved and ran up the trail. Dolly separated from Hannah and Mazie to search their respective wooded areas along the river.

As Hannah studied the ground for hoof marks or recent manure, she couldn't concentrate wholly on her task. She was still sorting out in her mind what Walking Owl had told her about the army's plans. He said that there was no indication that Order No. 11 would be lifted anytime soon, even through there was much indignation and outcry from some public sources in the state. In spite of the guerrillas' renewed activity, which the Order was designed to stop, Captain Murdock would continue to be in charge of keeping everyone out of the zone, land owners as well as outlaws. However, now Murdock's periodic forays into the zone were more specifically to spot any Bushwhacker activity, but he continued on his own to forage anything that might have been missed and to harass anyone foolish enough to dare defy the Order to see about their homes.

Walking Owl suggested that Hannah, as Hank Johnston, check with the major at Fort Scott periodically to see if he happened to find out any information about Paul.

"How will you get in touch with me if you find him?" Hannah had asked him. "Will you let the major know?"

"I'll get word to you," he had said with no more explanation. Hannah assumed by that he wouldn't send word to the major.

Though she really didn't expect any news from the major's efforts, she felt sure the Osage scout would succeed. She wondered what there was about him to elicit such faith. It wasn't only gratitude for his saving their house, and their horses, or even his offering to find Paul. His quiet seriousness and direct honesty won her over. Beneath his imperturbable face he let her glimpse some of the finest traits of humanity—gentleness, compassion, trust, and selflessness.

She believed in him. Now she needed to find the horses so when his message came, she would be ready to go wherever it was necessary to find Paul. In a way she was grateful for this job today; she needed to keep busy. Waiting was her most difficult task.

By noon she and Mazie had gone about a mile upstream without finding any tracks. Their faces were splotched with mosquito bites. Their feet were wet, their trousers muddy and torn from the briars. They were tired from the uneven and difficult walking. In many places they had to crawl to get through tangles of vines as they switched back and forth canvassing the timber area. Realizing that she had been out of range of the other girls' calls for at least an hour, she took a direct route back to the shack. Just before reaching it, seemly coming from their side of the shack, they heard the coyote call.

Leah was running toward them, obviously looking for them. "Hurry," she said when she spotted them. "Dolly's found the horses. She's been calling, but we were both too far away to hear her. She kept calling until I came home. She's with them, following them until we help her."

Hannah's aching legs sprang to life. Mazie's face suddenly became animated. They followed Leah downstream along the river bank beyond their favorite fishing place to where the river hit a sandstone bluff and veered south around it. There they joined Dolly who was sitting on a big rock where the broad river bottom ended at the raw rock bluff overhang. She pointed across the river to the bay gelding and mare who were contentedly grazing on the new growth of bluestem grass under a huge, black walnut tree.

Hannah scanned the river here to see if it was fordable, even though she knew it wasn't. They would need the skiff. "Mazie, stay here with Dolly. Leah, let's go back for the boat."

This was the same skiff the cavalrymen reported to Captain Murdock as unusable when they were taken prisoners six weeks ago. Not having any need for it, they hadn't used it since they returned from the detention camp. Hannah and Leah ran back upstream to where it was still submerged in the river. Only its bow was above water, held up by the stout rope tied to an overhanging sycamore tree.

Having emptied the skiff many times before, they both knew what to do. They grasped the rope and together, like a tug-of-war game, dragged the bow of the waterlogged skiff up the bank. When the front one-third of the wooden craft was out of the water, Hannah stepped into the river to turn it on its side. Giving less resistance as the water ran out, Leah pulled it farther up the bank. Together they turned it completely on its side until all water drained out. Leah pulled out a paddle that was tied to the underside of a nearby log.

Wet to her hips, but ignoring the chill, Hannah crawled in and sat on the board tacked across the back end. Leah gave the boat a push before jumping into the front herself. Hannah maneuvered the skiff to the center of the river to take advantage of the current and paddled down to Dolly and Mazie. She paused by them long enough for them to scramble in, and then she swung the bow out into the river. With several powerful thrusts, she crossed the current to an inlet where they could land without getting their feet wet. Dolly jumped out and pulled the skiff onto the opposite bank.

The girls needed no instruction on how to catch the horses. Each child positioned herself at different points around the more gentle mare and closed in on her to catch her first. To entice the mare, Mazie held out her bucket and banged on the side. When she got the mare's attention, she grabbed a fistful of corn, held it up for the mare to see, and then let the yellow grains dribble through her fingers to land noisily back into the bucket. The mare came willingly toward the bucket. While she ate the few grains of corn, Hannah tossed the halter's lead line around her neck to hold her and slipped the halter over her nose and behind her ears. She tied her to an oak tree while catching the gelding. He wasn't as easy to catch. Each time he stuck his nose into the bucket, he would snatch a bite and jerk back before Hannah could grab his mane or put the rope around his neck.

Leah watched while he outwitted Hannah several times. She climbed into a tree and told Mazie to bring the bucket under it. This time when the gelding stuck his nose into the bucket, constantly eying Hannah and Dolly and poised to jump back the moment they came within arm's length, Leah dropped out of the tree onto his back and threw her arms around his neck. Startled, he knocked the bucket from Mazie's hands and reared back, spun around, and started galloping. Hanging on to his mane with one hand, as she edged up his neck toward his head, Leah slipped the end of the halter rope around his nose.

The gelding was well trained. When he felt the pull of the halter, he stopped. Leah fitted the halter over his nose and ears. Then she slid off the gelding's back, handed the halter rope to her mother, and said, giving an exaggerated bow, "Your horse, sir."

Everyone laughed. They petted the horses and congratulated each other. "I don't think even Walking Owl would suspect you of being a girl after a stunt like that," Hannah said.

"I couldn't have done it wearing a dress," Leah said. "I like these britches." She looked down to her legs that were covered with river mud and newly ripped in the crouch when she landed on the gelding. "I like being a boy."

"I don't," Dolly said. "I'll be glad when Papa comes and we can go back to being what we are." Even after the tramping she had done looking for the horses, she still looked neat in comparison to the others who were wet, muddy, and covered with stick-me-tights. Mazie's cap was missing from her mop of short, straight brown hair. Hannah pulled a twig from her head and brushed off some sticky sycamore leaves that clung to her.

"We all will, Dolly, we all will. Now let's get these horses home."

Hannah converted the halters' lead ropes into temporary reins to control the horses. Dolly mounted the mare while Leah and Mazie rode the gelding. They were to travel the south side of the river to reach the ford by the paddock. There they would cross to their side of the river and release the horses in their enclosure. Hannah meanwhile paddled the boat back up the river, swamped it, and tied it again to the tree. She worried about the footprints all around the bank. Since they were sunk into the mud, she couldn't erase them. As a make-shift precaution, she threw some branches and fallen leaves around the area.

She stepped back to see if it looked natural. Not to her eye, it didn't. Walking Owl would spot it immediately, but she doubted that any other Indian would canoe by. The Osages had left the country over thirty years ago, and though they sometimes returned from Kansas to hunt or trap their ancestral lands, they were friends, not enemies. She decided that if it didn't rain in a day or two, she'd come back to further hide their tracks. This constant wariness was taking its toll on her. Like Dolly she longed for the time when they could resume being who they were.

Getting the horses back put them closer to that wished-for time. As she hiked back to the shack, she ran though her mind what she would do when she learned about Paul's whereabouts. If he was unhurt and hadn't been able to get word to her, then she would continue here as before until the war was over and he was free to return. But if he was a prisoner in a Confederate camp—she shuttered at that as the women in the detention camp told horror stories about Yankee prisoners at a place in Georgia called Andersonville. If he was a prisoner, she would go after him even if it meant traveling to Georgia. And if he was sick someplace? Again she most certainly would go to him wherever that might be.

How she wished the days would pass quickly to give her new friend time to find Paul and get word back to her! Time was almost a harder enemy to overcome than Murdock. She removed her felt hat and ran her fingers through her short hair. She brushed off some of the almost-dried mud from her trouser legs. Her recent exercise had warmed her up so that her damp feet and legs didn't feel the chill. However, she pulled her coat closer when the wind picked up. Cocking her head just a bit to show a manly pride, she practiced walking with longer strides the way Walking Owl had shown her.

"Remember," Walking Owl had said, "you are now the dominant

sex. Your posture should show that, even the way you hold your head. Be aggressive." He had demonstrated that by telling Leah to stand straighter but loose. When she did that to his satisfaction he added, "Now jut out your chin just a bit. Think all the time, 'I am a boy who will soon be a man.'"

When she did that even Mazie could see a difference in the way she held herself.

"You see," he continued, "by your posture, your body has been telling everyone that looks at you that you are submissive, even inferior. Never give that impression," he grinned at her, "even when you go back to being a girl. Your mother doesn't give that message with her body."

Hannah laughed. "Can you really see all that?"

Walking Owl nodded.

"You are right. Women act the way others think they should. I probably used to, also, but I've had to be the head of the family for so long, I can't think about how I should act as a woman."

"Exactly. That makes your disguise effective. And that also makes you more of a woman. Think of yourselves as human beings—people working in harmony with our mother earth to restore order." Walking Owl turned to Dolly to give her some coaching.

Hannah had never thought much about the roles of men and women. She did what society expected a woman to do without question or objecting. The Osage's words about how to hold herself in her masquerade as a man made her think. Were women submissive? Inferior? The message their body's movements gave certainly seemed to say that. But she felt like crying out loud to the river and trees all around her that she was a woman but she was not and never would be submissive. Or inferior. She had survived here in the burnt district when all others left. She outwitted the kindly officers, Lieutenant Knowles and Captain Cardwell, and so far had outwitted the murderous Carl Murdock. If she had to she would measure up as well to the whole Union Army or any Bushwhacker that might come her way. Inferior? Hogwash.

Then she remembered Walking Owl's comment about human obligation. "To work in harmony with our mother earth to restore order," he had said. He had put so succinctly what she was trying to do—live with the land as she preserved her family. And this comment explained more about him. It explained why he was temporarily a white man, helping to end the war. Only then could order be restored. Even his assignment to Murdock was helping, because in small ways he was restricting Murdock's influence.

Distracted as she was by her thoughts as she trod resolutely through the trees back to the shack, she still kept a part of her brain alert for any danger. She heard a muffled hiss or snarl which she couldn't identify. She stopped in her tracks. Nothing. But before she continued, she picked up a stick about three inches in diameter at the heavy end. As she grasped it in her left hand, she ran her right hand down to a smaller width to get a tighter grip. She glanced through the trees trunks to the shack which was about a hundred and fifty yards away. All was quiet there. The children probably hadn't had time to get back yet.

Hearing nothing more, she lifted her foot to take another step when she heard the sound again, only louder. It was above her. She looked up into an oak tree into the bright, round eyes of a panther. His grizzled gray body was crouched on a lower limb, not ten feet above and slightly ahead of her. The black tip of his long, heavy tail swished back and forth. She saw him open his black mouth and bare his teeth in a hiss. As she stood frozen, her mind was searching for an escape. She grasped the club, but doubted its effect on the animal which weighed at least as much as she. He was stretching and retracting the claws in his powerful paws. Like her, he seemed to be undecided what to do in this unexpected confrontation.

Just then Hannah heard another sound which she easily identified. It was the girls approaching the shack from the paddock. The panther turned his head to see what the noise was. He must have dismissed it as unimportant, for he turned back to continue staring at Hannah.

Hannah tried to remember what she'd heard about these big cats. They rarely attacked humans, she thought someone told her long ago. They fed on deer. Maybe she had disturbed him at his nap, or her stalking through the woods may have frightened his prey. Did he feel as trapped as she did? Was he wanting a means to escape, too? She stepped cautiously backward.

The big cat growled softly and hissed again. Wrong tactic. Hannah froze. The staring contest continued. The girls entered the shack. Just before Leah went through the door, she glanced down the river bottom to see if her mother was on her way back. Spotting Hannah among the trees, she waved. She took a couple of steps inside but stopped and looked back at Hannah again. Hannah wasn't moving and, holding a club, was staring up into the tree.

"Dolly, get me Mama's revolver," she said.

"Mama said not to..."

"Get it!" Leah's tone made Dolly hurry after the gun. When Leah felt the cold gun in her hand, she quickly loaded and cocked it. "Stay with Mazie," she ordered and slipped outside.

Hannah and the big cat had been staring at each other for several minutes, neither moving. Hannah hoped by not moving in any threatening manner that he would give up and leave. But in case he did leap onto her, so slowly that she hoped the cat wouldn't notice the movement, she raised the club until it was level with her face. That accomplished, and since the cat still moved only his tail and his claws which he kept extending and retracting in a threatening manner, she carefully brought her left hand around to clutch the stick firmly in both hands. Hannah and the cat continued the staring contest, both poised at readiness, one to attack and the other to defend herself.

Suddenly, with a snarl, the panther jumped. At the same moment Hannah swung the club with all her strength. Her blow struck the cat on his left shoulder hard enough to check the speed of his landing on her, but not enough to deflect his aim. His front paws spread apart as he leapt, struck her on each shoulder, and knocked her backwards. Losing her stick, she took two unsteady steps backward before she fell on her back, crashing into the leaves and debris. Her head struck a rotted log. Her hips were forced on top of a forked log that punched through her trousers to her skin.

The cat's body covered hers. His hot and feral-smelling breath washed over her face as his growl rumbled next to her ear. The claws of his right paw ripped through her coat and shirt and dug into her flesh on her left shoulder. She lay spread-eagled on the ground, her shoulders and head in a vise-like hug, her neck exposed for the cat's bared teeth.

Faintly, over the roaring in her ears from her fall, Hannah heard a shot. Instantly the panther's powerful arms lost their grip on her. His eyes, within inches of hers, became blanks as his face dropped down on hers. Lifeless, the big cat lay sprawled over her body, his front paws still on her shoulders, his back legs motionless beside her own thrashing legs. His dead tail, that was draped over her boots, whirled around as if alive as she kicked. It fell inert to the ground when she was free of it.

Unable to breathe, terrified and at the same time repulsed by the animal's weight and musky odor, and the spreading heat on her chest which she guessed was his blood, Hannah heaved her prone body up enough to push the dead weight partially from her. The cat's head rolled off hers to land right beside her head. It was still facing her. Staring unbelieving at the dead cat, as if mesmerized by him, she pulled her right arm from under him, spun her boots in the leaf-covered ground until she got a hold with her heels, and dragging her painful left arm, wormed her way backward from under him. Finally free, she sat up.

The scent of gunpowder reached her. She heard a rapid panting and a suppressed moan someplace above her. Understanding now what had happened, she was able to pull her eyes away from the panther's body. She looked into Leah's frightened eyes and into the muzzle of the revolver the child still clutched tightly in her hand as she knelt beside her mother. Then the lightheadedness that she often experienced with a sudden sharp pain overwhelmed her.

Chapter 12

HANNAH WAS no longer sitting up but stretched out on the ground, covered with blood from the panther and from her wounds on her shoulder. She put her hand to her shoulder and looked at the bright red blood on her hand with disbelief. Blood was oozing out onto her shirt from the long scratches. She looked into the eyes of her frightened daughters who were all three kneeling beside her. How did Dolly and Mazie get there so quickly? Leah, yes, she shot the panther. She was gently pulling off Hannah's coat and baring her shoulder to see how serious the panther's scratches were.

Hannah tried to sit up to reassure the girls. Her quick mental assessment as she paid attention to her body's painful points told her she had no serious injuries. Just bruises and scratches, and a bit of faintness. She was all right.

"Lay back, Mama," Leah said. Her hands were trembling as she pushed her back. Her eyes were full of tears and her lip quivered.

"Did I faint?" Hannah asked. Her head felt light. She was extremely weak and beginning to be nauseated. Her skin was clammy.

"Yes, Mama, but just for a minute."

"The panther? You shot the panther?"

"Yes."

Mazie said, "She just pointed the gun and shot. I screamed. I thought she was going to hit you."

"I had a clear shot. He was on top. Mama, we gotta get you to the shack. Can you walk?"

For answer Hannah raised to a sitting position, waited for the dizziness to subside, and then, with the girls supporting her, stood upright. She started to pull off her coat that was soaked with the big cat's blood. Then she vomited, Leah holding her until the retching stopped.

"My stick. Get me that stick." She pointed in front of her to the stick she had used against the panther. Holding it as a cane and with Leah on one side and Dolly on the other, she walked toward the shack. Hannah needed to get inside, lie down, and keep warm. She had prescribed this very treatment for many injured people, even Paul that time when the cow dragged him. She'd soon be all right as soon as her body functions returned to normal from her shock.

Her shoulder wounds were beginning to smart. When she moved her arm, the pain was worse. As she staggered to the shack door, she mentally checked the rest of her body. She couldn't feel any other injuries, just soreness in her hips and a knot growing on the back of her head from her fall. When her heart beat returned to normal and her color returned, she knew from experience that the nausea and dizziness would leave.

She forced herself to stay conscious to tell Leah what to do. "Build a fire," she said when they reached the shack. She removed the bloody clothing, lay on her bed, elevated her feet, and covered herself with a quilt.

"I'll be all right soon," she reassured the girls. "The shock of the big cat knocking me down and the sharp pain from his claws made my heart slow down for a bit. It's fine now." Though the meaning of her words was reassuring, the sound of the words spoken in a faint, breathless voice didn't convince the girls. They had never seen their mother sick before. "Really, children, I just need to rest."

But instead of lying back on the pillow, she leaned over the edge of the bed to look on the floor at the pile of clothes streaked with the panther's blood. "Dolly, take them outside and soak them in water."

"Mama!" Dolly cried, backing away from her, "I can't touch them with all that blood."

"Then go to the river for a bucket of water," Leah said eying her sister with disdain. "I'll take them out. Looks like you could do something for Mama. A little blood won't hurt you."

Dolly grabbed the slop bucket and ran out the door, glad to get out of the odious job. Leah bundled the clothes up and set them outside. Only then did Hannah lay her head back to the feather pillow Mazie fluffed up for her.

Now that she rested comfortably warm in her bed and no longer smelled the panther's scent, Hannah did feel better. Next she needed to tend to her wounds. Following her mother's instructions and using the herbs and medicines in her bag, Leah cleansed the shoulder scratches by applying Hannah's concoction of a bit of alum added to white oak bark that had been boiled down to a thick consistency in the iron kettle.

Her heart rate back to normal, her color returned, and her faintness gone, Hannah had some final instructions for the girls before she could fully relax. The panther's body had to be taken care of.

"Girls, we need that cat's fur. We can sell it at Fort Scott."

"Is it valuable?" Dolly asked. This was the first panther any of them had ever seen as they were scarce in this region.

"Not as much as beaver or mink, but they're valuable for rugs. We'll get a good price for it. We need to sell all the pelts we can to be ready when we hear from Walking Owl about Papa."

The girls didn't know how to skin the panther, but to protect its body until she recovered, Hannah gave Leah and Dolly directions to use the mare and drag it to the cellar at the main house. There it would be protected from other animals. "I'll take care of it tomorrow," Hannah said. Relieved that all necessary chores were taken care of, she let escape a deep sob-like sigh and closed her eyes.

Instead of immediately leaving the shack as Leah did to move the panther's body, Dolly sat on the edge of her mother's bed. Her usually cheerful face was serious, her eyebrows lowered.

"What's the matter, Dolly?"

"Everything's the matter," she exploded in tears. "Papa's gone, we can't live in our own house, or work our own land without sneaking around. We can't be our own selfs, but have to be ole boys and tell lies all the time. And now you almost got killed by a panther!" She laid her head on her arms and sobbed.

Hannah gathered her up into her arms in the bed with her. She rocked her, smoothed back her curls, and kissed her forehead. "I'm not hurt bad. I'll soon be fine again," she said. "Living like this is only for a little time."

"I can hardly remember living any other way," Dolly said. "We never play any games anymore. When we were coming back to the shack just before Leah saw the panther, we were telling Mazie about how we used to play 'King of the Mountain' with Papa. She couldn't even remember. That's how long it's been."

"Yes, it is a long time to a child."

"Why don't we leave here. Go to some place like the Kerrigans did? They don't have to hide anymore. They don't have to be scared every time they hear a noise."

"But they aren't home," Leah said. Coming back to see what was keeping Dolly, she stood in the doorway.

"And their papa won't know where they are when he comes home from the war," Mazie said, "will he, Mama?"

"That's right, sugar." She turned to Dolly. "I thought you wanted to be here for when Papa comes back," Hannah said, stroking her head. Dolly's sobs had diminished to an occasional quick intake of breath.

"I do, but not if you're going to get eaten by a panther." She clutched her mother and began crying again at the memory of the big cat sprawled over her mother.

"Then we'll take a vote. None of us should have to stay here in danger unless we want to. We could go to back to Clinton and join the Kerrigans. It's not so far but what I could come back every so often to see if Papa was here. Who wants to leave?"

No one answered, not even Dolly.

"Who wants to stay here?"

Hannah, Mazie, and Leah all quickly raised their hands.

"Dolly, you didn't vote," Leah said.

"I want Papa to come home and for us to be like we were," Dolly said.

"Would you like me to take you to stay with Beulah until he comes?" Hannah asked. "I can do that."

"NO!"

"Well, we'll just keep on as we've been doing." She kissed her again on the forehead. "I feel that things are going to change very soon. We've come so far all by ourselves. It's better now because we have Walking Owl helping us."

Dolly didn't say anything. "Dolly?" Hannah asked.

Dolly wiped her tears with the back of her hand. She kissed Hannah on her cheek and jumped off the bed. "Let's get that panther in the cellar," she said to Leah and went out the door.

After the girls caught the mare and dragged the panther's body to the cellar, Hannah was feeling much better. The scratches were not deep. If she moved her left arm with care, the wounds didn't pain much. She drank a soothing tea, and with the multicolored patchwork quilt tucked around her, determined not to worry but let the girls take care of her for the rest of the day.

She knew how Dolly felt. The time that Paul broke his leg when Dolly was a baby, she was ready to quit. She remembered that day very well. She felt then as Dolly did now. However, in retrospect, overcoming that misfortune nine years ago might have been what had kept her going the last two years. Would Dolly learn as much from this experience?

DURING THE spring roundup, Paul had rounded up all the cows except old Demon. This mostly black, mixed-breed cow was crazy, hence her name. Paul always had trouble holding her whenever he needed to handle her. He'd throw two, or sometimes three, ropes on her, and securely tie them in three different directions until she was immobile. There was invariably a rodeo exhibition when it was time to brand or castrate her calves. Paul always wished for her to drop heifer calves, simply because that meant no need for castration and one less time he'd have to confront Demon. When it was necessary to handle her calf, his procedure was to drive Demon and her calf into the corral along with several other cows and calves. Then he'd cut Demon out, keeping the calf inside.

He would work quickly, hoping to finish the job on the calf before Demon knocked down the wooden fence to get to it. Paul and Hannah both sighed with relief when the yearly job was completed. Paul vowed each spring to sell Demon before another year. But he didn't. Selling a good brood cow was not good business.

Usually Hannah helped with the sorting and branding jobs, but that year right after Dolly's birth, she was pretty well confined to the house. Neighbor Philip Newman planned to help. Thinking he was with Paul in the barnyard, Hannah prepared dinner for the men as she took care of the baby and toddler Leah.

Since Philip was late, Paul started without him. He and his stock dog had no trouble driving the cattle into the corral. All, that is, except Demon and her bull calf. Exasperated with her behavior, and afraid she would run off, Paul threw a rope over her. As usual, he quickly wrapped his end of the rope around the heavy gate post with a half hitch. Demon lunged until the rope tightened around her neck, jerking her head back toward the corral.

Paul threw the second rope. It also circled Demon's neck. But before he could fasten it to the corner post which would hold her as the point of a triangle, she lunged against the first rope. With his back to her, and the second rope in his hand still slack and part of it lying on the ground between him and Demon, the bug-eyed cow yanked out the loosely tied half hitch of the first rope. When Paul felt the rope in his hand tighten as Demon moved away from the corral, he swung around, stepping on the ground rope. He lost his grip. With no restraints on her, the cow began to run, the lassos still about her neck. As Paul swung around on one leg, dropping his end of the rope, the ground rope circled his ankle. The cow's movement yanked his feet from under him, throwing him down. Demon galloped toward the river woods, dragging Paul along the ground on his back. Paul whooped to Hannah.

When Hannah ran from the house, she vaulted on Paul's saddled horse and galloped after them. With her calf running beside her, Demon was bucking and bawling at the unaccustomed drag behind her. About twelve feet behind them in a swirl of dust was Paul, being dragged by his right foot as he twisted from side to side, his hat gone and his blond head thumping in the dirt.

"Cut her off!" Paul kept yelling. "Get in front of her." He tried to rise up enough that he could reach the rope around his ankle to untangle it, but each time he almost grabbed the rope, he was jerked back.

On Paul's horse, Hannah overtook Demon and cut right in front of her just as the cow was entering the woods. Demon almost rammed right into the horse before she veered him sharply to the left. Reining the horse to stay with Demon, Hannah forced her in a tight circle around a tree. One circuit around the trunk stopped Demon's head-on rush. The rope circling the tree entrapped her and brought her temporarily to her knees. Quickly righting herself, brown eyes bugged out in fright, she snorted, bawled, and pawed the ground. Even the calf beside her did not calm her.

Hannah jumped off beside Paul. The sudden stop gave the rope around Paul's leg some slack. Scooting forward on his seat to loosen the rope even more, he sat up and untangled the rope from his ankle. The legs of his levis protected his skin from more than surface burns, but when he tried to move his leg, he knew it was broken. Sweat popped out on his tanned face, now turned suddenly ashen.

"I've done it this time, Hannah," he said holding his full lips tight together from the pain. "Should have sold that bitch years ago." Leaning heavily on Hannah and using the stick she gave him, he tried to hop to the house since he couldn't climb on his horse. It was too far. Hannah convinced him to sit down and lean against a tree trunk while she harnessed the team to the wagon to carry him to the house.

That accident was the first time Hannah had needed to use her medicinal skills on Paul. When he was safely in their bed, she set his broken leg, dressed his bruises and scratches, and gave his some soothing herb tea to dull the pain.

A broken leg did not stop the work that had to be done. When Philip Newman arrived a half hour later, Hannah worked with him to finish the yearly branding and cutting, including Demon's calf, which they tended to while his mother was still bound to the tree.

In the days that followed, though often ready to quit, Hannah learned then what she could do with a strong enough incentive. Paul's encouragement and love kept her going. While Paul convalesced, they switched jobs, he taking care of the children and the house, while she did the ranch work. By supporting each other and sharing the work and responsibilities, they got through the spring and early summer until Paul could use his leg as before. After that accident, though they soon reverted back to their own jobs, she and Paul worked more as a team. Paul was teaching his daughters all about the ranch as Hannah was preparing them for being women.

HANNAH HADN'T quit before when Paul was laid up. Nor would she now while he was away, for Paul's need of her to keep the ranch and family together was much greater than when he simply broke his leg. The remainder of the day that the panther jumped her was all the time she would pamper herself. Tomorrow she would be back to normal. Dolly would forget her fright and discouragement, and they would continue getting ready for Walking Owl's message when it came.

After the girls returned from securing the panther, to show them that she was truly better, she led them in some guessing games. Dolly's outburst showed Hannah that the girls couldn't live in perpetual alertness. They needed to be normal children and to play. She held a spelling competition, with very easy words for Mazie, and finished up with a ciphering match. Instead of braiding rags into ropes as she usually did at the end of the day before time to go to bed, she fashioned a toy panther from scraps of material to join Mazie's toy horse the storekeeper's wife gave her.

When she drew a face on it using a burnt stick from the fireplace, Mazie said, "It looks like it's laughing." Hannah drew an open mouth with some teeth showing.

"Better?"

Mazie studied it. "Yes, a little. But it looks more like Puss meowing." She took it and the girls reenacted the scene with the panther. Only this time the panther talked real mean as the girls took turns being Hannah, the panther, and Leah. While the children played, Hannah planned out the next few days.

As Hannah expected, the next day she felt ready to work. Her first job was to skin the panther and stretch out his hide. It, along with the beaver, muskrats, raccoons, and the one beautiful mink she trapped, would bring them enough money to travel to Paul when they learned where to go.

In addition to the normal gathering of wood, hunting, and fishing, they set out more traps. Daily they ran the lines and prepared the pelts of their catch. Then in addition to that, now that they had the horses back, they needed to put up some hay for the winter.

Left free, the horses could survive on the dried prairie grasses, but to prevent their being stolen again, Hannah wanted to keep them penned up. The small amount of grass in their paddock wouldn't last much longer. She already planned to build another pen where she could move them, but even in the new area the grass wouldn't last all winter. With the unburned portions of the prairie still lush with stem-dried bluestem grass, the best solution was to cut enough hay to winter them over.

They knew how to cut the hay. The sores from the panther's scratches did not hinder as Hannah mowed. She swung the scythe, cutting with a strong forward sweep. She took two steps as she moved the scythe back into position, and swung again. She moved evenly, leaving behind her a three-foot wide row of stubs covered with the mowed hay. To pull behind the mare, they had fashioned a land sled using long saplings as runners with smaller limbs tacked across for the bed. Dolly drove the mare, while Leah and Mazie stacked the cut hay on the sled. When it wouldn't hold any more, the mare dragged the load to the woods. They forked the hay into small piles, in and around the paddock, rounded over so that the rain would run off. To disguise the piles, they threw limbs and vines over them.

Since the grass immediately surrounding their house was burned, most of the best grass still standing was near the main road. With one of the girls always on the lookout on the high ridge where she could see for a couple of miles in every direction, Hannah felt they could be warned in time if anyone rode by. She didn't work right by the road, as any passerby would recognize someone had been harvesting in the banned region. She picked spots that wouldn't be noticeable from the road. The only riders likely to come by were the Bushwhackers, whom she didn't worry about, and Captain Murdock. Walking Owl had said that unless Captain Murdock heard about any outlaw activity, he was not likely to make another trip though their area for a few days. So it was safe to work out on the prairie.

Four days into the haying, Dolly was on lookout when Hannah heard a bob white call, two times in rapid succession, a pause long enough to count to ten, and then a repeat. Warning! Hannah quickly led the mare into the protecting woods. She and the other two girls ran back to the edge of the trees to look out from behind the trunks. They could see the tall clumps of grass on the higher ridge where Dolly was hidden.

Captain Murdock's detail was loping leisurely west toward Fort Scott, the captain and young Lieutenant Knowles side by side in the lead with six men following two by two. When they reached the fallen entrance to Prairie Wood Ranch, the captain raised his right arm to halt the detail.

"Looks deserted to me," Knowles volunteered without dismounting. "No tracks."

"Yeah, it looks like it," the captain said, spitting a stream of tobacco juice on the ground. He scanned the undulating land of the ranch. "Has anyone been back since we cleared these people out?"

"I don't know, sir. I've not been on patrol with you since then," Knowles replied.

"We better check, just in case. Good place for Bushwhackers to hole up." Without looking behind him at the men waiting his orders, he said, "Walker, ride down to the building site to check it out."

"Walker didn't come with us today, sir. He's on leave," Knowles said.

"Oh hell! I knew that. Just habit. Damn it all, I still need him to scout out that Newman gang. His leave was against my wishes."

"Something to do about his enlistment," Knowles said. "The men of the Osage Nation serve as scouts on short enlistments so that they can take leave to tend to tribal affairs."

"I know, I know. Lord, man, do you think I'm stupid?"

"No, sir, far from it."

"What goddamn tribal affair was so important that he had to leave us?"

"As I recall, something about a neighbor missing in action."

"Humph! And that is more important than his duty?" Murdock scanned the empty country again. "He's the best scout I've had. Don't act like an injun, though."

"No sir, he doesn't. He's been educated, even gone to a university out east somewhere, I hear."

"Humph!" Murdock sent another stream of tobacco juice onto the ground. "I reckon I know this country good enough now that we can get along without him."

"Yes, sir, you do."

"I used to ride here some even before the war."

"I've heard of your work with the Redlegs," Knowles said.

The captain gave a smug grin. "We did the Lord's work here, and a goddamned thorough job, too, you can be sure." He paused. "But maybe not good enough in every instance. I should have sent that insolent pup to hell when I had the chance. These Bushwhackers think they're too smart."

"Which pup, sir?"

"Oh, the Newman boy. That was years ago."

Knowles didn't answer. "Well," the captain said, "since Walker's not here, send someone else to check out this ranch." Murdock jerked his reins to pull his stallion's head back to the west and continued down the road at a walk.

The men awaited their orders. "Continue as you were," Knowles said. "I'll check it out myself."

He trotted his sorrel down the trail toward the house as the others continued west. When he reached the mound where he could see the buildings, he paused and straightened up in his saddle as if surprised to see the house still standing. He scanned the nearby clumps of grass and the land between him and the house. He then covered the remaining distance to the buildings, walked his horse around the deserted lawn and burned out barnyard. Without dismounting he looked carefully at the ground for any tracks. He glanced at the garden plot. Then he whirled his horse around and galloped back up the trail. As he reached the rise where he could see in all directions, he stopped and carefully studied the expanse of prairie and the homestead by the woods.

A bob white call came from a heavy clump of grasses about twelve feet from him. Then after a brief pause it was repeated. The lieutenant sat quietly glancing curiously at the spot where the calls came from. At first he didn't see anything but grass waving in the persistent prairie wind. Then from a gap in the thick grass that was held open by two small hands, he made out a pair of eyes as blue as the wild asters along the trail. Around the rosy face was a fringe of blond curls just lighter than the burnt-golden dried grasses.

Knowles did not move. The smile that crossed the lieutenant's face was mirrored in the small face half hidden in the grass.

"Well, boy," Knowles said aloud to his sorrel, patting him on the neck, "all's as it should be. I see no problem here." He continued to sit still for a few seconds, the horse shaking his head with impatience to rejoin the other riders. Knowles scanned the prairie once again. From his vantage point he could see the patches of cut hay that weren't visible from the road.

"Did we get you into trouble?" a small voice asked.

Knowles smiled again, patting his horse once more. "No, no trouble. Nothing to report since it wasn't a military assignment." He tried unsuccessfully to see more than just the head of the small body that was hidden in the grass. Then, looking across the prairie to the military detail that was almost out of sight, he continued talking to his mount, "The ranch is deserted, boy. We'll report to the captain that all I heard was a lone bob white calling to his family."

He put his fingers to the brim of his hat. With a half salute into the clump of grass, he neck-reined his horse to cut across the prairie. When the horse had taken a few steps, Knowles pulled back on the reins, turned in his saddle to look back to the clump of grass. The grasses' heavily-laden seed heads waved lazily in the late October breeze. At the center of the clump a few stalks shimmered at a slightly faster rate than the others near it.

"C'mon boy." He clucked twice to his horse. "Let's get the hell out of here so that little quail back there on lookout can get back with her family."

He spurred his horse to a gallop to catch up with his captain. From behind him came a series of coyote cries, high pitched barks and yips getting louder and higher and ending with a long flat howl. The cries repeated after a short pause, carrying two or three miles over the empty prairie.

Chapter 13

"AND YOU'RE sure he saw you?" Hannah asked in alarm, looking about her as if expecting to see the soldiers surrounding them.

"Yes," Dolly said. She was breathless from running and excited about her daring in showing herself to the lieutenant. "He smiled at me and then talked to his horse, but I knew he was talking to me."

"What did he say?" Leah asked.

"He said that there was no problem on our place."

"You mean he isn't going to report us?" Leah asked. Just as her mother, she was ready to flee from the cavalrymen that would surely return for them as soon as the lieutenant informed the captain of their presence.

Dolly shook her head vigorously, grinning all the while.

"We saw him go up to the house," Hannah said. "I'm sure he knew we had been there for he stopped and looked so hard at the garden where we'd dug up the turnips. He could tell someone had been there since the fire."

"And when he didn't get off his horse or look around much more," Leah said, "we thought he'd figured it all out and was riding back to report to the captain. And then when he stopped at the ridge beside where you were hiding and just sat there for no reason, we just knew he saw you and we were caught."

"How did he happen to notice you?" Hannah asked. "I didn't think he could see you if you'd stayed down, unless he rode right through the clump of grass."

"He couldn't see me," Dolly said, "so I showed him my face."

"Dolly!" Hannah was aghast. "No matter how much you think you trust anyone, don't ever do that again. Do you hear me?" Her voice was stern and unrelenting. She clutched Dolly's coat and shook her slightly.

Dolly screwed up her face, her eyes on the ground. "But you trusted Walking Owl when he broke into the shack even before you knew he helped us. The lieutenant was our friend from the beginning."

"He treated us kindly, but that's no guarantee he wouldn't turn us in. It was his duty." Her voice was still stern.

"It was Walking Owl's duty, too. He is a soldier as much as my lieutenant." Dolly was ready to cry. "And we know that he likes us."

Hannah put her hand on Dolly's shoulder. "You are right, honey. I'm sorry. We do have as much reason to trust him as we do Walking Owl."

"Mama," Dolly said, "the captain called Walking Owl, Walker, and the lieutenant said he had asked for leave for tribal business to see about a neighbor missing in action." Dolly's eyes were eager. "Does that mean that he's already looking for Papa?"

Hannah forgot her anger at Dolly for putting them in so much danger. "Oh yes, it does. And that means that he asked for leave just to find Papa. Papa is the neighbor that's missing."

The girls danced with excitement. "We'll hear about Papa real soon, won't we?" Mazie asked.

"We hope so, sugar," Hannah agreed.

"And Mama," Dolly said, "the lieutenant didn't get into trouble about us running away from him."

"How do you know that?"

"He told me."

"You mean you had a conversation with him? You said he talked to his horse."

"Well, he did. But I asked him if he got into trouble, and he said..." Dolly frowned to remember the words he used. "... he said, 'No trouble. Nothing to report as it wasn't a military assignment.'" She grinned, pleased with herself. "That was his exact words. I memorized them."

Hannah didn't know whether to scold or hug her daughter. Hugging seemed to be in order since Dolly's bravery showed them that they had another ally and that they were not on Captain Murdock's wanted list. As far as the military authorities were concerned, the Rockforts were in Independence with Bill and Rhodie McGill. That knowledge meant that except in the military zone, she and the girls could resume their true identity.

"And that means that Captain Cardwell knows nothing about it," Hannah said. "No wonder he let the Kerrigans leave with us so easily. Yes, Dolly honey, your lieutenant is a friend we can trust."

"While you were talking to him," Leah said, "why didn't you ask him to hunt for Papa?"

"I didn't really talk with him. I just asked the one question. That's all. He talked to his horse."

Hannah took a deep breath of relief. "Well, let's finish up the haying. Murdock's not coming back this way today, for sure. With the lieutenant's report that our place is deserted, Murdock probably won't come back down our trail again any time soon. Dolly, come help us. No need for the lookout any more today."

Dolly grabbed the mare's rope to lead her while Leah and Mazie piled onto the sled the hay Hannah cut. When they paused to rest before taking the full load to the woods, Hannah noticed that Dolly wasn't talking and laughing as usual.

"What's the matter, Dolly?"

"While the soldiers were talking, they said something about the Bushwhackers."

"What did they say?"

"The captain sent the lieutenant to our house to see if there were any there. He didn't even think about us being there. It was to see about Bushwhackers."

"That's good for us, but it also means that there's some outlaws around. We better watch for them." Since she'd been home, the threat from the guerrillas never seemed as threatening as that of the military.

Now it seemed the opposite was true. "What did Murdock say about them?"

People-oriented as Dolly was, she could remember almost exactly what they said. "He said 'I still need him' he meant Walker, 'to scout out that Newman gang.' and then later he said, 'I should have killed that pup when I had the chance. These Bushwhackers think they're too smart.' Then he said the pup was the Newman boy from years ago."

"Oh, my!" Hannah put her hand over her mouth and with her tongue felt the gap in her lower front teeth. She could almost feel again the pain of that night.

"Who's the Newman boy, Mama?" Leah asked.

With this new threat, Hannah automatically searched the prairie for any riders. "Let's get into the woods, quick." When they were out of sight of anyone on the prairie, she explained, "You remember the story of the night when Mazie was born?"

"Yes." They had heard the story many times. They knew all about Carl Murdock's actions that night. "Well, the neighbors were the Newmans. Their boy, Bud, was that Confederate soldier that took Papa from us. He saw Murdock shoot his father."

"And now he's a Bushwhacker?" Leah asked.

"Apparently. Some of these outlaw bands are part of the Confederate Army. Their purpose is to cause the Union trouble any way they can. With young Newman heading up a gang, we may be in more danger than ever. He knows this country. He knows our ford. I don't think we can hide from him."

"But if he was a neighbor and saw what Murdock did to you, he won't harm us, will he?" Leah asked.

"Oh yes. Remember how he acted when he took Papa? He's become fanatic. And remember, Papa deserted the Confederate Army for the Union. To Bud Newman that means Papa is the enemy as much as Murdock." She looked at each child in turn. "And that hatred would include us."

Hannah reassessed their situation. Hopefully Newman would spend his energies against Murdock and the farms and ranches in Kansas. However, she feared that pinned down, he might come to the woods along her river to hide. The favorite hideout for Bushwhackers had traditionally been just south of her ranch along the Marmaton River. With military action against him, Newman might move up to the Osage River area, which would afford good cover and continue to keep him close to the military supply base in Fort Scott. Usually, when the leaves fell to make it harder to hide, the outlaw groups went to Texas to winter. Young Newman, knowing the country as he did, could probably evade the military while continuing to harass them even in the winter.

During the next two weeks Hannah rechecked the area along the river to obliterate any signs of their being there. She cut down a couple of cedar trees along the bluff and propped them beside the shack. The cold temperatures coming would preserve their color. She hoped that the needles would remain thick and green to camouflage the building while the deciduous trees were bare.

Avoiding the soldiers was not too difficult. Fooling guerillas from the area who were skilled in hiding was another matter. All she could do was anticipate where they might come and hope that they would bypass the shack. If not, they would have to bluff their way through. Dolly and Mazie had begun wearing their dresses some around the shack. Hannah insisted that they keep their male disguise at all times. If Bud Newman did discover them and believed that they were the Johnstons in hiding, perhaps he would leave them alone.

When she did all she could think of to protect themselves, she put her energies into preparations for finding Paul. She doubled her trapping efforts, each day increasing their take, until she had enough for another trip to Fort Scott. She and just one of the older girls could make the trip quicker than if all of them went, especially with their load of pelts, but she dreaded being separated, especially with the threat of Newman. The family discussed the pros and cons, finally deciding that separating was the better choice. With many orders and instructions from their mother, Leah and Mazie stayed at the shack.

"I know what to do, Mama," Leah assured her. "We've done it before. Don't worry about us. Just sell the hides." Leah kept their revolver.

Hannah constructed a travois like the Indians used from two long and slender oak trees. Across the poles she tied lighter poles with vines and flexible buckbrush runners to make a platform for the pelts. Though she had seen the primitive means of transportation, she had never used a travois because she always had a wagon. But with no wheels and too many pelts for the two horses to carry, she decided this was the best way to transport the heavy furs.

To avoid getting the pelts wet when they forded the river, they paddled them across in the skiff and packed the travois on the other side. She had to experiment how to place and tie down the hides so they wouldn't slip off. The rag strips she had braided added extra tying material to the few feet of rope she had. By dusk everything was ready for an early morning departure. The crossed ends of the travois poles were propped up on a forked stake driven into the ground. The poles of the crude sledge were ready to be tied together in front of the saddle horn when the mare was backed into place. Hannah didn't sleep much that night anticipating the many things that might happen both to her and Dolly on their trip and to the two girls left home.

One thing she didn't need to worry about was the weather. The cool, clear days had continued into mid-November. In the pre-dawn light, she and Dolly forded the river on the horses, hitched the travois to the mare, and traveled the back road to Fort Scott. Dolly was in the lead on the mare, Hannah following on the gelding. They moved slowly, not sure how the trailing oak poles would hold up, or whether the ends would wear off as they were dragged along the hard, dry ground.

Without incident, though much more slowly that Hannah wished, they arrived in Fort Scott in early afternoon. To reach the general store, she avoided the streets as they would further wear down the poles that were sagging dangerously by the time they reached town. Coming into town from the south also helped her avoid running into soldiers until after she sold the pelts. Most of the military was camped just north of the business area around the post headquarters at the old fort compound.

Her plan was successful. The merchant remembered Hank Johnston and his son Bob from the previous month's trading. As before, he and others in the store teased Dolly, ruffling her hair and laughing at her quick retorts which earned her a stick of striped peppermint candy.

While the storekeeper appraised the hides, he visited with Hannah. Several idlers and a couple of soldiers off duty gathered around to hear and share the general gossip. She learned of the increased activity of the Bushwhackers against Kansan citizens and the outlaws' continued irritation to the major at the fort. Order No. 11, whose purpose was to curtail the Bushwhackers, seemed to have had little effect. Several bands were mentioned, but the most vicious one, and one that she heard mentioned several times, was that of Bud Newman.

With her sale concluded to her satisfaction, she made some purchases. Discarding the travois, she strapped the larger of her purchased items onto the horses. The small items, like thread and needles, she put in the saddlebags. She secreted the twenty dollar gold pieces in a money belt she had made to wear under her clothing.

Going home would be much faster without the travois. But before heading back northeast toward the ranch, she walked to the major's headquarters. From the gossip at the store, she had learned that Captain Murdock was out patrolling. To see if there was any information about Paul, she would have braved going to the post even if Murdock was there, but with him gone, she felt there was little danger.

When announced by his aide, the major greeted Hank Johnston cordially, but regretfully told him that there was no word about his cousin's whereabouts. He had sent word to the district military headquarters at both Jefferson Barracks in St. Louis and Lexington. There was no reply.

Though Hannah didn't expect any news, she was nevertheless disappointed. Dolly's eyes started to fill with tears. Then she remembered that the man they were asking about was supposed to be a cousin. She quickly wiped her tears away and continued to suck on the stick candy, savoring every sweet and spicy lick with her tongue. Though she usually observed everyone within range, so intent was she on hearing the major's answer and sucking on her candy, she didn't notice the reaction to their name by one of the officers working at a conference table in the rear. He had his back to them. Nor did either Hannah or Dolly see the intent look on his face as he rose and followed them out. He loitered in the street where he could watch what they did.

As she limped out of the headquarters building, Hannah paused. She idly ran her finger over her mustache as she planned what to do next. She was convinced that she wouldn't find out any information from the officials. As Hannah Rockfort, she had tried this before with no success. If the officers had really wanted, they could have found some information. Even if Paul were captured, or dead, she shuttered, there would be a record of where he had been before that—his enlistment and assignments. He had been gone two whole years. And no information at all? How could that be? It was as if Paul never existed.

"If Papa were from Kansas," she said to Dolly when they crossed the street from the post to the business district of the town, "they would have kept after the higher up officials until they got the information."

"What'll we do now?" Dolly asked.

"Keep looking. Wait for Walking Owl."

She wondered how he planned to contact her. Short of his coming to her shack, she didn't know what else he would do. However, coming himself seemed unlikely. Would he send someone? Maybe, but whom could he trust? Fort Scott seemed to be the logical place to contact her as he knew she would come there from time to time. He even told her to check with the major.

Perhaps he sent a letter. Resolved to follow any lead, she tried the mail. Nothing there. She returned to the store. No, there were no messages there, either. Satisfied that Fort Scott was not the means of communicating with her, she untied the horses where she had left them behind the store and started for home. Knowing Murdock was miles away, she took the direct route out of town down the brick street. Among the townspeople and soldiers on the street, they saw but paid no special attention to a young officer who turned his back to them as they rode past.

Dolly was very quiet and hung her head as she trailed behind her mother. Hannah, though disappointed, brightened when she ran her hand over her waist to feel the bulge of the gold coins in the money belt under the fullness of Paul's coat and shirt.

"Cheer up, Dolly, honey," she said, standing up in her stirrups to turn around to face her daughter. "The hides brought us enough money to bring Papa home."

"But we don't know where he is!" Dolly could cry now that no one was looking at her.

"Not yet, but soon. We have to give Walking Owl time."

They rode at an easy-riding, ground-covering lope. Each was anticipating being home. "Won't Leah and Mazie be surprised at the stick of candy you bought them?" Dolly said.

"They deserve it," Hannah said absentmindedly for she was anxious about the girls being alone all day. What if Bud Newman came? They were out of sight of the town, though still in Kansas, and leaving the open grassland for a grove of trees near a draw, when Hannah became aware of a horseman behind her. He was traveling faster than they were, but did not seem to be pursuing them. As Hannah and Dolly turned the bend in the road, Hannah pulled into the trees and slid her gelding down the low bank of the draw. Though surprised, Dolly followed. Hidden from anyone on the road, they dismounted and, holding their horses noses to keep them from snorting, waited for the lone rider to pass.

The sun low in the sky behind the rider silhouetted him. They could not see his face, though they recognized that he was an officer. When he passed by them, he scanned quickly and automatically the woods on either side of him, but not noticing them, did not slacken his horse's gait. His cursory glance their direction was just enough for both of them to recognize him.

"Mama," Dolly said, grasping her mother's arm, her face in a broad grin. "It's my lieutenant!"

"Yes." Hannah had to hold Dolly from jumping out and announcing herself. She watched the young lieutenant ride out from the narrow wooded area beside the draw. When he peered ahead at the empty road, he slowed down, almost stopping.

"I think he was following us," Hannah said. Since he came from the post, he had undoubtedly seen them there. If he was on her tail, he obviously wasn't a threat to them. Besides, she reminded herself, she was Hank Johnston now, known in town by the major and several businessmen.

"Let's go talk to him," Dolly begged. She pulled on her mother's sleeve to get going.

"All right. It is always better to be the one in control of the situation. We'll pick the time, not him. But remember you are Bob." Hannah looked sternly at her until she nodded agreement.

They rode out of the draw, and resuming their previous speed, continued down the road. They soon caught up with the lieutenant, who slowed to a walk when he heard horses behind him.

"Good evening, Lieutenant," Hannah said in her male-sounding voice as she put her fingers to the brim of her hat in greeting.

She started to pull past him when the lieutenant said, "Good evening to you, too, sir." He looked a long time at Dolly and included her in his greeting. "And to you, buddy."

Dolly nodded her head, but she couldn't stop the grin on her face. "Are you following us?" she asked. "Pa and I hid from you back there thinking you were a Bushwhacker."

Both Hannah and the lieutenant were taken back by her directness.

"Why, yes, I was. I wondered where you disappeared to."

"What do you want with us?" Hannah asked.

"I understand that you are Hank Johnston." When Hannah startled at his knowing that, he quickly added, "I was at headquarters when you came in. I heard the orderly announce you." All the time he was talking he was studying her and Dolly intently.

"Yes, I had business with the major." She repeated, "And what do you want with us?"

"I have a message for you."

Hannah and Dolly exchanged glances. Hannah shook her head just enough to warn Dolly not to show any emotion.

"I see. Then why didn't you give it to me at the post if you knew I was there? Why trail us out here?"

"I thought I might put you in some danger if I confronted you there. The message asks me to be very discreet."

Inwardly Hannah's hopes were soaring. Still warning Dolly to keep calm, she waited for him to continue.

"It seems we have a friend in common. I received just this morning a letter from our scout Walker."

Dolly's eyes danced as if saying, "I knew it! I knew it!"

"Yes, we know him."

"He wrote for me to hold this," he handed her a small piece of paper, folded over twice and sealed, "until a certain Hank Johnston and his sons of Clinton come to town. Then I was to give it to him without the knowledge of anyone else. That is why I followed you out of town. I understand it is of great importance to you." He watched Hannah who stared at the note but made no move to open it. Seeing her assumed name written down for the first time in Walking Owl's beautiful script made her uneasy. "I have great respect for Walker, Mr. Johnston," the lieutenant said when she remained silent, "and I will not betray his trust, as you need not fear any betrayal on my part."

Although her mind was in a whirl of emotions, she had to continue playing her part. Her greatest problem was keeping her hand that held the note from trembling. "I appreciate your effort on our behalf. I wish I could thank you in a more suitable fashion, but right now my son and I have several miles to travel before we make camp."

The lieutenant smiled. "I understand. I was going to warn you about guerrilla bands along this road, but I see that is not necessary." He cocked his head back toward the grove of trees that had protected them from his discovery.

"We appreciate the warning. I heard about them in the store. We will be extra careful."

"I notice you do not carry a gun. Is that wise?"

"Perhaps not. I considered buying one at the store, but decided I needed the money for other supplies."

The lieutenant pulled out of his saddlebags a holstered gun and leaning from his horse handed it to Hannah.

"I couldn't take your gun," she said, pulling back.

"It's from Walker. He said to make sure you are armed."

"Oh." Hannah took the holster, removed the Smith & Wesson pistol and spun the cylinder. There were five bullets. Setting it on the empty cylinder, she thrust it into the holster and buckled it around her waist. "Thank you, lieutenant."

"Knowles, Micah Knowles."

Hannah nodded to acknowledge the compliment of his full name.

"I wish you success. If I can be of further help, let me know. When Captain Murdock returns next week from Bates County, I will once again be assigned to him." He moved his head to indicate the note in Hannah's hand. "I understand."

Knowles then turned to Dolly. He grinned at her just as she grinned back at him. "What is your name, buddy?" he asked.

"Bob." She giggled as if they were sharing a secret.

"Ah. What an appropriate name. You're small and wily with

inquisitive eyes almost like a bird." He winked at Dolly, grinned again and added, "Like a bob white."

Without waiting for an answer or even looking back, he spurred his sorrel back toward town, galloping into the sun around the bend by the trees. His silhouetted figure sitting erect in the saddle stayed in their minds long after he rode out of their view. Dust from his horse's hooves hovered in the still evening air.

Chapter 14

HANNAH'S hands trembled as she broke the seal on Walking Owl's letter. She and Dolly had dismounted and were standing by the side of the road. When the dust from the lieutenant's sorrel settled, there was nothing moving on the prairie. Even the ever-present breeze had stilled in the early evening chill.

"What does it say?" Dolly asked. "Did he find Papa?"

Hannah read aloud the few words. "The army hospital in Jefferson City." She turned the paper over. There was nothing more. But her heart soared. Her weariness from the day's efforts melted away. "He's alive! He's alive!" was all she could think.

Dolly hugged her as she danced crazily around her. "Papa's alive!" she said out loud so that Hannah didn't know whether the words were hers or her daughter's.

"And in Missouri! Oh my, oh my!" They hugged and kissed each other in their great relief, unmindful of the strange picture they made should anyone see them. But they had the prairie all to themselves.

"But, Mama, it says 'hospital.' Does that mean he's sick?"

"Oh!" She started to climb on the gelding as if she would ride this very moment to her husband. Was he sick? Or wounded? Perhaps both. "I don't know. Yes." At Dolly's stricken look, she added, "Probably recovering from wounds. It's all right, honey. I must get to him."

"Jefferson City's not too far, is it?"

"Quite a ways, but we can make it. It's about..." she thought for a few seconds "... a hundred and sixty miles. But come, let's get home and tell Leah and Mazie. We're going to Jefferson City!" She lifted her foot to the stirrup and swung easily into the saddle. Dolly was already mounted. They rode their horses as fast as they could along the more direct main road. It was near midnight before they turned onto their land, detouring around the ranch's sign which still lay across the trail.

Not being able to see well in the moonless night, they rode slowly side by side. "Why didn't Walker write more?" Dolly asked. "We don't know how Papa is or why he didn't write or anything."

"That may be all Walker knows. He could have learned only that Papa was there and sent the letter to the lieutenant right away. And even if he knew more, he wouldn't write it."

"Why not? He knows we'd want to know."

"To protect us and probably himself. Remember, he was supposed to be on leave for tribal business. He could get into trouble if Captain Murdock discovered that he was really helping one of his 'prisoners.'"

"But we're the Johnstons now."

"Still risky. Sending a letter during this wartime is very uncertain. He didn't know who might get ahold of the note. Actually, he didn't even know for sure that our lieutenant would deliver the message." Hannah had switched unconsciously from "the" lieutenant to "our" lieutenant. "He could have given it to Murdock or..."

"But he didn't. I knew he wouldn't." She puckered up her face and nodded her head to emphasize that she was sure of her lieutenant all along.

"Well, no he didn't, but Walking Owl might not have been so sure. Then there was always the possibility that Knowles might have been transferred to some other post. Or gotten hurt in scrimmages with the Bushwhackers, or killed. Walking Owl didn't take any chances that someone else would find the note and figure out what it meant. He knew that all we needed to know was where Papa was."

They rode over the rise, but couldn't see their house in the dark. "He's wonderful," Dolly said.

"Who is wonderful?" They had been speaking of two men. Hannah's thoughts were on the Osage, wondering what sort of magic he had pulled to find out in less than a month what she couldn't discover in two years.

"The lieutenant. Micah."

Hannah was surprised at her using his first name. "Yes, he's a good friend to us."

"I'm going to marry him when I grow up," Dolly said with the same certainty that she would use saying that she was going to be taller when she grew up.

"Oh, Dolly, that's foolishness. You're just a little girl. Marriage is a long way off and he's too old for you."

Dolly pouted as they rode along for a few minutes. "He's not old and I act older than my age. You keep telling me that."

"Yes, you certainly do."

"How old is he?"

"Oh, he's very young for an officer." She visualized the boyish face. "I'd say he's twenty or twenty-one."

"I'm almost ten. Lots of husbands are ten years older than their wives."

"Oh, Dolly, let's not think of such things. Be a child as long as you can." That was good advice, but for the past many months her girls hadn't lived as children. They had had to assume adult responsibilities even beyond what normal adults had to handle. They had been in a life-and-death struggle, physically, emotionally, and intellectually. In addition to the lives the war was taking, and beyond all the destruction of property and ordinary living activities, it was robbing her daughters of their childhoods. Perhaps that was the worst crime of all. Why couldn't slave owners, abolitionists, revengeful corporals, and murderous captains leave them alone. All she and Paul wanted was to live on their ranch and raise their family with moral standards. She trembled to think what standards her girls would learn witnessing what they had, not to mention their own play-acting and lying and defying the law just to survive.

"When Paul returns," she silently promised herself, "I will make sure they become children again. Marrying the lieutenant!" Hannah shuddered at the thought of time slipping away. In just six or seven years Dolly would be marriageable age. Just six years left to be a child.

"Mama, my lieutenant knows who we are—that we are not really the Johnstons but the Rockforts."

"Yes, he does. And I suspect he knows what Walking Owl's message says and what it means."

"He didn't break the seal. How could he know that?"

"It wouldn't be hard for him to put it all together. Maybe he and Walking Owl even talked about us. They were both at our house when Murdock first came, and since then they've done duty together out of Fort Scott. They are both educated. Not many of the soldiers are. Remember that Knowles—your lieutenant—said that he had great respect for Walking Owl?"

"He'll keep Captain Murdock away from our place. We can bring Papa home and live in the house again." Dolly's voice was happy.

"He'll help us if he can, I believe that now. He even said so. But we can't live in the house as long as Order Number Eleven is in force. And Dolly, we don't know how Papa is, or if we can bring him home."

Hannah knew she could trust Knowles. When he offered his help, without actually telling her to be careful on the trip, he let her know that Murdock would be in Bates County for the week. Her best route to Jefferson City would be through southern Bates County. The authorities learning that he revealed this military information to a civilian could result in his court-martial, or worse. Deserters and traitors were shot.

Two courageous men were risking their careers and perhaps their lives to help her family. Until now Hannah could think of no good coming from the war that seemed to be spawning evil in all directions. She had to admit that the war was bringing out the best in some people. The world after the war looked brighter.

Using only the light from the stars, they rode past their deserted house and in single file took the path to their shack near the river. "But Papa is alive," Dolly said. Neither of them tired of saying those words. "He is alive." They trotted their horses to the shack calling out, "He's alive. Papa's in Jefferson City."

Having fallen asleep waiting for her mother and Dolly to return, Mazie jumped up, upsetting Puss who was curled against her warm back. The homecoming was joyous. Their successful trip—selling the pelts, the lieutenant's friendship, and Walker's message were all reasons for celebration. Leah and Mazie sucked on their stick candy. Mazie even broke off a tiny piece to give Puss. The cat sniffed the candy and returned to Mazie's lap.

Hannah and Dolly ate a late supper of cold cornbread, turnips, and stewed rabbit. Though Mazie soon fell asleep again in her mother's arms, Hannah and the older girls talked for another hour telling one another every detail about the day's activities and planning what to do next. The fire died down before they settled for the night under the comforters, content and more optimistic than they had been since Paul left with Bud Newman's Confederates many months ago.

They spent the next day preparing for the trip. Until they crossed out of the burnt district, Hannah wanted them to continue with the male disguise. But depending on conditions outside the district, she thought they might wear their own clothes when they arrived in Jefferson City. She washed and mended their clothes. She sewed onto their winter bonnets the girls' braids she had saved from their hair-cutting. She experimented with her own cut-off, heavy braid to see if she could fasten it on to her short hair-do with hairpins. Though she had no mirror to see the effect, Leah said she looked natural, especially with her bonnet on.

Traveling in mid-November required more bedding and warmer clothes. The weather didn't usually become really cold until December, but there could be a cold spell anytime. And she did not know how long they would be gone or what she could buy along the way. They needed to take with them at least two days' worth of food for themselves and grain for the horses. Once they cleared the restricted zone, she gambled she could buy feed.

She had to be careful not to overload the two horses. When she collected and piled in the shack the absolutely necessary food, clothing, supplies, bedding, and other camping equipment needed, she knew their two horses could not carry the weight of the four of them and the bundles. She and one of the older girls would have to walk. The trip would take longer, but there was no alternative short of stealing a horse—an impossibility in the already looted country.

As before, when they left their home escorted by the soldiers, each one wore double sets of clothing, the most worn trousers on top. Only this time the extra clothing was welcome in the cold mornings and evenings.

An hour before light the next morning, they strapped their gear on the two horses. Excited about the adventure after the drudgery of all the work they'd been doing around the place for the past few weeks, and elated that they would soon see their father, the girls ran outside anxious to leave. Leah set Mazie in the mare's saddle and handed her the reins. They all giggled because she was almost lost among the packages and bundles. To save the horses' strength, Leah and Dolly both elected to walk, at least until they tired when they would take turns riding. Before leaving the shack, Hannah made a last look around to check that the window and door were shut against animal intruders. She scattered the coals in the fireplace and, holding the gelding's lead rope, led her family up the path toward the house. The shack disappeared among the oak trunks, cedar trees, and bushes.

Behind them they heard pitiful-sounding cries from Puss. The calico cat was following them, making quick running spurts to catch up. In the faint light of dawn they could see the white spots of her fur as she bounded behind them. Mazie tried to get off the mare to pick her up. "Mama, Puss wants to go, too!"

Hannah held her firmly in the saddle. "Puss will be much happier here. She'll watch the place for us."

"Yeah," Leah said, "she's just telling us goodbye and saying that she'll miss us."

"And telling us to bring Papa home quick," Dolly said.

"She'll be all right, won't she," Mazie said, uncertainty in her voice.

"Of course. Remember she stayed here when we were gone before."

"Yeah. And she'll keep the old dominicker hen company."

When they reached the main house, Puss stopped following. At the rise in the prairie where they could view the country for miles in all directions, they stopped to look as was their custom. The clouds on the horizon in the southeastern sky were red. Streaks of pinkish light radiated from the clouds, lacing the sky with fiery brilliance. "Red sky in the morning, sailors take warning," was the adage that ran through Hannah's mind. Perhaps the sunrise did mean that the fair weather was going to end. Rain and cold was no problem. She was prepared for that. At the store she had purchased outdoor wear. Packed in the bundles on the horses were slickers and sturdy, weatherproof boots for each of them.

In spite of the lieutenant's warning of Murdock's possible presence, because it was the quickest route, Hannah took the main road northeast across the military zone. Once into the next county, they could travel without interference from the army. As she pictured the various routes in her mind, she decided to go through Clinton, a two days' journey away. Though she didn't say anything to the girls, she hoped she could locate Beulah for a night's rest.

They made good time that day. The steady wind from behind helped push them along. The clouds at sunrise soon vanished, blown farther east by the southwest wind. With frequent short rests, Hannah kept them moving. Before cresting every ridge or hill, she went ahead to scan the road. Seeing no one, she waved the others on. Though they all made frequent glances behind, it was Leah's responsibility to watch the road behind them. At dusk Hannah pulled them off into a secluded spot in some cottonwood trees along a creek with scattered cedars to hide them from the road. She estimated they had covered almost twenty miles.

They ate the cold food she had prepared at home. After watering the horses, she hobbled them so they could graze during the night. Without a fire, the girls rolled up close together in comforters and quilts and were instantly asleep. Hannah listened to the night noises—a hoot owl close by and from the distance the cries of coyotes. She lay against Mazie's small body. Leah and Dolly were on her other side. She was not worried about being discovered during the night. It seemed a higher priority to her that they all get a good rest rather than anyone keeping watch. After reminding herself to wake up at five, a good two hours before daylight, she let herself sleep.

When the next day dawned to an overcast sky, they were already on their way. Mazie was so sleepy still, that Dolly had to lead her horse. They used a quilt to wrap around her and fasten her to the saddle. Dolly laughed at her. "She looks like a bug in a cocoon." But as she walked beside Leah, she looked longingly at her little sister as if she wished she were still small. She yawned, shook her head to clear out the sleepiness that persisted even after their activity in breaking camp, and took longer steps to keep up with Leah's long legs.

But Leah was also slowing down. Both children had walked every step the day before, riding the horses only to ford the creeks. Neither would admit to being tired. Hannah did not urge them to ride, knowing the load would be hard on the gelding, but she grieved to see them try so bravely to be adult. She slowed down a bit and rested more frequently.

Leah's steps lagged even more and she dropped behind the mare. She glanced back down the road frequently. Suddenly she got down on her hands and knees and put her ear to the ground. Hannah stopped, looking at her daughter.

"Hear anything?" she asked.

Leah motioned for them to be quiet. She listened some more. "Horses coming," she said, jumping up. "Quite a ways back."

Hannah searched the prairie for a place to hide. As far as she could see there was only the recently burned off land, now covered with short, new growth. She said, "Let's keep on. Maybe we'll find a spot. If we don't it'd be better to be traveling normally on the road than to be discovered in a hiding place." She pulled on the gelding's lead to break him into a trot as she jogged along beside him. When the mare started to trot, the jerk woke Mazie.

"Keep to the edge of the road in the grass where the horses' tracks won't show as much," Hannah told the girls.

They continued the trot for a quarter of a mile, slowed to a walk to catch their breaths, then resumed jogging. Leah dropped to the ground again to listen. She shook her head when Hannah asked what she heard. "I can't tell. They're still coming."

Hannah knew they couldn't keep up this rate of speed. The horsemen behind them were probably coming faster than they could go. Finding a place to hide two loaded horses and four people would take some doing. What she was looking for was a swell in the ground big enough they could get on the far side of the slope to avoid notice from the road. She finally spotted such a place to her left soon after Leah warned her that they would soon be in sight.

Pointing to the swell, she told Dolly and Leah to take the mare there. "Get completely behind the hill. Mazie, get off. Then wait for me."

"What are you going to do?" Leah asked alarmed. "The horses are not too far behind. I'd say not more than a mile. They'll see you."

"Go, quickly. I'll keep on a bit. If they do notice our tracks in the road, the gelding's tracks will go on. I'll come back to be with you, but if I can't get back in time, I'll get out of sight somewhere and give the coyote call when all's clear. Just stay there." She slapped the mare on the rump. "Go!"

With the impetus Hannah gave the mare, Mazie didn't need to do much spurring to reach the mound. Dolly and Leah ran behind Mazie and the mare. Leading the gelding, Hannah continued to run as fast as she could down the grassy edge of the road. When she looked back and saw that the girls were out of sight, she let out a sigh of relief and continued running until she found a thicker than usual patch of grass along the road. She turned abruptly to her left, heading for another swell she saw that was high enough to hide the gelding. She dared not take the time to cut back to the girls because the horsemen were close enough for her to hear the hoof beats. She ran at right angles to the road as fast as she could, the gelding right on her heels. Safely hidden, her heart racing and panting for breath, she peered over the rise.

The detail of soldiers she anticipated came into view about a mile back. Since there was little cover, she figured that Leah noticed where she had gone. She was sure of it when she heard the bob white call coming from their swell. To reassure them, she returned the call. Warning. Stay low. They all knew quite well what the call meant.

There were eight cavalrymen trotting leisurely along the road. When they got close enough, Hannah recognized the short figure of Captain Murdock in the lead. This was what she feared. No one but the captain or Bushwhackers would travel this road. Since they were too far east of the Kansas border for Bushwhackers, she knew from the moment that Leah's keen hearing detected them that it would be Murdock, especially with the lieutenant's warning that he was in this county. Of all the roads, it was bad luck he should chose this one. But then she told herself, this was the main east-west road through the county.

Hannah studied the men. She recognized them as the same ones she'd seen the two other times—all automatons obeying their master. Murdock's eyes were pointed up the road to the next rise, not on the ground. He didn't even look to his side when he sent a spittle of tobacco juice to the ground. Apparently Murdock hadn't replaced Walker, for a scout would have picked up her tracks. Though Murdock thought he knew the country and all its trails, he didn't know how to track. Without slowing down, he passed by the spot where the girls turned off. Hannah figured she had run almost half a mile before she veered off. When the horsemen reached her turn off, they paid no attention to the dusty tracks half concealed in the new grass on the left side of the road that turned abruptly to the north.

Hannah remained where she was for fifteen minutes. Her nervousness abated. She took a deep breath when she realized she had been holding her breath. The detail trotted on out of her sight and hearing. She waited five more minutes and gave the coyote signal. Before she counted to eight ready to repeat the call, she saw all three girls running to the road, Leah leading the mare. She also walked to the road and hunched down on her heels to wait for them to rejoin her.

Chapter 15

THREE DAYS later Hannah and Leah, rode over the last hill to see Jefferson City below them. Very conspicuous was the large rectangular state capitol building looming over the Missouri River with its fancy dome and broad, sweeping entrance steps leading to the door which was protected by a semi-circle of six large columns. They sat on their horses in awe of its grandeur. Neither had ever seen anything so splendid. Seeing the symbol of her state government, Hannah was proud to be part of it. Then she was angry that military outsiders now had control of it and felt a tinge of remorse that she had to delude the honest officials in order to stay in her own home. And here she was primed again to play any role she believed would allow her to find her husband and take him to that forbidden home.

The town was built along the south side of the wide Missouri River. Hannah and Leah were amazed at the size of the river. A steam boat was just arriving with much whistling and noise. There were several steamboats already docked with hurried activity on the wharf front street and in the buildings facing the river front. Strange to them was the bustle, the many houses, and the many businesses in this town of four thousand people, swelled by hundreds of soldiers. They had always lived in a sparsely populated region where the towns were only a few hundred people. During the past few weeks they had been alone in a completely deserted area. Fort Scott and Clinton were the largest towns they'd ever seen.

But what amazed them most was the military aspect—even more than Fort Scott. The capital city was guarded like a fortress. Leah trembled seeing the soldiers, especially the ones she would have to pass to enter the city. Most of her experience with soldiers had been disastrous to her family. Hannah neck-reined her horse closer to her daughter and reached out her other hand to reassure her.

"Papa is with these men. They have no reason to mistrust us," Hannah said.

Though still shaking slightly, Leah turned a determined face to her mother. She was ready and eager to play her part in finding her father.

Hannah took a deep breath of the frosty air. The smoke from the steamboats and the hundreds of chimney's carried even to their hilltop. She welcomed the scent for it meant her trek was over. She pulled Paul's felt hat down her forehead farther to almost hide her eyebrows. His great coat, split up the back to her waist, hung down on either side of the gelding, reaching to her boot tops. "Ready, Lee?" she asked, cocking her head toward the town below them.

"Yes, Pa." Then Leah added, "But I still think we could go in as ourselves. Surely the soldiers would let Papa's family in to see him."

If she believed her own words, Hannah Rockfort had nothing to fear. "Yes, I'm sure they would, but as men we can more easily get information about him and be allowed in to see him. Women are often ignored and barred from certain places we'll need to go." Though these arguments were true, she believed she could prevail as a woman, and seeing the military aspect of the city, she was beginning to doubt the wisdom of continuing the deception. Back in Clinton, Virgil had warned her of the military order to shoot persons discovered in disguised clothing. This order was intended as a deterrent to outlaw activity. To Union officers any woman dressed as a man was an obvious Bushwhacker. But in spite of the problem their deception might cause them if they weren't careful, she had decided to chance continuing the disguise. The risk to each of them of being two lone females was greater. "And, Leah—Lee—it is safer for us to be men. Especially you."

"Why? Would they put us in jail or shoot at us?"

"No, it's not that. Only twisted minds like Carl Murdock's would do that." She looked at her daughter, tall for eleven and beginning to mature. "You are growing up now and it's time you understood. Some men will do things to a woman that are worse than what Murdock did."

"What could be worse than knocking out your tooth or making us leave our ranch?"

"Tearing off your clothes and forcing themselves on you." When Leah didn't understand what she meant, Hannah said, "Like the bulls do to get the cows with calves."

Leah's eyes widened. Raised on a cattle ranch, she understood the function of the herd bull, though she had never associated the practice with people. "Oh!"

"So you can see that until we find out what the situation is down there in that town overrun with soldiers, we are Hank and Lee."

"Yes, Pa. But what will Papa... ?"

"Don't worry about him. He'll know us." Hannah scanned the view ahead of them.

"Also, Lee, strap Walker's gun on, but hide it with your coat." She pulled back her coat to show that she was wearing her gun.

"I'm glad you had Mazie and Dolly stay with Beulah."

"Yes, they are safe with her and Virgil in their house."

The picture of the comfortable house the Kerrigans had found to live in and their comparative contentment made Hannah almost envy them. With the assistance of his relative, Virgil found a job in Clinton and the use of an empty house. Virgil and Beulah had fixed up the house and reestablished normal family living. Each of the Kerrigans was a different person from the pitiful prisoners Murdock brought into the detention camp two months earlier. Virgil had regained his zest, Beulah her initiative. The children were free to run and play and were even attending school. When Beulah offered to keep all the girls while Hannah continued on to Jefferson City, Hannah agreed. For a time, the girls could be little children again while they played and learned with the other children in an environment free of fear.

Though worried about being separated and wanting to be with their mother, Dolly and Mazie were both willing to stay. Almost the moment they arrived at Beulah's house the evening after avoiding Murdock's troops, Dolly joined the Kerrigan girls to admire their new dresses some townspeople had gathered for them. She couldn't wait to get out of her britches.

Leah, however, didn't listen to any of the reasons the women used that she should stay. She would not let her mother travel alone. "What if another panther jumps you?" she said to prove how necessary she was to her mother. "I'm learning how to heal people like you do. Didn't I treat your scratches from the panther? And now they are completely well." When Hannah nodded to Beulah that what she said was true, Leah added, "And besides, Papa will need both of us, for you can't be by him all the time."

"She's right, Hannah," Beulah said. "You'll be safer with her along."

Virgil agreed. "Even going as men, it's a mite safer to travel in pairs. The lass looks more like a boy than the other girls. Let her go with you."

With everyone against her, Hannah relented. She and Leah could each ride, for without the little girls and the bulk of the gear they had brought to Clinton, they could travel lighter. Away from the restricted zone there were stores and farms where they could supplement their food supply and procure grain for the horses. After resting half a day with Beulah, she and Leah traveled rapidly, covering more miles each day than they could have with the whole family. They no longer had to watch the road for outlaws or Murdock's cavalry.

"I'm glad that the little girls are safe with Beulah," Hannah said. She dreaded what she might discover in this town spread out below her; at the same time she was eager to begin. "And I'm glad you're here." She leaned over to press Leah's hand.

"Me, too," Leah said. Her voice was tight with uneasiness as they touched their heels to their mounts. "What'll we do first?"

"Find a room and clean up."

"But that'll cost us. Do we have enough money?"

"For a time, yes, but it's necessary. It wouldn't be safe to camp out here so close to this city and military headquarters. After that we'll then find out where the army hospital is and present ourselves." She looked at the sun that told her it was still early afternoon. "We've got time today." She had to clasp her reins in both hands to keep them from shaking. She willed her stomach to stop churning. She should heed her own reassurance to Leah. But her uneasiness was not so much physical fear as from the possibility of actually seeing Paul today and learning his condition which was bound to be bad. She kept reminding herself that though he was in Missouri, he had sent no word to them. What did that mean?

Hank and Lee Johnston rode boldly up to the guards at the outpost. At the corporal's raised arm signal, they stopped.

"State yer name and where you're from," he demanded. He held his rifle in front of him at a slant pointed to the sky, butt end on the ground.

"Hank Johnston from Clinton."

"Missourian, uh?" When Hannah nodded, he said, "Where's yer certificate of loyalty to the United States?"

Hannah caught her breath. She had heard that some places demanded it. "We don't have any. Never been to a military post to get one. I didn't think I'd need it." When the guard showed no evidence of softening, she said. "I was one of only five men in our precinct that voted for Lincoln in eighteen sixty. We were considered traitors and our names were posted around town."

The guard looked at her closely. "Same thing happened to my pa." Apparently he believed her for he asked, "What's yer business in Jefferson City?"

"I heard that my cousin is in the army hospital here. I've come to see about him."

"You heerd wrong. Ain't no army hospital here."

Leah let out the beginning of a gasp before she could control it.

"And who're you, boy?" the corporal said. His tone was suspicious.

"That's my son," Hannah said.

"Let him speak fer hisself."

"Lee Johnston," Leah said. "I help my pa with our farm. He's got a bum leg, you know."

"I don't know nothin' of the kind." Ignoring Hannah, the corporal asked Leah, "How'd you hear about this cousin being in an army hospital?"

"A friend of ours sent word he might be here. He's been missing for two years."

"Since we were close..." Hannah started to explain.

"Let the boy tell it," the corporal interrupted her.

Without looking at her mother, Leah said, "Since we didn't live too far from here, we rode over to see if he was here then we'll fetch his wife and daughter if what we heard was true."

The corporal's manner was softening. He looked at Hannah who nodded her head agreeing to what Leah had said.

"If there is no hospital, is there a place for wounded soldiers?" Hannah could not believe that Walking Owl's message could be wrong or that they had come all this way for nothing.

"Naw, ain't had no fighting 'round here lately. Sent the wounded to St. Louis."

"Well," Hannah hesitated not knowing what to do next, "could we be permitted to see an officer in charge?"

"I reckon. Foller this here street straight through town. Headquarters is on yer left. You'll not miss it." He handed her a slip of paper. "This here pass will git you in. Even some of the merchants will ask for it if you try to buy anything."

Hannah and Leah rode on silently, passing two boarding houses without pausing. "Change of plans. We'll be going straight to headquarters," she explained to Leah. "If Papa's not here, we won't need a room."

After much interrogation from underlings and waiting for over an hour, a lieutenant finally spoke with them. He agreed with the guard that there was no army hospital as such, but there was a building under the supervision of a doctor of sorts where there were a few sick men.

Hannah's spirits soared. "Is Paul Rockfort one of the men?"

The lieutenant excused himself to look up the records. He returned fifteen minutes later. "No Paul Rockfort listed." When he noticed the despair on both Hannah's and Leah's face, he added, "But there are two sick men who are not on the list."

"Why?" Hannah held her breath.

"Don't know. Not my unit. All I know is that there are twelve men there, but only ten names." He wrote out a pass and handed it to them. "Here, go see for yourself." He gave them directions where to go.

Before they reached the building, they were stopped two times to show their pass. Paul's name meant nothing to anyone they met. At the door to the designated building, which turned out to be one of the barracks for the non-commissioned men, there were more delays.

Hannah whispered to Leah, "Good thing we're men. We couldn't get in here otherwise. Now, don't stare, no matter what you see. I guess you're old enough to know what a man looks like without his clothes."

"In the middle of the day?"

Hannah shrugged her shoulders. The delay and set-back of there being no hospital made Hannah revert to her former pessimism. During the time of his absence, she had insulated herself from deep disappointment by not really expecting him to be alive. Walking Owl's note had punctured that protection she'd built around herself. For the first time in months, she had really hoped. More than that, she was sure that she would find Paul. This disappointment was the most difficult of all to handle. But in front of the soldiers, and Leah, she dared not show it or behave in any way unsuitable to a man looking for his cousin. So she spoke to Leah of unrelated subjects, like men in their underwear.

Finally a man approached them. He confirmed that there were two unidentified men under his care who were not on the list. No one knew their names because since they were brought here, they were unconscious or incoherent with fever. "We call 'em Stony and Rocky."

Hannah staggered. Paul's last name was often shortened to Rocky by his friends. "Doctor..."

"I ain't the doc. I'm an aide, or orderly. Name's Weldon."

"Mr. Weldon, why do you call them those particular names?" she asked.

"Don't know."

"Is Rocky the nickname of one of them?"

He shrugged his shoulders, "Hell, man, I don't know. Gotta call 'em somethin'. The night man might know. That's what he calls 'em."

"Can I come in to see if one of them is my cousin?" She tried to look beyond Weldon into the door. She hadn't seem much inside when he came out the door and closed it behind him to keep inside what little heat the fireplace at the end of the barracks provided. She glimpsed an aisle with a row of cots on either side lined up head at the wall and foot to the aisle. In the nearest one she spied a body under dirty blankets.

"The doctor's the one to say and he's not here now."

"We've been traveling three days. All I need is to see if one of the unknown men is my cousin. If he's not here then we need to start back home today."

Weldon studied her for a few seconds. In spite of herself under his penetrating stare, Hannah fingered her mustache. He looked down the street to see if the doctor was in sight. Finding no higher authority to ask, he shrugged and gestured with his right hand. "Don't see why not. Won't do no harm." He put out his arm to bar Leah from following. "Jest you, sir. Pretty raw stuff fer the boy to see."

Hannah nodded and motioned Leah to stay outside by the entry.

The first man Weldon pointed out right by the door was either asleep or unconscious, Hannah couldn't tell. His breathing was labored; his cheeks had no tint of color. Though he was disfigured, and his face and neck, the only parts of his body not covered with blankets, was swathed with bandages, she knew he wasn't Paul. This man's beard was black, streaked with gray.

She felt both relief and despair—relief that this suffering human whom she feared could not live long was not Paul, and despair that he wasn't Paul.

"No, that man's not my cousin."

"The other 'un is down the other end." Weldon led her past some empty beds and ones where the men were awake, though most were coughing or moaning in pain.

As they moved down the long narrow building, Hannah looked carefully at each man, diagnosing what might be his ailment. From what she could see, they seemed to be suffering from illnesses rather than wounds. They had ugly rashes and sores, flushed faces, and feverish eyes. Some of them groaned and thrashed about on their straw ticks. Some attempts had been made to keep them clean, but the stench of urine, vomit, and unwashed bodies prevailed. The chamber pots at the foot of the beds were not emptied. On the rude tables between each cot, there were the barest of toilet articles—straight razors, combs, and brushes.

When Weldon noticed her dismayed look, he said, "This ain't a real hospital. And there's only me and the night man to look after all of 'em." Hannah nodded her understanding. At the last cot nearest the fireplace, he stopped and extended his hand. "This here is Rocky."

Hearing the name spoken caused Hannah's heart to leap. The man he indicated lay on his back completely still. The blood-stained and soiled blanket was up to his neck, still showing the indentations of fingers where someone had tucked it in. His head rested on a flat, uncovered pillow. The blue and white stripes of the ticking were soiled. His eyes were closed, his blue lips slightly parted as he breathed quietly without the rasp of some of his roommates, though his jaws were clamped tight together as if in pain. His lower face was covered with several days' growth of a pale beard that made his face look even more gaunt. His arms under the blanket were lying straight by his sides. As she stepped between his cot and that of his neighbor, she saw that his left arm nearest her seemed unnaturally large, as if wrapped in layers of bandages. Unlike the first unconscious man Weldon showed her, this one had no visible dressings on his face, but like the first, his face was deathly white. His short, light-colored hair was matted and dirty. The hair on the back of his head that was resting on the thin pillow was worn almost off, showing his white skin. But around his forehead a few blond wisps curled.

She didn't experienced either the relief or despair that she felt on seeing the other soldier. The dread and uncertainty of what she might find was gone the instant she saw this man. He was Paul.

Hannah had to steel herself from showing the emotion she felt. She wanted to throw herself on him and call out his name, to make him wake up and know her. In spite of her efforts at controlling herself, her hands flew to her face and tears sprung into her eyes. Her knees became so weak only her strong will kept her from collapsing. Turning her face away from Weldon, she nodded vigorously and said trying to control a sob, "That's Paul Rockfort." When Weldon looked at her display of emotion, she explained, "We grew up together. Like brothers."

Before she turned back to Weldon she noticed Leah sticking her head in the partly opened door. Hannah held both hands together up in front of her and shook them at the same time as she nodded her head. Leah's smile spread over her face as she closed the door.

Controlling her emotions Hannah said, "We thought he was dead."

"Funny thing," Weldon said studying Paul's inert form, "he was 'bout dead a couple o' weeks ago. We'd given him up, and then a tall soldier from some western outfit—the tallest feller I ever seen—he come in and talked to him fer a long time. Jest sat there aside him right where you are at and talked low like. Never stopped. Didn't seem like Rocky here knowed he was here or understood a word the tall feller said, but after that visit, he started gittin' better. Still didn't wake up or nothin', jest seemed less like a corpse. But he'd open his mouth when I'd feed him. You know, even when these here fellers can't talk and seem unconscious, they sometimes know what's goin' on around 'em."

"What'd the tall soldier talk about?"

"Hanged if I know. I was busy and couldn't hear nothin'."

"That was probably the soldier that got word to me that my cousin was here."

"How in hell did he know who this Rocky here was if we didn't? And why didn't he tell us?"

"I don't know, unless he guessed from the nickname," Hannah said. She did know though. When Walking Owl was at their shack, he extracted much information about him from her and the girls, including his nickname and exactly what he looked like. It wouldn't take the Osage long to figure out who he was. And maybe during his visit Paul communicated with him. Why Walking Owl did not tell the doctor who Paul was, she didn't know. She only guessed that he did that to protect himself. He wasn't supposed to be in central Missouri, but out in Kansas on tribal business.

"Well," Hannah said, "I can tell you that this is Paul Rockfort." She gave Weldon the last information that she knew of his regiment and rank. "His wife and daughter are here in town. Will they be permitted to come to him, help nurse him, and take care of him? She's a healer."

"Oh yes. The sooner the better. You say they're in town?" When Hannah nodded, he said, "Git 'em right away." He jotted down a note. "Give this at headquarters fer a pass fer 'em."

"How long can they stay with him?"

"As long as you want. We're short-handed here. We'd gladly turn his care over to you and his wife."

"My son and I may have to leave soon now that we've found our cousin. I'll make arrangements for his family." Weldon gave her directions to a nearby boarding house. Taking a quick look back at Paul, she swallowed a sob and pulled herself from his side to more quickly do the necessary arrangements to revert back to Hannah and return. In some way Walking Owl had reached Paul and started his recovery. How much more could she do. All she could think was that he was alive and, though very ill, he was not as bad as she had feared she might find him. He was already getting better, the attendant said.

She reached through the blanket to where Paul's left hand should be to grasp it before she left. There was nothing there! She looked up at the attendant in alarm.

"Better warn his wife," he said. "He lost his arm just above the wrist. The stump didn't heal, and he took the fever. He's still in a bad way. Two weeks ago I wouldn't give him a day to live. Now?" He held out his hands, palms up. "Maybe. Who knows? All I can say is git his woman here quick." He glanced again at the motionless man and patted the budge of the blanket where his leg lay motionless. "Rocky, ole feller, this is yer lucky day."

Chapter 16

HANNAH AND Leah stood by Paul's cot. They were in dresses and bonnets for the first time since they escaped from Lieutenant Knowles's detail on the way to Independence. They passed again a test of their disguise by switching in the same day from male to female. Expecting to see women, Weldon didn't look closely enough to the two to recognize them as the couple that came in earlier. Even if he had been observant, he had no reason to be suspicious. Hannah and Leah both positioned their long braids to hang down the front of their blouses. Leah had ribbons tied to the ends of her braids and had put on some aromatic powder that surrounded both mother and daughter. Neither walked nor acted like the Johnston men who had talked with Weldon a couple of hours before.

Even though her mother had warned her, Leah gasped and held on to Hannah's arm when she saw her vigorous, devoted father lying motionless and unresponsive on the sagging cot. During the time Hannah and Leah were gone to find lodging and change clothes, Weldon had made an attempt at cleaning Paul. There was a fresh blanket over him and the tangles in his hair were combed out.

"Rocky, ole feller," Weldon said cheerfully, "you better wake up. You're got some mighty important visitors." He put his hand on Paul's forehead and nodded to Hannah that there was still some fever.

When Paul gave no indication that he heard, Weldon signaled Leah and Hannah to try. Hannah reached under the blanket for his right hand and cupped it between her two strong ones. "Paul, my love, I'm here. We found you." Her whole body trembled as tears rolled down her cheeks. No longer worried about hiding her emotions, she laid her forehead on her hands grasping Paul's lifeless right one. "We found you," she repeated. She leaned over to kiss his forehead and run both hands lovingly over his face and beard stubble.

"Papa," Leah said, choking over the sobs in her throat and not knowing whether she should touch him. When Hannah let loose of his hand to fondle his face, Leah clasped it between her two, unmindful of the tears that dripped off her face. "Papa, we've come to get you well again and take you home." Her father did not move.

"I'll leave you alone with him, Mrs. Rockfort," Weldon said. He blew his nose and cleared his throat. As he left, Hannah sent him a glance of gratitude for not giving up on Paul.

"Mama, he won't wake up!" Leah cried, shaking his hand back and forth to make him notice her. "Papa, it's me, Leah. And Mama. Wake up."

"Just keep talking, Leah. I think he hears you. But we mustn't let him see us crying." She sat up straighter, wiped her face with her handkerchief, and tried to smile.

"But he doesn't do anything!" Leah said. "Papa squeeze your hand if you hear me."

Paul's hand remained lifeless. Leah gave her mother an anguished look.

"He's there, dear, just keep talking. Let him feel your hands on his face and head."

Leah rubbed his right hand and then cupped his hot face with her cool hands, stroking him gently, and closing his gaping mouth. Quieted by her mother's calm voice and purposeful actions of the healer that she was, Leah dried her eyes. No time to cry when her father needed her so badly.

While making Paul more comfortable, Hannah and Leah talked constantly to him. Hannah bathed him, shaved him, washed his hair, and changed his dirty nightshirt. Leah put wet cloths on his hot forehead. They spoke about the continued fine November weather, about their trip, and their impressions of Jefferson City. Hannah told how much the girls had grown, and that Mazie could now read. They stuck to pleasant matters that wouldn't distress him. Leah told funny stories about Puss. Hannah talked about the ranch—their new horses, how well the grasses were doing, and how much hay she put up. They told about visiting in Clinton with their former neighbors, the Kerrigans. Not once did they speak of the war, their difficulties, or Carl Murdock.

During the few hours they spent by his side, Paul did not respond, but Hannah insisted that his color improved slightly and his fever abated. Leah was convinced that his vacant face showed some understanding and that the pain lines around his lips relaxed. His mouth did not again gape open in the witless manner it had when they first saw him.

Early the next morning Hannah met the doctor. When she told him of her medical skills, together they unwrapped Paul's left arm. It was cut off above the wrist. Hannah could see that the stump was beginning to heal.

While they worked, the doctor told her what little he knew about his patient. Four weeks earlier, Rocky had arrived on the train with a group of other sick and wounded soldiers en route to Kansas City to convalesce before being discharged. He was part of a prisoner exchange. Apparently on the journey he had relapsed. His badly wounded hand developed gangrene. By the time his group reached Jefferson City and stopped over to spend the night in the post barracks, Rocky was delirious. Unable to travel farther, he and the other unknown soldier were left behind.

When the doctor reported to duty the morning following their arrival, the detail that carried the men in had left, leaving no record of who the two men were. Since both were delirious or unconscious, they hadn't been identified. During their semi-conscious states, the doctor and his two nurse-aides had been able to feed them liquids and enough solids to keep them alive, though they weren't able to talk.

When the doctor first examined him, Rocky's hand was in a bad way. It had taken a bullet, like a minié-ball, which crushed some of the bones. Somebody had gouged out the bullet with a crude, unsterilized instrument, probably a pocket knife. Infection from the wound was spreading up the arm and causing the high fever, delirium, and general nausea. To save his life, the doctor had no alternative but to remove the hand. The operation in Paul's weakened state almost killed him, causing him to relapse into a deeper coma. And to make his condition worse, the stump didn't heal properly. The pain and the infection throughout his body kept him in a state of semi-consciousness. He could not communicate, but responded just enough to take some nourishment.

"Strange thing," the doctor said, "for no reason that I know of, two weeks ago Rocky started improving. It was like he all at once decided that he wasn't going to let his body defeat him. That he had something to live for." He held up both hands to show his amazement. "The flesh on his stump even began to heal. His fever lessened. He still has a slight fever, but each day it is lowering. However, nothing I do brings him out of his unconscious condition."

"What about the other man left here with my husband?" Hannah had noticed that his cot by the door was empty when she walked by in the morning.

"The one we called Stony? He died last night. We couldn't get enough food into him. Now, Rocky... your husband... we didn't expect him to live either. But he began to swallow the liquids and soft foods we put into his mouth. He was unconscious, but it was as if back there in his mind he knew what was going on, but couldn't pull out of the fog all around him. About two weeks ago, when we put a cup to his lips, he began to swallow."

"Mama," Leah whispered, "that's after Walker..."

Hannah nodded quickly and shook her head to warn Leah to say no more.

Not hearing their exchange, the doctor continued, "And this morning he ate more than ever before. In fact, he seemed to want more, but I didn't want him to overdo it. His system isn't used to that much food all at once." He nodded as he studied his patient. "It's very fortunate that you've come here, Mrs. Rockfort. With you caring for him, I believe he will recover."

"We're going to take him home," Leah said.

For the first time the doctor seemed to notice the child. "Oh no, we can't let you do that, little missy. He's in no condition to travel. Moving him would kill him for sure. And he's still in the army. Now that we know who he is, we need to notify his regiment and go through the proper channels for his discharge. He can't just leave without the proper authority and permission." The doctor shook his head to emphasize the impossibility of them taking him home.

Hannah and Leah exchanged glances. Regulations and orders meant nothing to them. To the doctor Hannah said, "We can stay here and nurse him, though, can't we? Mr. Weldon said it was all right."

"Absolutely. We're short-handed. You and your daughter can be with him at any time. I saw how skilled in nursing you are, ma'am. We can use you here."

When the doctor moved on to his other patients, Hannah went to work. While Leah chatted a steady stream to her father, telling him to hold on that they would get him home no matter what the doctor said, Hannah put some of her salve on the open wound of the stump on his left arm, and wrapped it loosely in clean bandages. She massaged his arm above the stump to encourage circulation. She moved his legs and his other arm, bending them at the joints to strengthen the debilitated muscles. She rolled him onto his right side and gently covered the bed sores on his back with some soothing salve she had made from the purple flower of the balm of Gilead tree.

Sending Leah to the mess hall for broth and hot water, she fed him spoonfuls of the warm liquid. During the morning Paul gave no indication of awareness, though the vacant look was gone. His appearance was as of one sleeping. By noon, his fever was gone. Leah didn't have to hold his lips closed to prevent the broth she was spooning into his mouth from spilling out. He swallowed readily. Maybe it was wishful thinking, but they both believed his face had more color.

The bath, clean clothes, massages, as well as the salves and lotions Hannah put on him made him more comfortable, and definitely more presentable. Though much too thin and pale, he began to look like himself. Leah chatted gaily to him just as she used to do.

When she asked him questions, she answered them herself. "Papa, did you know that Mama cut off our hair? Of course you don't know." She touched one of her braids that were hanging from the back of her bonnet and leaned over closer to his ear. "I'll tell you a secret. These braids aren't fastened to my head. Mama saved them and sewed them into our bonnets. If I take my bonnet off, my hair will come off, too." She giggled. "Well, Dolly hated to have her hair cut. She pretended she didn't but when Mama wasn't around, she cried. But all of us cut our hair so we would look like boys." She fussed with her father's hair, letting the thick blond wisps curl around her fingers. "She looks more like you now than ever. Her hair curls around her forehead just like yours. But I'm tall like you. People say I'm extra tall for my age. Did you know that I'm almost twelve?"

THROUGH THE haze Paul heard his daughter's voice, just as he had been hearing it in his dreams. It couldn't be real. Back in the recesses of his mind he also heard his Hannah's voice. Stronger than ever. He was sure of it. Those strong fingers massaging his feet and legs were hers. Just as she used to do after a long day of swinging the scythe when cutting hay at the ranch. It felt so good he no longer wanted to drift back into nothingness.

He tried to speak, but nothing came out. Voices were speaking around him, first above him and then beside him. With great effort he pushed back his lethargy that was enveloping him to distinguished two voices, a child's and a woman's. Two familiar voices from long ago. A girl's face leaned over him, wavering in and out of view. Then it smiled a smile more beautiful than he ever saw.

The soothing fingers rubbing his legs moved up his body to his back. It caressed his throbbing left arm until the pain almost vanished. The hands manipulating his flesh cleared away the mist.

Paul moved his lips, but no sound came out.

"Mama," the child's voice said, "Papa's looking straight at me. He's trying to say something!"

Now there were two heads leaning over his face. Warm hands cupped his face as worried brown eyes smiled at him. "Paul, we're here. Leah and I are here." He heard the words distinctly. "Paul, my love, what did you say?"

He took control of his body, shifting it on the cot just a bit. He moved his lips again. This time he produced a slight aspiration of breath.

"He knows us!" the child said.

Then he knew who she was. This was his little Leah, not in a dream, but really there.

Paul tried again to speak. This time the words came out in an enfeebled whisper. "So big."

"He says I'm big!" Leah said. She hugged him and jumped up and down in her excitement. "Yes, Papa, I help Mama out all the time. She depends on me."

Though he tried to fight it, the haze descended again. Hannah and Leah disappeared.

AFTER THAT moment of lucidity, Paul's body became lifeless. Though they pleaded and coaxed, they could get no further response.

"He broke though his coma for just the moment," Hannah said. "He's there, dear, just under his sickness. He'll come back to us again."

"He woke up and talked to me!" Though disappointed that her father said nothing more, Leah was elated that his first words were to her. "He'll be all right, won't he, Mama?"

"Yes, I'm sure of it." Hannah stood up to her full height and glanced around the barracks. Today, since the weather was mild, it wasn't as chilly in the drafty barracks as it was the day before, but she could imagine how cold it would be in the winter days to come. The food from the mess hall was not good, with very little available that a sick man could eat. After all, this wasn't an official hospital.

Across the aisle from his cot two soldiers were coughing almost constantly. Hannah didn't want to expose Paul any longer to the illnesses of the other patients. The personal hygiene and elimination practices of the men appalled her. Men able to be up walked around in their long, unwashed drawers. Besides not being a healthy place for Paul to convalesce, this was no place for Leah. Yet she needed her daughter's help, and she dared not leave her alone in the strange city overrun with soldiers.

Wishing to take advantage of the unseasonably warm weather, and glancing again at Paul who now seemed to be sleeping naturally rather than in his former comatose state, she made a decision. "Leah, we're taking him home tonight," she said in a low voice.

When Leah looked toward the doctor, remembering his words, Hannah said, "We'll figure out a way. I won't leave him in this awful place another day."

"What'll we do?" Leah's eyes were dancing with anticipation of another of her mother's plans.

"First, let's see if we can get his cot moved up there by the door." She pointed to the empty cot on the right just inside the door where the other unknown man died. When Leah wondered why, Hannah said, "It'll be closer for us to carry him out later."

"Oh," Leah said with understanding.

Hannah asked the doctor if Paul could be moved. "My young daughter, you know," she explained. "If he's right there by the door, I can sort of screen out the rest of the men from her view."

The doctor agreed. "This is definitely not a suitable place for a young girl." He at the foot and Weldon at the head of the cot carried Paul to the front.

"It'll be colder here, ma'am, and drafty," Weldon said. "Farther from the fire and right by the door that will let in the cold air."

"If it gets too cold, I'll move him back. Today the weather's fine. It's not cold at all. I certainly do appreciate all you've done for my husband," she said to both the doctor and Weldon. "I'm sure that he wouldn't be alive without your help."

"Too bad he had to lose his hand," the doctor said.

"Yes, but better that than his life. I know about gangrene. You saved him."

After the men returned to work with the other patients, Hannah told Leah more of her plan. "There's enough time to do it today. It's only noon. Now, you stay here with Papa. Talk to him, tell him what we're going to do, but don't let anyone else hear you. He understands that we are here, maybe even some of what we're saying, even though he can't talk back. Get some more liquid down him. I'll go back to the rooming house and resurrect Hank Johnston. Then I'll buy a wagon and whatever supplies I can get with the money we have left."

Leah nodded agreement eagerly. More than anything she wanted to get back to her sisters and home. So used to playing these roles was she that she needed only to know her mother's newest script to play her part.

"Don't worry," Hannah said, "if I don't get back for quite a while. I've got lots to do. Can you take care of Papa by yourself?" When Leah nodded, Hannah hugged her, kissed Paul, and hurried out.

The doctor had left for the day, and it was almost dark when Hannah returned as Hank Johnston. She drove up in an old canvas-covered wagon and tied their horses to a hitching rail in front of the barracks. Weldon was still on duty. "Mr. Johnston," Weldon said in surprise when Hannah walked in. "I thought you'd left."

"Good evening, Mr. Weldon. I had some business to take care of, but I'm leaving soon." She expressed surprise to see Paul's cot moved. "My cousin looks much better."

"None of my doin's, sir. This here little lady and her ma was the best medicine." He indicated Leah.

"So I see. I just came by to see how he was before leaving and to sit here with Leah until her mother returns."

While Weldon finished up his duties, Hannah filled Leah in on what she had done and her plan of action. They had positioned Paul on his right side, with the side of his head resting on the pillow. He was facing them as they were both seated near him. She spoke quietly, but loudly enough that if Paul was aware of them, he could hear what she said as well.

She knew from the procedure of the night before that Weldon would leave as soon as all the men were asleep for the night. Until the night nurse reported a couple of hours later, the barracks had no other supervision than the routine check of the night guards as they made their rounds. Hannah waited for that unsupervised time.

"Did Papa say anything more?" Hannah asked.

"No, but I know he hears me. I think he knows what we are doing. Once his fingers moved while I was holding his hand."

Weldon came by with his coat on ready to leave. Seeing the team still tied outside, Weldon asked Hannah, "You surely won't start out tonight, will you, sir?"

"No. I'll wait until morning. I expect Mrs. Rockfort is indisposed. I'll sit here a few more minutes, and then we'll go back to our lodgings."

"Have a pleasant trip, sir."

"Thank you, Mr. Weldon. We are greatly in your debt for caring for my cousin."

Weldon nodded and left. Leah went to the door to watch him disappear into the darkness. She expected her mother to move her father immediately. Instead, Hannah sat there quietly on her stool for over fifteen minutes, listening to the snores and breathing of the men left in the barracks. All seemed to be asleep.

"Now," she said. She propped open the door. Carefully she placed Paul's injured arm by his side and tied it in place with strips of bandages. She wrapped the blanket around his body from his chest to his knees and fastened it with more strips to keep it in place. They put socks on his feet and a stocking cap on his head. Hannah grasped the pits of his arms to carry the heaviest part of his body, while Leah clutched his feet. From the cot by the door to the back of the wagon where she had parked it parallel to the building, it was only a few yards. Though Paul normally weighed a hundred and eighty pounds, he probably didn't weigh more than a hundred and twenty now. Still he was a dead weight. Hannah stumbled and almost dropped him. She had trouble keeping a grip on him with his arms bound in the blanket.

They took only a few steps before she knew she couldn't carry his upper body alone without the risk of opening his wound. She carefully lowered him to the floor. "Come here, Leah," she said. "It won't hurt him if we let his feet drag."

With Leah at his head to help with the weight, they half lifted and half dragged him out the door. While Leah steadied her father in a sitting position, Hannah climbed onto the back of the wagon and leaned over to hold him. Leah then climbed in beside her. Together they pulled him up into the wagon. Once he was inside, they had no trouble scooting him onto the pallet Hannah had fixed for him. While Leah quickly untied the strips holding the blanket, covering him up with the extra blankets Hannah had provided, positioning his wounded arm on a pillow to protect it, and otherwise making him comfortable, Hannah inserted the wagon's tail boards, and returned to the barracks. The breathing of the sleeping men had not changed. She cleaned up around the now empty cot, spreading the blanket over it so that it looked as it did in the afternoon before they moved Paul. The night nurse would not know he had been moved and would assume Paul had died as did Stony, the other soldier. Hannah hoped no one would miss Paul until Weldon reported in the morning. She quietly closed the barracks door.

She returned to the wagon just as Leah finished making her father comfortable. A cursory glance into the dark bed of the covered wagon showed among the usual camping supplies just a pile of bedding. "Come back inside the barracks," Hannah said.

They put the stools they had used to sit by Paul's cot beside another sleeping soldier and sat down. The young soldier tossed in his sleep, moaning and coughing. Hannah wanted to help him, to ease his pain and give him some of her medicine, but dared not. As she did in the detention camp when getting the Kerrigans out, she steeled herself against the sufferings around her. Helping others would jeopardize those she could help.

"This awful war," she said to Leah. "This boy ought to be home helping his father on the farm instead of here."

In just a few minutes they heard the approaching steps of the night guard. He stuck his head into the barracks. Before he could say anything, Hannah stood up so he could see her.

"Hey, feller, what the hell is this wagon doin' here?" he asked.

"Sorry. I didn't realize it was so late. Just keeping my poor cousin company."

"Well, git goin' now. C'mon, I'll escort you off the base. Hell of a time to be out."

"We've got rooms booked for tonight," Hannah said.

"Humph. Time to git to 'em."

Hannah and Leah followed him outside and quickly climbed onto the wagon seat while the guard untied the team. Then he ordered, "Foller me." He led them to the edge of camp and waved them on as he turned back to complete his rounds.

Hannah drove the team west out of the city on a different route from the one they entered the day before. During her busy afternoon as Hank Johnston, besides buying the wagon and harness, bedding, and some other supplies she would need to care for Paul, she had asked around for information about some little-used route out of the city that would not go past any sentries. Finding the directions she needed, she had scouted out the route on the gelding so that she would not get lost at night. Returning to the rooming house, she had inserted the ribbings on the light wagon and put up the canvas cover. She had packed all their gear as well as her new purchases in readiness for travel. After explaining to the landlady that she was escorting Mrs. Rockfort and her daughter back home, she harnessed the team and hitched them to the wagon.

All points covered, she used her pass as Johnston to drive into the military base to pick up Mrs. Rockfort and her daughter. Everything went smoothly. The only problem she had in the hectic afternoon was remembering who she was and getting Hannah and/or Hank into and out of the rooming house without suspicion. As she had hoped, all the people she met and did business with were too busy with their own affairs to pay close attention to her. She told one story after another, inventing them as needed to explain her need of various purchases. As long as she had the money to pay, no one cared about her reasons. However, she didn't want to cause anyone to wonder or even remember either Hannah Rockfort or Hank Johnston as anybody out of the ordinary. In this military station and the seat of the state government, people were used to strangers coming and going. No one questioned her.

Her afternoon's work was successful. They were now on their way. "Quick now, Leah," Hannah said after they had gone about three hundred yards after the sentry turned back, "crawl into the back. See about Papa. Change into your britches as soon as you can."

It was too dark to see each other's faces. Leah put her hand on her mother's arm and said, "Hank and Lee came into town, and Hank and Lee are leaving." Her voice was elated as she felt her way through the circular hole in the canvas wagon cover behind them and crawled into the back. "And going home we've got Papa!"

Over the rumble of the metal wheels on the hard-packed earth and the jingle of the team's harness, both she and Hannah heard distinctly a hoarse voice from the back. "Yes," it said. "Oh, yes. We're going home."

Chapter 17

LEAH KNELT beside her father and leaned over to kiss him. "Oh, Papa."

A jolt of the wagon caused her to fall against him. His right arm circled her thin shoulders, and as if the effort was all he could muster, he let it lie there. Though unable to see his face in the darkness, she knew he was conscious by his irregular breathing and the slight pressure of his fingers.

"Rest now, Papa," she said, kissing his cheek. "We're going home."

Though Hannah wanted to stop and join Leah during Paul's lucid moment, she dared not. Nor on the dark road, did she risk letting the horses go faster than a brisk walk. Turning around on the wagon seat, she poked her head through the canvas opening. "Yes, Paul, my love, rest if you can. We'll go on a few miles until I find a good place to stop."

"Hannah," Paul said so softly they could hardly hear him over the creak of the wagon and the thud of the horses on the road, "I'm... all... right... keep on."

Leah stretched out beside him, pulling the blanket over both of them. She put her arm over his chest and snuggled her head in the pit of his right arm.

"Try to sleep," Hannah said. She clucked to the horses who almost stopped when they felt the slack in the reins.

Though the team was fresh from their day's rest, Hannah was afraid to travel too far for Paul's sake. Jolting in the rough wagon was hard on him. She was afraid that the bumps would aggravate his bed sores. She needed to be beside him to monitor his condition and care for his left arm to be sure it did not fall off of the pillow and open the wound. If it were daylight, Leah could drive the team, but she didn't want to give her the responsibility on this strange road. Instead she gave Leah so many instructions that the child moaned.

"Mama, I'll see to him. You drive."

Weary herself from all her activities and preparations during this long day, and trusting Leah to warn her of any change in her father, Hannah drove on doggedly. Her elation over Paul's conscious state and her resolve to get him home kept her alert. Up on the spring seat of the wagon, she urged the horses on into the night. After a few miles, far enough to be out of range of any patrol, though she didn't expect any pursuit, she looked for a place to stop. She believed that Paul would not be missed until morning, and even then she doubted that the officer in charge would mount a search for a dying soldier that was not in his unit.

After passing a long stretch with no buildings, she sighted a light about two hundred yards to the right of the road. She pulled into the lane through the scattered trees up to the house and shouted in her man-like voice, "Hello, the house."

The front door opened, releasing a stream of light that flowed across the yard to the horses. "Who's there?" A man held up his lantern to see better.

"Hank Johnston and son from Clinton," Hannah answered. Leah poked her head out of the canvas opening behind her mother. "In the wagon we've got my wounded cousin that I'm taking home. Could we put our horses in your barn and camp here in your yard for the night?"

A woman appeared behind the man. "Wounded?" she asked.

"Yes. He lost his left hand."

"In the war?"

"That's right."

"Which army?" the man asked. His voice was guarded.

Because of the divided sympathies of Missourians, Hannah needed to give the correct answer. Before the war began, many people here in the Missouri River valley were slave owners. The Union Army's subsequent marches across the state and their capture of Jefferson City further alienated many local people. But with the state capital so close, she gambled that these people were loyal to the United States. Regardless, the truth about Paul seemed the best course in this situation.

"Union," she answered, "Eighth Missouri State Militia. He was a prisoner of war but was exchanged because of his injury. We're taking him to his family to recover." Without getting down from her seat, as doing so without an invitation would have been a discourteous as well as a hostile action, she added, "He's in the back. Look for yourself." The man walked to back of the wagon. "He may not be conscious," she added.

As soon as Hannah said, "Union," she knew she had gambled correctly. The woman relaxed and draping a shawl over her shoulders, followed her husband. He held up his lantern to view the inside of the wagon. The beam fell on Paul's wrapped up form. The imperfect light cast deep shadows on his face, giving him an even more spectral appearance than normal.

"Sergeant Rockfort, sir." Paul's voice was weak.

"It's too cold out here for him," the woman said wrapping her shawl tighter around her. "Let's get him in by the fire. Mr. Johnston, you and the boy can spread your blankets beside him."

Greatly relieved, Hannah and Leah jumped down. They were beginning to feel the chill as the temperature was near freezing. The man helped them carry Paul into the house. After fixing a pallet on the floor for him, the woman prepared some warm food. Leah and the man tended to the horses. Fed and warm, everyone retired for the night.

Three days later, traveling slowly by day and stopping at farm houses at night, the Rockforts reached Clinton. The journey was harder on Paul than Hannah anticipated. She had not taken into account the effect of the constant jolting that rubbed his bed sores and caused his wound to throb, nor the sudden cold temperatures the thin blankets could not block out. Though she and Leah believed that Paul knew what was happening, he said nothing more. Most of the time his eyes were closed. Lines of pain creased his face, especially when the wagon lurched as one of the wheels struck a rock. When Leah drove, Hannah tended to Paul's needs, fed him as often as she could encourage him to swallow, and tended to his bodily needs. Twice daily she dressed his wound. Though his awareness didn't improve, his arm was healing nicely.

By the time they reached the Kerrigan house, Hannah had given up her plan to take Paul straight home. Each day's ride seemed to undo a bit more of his feeble progress. She was afraid two more days on the trail would send him back into his coma. She accepted Beulah's invitation to stay a few days.

Beulah helped her recognize the wisdom of this. "I don't know why you think you have to get home so bad. It'll be there later when Paul is better. Now you have your whole family together. That's what's most important." She sighed.

Hannah knew she was right. No one knew where Beulah's husband was. She had not heard from him in months, nor did she expect to hear since he was with General Price in the Confederate Army somewhere in the South. Hannah agreed that her family came first, but she refused to look for a house to stay in Clinton as Beulah and Virgil urged her to do. "You can stay here just until the war is over," they tried to persuade her. "You will be safe here. Order Number Eleven did not include this county."

That was true. She did feel safe. No need for disguises or role-playing here. The girls were enjoying being themselves and playing with the Kerrigan children like carefree children should be able to do. They attended school. With no chores to do, they studied hard. Leah read through the fourth reader and enjoyed spelling down the whole class. Dolly, ashamed to be behind the other children her age, tackled the hated long division. Mazie's progress showed every day when she came home telling her parents everything she learned.

Hannah hardly recognized the young Kerrigans from the thin and sad-eyed children of the detention camp. Filled out and eager, they and her girls kept the crowded house in an uproar when they were home.

"Think of your children and your husband," Virgil said one evening after supper when the five younger ones were listening to Leah reading them a bedtime story. He spread out his hands to show the contented and unafraid group. "A spell here will do 'em all a world of good."

"I'm thinking of all of us," Hannah said looking over at Paul, who though watching the children, lay quiet, his face unresponsive and his crippled arm held stiffly against his side as if shielding it from view. "He's lost here, unimportant and not needed."

Virgil nodded. He understood. For a time his self-worth was stripped from him. "But the border region will never be the same. The hatreds and raids will continue. Beulah and I aren't going back."

Hannah was shocked. "Not come back to your home?"

"Our home is gone. All destroyed. There's nothing there," Beulah said. "We have more here in the short time we've been here, than we have now at home."

"But the land?"

"Aw, the land," Virgil said. "When it's safe to go back, the region will be overrun with land grabbers. All the records were burned with the courthouse. Our claim wouldn't stand up. An old southern man and a woman with young'uns, we'd be run off again."

"It isn't worth it," Beulah said. "We like it here."

The Kerrigans couldn't discourage Hannah from going home. She had resolved not to be a victim again—not to give in to greedy and corrupt people. Somehow she would prevail. Restless during the mild November days that followed the first cold spell, she counted the days until Paul would be well enough to travel again. She wanted to take advantage of the fine weather to get home. Knowing that at any time the weather could turn bad, she merely endured each day. Her deadline was no later than mid-December. After that she could expect snow and continued freezing temperatures which would make traveling with an invalid impossible.

Paul improved daily. Warm surroundings, hot, solid foods, and the company of his daughters, kept him conscious. He pronounced their names when they hugged him, even frowning with displeasure when he ran his hand over their cropped hair. Dropping off frequently into a natural sleep, he awoke each time more alert than before. His sores healed from Hannah's salves. He was soon well enough to sit up most of the day, and with support from Virgil and Hannah, took a few steps.

What worried Hannah the most was the slowness of his mental recovery. He was gaining strength and his wound was healing, but he still said very little. He seemed to have trouble formulating the words. So as not to distress him, Hannah urged everyone to keep a steady stream of chatter when near him, but not ask direct questions, especially about his war experiences.

Beulah advised her not to worry so much because Paul smiled often and understood what people said to him. Hannah said, "That's just the trouble. He's acting like he is at a play. Like he's sitting in the audience watching the rest of us. He smiles when things go right, but he isn't taking part. He's just observing."

"Maybe that is how he survived all the things he's gone through," Beulah said. "The war, getting wounded, being in the prison camp. It must have been terrible."

"So he played like he wasn't part of it, you mean?"

"Yes. Then when it got really bad, losing his hand, and all, he retreated into himself. That's what Virgil did when we were forced off our farm and taken to the military camp. He pulled into himself and wasn't himself until you came and took us away. I think that's what Paul did."

Hannah agreed that was a good explanation. "And it will take time for him to emerge?"

Beulah nodded. "He went through much more than Virgil did. It'll take him more time."

With that understanding, Hannah changed her tactics. Instead of shielding him, she put Paul in the midst of the activities. She let the children play as actively and loudly as they wanted around him. She encouraged him to dress himself and do any task he could, each day challenging his strength and his ingenuity of how to manage with only one hand. She gave him small tasks he could do, like putting wood on the fire, or combing Mazie's short hair. She talked to him, asking his advice, and trying in every way she could to bring him out of his shell.

At first he spoke in monosyllables, or single words as if reluctant to leave his mental sanctuary. When Hannah and the others kept after him, asking questions that required more words, he replied in short sentences.

"His mind is there," Beulah said. "It's just buried."

As he improved, Hannah's restlessness increased. Though she admitted that Beulah was right about the importance of the family being together, Hannah knew that Prairie Wood Ranch held the key to Paul's complete recovery. Maybe the Kerrigans didn't need the land, but she and Paul did. To feel like living again, he needed to be where he was a man. At the army barracks and here in the Kerrigan house, his every need was taken care of. In this small house full of women, there was very little he could do to help out, for he wasn't well enough to help support the family with a job as Virgil was doing. But at the ranch he would again be important. He would see hundreds of tasks he could do, and with Hannah he could make the important decisions about their future. Even without his left hand, he could function on his own place.

Two weeks after arriving at the Kerrigans, Hannah decided she could stay there no longer. Paul was walking across the room by this time and taking complete care of himself. His color had returned and his gaunt face and body was filling out. Whenever anyone approached him, he flashed his charming smile and said a few words of pleasantries. But when left alone, he slumped in his chair and stared at the bandage on the end of his lifeless left arm, his eyebrows lowered into a frown. The lines of pain returned to his face. He retreated into himself until one of the girls climbed into his lap or otherwise demanded his attention.

Afraid that learning about their trials and hardships would cause Paul to relapse, Hannah had said very little about her experiences since he left with Newman's Confederate detail. She too had erected a barrier around her recent life so that neither knew what the other had gone through. She was constantly tip-toeing around him to create an artificial security. Until now that course of action had worked. Paul was far from the pitiful creature at death's door that she and Leah first saw in the army barracks.

But as he became better, the fact that he did not ask her anything was another cause of worry. Since Paul was always considerate and solicitous of the family's welfare, to ignore what happened to them in the past two years wasn't like him. He was strong enough to knock down all his mental barriers. Now was the time for reality.

She told him how she and the girls lived and what happened to them from the day he was taken by young Corporal Bud Newman until she found him in Jefferson City. As she talked, Paul listened carefully. He asked a few questions. His apathy disappeared when he learned that he was not the only one in the family that suffered in the conflict. His vitality seeped into him with his indignation and the realization that his family endured many hardships and dangers to keep the ranch and family intact for his return. Whether he was maimed or not made no difference to them. They lived for him. They needed him.

Hannah skimmed over the earlier raids of the two armies and subsequent forays of the Bushwhackers and concentrated on the events since September when Carl Murdock ordered them off the land.

"You mean no one can live on their own land?" he asked. The injustice made his voice strong. This was not right!

"No one. Everyone had to leave or be taken prisoner. The children and I have been hiding there in the shack by the river since we escaped the detention camp."

"And if we go home now?" His mind was clear and sharp.

"We'll have to continue hiding out there."

Such an outrage ordered by his own army was impossible for Paul to grasp. This was his beloved country dedicated to the rights of the individual—white and black. While he had been off fighting for those rights, his own family was taken prisoner by his army just as he had been captured by the Rebels. He shook his head in dismay. His weakened intellect could not understand the reasons and the subtleties of such an action against loyal citizens. Even he, a legitimate prisoner captured in battle, even he had been released to his own side where he could eventually go home.

But he couldn't go home! His land was under military guard, ruined and controlled by a madman. His wife and daughters were escaped prisoners living in disguise for no reason other than they wanted to stay home.

Paul rose in indignation as if he would go right then to avenge this injustice. For a moment he felt like his former self. He wasn't dizzy nor did the hovering mist threaten to engulf his mind. He was again confident that he could do anything. He raised his left arm, ready to take some action. The neat bandage on the stump waved in the air as he started to speak. The reality of their situation was obvious in his ruined hand. His resolve gone, he fell into a chair. "What can we do?" he asked feebly.

"That's what we need to decide. We can stay here in Clinton, like the Kerrigans, safe until the war is over. We could even make our permanent home here. Virgil thinks that is best. Or," she paused when his face formed into a frown and he shook his head slowly as she spoke, "or we can return home and live in the shack just like the girls and I have been doing."

Paul's frown disappeared; he straightened up in his chair. Encouraged, Hannah continued. "We'll be fugitives and have to be on the alert all the time, but we can hunt and trap to make a living. Then when this war is over, we will already be there to protect and build up the ranch."

"They didn't burn the house?" Paul stopped shaking his head. He saw some hope in all these catastrophic events.

"No."

"That was lucky."

"No, not lucky. It was saved on purpose. We have a friend in the army at Fort Scott. No, two friends. I think we'll be safe from Carl Murdock. Our friends will warn us."

Hannah paused while Paul sorted out all she'd told him. "Do you remember a tall soldier visiting you in the barracks about a month ago?" she asked.

"No. I don't remember anything after being on the troop train and getting very sick." He thought for a minute. "Yes, maybe I do. But it was more like a dream. I remember a man said you would come get me. He said over and over, 'Your wife, Hannah, will come get you.'" He grabbed her hand. "I thought I was dreaming. Did that really happen?"

"Yes. That really happened. And the doctor said you started getting better right away. That man was Walking Owl, an Osage scout under Murdock. Most people call him Walker. He put out the fire in our house. Then later, after we escaped from the detention camp, he came to the shack to see us. He took a leave of absence just to find you. Somehow he traced you and sent me word. That's how I found you."

"We must thank him." Paul was having difficulty sorting out in his mind all this information. He passed his right hand over his brow and frowned as he forced his mind to work. "You said there were two friends. Someone besides this Walker."

"Yes, a young lieutenant, Micah Knowles, the one that Murdock ordered to take us away. Later when we ran away from him, he didn't report us. And he knows we returned home but didn't tell Murdock. He was the one that gave Dolly and me Walker's message that you were in Jefferson City."

"We are fortunate to have two such allies." Paul smiled pleased with himself that he understood these complicated relationships.

"Yes, we are," Hannah said. She wondered how much to tell Paul of the other dangers at home. He was responding so well to what she told him of the past, that she decided he needed to know everything. "Murdock is not the only threat at home. The Bushwhackers are riding again. Bud Newman is almost as fanatic against the Union Army as Murdock was against slave owners."

"But isn't Bud in the Confederate Army down in Arkansas?"

"Yes, and no. He claims he's with the Confederate Army. But he's more an outlaw now heading up a band of Bushwhackers in our area. He's doing all the damage he can to the Union soldiers stationed at Fort Scott."

"And if he knew I was back home?" Paul asked, though he knew the answer.

"He'd come for you, that is certain. He considers you a traitor for changing sides—worse than Murdock. He knows the country, and we don't have any friends in his band to warn us."

"I remember him as a child when he used to come with his father when we traded work. He's not too smart. We should be able to outwit him."

"I don't worry too much about him. He's out to get Murdock, not us, but he's mean. We can't ignore him."

More and more he was feeling like his old self, head of the family.

Yet he couldn't take complete control yet. Hannah was strong. She'd know what is best for them. "So what do we do, stay here or go home?" Paul asked.

"Go home," Leah said. Neither Hannah nor Paul had noticed that she and her sisters were listening to every word.

"Go home," both Dolly and Mazie said running to him and holding on to him as if ready to lead him there at that moment.

Paul laughed out loud for the first time. The sparkle returned to his eyes as he gestured with both arms. He was using his left arm instead of holding it close to his side as if ashamed of it.

Mazie crawled into his lap. Leah and Dolly stood beside him, each one holding an arm. Leah was very careful of his left arm, but she moved it up and down. "See, Papa, it still works."

"Yes, Sister, it does." He gestured with it again. Everyone laughed. Paul turned to Hannah. "And you want to go home, I know."

"Oh, yes."

"Then we'll go home." Paul was again the head of the family, making the crucial decision.

The girls whooped. Dolly and Mazie left immediately to gather their few belongings. "I'll harness the team," Leah said.

"Whoa, there, girls," Hannah said. "Come back here. Tomorrow is soon enough."

"But Virgil said it is going to rain tomorrow," Dolly said. "Shouldn't we get going?"

"All the more reason to be prepared. We couldn't get very far today anyway."

Everyone scurried around. Hannah gave the little girls instructions. Paul accompanied Leah to the wagon as she greased the wheels and tightened the canvas cover where it sagged between the ribbings. When they returned to the house, Hannah was gathering up enough food to last the trip and checking over their shirts and trousers. While in Clinton they wore dresses all the time. But on the trail and at home, she and the girls would revert again to their male disguise.

"I don't want you to wear those clothes," Paul said. "It isn't fitting for women to dress like that. It's bad enough you cut your hair."

Leah looked at her mother in alarm. "But Papa," she said, "If we don't..."

Hannah held up her hand to silence Leah. Though pleased that Paul was making decisions, Hannah knew she couldn't turn complete control over to him yet. He wasn't well enough and didn't know the present situation. She knew better what to do. Patiently, and trying not to offend his position as head of the family, she explained again to Paul the danger of traveling through the military zone and why the male clothing was necessary.

The day's physical activities and mental stimulation were taking their toll on Paul. He merely shook his head in disapproval as he lay down on the divan and closed his eyes in weariness. In a weak voice he reasserted his authority by saying, "We'll leave at dawn tomorrow."

Chapter 18

IT WAS three days later in a cold drizzle that the Rockforts urged the team across the ford on the Osage River just above their shack. The horses balked at entering the current. From the southern side they couldn't see that thirty inches under the slightly swollen water rolling by was a solid rock surface.

Leah and Dolly each had to sit astride one of the horses to convince them with repeated jabs of their heels in their flanks that it was safe to cross. Hesitantly they pulled their feet from the mud on the slanted southern approach and stepped into the brown water. As soon as the gelding felt the solid rock with his front hoof, he willingly went forward. Like the people in the wagon, he knew he was almost home.

Slowly the gelding and mare pulled the wagon across the river. The recent rains made the crossing more difficult. Just upstream they could see the surge of water from Duncan Creek spilling into the river. The water level reached almost to the wagon bed, and its force against the wheels pushed the wagon downstream a few inches. Hannah's shouts from the seat as she slapped the reins across their backs and the girls' spurring them encouraged the team to pull with all their strength. Scrambling on the slippery rock surface with their front hooves, they reached the northern bank and started up the muddy incline toward firmer ground. Each step squished into the oozy mud, hampering their progress. When the wagon wheels left the rock stream bed and reached the bank, they sank six inches into the mire. The horses strained and pulled, but could not move the wagon.

"Everyone out," Paul ordered. The nearer he got to his land, the faster he seemed to regain his strength. "We'll have to help push."

"Unload everything," Hannah said.

By crawling out the front and stepping onto the wagon tongue between the horses, they avoided having to wade in the water. But the moment they stepped onto the bank, they, too, sank into the cold mud. Afraid that he would overexert himself, Hannah convinced Paul that he could help best by persuading the team from the front. Hannah and the girls made an assembly line to unload their few belongings and supplies.

Already wet and muddy, Hannah, Leah, and Dolly waded into the water to heave on the front wheels of the lightened wagon while Paul urged the horses to pull. Helped by Hannah and the girls, the team pulled the wagon onto firmer ground.

"Hooray!" Leah shouted and without waiting for instructions from her parents, ran ahead to the shack. She quickly disappeared in the vegetation. It was safe, for Hannah had already scouted out the area and determined that the shack hadn't been touched since they left. Leah's cheerful voice came back, "I'll start a fire."

Mazie ran behind her. Even before getting in out of the rain or building a fire, Mazie had to find her cat. "Here, Puss, kitty, kitty, kitty," she called as she ran.

So that Paul wouldn't overtax his strength, Hannah convinced him get back on the wagon seat while she and Dolly reloaded their belongings through the back opening. Just as he had been doing all day as they drew closer to his acres, Paul sat on the seat wrapped in a rain slicker, a grin on his face as he moved his head from side to side to see everything that was visible in the mist. He stared at the river as if it appeared there by magic just for him. He greeted each tree as an old friend. He kept looking north through the woods to catch a glimpse of the house, although he knew even with the leaves gone, that he couldn't see it.

Nor could he locate the shack, though he remembered where it should be. Suddenly Leah appeared from between two huge tree trunks when Hannah stopped the horses. "We're home," Hannah said and jumped down.

Dolly laughed at her father as he looked around in awe, seeing nothing but a thick grove of tree trunks, cedar trees, and brush. Though he could not see her, he heard Mazie's voice from inside the grove still calling for Puss. Paul looked at Hannah, shaking his head in amazement and admiration. "Marvelous." Everyone laughed.

"Now gang, let's unload and get inside," Hannah said. "Change quickly into dry clothes. Mazie, don't worry about Puss. She'll show up as soon as she knows we're back. Sugar, I'm putting you in charge of Papa. Get him some dry clothes and fix him some hot tea. And most important, make him lie down."

While Mazie proudly escorted her father into the shack that was already warming up from Leah's fire, the other girls started unloading. Hannah's task was to find a place to hide the wagon. Elated that they were home again and that once more she had a wagon to help with the farm work, she drove the team downstream to the bluff overhang. It would be a perfect place to protect the wagon—dry and hidden from view even from the river. She had to swing around the marshy areas and zig-zag through the trees to find passages wide enough to admit the wagon. Finally at the bluff, she backed the wagon into place. Unhitching the team and removing their harness except for their halters, she climbed on the wet, bare back of the gelding and, leading the mare, backtracked upstream to the paddock. She turned the horses loose to rest from their long journey and to feed on the prairie hay she and the girls had stacked nearby.

Before returning to the shack, she wondered if she had chosen wisely to take the extra day to come home the longer route. Instead of cutting across the military zone as she had done on the way to Clinton, she stayed in the wooded hills of Cedar County until crossing the Osage River. Then she headed west over the prairie to come to their place from the south. Although they had to ford the river twice and travel an extra day, this route through the hills completely avoided the military zone.

She decided that she had made the right decision. The possibility of running into Murdock again on the more direct north road was too great.

The rain that Virgil predicted came at the end of their first day of travel, an unceasing, slow drizzle that kept them uncomfortable and slowed their progress. Now, a day longer on the road, though more tired and certainly much wetter, they were finally home and safe. On the hill route that was not in the restricted region, the local people and the soldiers they met did not stop them or question them. The few travelers on the narrow, wooded roads merely exchanged friendly comments about the weather or made some cheery remarks to the children as they pulled to the side to let them pass.

Posing as Hank Johnston and his sons with his injured cousin, they found shelter one night in a farm home. The second night, not finding an occupied house place in the semi-deserted area nearer the military zone, they located a secluded spot near a spring and slept in the wagon. To keep Paul warm in the bed of the wagon, Hannah and his daughters almost smothered him with their bodies.

The persistent cold drizzle was the main hazard. Though Paul and the children stayed under the wagon cover where they were fairly dry, Hannah, on the exposed spring seat, was wet through most of the time. Rain dripped down inside the collar of her slicker. Her boots and jeans were never dry. The wet clothes did not dry completely even when hung by the fire at night. Though Mazie had the sniffles and Hannah's throat was raspy, Paul didn't seem to suffer from the dampness or the trip. In fact, he continued to get stronger each day. His mental barrier was completely gone. Except for his missing hand and weakened physical condition, he became the assertive husband and father they knew. Everyone rejoiced in his presence. The rain, mud, cold—nothing discouraged them. Papa was with them and they were on their own land.

The first night home to forestall any sickness, Hannah dosed everyone with hot tea from the bark of wild cherry. The children willingly sucked on sticks of horehound candy she gave them from her bag to prevent colds. Everyone changed into the dry clothes left in the shack and basked in the luxury of the fire. All was right with their world.

Well, almost. Mazie still couldn't find Puss. But for a few hours that night they forgot that they couldn't live openly in their big, comfortable house. They put on hold their worry about Murdock or the Bushwhackers discovering them. After everything they had accomplished, those were problems they could handle.

Home and safe with her complete family, even before letting herself sleep as she lay snuggled against Paul's right side with his arm around her, Hannah began planning how to survive the winter and get the ground prepared for spring planting. First, she would need to set more traps. Fur was at its best now. They should get as many pelts as possible to trade for supplies and seed. Constructive plans for the ranch whizzed through her head as she drifted off to sleep.

The next morning seemed to echo the Rockforts' optimism. The December sun rose in a clear sky. The golden light filtering through the bare tree limbs crept through the shack's one window to brighten up the room. And to cheer everyone, while the family was eating breakfast, there was a scratch on the door followed by an insistent yowl to be let in.

"Puss!" Mazie shouted. She jumped up, upsetting her bowl as she ran to the door. The cat strode into the room meowing her displeasure at having been deserted again, her orange and black patches shining in contrast to her immaculately clean white coat. She held her tail high as she set each white paw possessively on the puncheon floor of the shack. After thoroughly bawling her family out with a series of meows, she stopped to glare at each of them in turn. Mazie scooped her up into her arms and buried her face into her soft fur, murmuring endearments to her. Puss allowed Mazie to squeeze her for a few seconds and then squirmed out of her arms. She walked sedately to the fireplace to sit on her haunches in the warmth. But seeing Paul, she decided she had punished them long enough for deserting her and jumped into his lap. She rubbed her cheeks on his neck, and purred loudly as she worked her claws in her happiness.

Everyone laughed as Paul shook Puss's paw and said, "I'm glad to see you, too, Puss. It's been a long time."

"Puss is wondering why you didn't write to us," Mazie said.

The laughter died. Though Hannah and the girls had shared everything about their lives with Paul, they had been careful not to question him about his experiences. Hannah believed it better to wait until he was ready to tell them himself. She still feared the memories might cause him to relapse.

"Mazie," Leah scolded in an undertone, pushing her to emphasize her meaning, "we're not supposed to talk about that."

Mazie started to cry.

"Why not, Sister?" Paul asked Leah.

Leah glanced at her mother. Hannah held out her hands to indicate she might as well tell him. "We thought talking about what happened to you would make you..." she hesitated whether to mention the coma. "Make you sick again, Papa."

Paul stood up, placed Puss in Mazie's arms, and hugged his daughter, automatically using his crippled left arm. "No, it's all right. I won't retreat again into myself. You children have cured me. There's too much here to live for. I don't want to miss a single moment. We can talk about anything that bothers you."

"Well, why didn't you write to us?" Mazie insisted.

"I did, little Amazing." He paused for Mazie to frown and pucker up her face as she did whenever he used her full name. "I wrote several letters. Before I was captured, I assumed they reached you." When Hannah and the girls all shook their heads, he continued, "Apparently they didn't. I didn't know how unsettled things were here on the border. After I was taken prisoner, I wrote lots of letters. While writing them I felt like you were all beside me listening to me. But there was no way to send them across enemy lines. I had them all packed carefully in my knapsack, but I guess everything got lost in Jefferson City. Probably the knapsack stayed on the train."

"No one there knew who you were," Leah said. "They called you Rocky, though. How did they know that?"

"That's what the fellows all called me. You know it's been my nickname all my life. Probably one of my buddies said that as he carried me off the train. Maybe the aide heard him."

After a pause Hannah asked softly, "Do you feel like telling us what the letters said?"

Paul studied his family. Each of his girls looked steadily at him begging him to tell them. "I've tried to block out the past two years, but I can't. At Jefferson City, every time I'd wake up, I'd remember. So I'd block it out and drift off again. But now, in the daytime, I don't think about them anymore, but at night I keep having nightmares about them. The war and the prison camp still seems more real to me than this." He used both arms to show he meant the family, the ranch, and being free. "I can't believe that it's all over and I'm back at Prairie Wood."

"You are, my love, and for you the war is over," Hannah said, kissing his cheek and holding him. "Perhaps you might be able to put it behind you by telling us about it."

"Yes, maybe I can." A sadness spread over his face as he studied where to begin. Mazie crawled into his lap. He mussed up her short hair and kissed the back of her neck. She giggled. "You got my letter telling that I escaped from Bud Newman's outfit after the battle at Lexington?" They all nodded. "That was in September eighteen sixty-one—more than two years ago, up there on the Missouri River. Well, after I got safely away—I went to Kansas City—I knew I couldn't come home with both armies running over the state. I didn't want to go West as my buddy did that escaped with me, so in order to help get the war over quicker so I could come home, I hid out until the Rebels pulled back south toward Arkansas. Then I joined up with the Union forces. I was assigned to the Fourth Union Division and went south in the campaign to run the Confederate forces out of the state and keep Missouri in the Union."

He leaned over to pat Dolly's arm. "And Dolly, since I still had Black Laddie, I was in the cavalry. We rode south in Kansas just across the state line near here, but I couldn't get away to see you. We were in a big hurry chasing General Price. I figured after we whipped him down in Arkansas, I'd be able to come home. We all thought that would end our part of the war."

Hannah sighed, "That was only just the beginning."

"We didn't know that then. At the Battle of Pea Ridge in Arkansas, we defeated the Confederates all right and saved Missouri for the Union. During the fight our division was hit the hardest. By my estimate, about fifty of us were captured. Several were wounded so badly that they died, but the rest of us were sent farther south and held in a prison camp." He visibly shuddered.

"What happened to Black Laddie," Dolly asked.

"I don't know what happened to him after they captured me. I saw a Rebel soldier catch him, jump on him, and ride off. He took my saddle and all my gear. I suppose the Rebels used him. He was a fine horse."

"I'm glad he wasn't killed. Is that when you got your hand shot?" she asked.

"No. I wasn't wounded in that battle. That happened several months later when six of us tried to escape from the prison camp. We got away all right, but the Rebs trailed us and ran us down. We got almost to the Missouri state line before they recaptured us. Three men were shot dead, but I was lucky. I just took a bullet in my hand as I dived into a ditch."

"Did the doctor cut it off then?" Mazie asked.

"No. They didn't have many doctors. The Rebels had so many of their own men wounded and sick the few doctors didn't have time to help the prisoners—especially those of us that tried to escape. We were lucky they didn't line us up and shoot us, or hang us. I'll give that to them. They just left us alone. I dug out the bullet myself with a pocket knife and tried to care for the hand the way I'd seen Mama do. But I didn't have any of her remedies or salves. Not even clean cloths for bandages. I used the tail of my shirt and tried to keep it clean by washing it out when it got bloody. But that wasn't very satisfactory."

Dolly picked up his stump that had a fresh clean bandage on it and cradled it close to her chest. There were tears in her eyes. "Did it hurt?"

"Oh yes, it hurt. Never stopped. But for a spell the wound in the hand seemed to mend, though the broken bones made it deformed. Then it started festering. About that time there was an exchange of prisoners. Those of us that were sick or wounded were exchanged first. The Rebs thought it was a good exchange to get rid of wounded men for healthy Confederate soldiers."

"Lucky for us," Leah said.

"Yes, more than I ever hoped for. We were put on a freight train for St. Louis. I remember part of that trip. It was long, with many stops and delays, and very hot. Swarms of flies on us all the time. My hand got worse. Long red streaks ran from it up my arm. I knew it couldn't be saved. It hurt so much that I begged the men around me to cut it off. Of course, no one did. There weren't any doctors. When we changed trains in St. Louis, I knew from the red marks that gangrene was spreading. I don't know why I wasn't taken to a hospital in St. Louis. I was not conscious part of the time. I supposed they thought I was just sleeping."

He rubbed his right hand over his brow and held out his left arm. His voice was beginning to get thin from the unaccustomed talking. "I don't remember being taken off the train in Jefferson City. I guess I was delirious. The next morning I was aware where I was and that the others had gone on without me, but I couldn't break through the thick layers surrounding me. I couldn't speak. It was like being in a nightmare when you try to shout and you can't. Have you ever dreamed that?"

"Yes," Leah said. "And sometimes my legs won't work and I can't run."

"Exactly. That was how I felt. The doctor in Jeff City cut off my hand." When Mazie started to cry, he said, "If he hadn't, I'd be dead now. He saved my life."

"Did you know Mama and me when we came to your cot in the army barracks?" Leah asked.

"Yes. I knew you. First I heard Mama's voice. I thought it was a dream. Then it seemed like a long time later I heard your voice, Sister. I guess I opened my eyes and saw you because I remember wondering how you got so big."

"That's what you said, Papa. The first thing you said was 'So big.'"

"Did I?" When she and Hannah both nodded, he said, "Again I thought I was dreaming, just as I had supposed the Osage scout coming to me was a dream. I thought your being there was just part of that dream. I kept trying to talk to you, but couldn't. Then the dream would go away and I wouldn't know anything again."

"And then what?" Mazie asked when he stopped.

"That's all. The dream kept recurring. I'd see Mama and Sister, but I couldn't see you and Dolly. I worried why I couldn't dream you girls as well. I thought maybe something bad had happened to you. Then I knew for sure I wasn't dreaming when I found myself in the wagon bumping along the road. Those jolts, the smell of the horses, and the cold night air, all that was real." He squeezed Mazie and patted Dolly's arm. "And then I saw you two and here we all are together without having to dream it."

Their questions answered, the girls sat quietly thinking over what their father had said.

Hannah pushed away from the table and said, "And in order to get through the winter, we better get to work right away."

"Yes," Paul agreed. "We've much to do. I've much to see."

"Dolly, you and Mazie stay with Papa," Hannah said. "As much as he feels able, take him around the place, but don't let him overdo it. Leah and I will set some traps. We'll be back by noon."

"Can we use the horses?" Dolly asked her mother. "Papa will want to see our house and that's too far for him to walk."

Hannah started to answer. She recognized on Paul's face the disapproving expression he wore when upset. Creases appeared on his forehead when she started giving orders. Changing her tone she turned to Paul. "Whatever Papa says, honey. Ask him."

"Can we, Papa?"

"Yes, Dolly," Paul said his frown gone, "that's a fine idea. It'll be good to ride a horse again. I can go as far as the house, I'm sure."

Hannah formed the words to warn them to look out for any riders, but held her tongue. She needed to proceed on a tight course not to be too assertive. Though she was better able to handle their survival than he, she must give Paul back his place as head of the family. He would know to be careful, or if not, Dolly would warn him. Though she knew Paul disapproved, she and Leah were dressed in trousers to better do the outside work. They gathered up their traps and headed to the river to set them.

Hannah walked as if on air, the metal traps clanging together as they hung on a rope down her back. Setting the traps and looking over the woods for danger were tasks she'd done for years. After so long being constantly on alert and fearful for Paul's condition, she almost floated along the river bank in her new sense of well-being.

Hannah expressed her relief. "Just like Papa coming out of his fog, I feel like I've cut through layers of fear."

"Me, too," Leah said as she set a trap in a quiet pool under a ledge where the river had eaten out a hole. It was a good spot for a mink or raccoon to walk by and step on the hidden trap. "It's like a heavy black cloud has been lifted and the bright sunlight is shining through." She laughed as she glanced up at the bright December sun in a cloudless sky. Its warmth and their exertion caused them to unbutton their coats. "And that is really what happened, isn't it?"

"Yes. The weather is perfect. And Papa is getting well. Did you notice he's beginning to use his left arm to help hold things?"

"This morning he held Puss in the crook of that arm when he got up to put another stick of wood on the fire. Did you see that, Mama?"

"I did." Hannah spied some mink tracks along the bank that disappeared into the river. She placed her last trap under about a foot and a half of water. Then she fastened the trap to a submerged root and carefully covered it with some rotted leaves. Over the entire area she sprinkled a thin film of mud to make the leaves look like the river bottom. Anxious to get the job done, this time she did not use any bait. She planned later to catch some suckers as a lure. Since the traps were set in the animal's paths, she figured that she would probably catch some as they stepped into them.

Hannah was so intent on setting her traps and congratulating herself on their good fortune that she didn't heed a high-pitched coyote cry. Leah didn't miss it. She grabbed her mother, pulling her up from the water's edge. "Listen," she said. When the first calls subsided, they held their breaths as they counted to ten. The calls repeated. The signal to come!

Was Paul worse? Murdock here? Both raced back up the river, keeping behind tree trunks and looking in all directions for any disturbance. Half way back they heard horses coming toward them. The coyote call was repeated, so they knew Dolly was riding. She soon appeared riding the mare and leading the gelding. Paul and Mazie were not with her.

"Bushwhackers up at the big house," she panted. "Papa said to stake the horses under the bluff, get you, and come on back to the shack. He and Mazie are already there."

"Quick, girls, get back to them," Hannah said. "I'll take care of the horses."

Dolly slid off as she and Leah ran back to the shack. Hannah led the horses the short distance to the bluff overhang where she had put the wagon the day before. She removed the bridles and saddles, tied ropes to their halters and fastened each horse to a tree. When she ran back around the bend of the river and looked back, she couldn't see horses or wagon. Near the shack, she stopped to look and to listen. The cut cedars she had propped around the shack to camouflage it were still green and standing. Only a discerning eye would notice that they were not naturally growing there. From their big house about a quarter of a mile north, she believed she could distinguish men's voices. Satisfied that no one had come this far down to the river, she entered the cedar grove around the shack.

"It's young Newman," Paul said as soon as she entered the shack. "We were looking over the yard when Dolly heard his outfit coming down the trail from the road."

"They were talking and making so much noise as they came that they didn't hear or see us," Dolly said.

"And we got the horses and hid in the edge of the woods to watch them," Mazie said.

"They weren't soldiers?" Hannah asked Paul.

He shook his head. "It was Newman. Him and six others."

"They acted like they were going to stay there," Dolly said.

"They took their bedrolls inside and hobbled their horses," Paul said.

The euphoria of the morning disappeared. Hannah wrung her hands and paced back and forth in front of the fireplace. Paul or Dolly had already doused the fire so there would be no smoke to give them away. "We can't stay here. Bud will find us."

"Do you think he'll remember this shack?" Paul asked. "He was just a kid when he left."

"He knows the ford. He and his dad used to hunt and fish along here. He knows about it."

"Maybe he won't remember it."

"He mentioned it when he came to get you. He called it our crossing down by the draw."

"What'll we do?" The girls looked first at Hannah for instructions as they had been doing for two years. Then they remembered that their father was back. They looked to him for direction.

He started to speak and then hesitated. "You know the situation better than I, Hannah. What do you think?"

Since Paul asked her, she felt free to make the decisions. "The girls and I will be safe as the Johnstons. This time we'll be Confederate sympathizers forced from our home in Bates County. We just found this shack to winter in." Paul agreed to the plan. "But Bud will know you," she added.

"Yes, he will. Then he'll figure out who you are and spoil everything you've done," he said, once again dejected.

"Why not have him put on your dress, Mama?" Leah suggested.

In spite of their eminent danger, Dolly and Mazie giggled at the picture of their father dressed like a woman. Paul shook his head at the thought.

"That's a good idea, Leah," Hannah said. "He can put on my dress and bonnet with the braids hanging from it. Our story will be that the hated Captain Murdock cut off Mrs. Hank Johnston's hand and we couldn't go any farther. We're staying here for her to recuperate."

When everyone looked dubious, Paul said, "I hate it, but we haven't time to do anything else. It's one thing for you to travel over the state as men, but for me to masquerade as a woman?"

"I don't see how it's any different." Hannah said.

"It's degrading for a man," he said.

Leah looked hurt. "Why Papa? Why is it degrading to pass for a woman?" She looked down at the trousers she was wearing.

"No time for this now," he said gruffly. "Can't be helped. Dolly, help me get dressed. And you and Mazie put on your boy clothes."

Two years before Paul's words would not have bothered Hannah, for she would have agreed with him. She realized then how much she had changed. But now was not the time to pursue this male dominance thing or worry about Paul's feelings by giving orders in front of him. He certainly wasn't thinking of her or the girls when he implied that women were second class. Newman's arrival was eminent. There were preparations to make.

"Dolly," she said, "be careful of my bonnet so that the braids don't come undone when you put it on Papa. Leah, go out and get rid of any sign or tracks you see. I'll go scout around up at the house to see what I can find out. I guess you told Papa about our warning signals?" Dolly nodded. "Good. If they head this way, I'll give the bob white call."

She followed Leah out the door and hurried toward the house.

Chapter 19

HANNAH CREPT up to the edge of the woods where she had a good view of the house. There were seven horses tied to a rope strung between two apple trees behind the house. The men were all inside, talking loudly, obviously not worried about being heard.

Hannah crept up to the horses, using them as a screen to get closer. She counted seven men seated around the kitchen table, laughing, drinking, and playing cards. Smoke was coming from the kitchen chimney. Knowing that all the men were together and busy concentrating on their game, she ran crouched over to the back porch and crawled under its wooden floor where Leah and Dolly could always find Mazie when they played "I spy." Through the small opening, Hannah squirmed on her stomach to clear the joists resting on the limestone corner foundations until she was close enough to the men's conversation. She had a limited view of the men through the cracks in the porch floor.

Their talk was about the poker game they were playing. Hannah was just about to back out when one of the men stretched out his feet and said with satisfaction, "Best place we've had to hide out in since everyone left."

The other men murmured agreement. "You said it, Collins."

"How'd you find it, Bud?"

"Used to live 'round here. Thought maybe the Feds would miss this here place, being off the road and all."

Another man said, "Lucky fer us Murdock didn't burn the house along with the barn."

"Yeah," Bud said. "We'll bunk here fer a spell, then when we git done with Murdock, we'll finish the job fer him." He laughed. "It's only fittin' that we burn it down."

"What fer?" Collins asked.

A look of hatred crossed Newman's face. "A turncoat lived here. A neighbor, name of Rockfort. He joined up with us all buddy-buddy and went up to the battle at Lexington with us. But he cut out during the fight there and went over to the Yankee side." The venom in his voice was reminiscent of Carl Murdock's when he killed Bud's father several years ago. "Though we licked the Yanks good and proper there, when we pulled back to Arkansas, they chased us all the way. This here Rockfort, knowin' the country, probably helped 'em keep on our tail. By the time we got to Arkansas it was like we lost the battle 'cause the Yanks was still in charge of all Missouri."

In his anger Newman didn't look carefully at the cards in his hand and asked for only one card. "Don't want this Rocky to come home and find his fine house standin' when ever'body else lost theirs." Bud almost snarled when he pronounced the word, "fine."

Hannah shivered at the hatred in his voice. Paul was right. This man was as dangerous as Murdock.

"What happened to him?"

"Don't know."

Collins laughed and threw down his cards which won the hand. "I'd not want to be in his shoes when you catch up to him."

Newman sneered, "Nothin' worse'n a traitor. Him fightin' on the same side as Murdock, and his own woman gittin' knocked plum out by that preacher bastard."

"When was that?"

"Same time Murdock murdered my pa. 'Bout seven years ago. And this Rockfort and my pa worked together all the time helpin' each other out. His own wife seein' the killin' and gittin' beat up herself!"

"What kind o' man would fight fer the Yanks after that?"

"One that needs shootin' or better yit hangin', if I run into him," Newman said.

Collins scooped up the cards and dealt them out again. "Seems like some kind o' justice fer you to use his house."

"Yeah." Newman picked up his cards, studied them a few seconds and then looked around the room. "But when he gits home, he don't deserve findin' no house still a-standin'."

The men laughed and continued their game. "But yer right, Collins," Newman said, "this here's a good place fer now. We can winter over here and cause the Yanks at Fort Scott some grief at the same time. We won't burn it long as we can use it."

Hannah backed out from under the porch and sprinted across the open yard back to the protection of the horses. This threat was the greatest so far. Newman's words left no doubt in her mind that he would shoot Paul on sight. And the men with him looked vile enough to commit any atrocity. When she thought of the danger to her little girls, her right hand trembled so that she had to hold it still with the other. She needed to get to the shack.

As she crept behind the shield of the horses, she thought about untying them but decided against it. The missing horses would put her family in greater jeopardy than they already were. With no means of transportation, the outlaws would comb the area for their mounts and would undoubtedly find the shack and her own horses. Then their scheme of posing as the Johnstons would backfire. Newman would know that one of them stole the horses and he would deal quickly with them. She had heard stories of Bushwhackers shooting everyone in a house they plundered, even children. Tempting as it was to take the horses, she decided to bide her time. Maybe later when the men were camped somewhere away from the ranch she could sneak up to the horses while the men slept.

One of the horses nickered as she crept beside him. She spoke softly to him and dropped to the ground out of view of the house. Busy with their game, the men paid no attention to the horses' customary sounds. Rising up behind the animal, Hannah patted his black rump. She gently ran her hand along his back and neck until she reached his head. The horse nickered softly again and nuzzled her as she stroked his nose and forehead. Surprised, she looked more carefully at the close-made body, at the long joints at his knee and ankle, and at the two white stockings on his back legs, the only markings on his solid black coat. Her hand stopped in mid-stroke. This was Paul's horse, Black Laddie! He had recognized her before she knew him.

Excited at how pleased Paul would be to get his horse back, Hannah started to untie his lead rope. Then she stopped. No, she dared not do anything to make Bud Newman suspect their presence. Later, she promised herself, she would follow the outlaws out on the trail and steal him back. A few more days wouldn't matter. "I'll be back for you, Laddie," she whispered in his ear. He was in good shape and had been treated well. His present owner had shod his right back hoof with a special shoe just as Paul always did. It had a trailer to make him point his foot straight instead of toeing in.

Paul and the girls anxiously greeted her return. "They're playing cards," she said to allay their worry of immediate danger.

The girls were waiting Hannah's reaction to their father's transformation. She could not take her eyes off of Paul, now changed into Mrs. Johnston. The girls had arranged the braids and bonnet and dressed him in Hannah's blouse and skirt. Since he was sitting down, the shortness of the skirt did not show. Paul's thinness allowed enough room across his normally muscled shoulders for him to move his arms without straining the material, and the girls had tied an apron over the skirt's waistband that wouldn't quite meet to button.

Hannah stifled a giggle when she noticed how embarrassed Paul was. The girls loved dressing up their father as they did their dolls and the ever patient Puss. His discomfort didn't bother them. "We wanted to make him some breasts," Dolly said with a giggle, "but he wouldn't let us."

"This is bad enough," Paul said, indicating the shirt and bonnet. He was very uncomfortable and embarrassed.

"If the men don't look too closely, they won't notice." Hannah didn't have time to worry about Paul's insulted manhood. "You'll do. You look like a big, raw-boned woman who has been ill."

"The girls decided I should be Polly," Paul said.

"We're trying to get him to talk high like a woman," Dolly said.

"How's this," Paul said in a falsetto voice. In spite of his resistance, with his family all smiling at him, he was beginning to get into the act.

"That's better." Dolly laughed.

After Hannah told them what she had learned from the outlaws, they all agreed that their best option for now was to stay close to the shack, hope Newman didn't find them, but keep a constant watch on them. They all rejoiced to learn that Black Laddie was still alive and cared for.

"We've got to get him back," Dolly said.

"We'll figure out a way," Paul said. Bowing to the inevitable, he no longer objected to the clothing. Hannah's report convinced him the disguise was vital.

"But our house?" Leah asked. "He said he'd burn it."

"We won't let him," Paul said.

"How can we stop him. It takes only a second to start a fire," Leah said. "By the time we'd see the flames, it would be too late."

"We'll figure out something, Sister."

Hannah said, "I don't think there's any immediate danger. They won't burn it as long as they want to use it. Our chance will come when they are away..." She knew killing Newman was probably the only way they could prevent him from setting the fire, but she didn't want to use the word. She pushed the thought away.

"Maybe my lieutenant will capture them and put them all in jail," Dolly said.

Hannah and Paul exchanged glances. That would be a perfect solution. Perhaps one of them could warn the post of the outlaws' presence.

But not today. There were more urgent matters. To keep an eye on the men, Hannah, Leah, and Dolly would take turns watching their activities from the cover of the woods. To determine if they could hear the bob white danger signal from that distance, Leah ran to the edge of the woods to test it. They heard her if it was quiet inside the shack or if the listener was outside. They next agreed that Paul and Mazie were the logical ones to be responsible for listening for the signal should it come because they would both be close to the shack at all times. Since Paul's major task was to get well and strong, he could rest and yet move about as much as he was able. Too small for most tasks, Mazie could help him learn to move about in skirts. This arrangement had another advantage. The father and youngest daughter could look out for each other, allowing Hannah and the older girls to keep watch, run their trap lines, and care for the horses.

Leah took the first watch. Hannah's and Dolly's job, since the horses could not be left tied up all the time, was to build a temporary fence under the bluff overhang. The outlaws would not be as likely to spot the horses in this location as they would in the paddock near the ford. Though there was water there in the river, the bluff had the disadvantage of having no grazing area. They would have to carry in hay.

By dark, when it was obvious that the Bushwhackers were settled in the house for the night, Leah returned to the shack. After covering the window with a comforter to hide its light, Paul rebuilt the fire to warm the chilly room. The Bushwhackers could not see the smoke at night. The family discussed what to do next. Dolly insisted they go this very night to Fort Scott to tell Lieutenant Knowles. Leah believed that they should stay hidden here together. She reasoned that they wouldn't need to make the trip because Walking Owl would scout out the outlaws and inform the major at the fort.

Neither plan, even if it succeeded in removing the outlaws, was acceptable, for both plans would bring the soldiers to Prairie Wood. None of them wanted that. Murdock would discover the house was still standing and would surely burn it if Newman didn't beat him to it. Then all the activity around the house and the attack would put the family in greater danger. Their horses and the shack would be discovered. Dolly worried that Knowles would get hurt, or at the very least would get a demotion for not being truthful to his captain when he knew the house was not burned. Hannah and Leah worried about the danger to Walking Owl.

Each plan suggested had flaws and risks. What they needed was a plan for the soldiers to capture the Bushwhackers when they were well away from the ranch, perhaps on one of their own raids. They needed a plan that would not risk revealing the friendships of Lieutenant Knowles or Walking Owl and, as a bonus, somehow stop Murdock. Secretly Hannah hoped that in the skirmish Captain Murdock might be eliminated. She couldn't bring herself to think of "killed," as much as the prospect would ease her burden. "Eliminated" was a euphemism that could mean many things.

As they discussed pros and cons, it became clear that whether the Bushwhackers stayed or not that before too long Hank Johnston needed to travel to Fort Scott. After their long separation, the thought of splitting up again was almost unthinkable, but for the whole family to make the trip seemed equally untenable. Their two horses could not carry all of them. Going by wagon would take too long and cause more complications. Walking that far was out of the question for Paul. Besides, how could they explain Paul's presence? With his missing hand, he would be conspicuous. Paul's showing up as himself might put them all in danger if the doctor at Jefferson City had reported he was missing. Learning that he was in the area might cause Murdock to become suspicious and investigate Prairie Wood more closely. Paul posing as Polly Johnston wouldn't work. The major already knew Hank Johnston had no wife.

Their immediate plan was to sit tight and wait. No way would Hannah leave Paul while Newman was around. At least not until Paul was fully recovered. They would wait, hoping the outlaws would leave, not for good, because then they would burn the house, but leave on a raid against the soldiers. When the outlaws rode off, then Hannah and one of the girls would hurry to Fort Scott to warn the major.

The fine December weather continued. Hannah ran her traps, preparing and storing the pelts at the overhang. The girls fished, and dried the flesh by sun during the day and by the fire at night. Hannah kept only a small amount of their precious salt, cornmeal, and flour in the house. The rest she hid with the pelts, for they knew, if Newman discovered them, he would take whatever he wanted.

Hannah fretted at the outlaws' continued inactivity. "Maybe they are settled in for the winter," she said. "Surely they aren't going to waste these nice days if they want to harass the soldiers."

"They are waiting for bad weather," Paul said. "When it's raining, or better yet, snowing, they can more easily strike and get away. The soldiers won't be expecting them under those conditions."

It appeared that Paul was right. After four days of idleness and card playing, when the temperature dropped and clouds gathered, Newman and his band began making arrangements to leave. Dolly ran home from her lookout post to tell the others.

"They're saddling their horses," she exclaimed while catching her breath from running.

"Did they take their bed rolls?" Paul asked.

"I don't know."

"Which way did they go?" Hannah asked, grabbing her with both arms.

"They haven't left yet. I came back as soon as two of the fellows came out and picked up their saddles." Dolly started to cry when she realized she should have stayed longer to learn the outlaws' intentions.

Paul put his good arm around her. "That's all right, Dolly. You did good. Now be very careful and run back to see what they're taking and which way they're going."

For convenience in doing the outdoor chores, and because of the ever-present danger of the outlaws discovering them, Hannah and the girls continued to dress in male clothing. Though Paul didn't wear his disguise all the time, the skirt, blouse, and bonnet were always hanging on a nail ready to put on. As Dolly ran out, Leah helped her father into the clothes. Hannah stuck on her mustache, pulled down to her eyes the stocking cap she wore for warmth in the fireless shack, and glanced around the room for any clue that would give away their real identities. Mazie was stationed outside to listen for any signal from Dolly.

Dolly hadn't been gone five minutes until a bob white call came distinctly even to those in the shack. Immediately after, they heard men's voices and horses coming down the path toward them.

"Leave me alone. Let me go," came Dolly's shrill voice.

"Newman," one of the Bushwhackers called, "look what I found. A lost pup." He had reined his black horse after her, leaned over the saddle to grab her and lifted her up by her coat collar. She was kicking and batting him with her fists.

"Let me go," Dolly screamed.

"One boy out here means there must be adults nearby." Newman immediately signaled his men to spread out to search. "Bring him here, Collins," he said as he eyed the cedar grove that concealed the shack. Giving his men silent directions, he pointed to the grove and sent two men in one direction and two in the other around the swampy area where the shack was hidden.

Collins dismounted and half dragged, half carried the kicking and yelling child to Newman. Still astride his horse, Newman leaned over and slapped her across the face. "Shet up, boy!" he ordered. Dolly didn't make another sound. There was no more need. Her screaming had alerted her family and they could see what was happening. "What's yer name?"

"Bob."

"Bob what?"

"Bob Johnston."

"And what the hell you doin' here spyin' on us?" Newman dismounted and handed his reins to Collins.

Dolly clamped her mouth shut.

"Yer pa in that there shack?" Newman asked cocking his head in its direction.

Dolly nodded.

"He got a gun?"

Dolly kept her mouth closed, her head down.

"'Course he's got a gun," Collins said, tying the two horses to trees and standing behind a trunk big enough to protect himself.   "He jest ain't used it yit. Too many of us."

Newman held Dolly in front of him with his left hand. Holding his revolver in his other hand, he sloshed through the marshy water left from the recent rains in the low bottom around the shack and walked boldly through the trees and brush until he saw the shack.

"Johnston, throw out yer gun and show yerself," he yelled, "or I'll shoot yer brat."

Hannah opened the door, and limping badly, stepped on the log doorstep. She held out both hands to show she had no gun. "Don't harm the boy," she said in her deep voice. "We don't want to shoot you."

"What're you doin' here?"

"Hiding out from Carl Murdock." She said the name with a snarl.

The surprise of hearing Murdock's name, caused Newman to lessen his clutch on Dolly's coat. She wriggled from him and ran to Hannah. "If I'm not mistaken," Hannah said calmly while shielding Dolly with her body, "you fellows are the famous Newman Band. We've heard lots of good things about you. Trying to rid the country of the Feds, aren't you?"

As Hannah intended, Newman eased his grasp on his gun and smiled just briefly at the compliment.

Newman's other men were creeping up on the shack from the back and sides. One man looked into the window. "Hey, Bud, they's a woman and some more young'uns in here."

Collins and the speaker stepped into the shack followed by Newman who pushed Hannah and Dolly in before him. Paul was seated in a chair with the rifle lying untouched on the faded calico apron stretched across his lap. The bonnet was pulled tight around his thin face to hide his blond curls. One long, thick brown braid hung down his back over the unbleached muslin blouse. His good right arm was around Mazie. His left arm lay lifeless in his lap on the rifle, the bandaged stump resting on the worn wooden butt. Leah knelt beside him, holding on to his butternut skirt.

"Here's our gun, mister," Leah said. "We're not going to use it against you. We want to help you lick the Feds."

Newman studied the scene in silence. He motioned Collins to take the rifle. When Paul made no effort to hang on to it, but cringed with pain when the outlaw pulled the rifle from under his wound, Newman said, almost courteously, "Mornin' ma'am."

Paul merely nodded his head to acknowledge Newman's presence, his hollow eyes staring at the outlaw from beneath the wide brim of the bonnet.

"You leave my ma alone," Leah said. "Can't you see she's been through enough from the Yankees already. No cause for her own people to hurt her." She stood up ready to attack Newman if he took a step closer.

"Whoa there, sonny," Newman said. "I ain't gonna hurt her."

Newman turned to Paul and pointed to his crippled arm, "Murdock do that to you?"

Hannah said, "He run us off our place up in Bates County. When we wouldn't leave quick enough, on account of my bum leg and the young'uns, he shot at us. She took a bullet in her hand. Had to cut it off."

"Murdock," Newman spit out the name as if the sound of the word was bile in his mouth. "He killed my pa when I was 'bout this boy's age," Newman pointed to Leah. "And my ma was never again the same."

Collins checked with one of the men who had been scouting around outside. To answer Newman's look, he said, "Nothin' out there."

"How'd you find this place?" he asked Hannah.

"Just lucky. We got away and headed south intending to get to Arkansas and find our oldest son who's with Sterling Price's army. Murdock and his soldiers chased us this way. We hid in the woods, but couldn't get across the river. Then Bob here found this shack. My wife was so sick we couldn't go farther, so we've been here a spell waiting for her to get well enough to move on."

"You didn't walk here with yer limp and her in that shape," Newman said.

"No. We came this far on our horses, but they got away and Murdock's men caught them. We couldn't go farther."

"Humph," Newman said. He was looking around the shack. "Well, you better git a-movin' now. You cain't stay here in our territory." He turned to his man, "Collins, search the place and take all the food they've got, and anything else you can find."

"We haven't much, just what we could carry and scrap together," Hannah said.

For the first time Paul spoke. In an enfeebled high voice he said, "The young'uns will starve."

Newman laughed and stashed into his knapsack the three loaves of bread that were on the table and the salted deer ham that was half left. "Fer a good cause." Then he noticed the container of honey. Even before putting it in with the other food, he stuck his dirty finger into the golden syrup and sucked on it. Then he stomped out the door without discovering under Hannah's jacket, stuck in her belt at the hollow of her back, Walking Owl's pistol that Knowles gave her. "You'uns be gone when we git back, you hear?"

Hannah nodded. "You going after Murdock?"

"One of these days. Time for another army patrol to head out north along the border on the military road. We'll be ready. Maybe he'll be heading it. If not now, later."

"Good." When Newman took a few steps toward his horse, Hannah added, "The recent rise in the river washed out a deep hole in the ford on the far side of the rocky bottom. Your horses will have to swim to get to the south bank."

"Damn," Newman said.

"You'd do better to go back by the house and take the main road to Kansas," Hannah said. "It's almost as quick, and you'll likely run into the patrol on that road."

Newman swore. "Sure don't want to git wet in this weather."

"Can we have back our rifle," Hannah asked. "Pretty dangerous in these parts unarmed."

"That's your problem. We need the rifle." He turned toward the door. "C'mon, men, we've wasted enough time. Let's ride." He jumped onto his horse and spurred him north back toward the house. His men followed, Collins riding Black Laddie, who nickered as he left. Just before Newman rode out of earshot, he yelled back, "Johnston, you and yer family be gone afore we git back. You hear me?"

Chapter 20

"WE MUST hurry," Hannah said. "They plan to be gone a few days because they took their bedrolls."

"Yes," Paul said, "this is the time to warn the major."

"Are you ready to go, Dolly?" Hannah asked.

"It's my turn to go with you," Leah said, shoving Dolly out of the way. "Besides, I'm oldest."

"She got to go to Jefferson City," Dolly said. She pushed Leah back causing her to fall.

"Stop that this minute. Dolly is the one going. The people in town know Bob," Hannah said with the tone of voice that boded no argument. Then she looked at Leah and softened her voice. "Can't you see that it's better Dolly goes?"

When Leah said nothing, Paul took her hand. "Sister, because you're the oldest, Mazie and I need you here."

Dolly made a face at her sister. She was ready to go, though Hannah made her put on another shirt for warmth. Hannah kissed Paul and the other two girls. "I'll try to get back tonight. It may be late. If we don't, don't worry."

"I won't do anything but worry the whole time," Paul said. Even if he were strong enough, he couldn't do this job. It had to be Hannah. She could go more quickly and she had made all the contacts. Whether he liked it or not, he could not resume the family leadership yet.

"She's done it before, Papa," Leah said, patting his arm. "They'll be fine. The outlaws rode out by the main road. Mama will cut across the ford and beat them to Kansas. She won't even run into them." When Paul still looked worried, Leah continued. "Papa, they'll be all right." Then she turned to her mother, "And Mama, so will we."

Hannah smiled at her, "You see, Leah, this is why I want you to stay here? Besides being oldest, you keep calm and think clearly." She pulled out Walking Owl's revolver and held it out to her and Paul. "You should keep this. You may need it more than I. I'll try to trade for another rifle in town."

Paul motioned for Leah to take the Smith & Weston. "Don't worry about us, Mama," Leah repeated. She pointed the revolver toward the door and sighted down it.

"I won't," Hannah promised. She meant it.

"Go," Paul said, urging Hannah outside.

In the cold drizzle, Hannah and Dolly ran along the river bank to reach the bluff overhang for the horses. In less than fifteen minutes they galloped back to the shack where Leah helped them load the pelts and gear. Hannah waved to Paul and Mazie as they watched from the window and then galloped her horse to the ford. The crossing on horseback was easy this time. The river was at its normal eighteen inch depth. With Hannah leading on the gelding, they splashed across the river that had no sign of Hannah's mythical washed-out hole. They climbed the opposite incline and headed west on the faint, rarely used back trail to Fort Scott.

It had been a month since they had been to town, and they did not know the local conditions that often changed rapidly during the war. To avoid attracting notice, as before, they entered the town from the southeast rather than the main street. Even though Hannah wanted to alert the major as quickly as possible, before going to his headquarters, she needed to assess the situation. That was best done at the general store while she did her trading. As it was on her other visits, the town was overrun with soldiers and civilians. She believed there were even more tents than before pitched in vacant lots and in the parade ground at the old Indian frontier fort. Every available building seemed to be occupied with military business. Since the eruption of the border troubles and the outbreak of the war, Fort Scott had again become an important military base. The army was occupying the former barracks, the officers' quarters, post headquarters, and other buildings still remaining from the old fort that several years earlier had been sold for civilian use. In addition to these buildings, soldiers were encamped all over town. Business was booming for civilians.

With so much activity, Hannah was surprised that the storekeeper remembered her name when she piled her pelts on his counter. "Ah, Hank Johnston and young... eh, Bob, I think it is." He examined the fur and told them their value. It wasn't as much as Hannah hoped, but sufficient to buy more meal, ammunition, an old pistol, and some medical supplies, as well as jeans and boots for Paul.

While Dolly stood by the pot-bellied stove to listen to the chatter of several older men who were visiting and playing checkers, Hannah encouraged the talkative merchant to tell the latest news. As Hannah and Dolly packed their purchases on the horses, protecting them from the now spitting snow, they shared the information they heard.

A couple of patrols did leave that morning, one going north and other south to look for Bud Newman's band. The band had been causing much alarm in the town, sometimes raiding farms within sight of the post. The soldiers could never catch them, for the Bushwhackers struck quickly and scattered in all directions before the alarm reached the major. The townsmen welcomed the coming snow storm, for then they believed that Newman would head to Texas for the winter as the other guerrilla bands had already done. Maybe then they would have some peace. Some of the men grumbled that Order No. 11, which was supposed to clear out the Bushwhackers, only made it easier for them to operate. Newman's band was more active than ever. He hit the eastern Kansan farms and towns and then almost magically disappeared into the uninhabited burnt district where there were no loyal citizens to report them. The men around the stove theorized that his band was holed up in some partially burned building no longer visited by the army.

"It's a made-to-order area for outlawry," the storekeeper had said.

"Johnston, you were lucky Newman didn't ambush you on your trip here for your horses and pelts."

"Yeah. I reckon so."

"His last several strikes have been south of town. I figure he's going to concentrate now in the north end of the county. I'd stay clear of that area if I was you."

"I will. Thank you for the warning."

Leaving the horses at the blacksmith to get their feet trimmed and reset their shoes, Hannah and Dolly walked down the main street to the old fort. Snow was falling in earnest, gathering on Dolly's stocking cap and dusting the brim of Hannah hat.

"What're you gonna say?" Dolly whispered as they asked permission to see the major.

Hannah just had time to briefly answer Dolly when she was ushered limping into the post headquarters building across the old parade ground which was now covered with rows of enlisted men's tents. "Hank Johnston from Clinton," the orderly announced.

"Ah yes, Mr. Johnston." The major shook hands. "You were here a while back wanting information about your relative, I recall."

Hannah nodded and started to speak when the major continued, "I'm sorry to tell you that we've had no success in tracing him. There's been no answer to the dispatch I sent to General Ewing's office."

Hannah put up her hand to interrupt him. "I've come on another matter entirely, sir. And I thank you for your efforts on my cousin's behalf, but I have located him myself, in Jefferson City, wounded and almost dead. He is now recuperating in my home in Clinton."

The major looked at him in amazement. "How did you find him when I couldn't through army records?"

"Because there were no records of him. He was taken off a prisoner exchange train on route to Kansas City. He was in a coma for many days, and no one knew who he was. I got word through a friend that a man matching my cousin's description was there. So I went to see and found him."

"Remarkable." The major looked more closely at this man before him. He paid no attention to his small son, who eased out of the room looking for Knowles.

"You said you had another matter to speak to me about?" the major asked.

"Yes, I do. On our way here my son and I just avoided a group of armed riders. We believe them to be guerrillas. They weren't in uniform, though some wore Confederate caps and jackets. We heard them coming toward us and hid until they passed. We heard portions of what they said. They were headed toward the Kansas line north of town. They seemed to have knowledge of an army detail in that vicinity. I believe they intend to ambush it."

The major stood up quickly, motioned his aide to his side in readiness to send an order. "Describe them," he said to Hannah.

Hannah gave careful descriptions of the seven men and their horses and made up a location south of the military zone where she "saw" them.

"That's Newman's band of Bushwhackers. I send out patrols every day looking for them, but haven't heard anything about them in the past few days. With bad weather coming, we hoped they had gone to Texas for the winter." Excusing himself for a moment, he gave his aide some hurried orders. He then shook Hannah's hand again and thanked her for the information. "You heading back today?"

"Yes."

"Then be careful. I'd give you an escort for a few miles, but I need all the men I've got. And if they're going north as you think, your route east should avoid them."

"I understand, sir," Hannah said. "I'll keep an eye open."

The major accompanied Hannah to the door. "Looks like we're in for our first storm."

As Hannah left to rejoin Dolly, some soldiers hurried into the major's headquarters to receive their orders for immediate departure. They quickly mounted and galloped up the north road. None of them was Knowles or Walking Owl. Dolly's face told Hannah that she hadn't found their friends.

Before starting home, Hannah made a final attempt to find them. She said to the friendly sentry, "There was a lieutenant the last time we were here. Tall, thin, very young. He was kind to Bob, my son here, and we hoped to see him again. Is he still at the fort?"

"You probably mean Lieutenant Knowles?"

Hannah said, "Yes, I believe that was his name." Dolly nodded eagerly.

"He's still stationed here. But he's out on duty today. Won't be back 'til night."

"Oh, too bad. And Bob was also taken with a very tall, black-headed scout. Indian, I think?"

"Yep, Walker. He's been away on leave, but he got back a week or so ago. He's on patrol, too."

"What a shame! Do you know when either one will be back?"

"Hard telling. Maybe not today."

"I hope they catch these Bushwhackers." Hannah started to walk away, but turned back, brushed the snow from her shoulders and asked, "Corporal, could you tell this Walker that we asked about him? Hank Johnston. But he probably won't remember us."

"Oh, Walker will. He's got a mind that never forgits nothin'. Why he hasn't lived in this country since he was a young'un, but he remembers each bend in the river and each swell in the prairie."

"Thank you. We'll appreciate it if you tell him, corporal."

"Jest private, sir."

After stopping at a bar to get some hot coffee and a bowl of beans, they returned to the blacksmith to find their horses ready. Then without incident, they retraced their route back to the river and their shack as fast as the horses could go. By the time they forded their river, the snow was coming down fast enough to cover their tracks in just a few minutes. To guide them to the shack, Paul had a candle burning in the window with the comforter draped over the glass so that it let just a shaft of light escape.

After Hannah and Dolly warmed up, showed off their purchases, and told everything that happened to them, Leah expressed the despair of all of them. "But your warning really didn't help. The major already knew Newman was in the area. The patrols were already out, and you got there too late in the day for the reinforcements to help. Newman will come back to our house and find we're still here in the shack. And worse than all, you didn't see the lieutenant or Walker."

Though they didn't know just what they expected from their two soldier friends, not seeing them was the greatest disappointment.

Like her sister, Dolly feared the worst. "And, Papa," she said, hanging on to him, "the lieutenant was probably in that patrol that Newman was after. He could be dead."

"We don't know that," Paul said. "Maybe he was in the other detail—the one that went south. And if he's as good as you say he is, then even if he did come upon Newman, maybe he captured the band."

"Maybe, maybe," Leah said. "That's not good enough."

The constant dangers were taking their tolls on the girls—the trip, worrying about their father, and when finally reaching home, finding a still greater threat to them from the Bushwhackers. Hannah wondered if she had made the right decision to bring them home from the comparative safety of Clinton. "We did what we could, Leah."

She needed to be optimistic for Paul's sake, too. Though much improved, he was still weak. "Let's look on the plus side. I think the trip was a success. We've replaced the rifle with another gun and now have enough supplies to last us a few more weeks. The major will search even harder for Newman now that we've warned him he's still in the area. And, I'm banking on Walker getting my message from that nice sentry. You'll see."

"What good will that do?" Dolly said.

"If Newman doesn't kill him today..." Leah said.

"None of that, Sister," Paul said and held out his right arm for her to come to him. "We can't think like that." He held her with his wounded arm. "Mama is right. The trip was a success. You took care of Mazie and me here, and she and Dolly got home with no trouble, even in the storm."

Her daughters' pessimism spoken aloud was what Hannah was also thinking in spite of Paul's comforting words. This was more than any person should have to endure. Everything depended on her. Straightening her shoulders and lifting her head, she pushed aside the despair about to overcome her to think what more they could do. They couldn't merely sit idle waiting for some possible help from their friends. She knew where Newman planned to operate and where he was headed this morning. And she knew the country better than Newman. Now that the snow had stopped, she might find their trail to track them.

"Let's get some sleep," she said. "And Leah, now it's your turn. Before light, you and I will ride out after Newman ourselves."

"No," Paul said vehemently. "No, you won't. They are seven

desperate men."

Hannah put her arms around him and kissed him. "We won't confront him, my love. He won't even know we're near. We'll just keep track of where he is and maybe hamper him a bit, like make things disappear."

"Like a black horse?" Leah said, brightening up, her gloom gone.

"Something like that."

"And get back the food he took from us?" Mazie asked. Curled on the bed with her arms around Puss, they all supposed she was asleep.

"And..." Leah started to say.

"I get the idea," Paul said. He laid his head against the back of his chair. "What about it, Dolly, dare we let them go."

"Yeah, Papa. Mama is good at tracking and stuff like that. If she knows where they are, the Bushwhackers can't be surprising the soldiers, or coming back here to us."

Outnumbered, Paul said nothing more. Each day since he had reached his own land he had been getting stronger and putting on weight, though he could take only a few steps without resting. His arm was almost healed, but still too tender to put any pressure on it, though he was now exercising it at the shoulder and elbow joints to rebuild his muscles.

By five o'clock the next morning Hannah and Leah rode past their big house on their way to the main road. Although the sky was still overcast, and the temperature in the upper twenties, the snow had stopped with about four inches on the ground. The pre-dawn glow reflecting off the white cover gave enough light for them to follow their familiar trail. By the time they reached the main road, there was enough light to guide them.

The prairie stretched before them for miles. Hidden by the snow cover, the burned areas and grassy ones all looked alike. Occasional stalks or bushes protruded, but as far as they could see, the white blanket covered everything. Hannah chose their route from remembering the contour of the land as the road was indistinguishable from the prairie. When she wasn't sure of her way, she dismounted and dug into the snow until she found the rutted tracks of the road. When she neared the Kansas line, as she was brushing aside the snow, she found fresh horse tracks. She dug more until she found Black Laddie's track, the one with the trailer on the right back shoe.

Each time they crested a rise, Hannah scanned the area. She was following a track that was twenty-four hours old. She didn't want to follow them where the men must have swung wide into Kansas during the day. She was looking for tracks leading back to discover where they had spent the night. She remembered what the men in Fort Scott had said. After striking, the band would scatter, disappearing into the burnt district. She knew they had a rendezvous. To find that was her goal. But if she wasn't careful, she might run into them.

When she traveled a short distance into Kansas without finding any tracks leading back, she tried to recall other roads heading back east and think of likely places the band might hide out. Since there was no alarm yesterday while she was still in town, she knew his strike, if he made one, was far enough north that the news hadn't reached the post. So used to running from soldiers and hiding was she that she could think like Newman, a man on the run. Guessing what he might do and where he might go, she left the road to cut north across the prairie to intersect another east-west road. She remembered a barn in nearby Bates County that was constructed entirely of limestone. It was the talk of the country when it was first built over ten years ago. That barn wouldn't have burned, nor could the soldiers destroy it. Perhaps Newman was using that as his base.

The only tracks they saw in the snow were those of animals—deer, wolf, coyote, 'possum, rabbit, and raccoon. As the sky cleared and the temperature climbed above freezing, the snow began to melt both from the heat of the sun and underneath from the still warm ground. Hannah was glad the snow was melting, for a baby could follow the trail she and Leah made, leaving them vulnerable if she miscalculated and Newman was behind her. But she needed to hurry because any trail the outlaws made after it started snowing would also disappear.

"Mama," Leah said, pointing to the next rise. Her sharp eyes had discerned what Hannah had not yet seen. There coming down the slope were the clear tracks in the snow of several horsemen. The tracks pointed east, away from Kansas. When she examined them, she counted seven different horses, and spotted Laddie's mark among them.

"What does it mean?" Leah asked.

"They weren't in a hurry, an easy jog, and they didn't fear being chased as they made no effort to hide their tracks. There's not much snow in the tracks, showing they were made as the snow was stopping, about dark last night. So there's three possibilities."

When Hannah said nothing more, Leah asked, "What possibilities?"

"Well, their raid into Kansas was a complete success and they were going to their camp to celebrate." When Leah looked aghast, she added. "But that's not likely. They would have more horses and be loaded with their spoils."

"What are the other possibilities?"

"Second, Newman saw the patrol but for some reason, perhaps there were too many soldiers, he calmly retreated without attacking. Or, the most likely, Newman didn't find them and discouraged, they headed back to their hideout. We'll follow the tracks and likely find them. Keep alert."

After about a mile, Hannah guessed that the tracks led to the stone barn she remembered. The sun was high in the sky, burning away most of the snow. Though the tracks led straight across the prairie, Hannah detoured by way of a wooded draw. If the men were still in camp, she didn't want to be a target approaching them. And, the more likely alternative, if they were riding out again, she didn't want to run into them on the road.

Riding slowly and cautiously, she and Leah approached the deserted homestead. As everywhere, the house, small outbuildings, and rail fences were burned. However, the stone barn was untouched. Tying their horses in the draw, they crept up to the barn. There were tracks of boots and hooves everywhere going in all directions where the men and horses had milled around. It was very quiet, but Hannah couldn't determine whether the men were still there.

She watched for half an hour before deciding that they were gone. But to be sure, she held out her hand for Leah to stay put while she circled around to come upon the barn from its back. Reaching the solid rock wall, she listened. Still no sound. Then she moved around to the side to a window opening covered with a board. Through a knot hole in the board, she peered inside. There were no horses nor men, however the bedrolls were still rolled out on the straw-covered floor of the feed way and the remains of their breakfast were still beside the dead ashes of a fire. There remained a half loaf of her bread and some honey left in the jar.

Hannah crept back to Leah. "They're not here but plan to come back."

"What'll we do?"

"Stay here until they come back."

"What'll we do then? Get Laddie?"

Hannah nodded. She was trying to decide the best plan. Getting Black Laddie was her first priority. Somehow she needed to keep them holed up here until she could get word to the major. Perhaps she could make it look like the other horses got away on their own? That was a good idea, but the men would strike out on foot looking for their horses. In time they would probably catch them. How could she assure they would stay here?

"I'm hungry, Mama," Leah said. The breakfast they had eaten was hours ago.

Hannah pulled out the cornbread and dried meat she had packed. Though Leah ate it hungrily, she complained how dry it was. "That's it!" Hannah exclaimed. "The bread!"

"What?" Leah held the cornbread midway to her mouth.

"The bread, Leah. That's how we'll do it. They haven't eaten all of our bread and honey they took." She took a vial from her saddle bag and ran back to the barn, Leah closely following. "Watch for them returning," she said.

Being careful not to disturb anything or leave any tracks, she entered the feed way of the barn where the men had slept. She opened the half-empty honey jar and poured the complete contents of the odorless liquid from the vial into it. To thoroughly mix it in, she broke off a twig from a bush and stirred it. The consistency of the honey did not change, though her dark tonic made the honey less golden.

"They won't notice it," Leah assured her. Hannah agreed for the light in the barn was poor. She set the jar back exactly as it was.

Leah giggled. She knew what was in that vial. Each spring her mother dosed the whole family with just one teaspoon of her powerful spring tonic mixed in a glass of water to "thin the blood." Her concentrated syrup boiled down from a mixture of roots of may apple, sassafras, and burdock and wild cheery and dogwood bark caused those who drank it to make many trips to the outhouse. The large quantity she mixed full strength into the honey would be a powerful purgative, enough that when spread on a slice of bread and eaten would almost make one incapacitated for many hours.

Their horses hidden well away from the barn, Hannah and Leah waited where they could watch from a cover of charred boards from the fire. In mid-afternoon the men returned, riding boldly to the barn, splashing the puddles of water left from the melted snow. They were grumbling to one another about their lack of success.

"Ain't no good here," one of the men grumbled as they dismounted. "It was almost as if them soldiers were waitin' fer us."

"Yeah. More of them than usual. Two days and nothin' to show fer it," Collins said.

"We should'a tried somethin' instead of jest sneakin' off," another said.

Newman's face was set in anger. "And git killed? We'll give it one more try. Tomorrow we'll hit just south of town. They seem to expect us up here. Bigger patrols than usual. So we'll fool 'em and hit clost to home while they's all out lookin' fer us in the wrong place." He laughed in anticipation. "Maybe even hold up the store in town, what'cha say?"

The men laughed, their spirits brightened again. "That's the ticket. Now let's eat. Anything left?"

"Enough fer tonight." They led their mounts to the open shed on the side of the barn, closed the broken-down gate to hold them in, and tossed them some loose hay from the loft.

After waiting to make sure the men wouldn't come out again, Hannah whispered to Leah, "Go back to our horses and stay there until I come. I'll wait until almost dark, and then we'll go home."

Leah nodded and left. An hour later, when the sun was low in the west, Hannah slipped inside the shed with the Bushwhackers's horses. Black Laddie nickered. The other horses were eating their hay and nudging one another, making their usual noises. The men on the other side of the stone partition were talking and laughing loudly. Hannah didn't have much time. She wanted to get away before the effect of the tonic took over and the men would have to come outside to go to the brush. They had eaten up all the bread and honey. Newman even wiped the inside of the honey jar as far as his fingers could reach to get every bit of sweetness. Then he licked his fingers with satisfaction.

Instead of completely opening the gate, Hannah dislodged a couple of boards in the dilapidated gate to make a vee-shaped opening the horses could step over. She wanted it to look like the horses got away on their own. Easily catching Laddie, she made a halter for him from the rope she had tied around her waist just for this purpose. She did not touch the saddles and bridles hanging on pegs against the wall. She carefully led Laddie outside, encouraging him to hop over the section of the gate she had worked on. She quietly led him around to the back of the barn, and then, with the barn as a screen, hurried down the slope.

When she reached the lower level, she ran with him toward the draw where Leah and their two horses waited. A glance backward showed that the other horses were investigating the low place in the gate. One horse jumped over it and started ambling away from the barn to graze. Mounting the gelding, while still leading Laddie, and with Leah following, she rode him at a fast walk for a mile and a half, far enough that the sound of running horses would not carry back to the barn. Then they spurred the horses as fast as they could go across the prairie. The sun to their right was a big red ball just dropping behind the wet and soggy prairie. To their left a full moon was rising.

Chapter 21

ALTHOUGH THE night turned cold as soon as the sun set, neither Hannah nor Leah noticed it. They cut across the prairie to hit the Fort Scott road and turned east toward Prairie Wood. They were jubilant with their success in putting the men out of commission. The knowledge that their friends had not been involved in any fighting eased their worry. Now they must get home, for tomorrow would be soon enough to ride to Fort Scott to tell the major where he could find Newman. Hannah had at least one day, maybe two before the Newman gang would be in any condition to ride. And even if they managed to catch their horses, they would be one horse short. Like birds with clipped wings, Newman and his men were easy targets for the cavalry.

A great load lifted from Hannah. Newman would not return to Prairie Wood, and she wouldn't have to worry about the other outlaws returning from winter headquarters until spring. With cold weather arriving and with neither Bushwhackers nor illegal inhabitants coming back, Murdock should ease up on his patrolling the border counties. She had overheard a soldier at the store brag that there wasn't a single family still living in Bates County from the over six thousand people before Order No. 11. She doubted that there were more than a dozen other families living in all of northern Vernon County. She knew for certain there were no others north of the Osage River. Murdock had done his job well.

From now on, Hannah could devote her time to her family—help Paul fully recover and learn to use his crippled arm, let the girls revert to being themselves, playing, studying, and helping in normal family living. She regretted that the big house would still be off limits, but that was a minor annoyance. They would be warm and reasonably comfortable in the shack.

As they drew near the shack, Leah gave the bob white whistle to signal the family they were back. Immediately light from the opened door of the shack gleamed through the tree trunks and cedar foliage as Dolly ran happily to greet them. Her joy at seeing Black Laddie was almost as great as seeing her mother and sister safely back, for she expected them to return unharmed. She never doubted her mother's ability to accomplish whatever she set out to do. She called back to the shack. "Papa, I told you not to worry so much. Mama even got Black Laddie back." She grabbed Laddie's lead rope, rubbed his head, and ran her fingers through his long, black mane, all the time crooning to him. He nickered softly and rubbed his head against her arm.

Paul stood grinning in the doorway, holding on to Mazie for support. Jumping off her horse, Leah ran to him. He hugged her and let her help him back to the chair. "We found them, Papa. And they won't be going anywhere for awhile. Mama put her spring tonic full strength in the honey jar." He and Mazie both grimaced. They knew the power of Hannah's potions even when diluted. They could only imagine the effect when taken at full potency.

While Leah stayed in the shack to tell their story, Hannah took care of the horses. Without the danger of the Bushwhackers, she could turn them loose in the more convenient paddock. Still excited about her long day's work, she did not notice how weary she was as she rejoined the family or that she swayed slightly from side to side as she walked to the warmth of the fireplace. Paul and the girls were laughing at Hannah's clever use of her herbs as they pictured the distress of Newman and his men.

"And they have no idea that you were there?" Paul asked Hannah.

"No. I was careful not to disturb anything." Hannah crouched down beside Paul who was sitting in their only chair near the fire. He pressed her against him with his good arm. That comforting gesture that he used to use so often when he saw how tired she was after a long day's work allowed her to give in to her fatigue. She was back with Paul. She sat on the floor and rested her arms and head on his leg while he massaged her shoulders with his hand just as he used to do to relax her before going to bed. Hannah luxuriated in the returning strength of his fingers and for the first time was fully aware that the old Paul was with her. She was no longer alone with all the responsibilities.

"The men will probably just think they drank some bad water," Leah said, "and that the horses got loose all on their own."

"And when they can't find Black Laddie, they'll just think he ran off farther than the others, huh?" Dolly asked. The girls were sitting cross-legged on the floor in a semicircle around their parents.

Hannah nodded. "It all went off like clockwork. Nothing to it, huh, Leah?"

Paul cocked his head toward Dolly and shook his head in amazement. "And, Doll Baby, we spent the day worrying about Sister and Mama, when we should have been worrying about the poor Bushwhackers." Everyone laughed at the picture of the ruthless and murderous men helplessly running out frequently to squat in the brush, their bare bottoms exposed to the freezing air. The idea so delighted Dolly that she forgot to frown in disapproval at her father's use of her baby name.

"Listen," Leah said, suddenly sobered. She raised to her knees to hear better.

They all heard what alerted Leah—a soft bob white call north of the shack. Though everyone knew the family was all together, each checked to see if one of them had stepped outside. The call came again, closer this time. Before they had time to rise to their feet, the call was followed right on their doorstep by the hoo, hoo-oo hoo-oo of the great horned owl.

"Walker," Hannah exclaimed, jumping up, all weariness forgotten.

The soft hoot came again as the door opened and the tall Osage ducked his head to enter the room. He held his army cap in his hand.

"I knew you'd come," Leah said, running to him and grabbing one hand while Mazie took the other.

"I hope I didn't startle you, ma'am," he said to Hannah, grinning at the girls and pleased at his reception. "I got your message and figured that you were expecting me."

"Oh, no, I mean, yes, we were expecting you. However, I just got back and we were talking." She walked over to him to invite him in. "Dolly and I missed you in Fort Scott yesterday. We had much to tell you then, but after today we have still more news. Welcome, my friend, sit here by the fire." She indicated the crude bench by the table.

"Yes, welcome," Paul said, trying to stand up.

Walking Owl stepped over to Paul. "Please stay seated, Sergeant Rockfort. You look much better than when I last saw you."

"You know Papa almost died?" Mazie asked. "Mama and Leah stole him out of the hospital and he's almost well now."

"So I can see." Walking Owl shook Paul's hand.

"I don't know how to thank you, sir," Paul said. "I owe you my life."

Walking Owl waved his hand as if dismissing what he had done. "You may not remember, but my father and I visited your father when you were very small."

He didn't elaborate, though the girls were anxious to hear. He had more urgent matters to discuss. Without asking about how Hannah managed to get Paul home, he went immediately to present business. "Mrs. Rockfort, you needed to see me, I gather, or you wouldn't have left the message with the sentry. We've been out all day on a fruitless search for Newman. When my unit turned back to the fort, I came as soon as I could get away."

All of them started at once to talk. When he finally understood what Hannah had done and learned where the outlaw band was holed up, Walking Owl smiled. "Mrs. Rockfort..."

"Hannah," she interrupted. "Please call us Hannah and Paul."

"Hannah." He rolled the name over his tongue so that it sounded regal. With a nod of admiration he said, "You have done what the entire regiment at Fort Scott hasn't been able to do. I remember that stone barn and should have thought of looking there as you did." He turned to the girls and Paul. "Don't worry any more about that band of guerrillas. We'll clear them out tomorrow." He rose to leave.

"Don't go yet," Leah said, grabbing his hand and pulling him back toward the fire.

"No," Paul said, "do sit back and rest awhile. We have much to talk about."

Walking Owl accepted the hot drink and the chunk of yellow cornbread smeared with honey that Dolly put on the table before him.

"I'll guarantee there's no spring tonic in that honey," Paul said as everyone laughed.

"Since there's nothing the patrols can do until morning," Walking Owl said, "and Hannah has immobilized Newman for now, I can stay a bit."

"Is Lieutenant Knowles all right?" Dolly asked.

Walking Owl turned toward her. "He's fine."

"Does he know you came here?"

"No, but if you want, I'll tell him." Dolly smiled and nodded. "I'll not reveal to the major or Captain Murdock who gave me the information about Newman. I won't mention either Rockforts or Johnstons," he said to Hannah. "Only Knowles and I know you're here though neither of us has spoken of it to the other."

"How will you let the officers at the post know about the outlaws if you don't tell them we told you?" Leah asked.

"I'm the company scout. It's my job to find out these things. I'll simple report where the Bushwhackers are. They don't ask how I know. The captain will assume that I've spent the night scouting them out."

Hannah said, "You mislead people by saying very little. So they assume things that aren't so."

"Something like that. I have the reputation of being taciturn. If people come to the wrong conclusions..." He spread out his hands to indicate that was their problem and not his.

"And the girls and I have survived by actually playing different roles and telling one false story after another."

"We each do what succeeds for us."

"But everyone should know that Mama found the outlaws and got them sick," Dolly said.

"No, Dolly," Paul said, "Walker is right. No one must know. Not Newman, not Murdock, not the major. It's much safer for us that the army takes the credit. Remember we aren't even living here."

"People should know," Dolly mumbled.

"I'll know," Walking Owl said to her in his soft deep voice.

"And my lieutenant?" Dolly asked.

The Osage nodded. "I'll tell him when it's the right time." He ate with relish the last bite of the sweetened cornbread. "You're a good cook," he said to Dolly.

"How'd you know I made it?" she asked in amazement.

"Easy. A scout is observant, like a detective. The cornbread is fresh made, but not hot, meaning that it was baked this evening. Your mother and older sister couldn't have made it for they just returned from being gone all day. Mazie here is too small and your father hasn't yet learned to do things with just one hand. So you baked the bread."

Dolly looked at him with awe. Walking Owl grinned and said, "But the telling clue was this fresh dough right here." He pointed to the smeared apron she still wore over her boy's shirt and trousers. Everyone laughed at her dismay when she tore off the apron and threw it on the floor.

While the temperature outside dropped steadily, the family around the fire visited and enjoyed their friend's company. Seated on the floor, Hannah rested her head on Paul's knee on one side while Mazie on the other side held his leg with both arms as if physically holding him with them. Curled up as close to the fire as she could get without scorching her fur, Puss added the right touch of family unity to the scene—a white, black, and yellow splotched ball of fluff. Her eyes were closed, but the tip of her tail flicked now and then to show her awareness.

"Tell us how you found Paul." Hannah asked the question everyone wanted to know.

"Yes, kind friend," Paul said. "tell us how you happened to enter my dreams as I was dying on that army cot."

Walking Owl pushed the bench back so he could lean his back against the rough logs of the shack wall. "As I told the ladies when I was here last," he said, "my enlistment was up. During this war, that doesn't mean I can leave the army, but being an Osage on temporary loan, I asked for a few weeks' leave. The major granted my request on the condition that I re-enlist. I intended to do so anyway."

"So you spent your furlough looking for me?" Paul asked.

"Part of it. After I found you, I did visit my family in Kansas before coming back."

Walking Owl told his story briefly. He first went to General Ewing's army headquarters across the Missouri River from Kansas City and then to the military post just east at Lexington. With his educated English, his military bearing and credentials, and his army name of Walker, no one suspected that he was an Indian. He did not need to tell the family that an Osage would not have been able to see the officials that could help him. Knowing which state militia Paul enlisted in, he learned that in March 1862 Paul, by then with the rank of sergeant, was reported missing at the battle of Pea Ridge down in Arkansas. Since the information did not indicate whether he was killed, was taken prisoner, or simply ran away, Walking Owl sent a telegram to Paul's commanding officer who replied that he didn't know for sure, but believed that Paul was taken prisoner.

Walking Owl sent more telegrams and spoke in person with several officers in the Western Missouri Military District. No one had any further information about Paul. However, he learned that a month earlier a group of wounded Union soldiers came through Kansas City. They were released exchange prisoners from the battles in Arkansas. Most of the men were sent on to Fort Leavenworth in Kansas, where three subsequently died. The rest recovered and were sent home with honorable discharges. Paul's name was not on any of the lists. Since this group was his only lead, Walking Owl searched for the officers in charge. They had all been reassigned elsewhere, but he found one private who was on the train with the unit in charge of the freed prisoners.

"Do you remember a Paul Rockfort among the men?" Walking Owl had asked.

"Naw, I don't remember no names. They was too many of 'em and they was in bad shape. I jest helped 'em on the trip, you know, things like gittin' on the train, givin' 'em their grub, and stuff like that. Sort of an attendant to 'em."

"Did any die on the way?"

"No. As I recall we got here with all we started with." Then he paused. "'Cept two."

"What happened to them?"

"They got so bad we had to leave 'em when we stopped over in Jeff City."

Walking Owl asked the soldier to describe the two men. One of them fit the description Hannah had given him of Paul—tall, thin, with curly blond hair. He especially remembered the curly hair. The Osage then wired the post at Jefferson City. The message he received read, "Two unidentified men STOP very low STOP probably won't survive STOP."

Though it was a slim chance, since this was the only clue he had found and all the facts he knew made it possible that this blond man was Paul, Walking Owl went to Sedalia to ride the newly completed Missouri Pacific Railroad to Jefferson City. The doctor in charge of the troops stationed there confirmed the soldier's story that two men had been left from the troop train. All he knew about their identity was that the aides called them Rocky and Stony. Even before the doctor took him to Paul's bedside, Walking Owl knew it had to be Paul. The nickname, along with the other facts, made a coincidence unlikely. Though the man lying on the cot was burning with fever, tossing in delirium and pain, Walking Owl was sure that it was Paul.

He sat beside him for several hours, talking quietly. He called him by his name, spoke the names of his family, and described the beauty of Prairie Wood Ranch. Almost immediately Paul quieted, though he did not open his eyes, speak, or respond in any other manner. Walking Owl rubbed the sick man's lifeless right hand, hoping for some response there. Although there was no physical reaction, the Osage was sure that some of the things he was saying got through. Paul lay still and for the first time in several days, allowed the aide to feed him spoonfuls of liquid, swallowing willingly.

"I remember," Paul said. There were tears in his eyes. "I thought I was dreaming. I still can't separate out what was real. I couldn't see you through the dense fog and, though I tried, I couldn't open my eyes because of the heavy weights on my eyelids. But I knew there was some..." he struggled for the correct word.

"Fairy godmother?" Mazie said. Her favorite story was the one Leah told her of Cinderella.

"Yes, fairy godmother." Paul cocked his head playfully to one side as he looked at the dark, rugged features of Walking Owl. "You're the most unlikely-looking fairy godmother I've ever seen." Everyone laughed.

Mazie said, "And then you sent the letter to our lieutenant?"

"Yes. But first I stayed a couple of days to see that Rocky was in truth getting better. I didn't want Hannah to travel all that way and find he had just died."

"How'd you happen to think of getting the message to me through Lieutenant Knowles," Hannah asked.

"I knew I could trust him. He and I were both assigned to Captain Murdock's unit about the same time, just before Order Number Eleven. We were not like most of his men who had been with him since before the war. I saw how Knowles hated his job of enforcing the Order. When he discovered how brutal, how fanatic, the captain was against the Missourians he deposed, Knowles asked for a transfer. It wasn't granted."

"I'm glad he wasn't transferred," Dolly said. Everyone agreed.

Walking Owl continued, "So, to compensate and without the captain's knowledge, Knowles did what he could to make things easier for the displaced people. By the time we got to your ranch, both of us had had all we could stomach of his brutality and greed. We admired you, Hannah, and your plucky daughters. I noticed how he took to you and took care of you when he was ordered to move you off your ranch. And, though he thought no one knew about that later business when you got away from him up near Independence, I heard about it from Jenkins, one of his men. The story of finding an empty dress and bonnet instead of his charge and losing all his horses to a woman and little girl was just too good to keep. Jenkins told me, but he was careful the story didn't reach the officers.

"Now the fact that Knowles didn't report your escape was significant, and more dangerous to him that he didn't tell it than if he had. If Murdock learned that he'd kept it secret, he'd have court-martialed him for aiding a Bushwhacker. So I knew I could trust Knowles. I also knew that Hank Johnston would come to the post and that Knowles would give him the message."

"How did you find out that the lieutenant also knew I was Hank Johnston?"

"I guessed it. I don't know how he figured it out, but he knew."

Mazie said, "Dolly was hiding in the grass and talked to him when he came back and found our house wasn't burned."

Walking Owl turned to Dolly in amazement, "You did?"

"I knew he wouldn't tell," Dolly said, "and I was right."

"Yes, we judged him correctly." Walking Owl stood up to leave. He shook Paul's hand. "Once again, Paul, I'm happy to see you so well. You can rest easy now. We'll take care of this Bushwhacker for you." Then he was gone. They didn't hear his horse heading for the ford and the back road toward Fort Scott, but they did hear distinctly from that direction the hoo, hoo-oo, hoo-oo of the great horned owl.

"A remarkable man," Paul said. "I do remember his father and old grandfather stopping by to see my father when I was a boy."

"How'd he learn so much?" Leah asked. "He talks like a professor."

"A few years before your grandfather came here there was a mission school down the river a few miles called Harmony Mission. It was about the first settlement of whites in this region. I think the Osages themselves asked for the school. I figure that Walker went to it. He would have been about the right age."

"Why would the Osages ask to be converted?" Leah asked. She knew she wouldn't ask anyone to change her beliefs.

"They believed that our God had some special magic that made the white man so much more powerful than the Osages," Paul said. "So they surmised that they could send their children to discover what that magic was and then use it for themselves."

Hannah said, "And when they found out that we had no special magic, and after they ceded this area and moved to Kansas back in the late 1820s, they continued their own ways."

"Well, I'm glad Walker is our friend," Mazie said.

"As we all are," Paul said. He sighed with relief, the worry lines on his forehead gone. He turned to the girls with the twinkle in his eye they hadn't seen since his return. "Now, my chickies, it's time to fly up to roost. We can look forward to some days of peace and safety here on Prairie Wood Ranch." After he kissed each child good night, he pulled Hannah to him and gave her a long and ardent kiss on her lips, his first truly amorous display.

With the candle out and the fire banked up to last the night, Hannah nestled up to her husband in their bed while the girls slept on their pallets by the fire. In spite of her weariness, Hannah could not immediately sleep. She kept reliving the day's activities. Images of the stone barn and the Bushwhackers crowded her mind. After so much initiative on her part from all of her recent activities, she knew that she couldn't stay home while the soldiers finished the job. She had to be there, too. Deciding that, she let herself sleep.

Chapter 22

"BUT YOU absolutely mustn't go," Paul said very early the next morning after Hannah sent Dolly after the gelding and was packing her saddlebags.

"I promise I won't participate. I just have to see it through."

"The army will take care of it."

"I can't be sure. I have to know."

Paul's anger showed in his eyes. "That is no place for you."

Hannah was too much in a hurry to argue. Though glad that Paul was well enough to reassert himself, she would not be overruled in this. Holding her anger in check, she said, "I lost my place when Bud Newman took you off. Since then I could not be concerned with what my place was. Yes, Paul, it's my place to see this matter through. I've had to be many things—woman, man, Fed, Reb, or Bushwhacker, whatever was needed. It's been me and me alone to manage the family. Maybe I'll find my place again when this is all over, but for now I'm going."

Paul backed up, holding his hand up in defeat. "At least let Leah go with you."

"No, no reason for her to come. I'm just going to watch. I'll be back before night, I promise." Helpless to prevent her going, Paul stood grim and unyielding as she kissed his cheek. "Don't worry."

In spite of Paul's objections and Leah's begging to go with her, Hannah saddled the gelding when Dolly brought it to the door. She fastened extra coils of rope to the saddle before mounting. She threw a kiss toward the girls gathered beside her. Paul nodded, not to her but to Leah. Leah grabbed her heavy coat and cap and ran around the shack toward the paddock.

Hannah rode as directly as she could the ten miles to the stone barn. The cold was bitter, all the more penetrating for being the first major freeze of the winter. She figured that she would reach the barn well before the soldiers could since she was closer. She was right. At eight-thirty when she tied the gelding in the copse of trees she and Leah had used to hide the horses the day before and crept closer to a patch of tall grass to view the barn, there was no sign of the soldiers.

She settled down to wait and watch. Smoke oozed out of the barn door. One of the men stumbled out and ran, doubled over, toward the patch of brush to his right. She heard groans and curses from inside the barn. The shed where the horses were penned the day before was empty. Presently another man ran to the brush. The first man returned, opened and stepped through the barn door, only to retrace his steps within minutes.

Hannah smiled. Her tonic was doing its work. She estimated several more hours of acute diarrhea before its effects would ease off and allow the men some relief. She listened to the sounds around her, hoping to hear the approach of the cavalry. The prairie was unnaturally quiet. Then a bob white whistle from behind her caused her to hold a gasp that came from her mouth. After a count of ten, the call was repeated and Leah crawled beside her.

"What are you doing here?" Hannah asked in anger. She glanced toward the barn to see if the outlaws had noticed her. Another man running to the brush was the only activity there. Then she turned her angry face to Leah. The girls had always obeyed her even though they often didn't agree. For Leah to flagrantly disobey her bothered her more than any danger the child's arrival might have brought. "I told you to stay home."

"Papa sent me," Leah said. "He said you shouldn't be alone." Leah was almost crying, torn between conflicting orders from her parents. Since her father's wishes were also hers, she had obeyed him by following after her mother.

"You must never disobey me," Hannah said. Her voice was stern.

"But Papa told me..." Leah was crying now.

Hannah relented. It wasn't the child's fault. Hannah had been solely in charge of her small girls for so long, she almost forgot that before the war Paul's voice had been the deciding one. And she forgot that Leah was old enough to make decisions on her own. She decided then to never again put the girls in a position that they had to choose between their parents. And perhaps Paul was right. Since Hannah was determined to be here, it was safer to have someone else with her. She admitted she could use Leah, because she hoped that she could find and catch some of the horses. She needed help to do that.

"I'm sorry, Leah." Hannah hugged the weeping girl and dried her tears. "You are right. You must do what Papa says." She looked at her daughter in admiration. "I didn't hear you following me."

"I stayed far enough back that you couldn't see or hear me. I didn't worry about losing you, for I knew where you'd be."

"You're getting good."

Since everything was still quiet, Hannah explained what they might do. "Newman won't be looking for anyone to ambush him. So, let's see if we can find any of their horses." Leah straightened up, eager to help. "I figure it'll be at least an hour before the soldiers get here."

Keeping well out of earshot of the outlaws and out of their view over the swell of land, Hannah and Leah searched the prairie for signs or sight of the horses. Hannah found a trail that ended by a draw where they saw three of the horses together, contentedly grazing on the dried grasses beside one of the natural pools of water in this area. One of the horses nosed through the skim of ice over the water to drink.

Dismounting, Hannah and Leah each armed themselves with a coil of rope draped over their shoulders and fistfuls of corn they took from a sack hanging from the gelding's saddle horn. They separated to come upon the horses from different angles. Hannah spoke gently to the horses and held out her open palm showing the yellow kernels. She and Leah each easily caught a horse by the mane. Gentle and accustomed to handling, the horses stood still for Hannah to slip a rope over their heads and loop it over their noses for a temporary halter.

Leah held the lead ropes for Hannah to catch the third horse. He had moved away, but stood watching from beyond arm's length. She returned to her gelding for more grain. Crooning to the free horse and holding out her hand, she approached him, enticing him with the feed. As he greedily ate the shelled corn in her right hand, Hannah slipped a rope over his neck.

The horses were well-bred, young, and recently shod with heavy-duty shoes. She expected no less. Bushwhackers used the finest of horses as the rapid get-away after a sortie was their major defense. Their horses were all important.

"Only three more," Leah said.

"We better not try for any more now," Hannah said. She left unspoken that maybe later they might search for the others. "The cavalry will soon be here. We'll have to hide these from Newman as well as the soldiers." She looked around for a suitable place. They had too many horses to hide in the copse she had used before. The cavalry would arrive from the southwest, and since their first action would probably be to surround the barn, Hannah knew she had to get the horses a couple of miles away. Farther than that would be safer.

"After they capture the outlaws, the soldiers will look for the horses, too," Leah said.

"Yes, they certainly will, and Murdock will scour the country, for you can be sure he'll want the horses. Knowing they are loose, he may even send some men to look for them at the same time he's surrounding the barn."

"I bet he will," Leah said anxiously looking over the expanse of prairie. "Where'll we put them? There's no place to hide all of them."

"No, there isn't." Hannah searched the prairie for sight of the soldiers. She laid her ear on the ground to listen. "Nothing yet, but we haven't much time."

"I could take them home," Leah suggested.

"Yes, that's it. You must go right now." Leading two horses with Leah following with the third, Hannah ran back to their own horses they had tied to some saplings growing beside the draw. She refastened more securely the captured horses' rope halters, tied the horses in a string, and handed Leah the lead rope of the first horse. "Now ride as fast as you can home." She pointed down the draw and swung her arm to the east toward a lone mound about the size of a two story house. "Keep to the lower ground out of sight."

Leah nodded. "I wish I could stay, but this is the only way we can keep the horses, isn't it?"

"Yes," Hannah said, glad for this excuse to get Leah out of danger. But she admitted she was glad Leah had come. She needed her to get the horses home. Even if they hadn't needed the animals to rebuild their ranch and for each member of the family to have a mount, the horses would trade for three or four hundred dollars in town—a veritable fortune. It wasn't stealing. Soldiers from both armies and outlaws alike had taken more that this many horses from them. These horses were roaming the prairie with no identifying brands. If they didn't take them, Murdock surely would.

"I'll get them home, Mama. You be careful." Leah hugged her mother and mounted.

"Leah, dear, I'm glad you followed me."

Leah nodded and loped down the draw and around the mound, the outlaws' three horses following in a string behind her.

Left alone, Hannah wondered what to do with her gelding. Since one horse was easier to conceal than five, she gambled that her original copse where Leah found her was as safe a place as any. It also had the advantage of being closer to the barn. She wanted the gelding handy in case she needed to retreat in a hurry. She mounted and returned to the copse.

The dried grasses and brush were enough to hide her, but if a rider came near, he would see the tall horse. If only the horse would lie down. Since she knew he wouldn't do that, she tied him in the lowest spot in the copse. His bay coloring blended in with the dried vegetation, but to help conceal him, she pulled some branches and other debris and fastened them to the gelding's bridle and saddle. He wouldn't pass a close inspection, but from a distance, he wasn't noticeable.

Then she crept within earshot of the barn and lay on her stomach in a patch of tall grass. The sun showed that it was past mid-morning. The army should be here by now! She worried that the effects of the tonic would soon be worked out of the outlaws' systems. If the soldiers didn't hurry, the Newman band would not be so vulnerable.

She lay on the frozen ground watching the Bushwhackers trot between the barn and the brush.

"Hey, Bud," one of them said on returning. "I heerd one of the hosses back there."

"Well, go back and git 'em," Newman said. "He won't go far. I'll help jest as soon as..." The rest of his words were a string of curses.

The man soon returned to the barn leading a horse. He put it in the shed and propped some boards into the hole in the gate to keep him penned in. He groaned and leaned over from the pain in his stomach.

Hannah waited. To help pass the time she began to keep track of the men's trips to the brush. Four men, including Newman, were in the barn, three still in the brush. Another man hurried from the barn, lowering his britches as he went. That left only three in the barn.

"I wonder why I'm not surprised to see you here," came a soft, deep voice crouched in the grass behind her. "Or that you got here before us."

Hannah jerked around, her whole body trembling. Walking Owl was grinning at her. She should be getting used to his appearing without warning. He pointed to the high points in three different locations surrounding the barn. Hannah knew he meant that soldiers were waiting there. Then he pointed to the line of brush the Bushwhackers were frequenting and grinned. "Lieutenant Knowles is picking them up there one by one."

"How long have you been here?" she whispered.

"Me, a couple of hours. The rest just in the last half hour."

"So you know..."

"That you caught three horses? Yes. No one else does. Good work."

"Did Murdock come?"

"Yes. When he heard how Newman was stuck here ripe for the picking, he insisted on heading up the unit. He's very angry. Not one to cross today."

"Two mad fanatics confronting each other. Should be interesting."

They watched another outlaw run out of the barn. "There's only Newman and one other man left in the barn," Hannah said.

Walking Owl nodded. "That's my count, too. It'll soon be over. Keep low," he said and melted back out of her sight into the grass.

Suddenly cavalrymen materialized in a circle around the barn. Each mounted man held a rifle pointed at the barn door leading into the feed way where Newman was. Captain Murdock spurred his bay stallion a few steps in front of the others. He sat rigid surveying the scene below him, his short form reminding Hannah of children playing king on the mountain, daring anyone to depose him. But this arrogant officer's deadly game had begun years ago. The mountain he kept under his control was now expanded by official degree to four counties.

As he sat his horse, he presented a picture of eagerness to begin the bloody slaughter, his mission from God. He glanced around at the men encircling the barn, each one of them also savoring the coming conflict that they couldn't lose. Most of the men had been with him from his Redleg days of the fifties.

Captain Murdock smiled, sent a stream of tobacco juice expertly to his side, and shouted, "Bud Newman, I order you to surrender in the name of God and the cavalry of the United States of America. You are now my prisoner."

In spite of herself, Hannah cringed at hearing again that hated phase.

"Come and git me if you can," Newman yelled. He and the one outlaw still in the barn sent warning shots at Murdock through the partially opened door. Murdock had halted just out of range. "You're a chicken-livered coward," Newman yelled, still not showing himself. "You ain't got the guts to meet a real man. You even need an armed cavalry to give you enough nerve to murder old men in their nightshirts and knock around pregnant women."

"Should'a killed you along with yer border ruffian, slave-lovin', heathen pa," Murdock yelled back. His body was tense with fury, his thin lips pressed tightly together. Amber-colored tobacco juice oozed out of his mouth and dripped off his chin, for he was too obsessed with Newman to take the time to spit.

"Yeah, you should'a," Newman screeched, "'cause now I'm gonna kill you."

The captain sat his horse, his hand up indicating to his men not to fire. He obviously wanted the pleasure of capturing or killing this man himself.

Lieutenant Knowles stepped out of the brush on the captain's left where the circling cavalrymen could all see him. "Hold your fire until my command," he ordered the men who were prepared to fill Newman with bullets the minute he showed himself. The captain nodded agreement, savoring the coming duel he would surely win with his more powerful, long-range rifle against a sick man on foot.

Newman bolted out of the barn, firing his rifle rapidly as he ran toward Murdock. Dodging the warning bullets Murdock fired at him, Newman, still out of range, emptied his gun. Murdock sat patiently, a smug grin on his face as he sighted down his rifle waiting for Newman to get within range. Newman threw his empty rifle aside, jerked as one of Murdock's bullets struck him in his side, but rallying, he pulled out his revolver from a holster. Standing still, his eyes wild and his hair sticking up in all directions from his hatless head, he aimed carefully, ignoring two of Murdock's shots which whizzed past his head. His shot was true. The bullet entered Murdock's chest. Murdock fell off his horse, his last shot going wild. Newman collapsed to the ground.

Still on foot at the line of bushes, Lieutenant Knowles shouted an order that tightened the circle of cavalrymen on the one remaining outlaw. As soon as his leader fell to the ground, the outlaw dropped his rifle without firing and threw up his arms. "Don't shoot," he begged. "Don't shoot."

Knowles and one of the soldiers on foot near the brush ran to Murdock who was already being tended by his aide. Murdock's blank eyes stared at the sky. His face was frozen in a mixture of hate, triumph, and surprise. Amber liquid rolled from the corner of his mouth unchecked across his chin and down to stain the frozen ground. After a brief examination, Lieutenant Knowles walked over to Newman lying in the barnyard muck.

"Is he... ?" Newman gasped as Knowles knelt beside him.

"Yes," Knowles said, "he's dead."

"He murdered... Pa invited him... in from the storm... just shot Pa... claimed to be a preacher." Newman had difficulty saying all the words.

"I know," Knowles said, examining Newman's stomach where the bullet entered. Blood was seeping out over his trousers.

Newman grabbed his stomach and looked at his bloody hands in surprise. "No cause... to kill... Pa," he panted for enough breath to speak.

"No, Newman, no reason."

"He won't kill... no more..."

"No, he won't."

Newman said nothing more.

"Is he dead?" asked the soldier accompanying Knowles.

"Yes, Jenkins, he's dead." Knowles remained kneeling beside the body.

Jenkins stood up and looked around him. The five men captured in the brush were being led out. They were joined by the one that surrendered at the barn. The other cavalrymen were still sitting on their horses, rifles cocked and pointed at the barn but not fired.

"At ease, men," Knowles said. The cavalrymen lowered their guns.

There was admiration in Jenkins' eyes as he said, "Lieutenant, I never seen nothin' like it. You cleaned out the last nest of Bushwhackers without firing a shot." He looked toward the men who were strapping the dead captain to his stallion's back. "'Cept him," he added.

"We were all just obeying his orders not to interfere," Knowles said, raising up. "We had already caught most of Newman's men back in the brush. The fight was between the captain and this poor fellow."

Jenkins scoffed, "Poor? He murdered and robbed as much as the cap..." When he realized what he was saying, he stopped. Since the other men paid no attention to his words, he finished lamely, "Well, he shore done his share of murder."

"Yes, he did. Like many men, this young man wanted an eye for an eye. The border troubles before the war started it and now this full-scale war justifies his actions." Knowles sighed. "But now he's paid for it." He quickly scanned the charred ruins of the farm house and the horizon where the only sign of the former life and human industry on the farm was the stone barn with one horse in its shed. "And so have many innocent people."

A sergeant stood at attention beside him. "Lieutenant, sir, we are waiting for your orders."

The captain's death put Knowles in command. "Sergeant, detail four men to look for the other horses belonging to the Bushwhackers. There should be six more. Then bury this body," he pushed Newman gently with his boot, "and escort these six prisoners to the fort."

"Why don't we just shoot 'em here and save the trouble?"

Knowles whirled on him. "Treat the men as prisoners of war. That's what they are."

"Outlaws and murderers is what they are," the sergeant sneered.

"They work for the Confederacy. As such they are doing nothing more than we are doing in the name of the Union." Knowles's voice was brusque. Then he moderated his tone. "When you have turned the prisoners over to the major, report to me at the post headquarters as soon as you can."

"Yes, sir." His voice showed disapproval.

"Mind you do not mistreat the prisoners." As the sergeant was saluting to carry out his orders, Knowles asked, "Have you seen Walker?"

"No sir, not since out on the trail when he reported to the captain that the Bushwhackers were spending time in the brush." Remembering the plight of the Bushwhackers, he grinned. "Then he rode off again, and I ain't seen him since."

"Very well, dismissed."

The sergeant detailed the men necessary to carry out the lieutenant's orders. The remaining cavalrymen lined up behind Knowles awaiting his order to return to Fort Scott.

"Jenkins, do you know where Walker is?" Knowles asked.

"No one ever knows where that feller is," Jenkins said.

"You're right. He'll show up." A backward glance showed him that the men left behind were going about their duties. Just southeast of the barn from behind a copse of trees he noticed a horseman racing off. Probably one of his men looking for the stray horses. He reined his horse away from the stone barn and gave the order to march without mentioning to Jenkins that the lone horseman wasn't wearing a uniform. The column of soldiers started back up the slope two by two.

Walking Owl materialized beside Knowles leading two of the Bushwhackers horses that got loose. The Osage said nothing, but sat his horse awaiting further instructions. The lieutenant and scout trailed behind the returning cavalrymen. Neither man said anything. Knowles started the conversation.

"Walker, how in the name of all that's holy did you manage to get all of Newman's band sick at just the right time for us to nab them?" When Walking Owl didn't answer, he added, "I know it wasn't just luck that you happened to find them at this opportune time and that their horses just happened to get loose." When Walking Owl continued riding silently without answering, Knowles said, "There's evidence that Newman has been using this barn before but you didn't find him."

"No, I didn't. I admit I should have thought of this barn as a possible hideout."

"So you didn't find it?" Knowles said grinning. Walking Owl still didn't answer. Knowles laughed. Since he would get nothing more by direct questions, he tried another tactic. "You had help?"

Walking Owl's answer was a grin and a glance to the southeast where the lone horseman had disappeared behind the mound.

"I thought so," Knowles said. Then changing the subject, he waved his arm behind him to indicate the prairie and asked, "I don't suppose there are any more of Newman's horses out there?"

"No, the other four got clear away. Lost the tracks over east of here."

"I see." Lieutenant Knowles grinned, but saying nothing more, spurred his horse to catch up to his unit that was about half a mile ahead of him.

THE MOMENT Hannah had heard Knowles give the order to search for the outlaws' missing horses, she crawled back to the copse, removed the brush from her gelding, and walked him as quickly as she could behind the protection of the trees until she reached the mound that she had pointed out to Leah. She followed along the lower land until it gave way to the open prairie. She hoped she was far enough away from the soldiers that she could get on the other side of the rise without being seen. She reached the crest and galloped down the far slope without hearing any shouts or pursuing hoof beats.

She loped the gelding most of the way home, slowing down only long enough to give him short rests. Ten miles never seemed so long, anxious as she was to reach her family and tell them the good news. Or so short. She literally flew home, the frozen sod under her eaten up by the gelding's racing hooves. She didn't need the afternoon December sun to warm her body. Her elation sent hot blood to her finger and toe tips. Free!

Free of both Murdock and Bud Newman. With a bonus of three—no, counting Black Laddie—four horses. She was going home to her husband and children, to their own land. She wanted to hug something. She'd have stopped to hug the gelding, only that would have taken too much time. She settled for patting his neck and talking to him.

Her long range planning and strategy ever since Carl Murdock marched on Prairie Wood last September had succeeded beyond her hopes. She and the girls were able to return to the ranch. She found Paul and returned him to the family and to health. Even this latest conflict between Murdock and Newman ended in her favor. Her part in the Bushwhackers' capture remained secret as she wished. The soldiers would credit young Micah Knowles with their success. He'd probably receive a promotion. Hank Johnston and his boys could disappear into the limbo from which they were fashioned, for the two major enemies of Hannah and Paul Rockfort were dead.

She was sobered with the knowledge that the war was a long way from over and Order No. 11 was still in effect. But with no enemy captain in Fort Scott and no fanatic guerrilla roaming the prairies, they could survive.

The tingle in her toes made her aware of how cold it was getting. Clouds were gathering rapidly in the southwest as the persistent wind blew colder. By the time she turned onto their trail from the main road, flurries of light snow eddied around her. She pulled her hat farther down over her head, turned up her coat collar, and fastened the top button. She held her hands inside her coat against her chest. The gelding needed little guidance or encouragement. He knew the way home.

Nothing in her life ever looked so comforting to her as the scene in the shack. Big logs blazed in the fire, while the kettle spewed out its cloud of steam. Pleasant aromas were coming from the pots hanging over the fire. On the bed Mazie and Dolly were curled up on either side of their father, listening intently to him reading to them. Leah, on the floor with her side to the fire, leaned against the bed, stroking Puss.

At Hannah's quiet entrance, they all looked up surprised. She shook the snow from the brim of the old felt hat and hung it on the peg by the door. She ripped off the mustache and let the great coat drop to the floor. Startled into silence more by her actions than her sudden appearance, her family watched her walk to the chest, open the lid, and pull out a dress. She held it up to her, modeling it as if asking them if it still looked good on her. Her heavy, mud-encased boots stuck out from under the hem.

"Hank Johnston is no more," she said, looking straight at Paul. "Hannah can come back." She ran her fingers through her matted-down hair that was already growing out of its mannish look. "And we can all live again." She smiled, showing the gap in her lower teeth. This time she did not run her tongue over the space as she usually did.

Paul started to get up, but instead grinned, patted with his crippled arm a spot on the bed beside him for her to sit, and holding out his right arm to her, said, "I'm reading the girls a once-upon-a-time story where a beautiful young princess is imprisoned by an evil king. Her handsome prince rescues her and they live happily ever after. But, girls, your mother has a much better right-at-this-time story of a beautiful queen mother also imprisoned but by two evil soldiers. In Mama's story, this brave mother, with her own brand of magic, saves not only herself, but her wounded, but still handsome, king and her three beautiful little princesses."

"That's a story about us," Mazie said, "and we are the beautiful princesses, aren't we, Papa?"

"Of course it is, you silly," Dolly said. "Tell us what happened, Mama."

"Did the soldiers get Newman?"

"Did my lieutenant get hurt?"

"Is Walker all right?"

To her rapt audience Hannah described with careful detail everything that happened. Puss jumped onto her lap and climbed up her shirt to her shoulder. Draping herself around her neck, the cat purred her contentment. There was a pounding on the roof as it began to sleet. The fire hissed as some of the frozen pellets fell down the chimney. The wind howled around the shack and found its way into some of the cracks, but the family didn't notice. They almost welcomed the coming isolation of winter, for they were prepared and safe from human assault.

Chapter 23

AFTER THE coldest winter either Hannah or Paul could remember, the weather moderated. Normally the few snowfalls of each winter would melt during the intervening periods of above-freezing weather before the next cold spell. Beginning with the storm in mid-December, the winter of 1863-1864 had snow and cold that persisted well into February. Under the snow cover the renewing grasses, seeped in moisture, had lain dormant awaiting the sun. Late in February the snow cover vanished into rivulets of olive-colored water the soggy ground could not absorb. Tiny streams joined larger ones and, like an intricate, winding network of veins and arteries, they carried away the remaining sooty evidence of the wholesale burning during the autumn. The flourescent green grass deepened and lost its yellow tint when it resumed its yearly assignment of growing to waist height by summer.

Urged by the nearness of spring, Hannah and Paul saddled the gelding and Black Laddie to ride over the ranch. Fully recovered in strength, Paul did not wait for Hannah to help him, but threw his saddle over Laddie with his right arm, using his left to steady it.

"I can bridle him," he said, pushing Hannah away when she started to slip the bit into Laddie's mouth. He had been practicing with the hook the blacksmith in Fort Scott fashioned for him. Using soft deer hide, Hannah had sewn a holder for the hook that capped his stump and extended in a sleeve-like tube that fit his arm snugly. Now that the flesh over the stump was no longer tender, Paul could exert pressure on the hook to hold and lift things. Once again he had the use of two arms.

Hannah stood back ready to steady Laddie if necessary. Twice she started to reach out to him when he snorted and reared back, but refrained. Paul spoke soothingly to the horse, showing him the strange hook. He laid it flat on Laddie's forehead and rubbed it gently back and forth so he wouldn't be afraid of it. He gently scratched Laddie's neck with its blunt point and used the hook to comb out a tangle in his mane. Then Paul slipped the brow band over the hook to hold it steady while he forced the bit between Laddie's teeth with his good right hand. The bit in place, Paul slipped the head piece over the horse's ears and buckled the strap in place.

Grinning with his success, Paul then tossed his pad and saddle over Laddie's back, tightened and clinched the girth straps, and holding to the saddle horn, jiggled the saddle to see if it was tight enough. It was. With a sigh of contentment, he grabbed the horn with his right hand, put his right foot into the stirrup and swung into the seat. Paul's elation at being mounted again showed as he clamped his knees against the saddle leather, as he held the reins together in his right hand, and as he surveyed the woods and river from his higher perch on the horse.

"Let's ride, Laddie," he said gleefully and neck-reined the horse toward the path out of the woods onto the prairie. Hannah mounted the gelding and followed Laddie's easy slow pace.

DURING THE weeks following the double shootings of Carl Murdock and Bud Newman, the Rockforts had spent a quiet winter. They were isolated both by the severe weather and by choice. They needed time to become re-acquainted after such a long absence. They needed time to establish new working relationships. Paul wasn't the only one who had changed. The experiences of the past two years had changed Hannah and the girls. Although they consciously tried, they could not revert back to the earlier system of Paul's undisputed leadership of the family and ranch. The girls, even Mazie, had assumed so much responsibility that though still children, they could not be excluded from family decisions. Hannah had long been in charge of the family, and during the last few weeks while he was recovering, that included Paul. Since the family depended on her for their very lives, she could not revert to her former position.

Paul's adjustment was the hardest to make. Hannah and the girls continued as they had been doing, with minor concessions to Paul, while he had to adapt to the more democratic partnership as he reestablished his place of authority in the family. But everyone agreed, his priority was to recover both physically and mentally. Though regaining his physical abilities seemed the most difficult, in some ways it was the easiest. All he needed was time to heal and practice to acquire agility with his crippled arm. The inactive winter months gave them time. The girls helped Hannah work with him daily in exercises and drills to recoup his strength and to learn how to use his left arm to be completely independent.

His mental recovery was slower. Throughout his ordeal in the army—the fighting, his capture and experience in the prison camp, loss of his hand, and the illness relating to it—Paul's constant hope was returning to his family, his land, and his life. When he found himself back home, his family had grown and become independent, much changed from his idealized memory, his land was ravaged, and his life became one of hiding and deceit just to survive. Accepting his new life and status also took time.

Although the children grew restless during the winter idleness in the crowded shack, Paul and Hannah welcomed the storms that kept them confined. Excluding the daily chores of wood gathering, fishing, and hunting for meat, Hannah's main job was running the trap lines. While she was out, Paul became reacquainted with his girls by taking the major share of teaching them their lessons.

Hannah and the children put aside the male clothing. Dolly hated the drab britches she had to wear. She gleefully put on her dresses and petticoats, and she rejoiced as her hair grew shoulder length and began to reform into ringlets. Mazie didn't care what she wore, but Hannah and Leah preferred men's clothing for outdoor work.

In spite of Paul's protests, they wore trousers when running the trap lines on the river or doing other heavy outdoor work in the cold. When Paul objected that it wasn't seemly, Hannah won her point by explaining how she was warmer and was less tired at the end of the day after wearing men's clothes that were more suited to the work she was doing. The long skirts hampered her movements, sometimes even causing her to fall. What finally convinced Paul to their way of thinking was his experiences when he had been forced to put on Hannah's clothes to hide his identity from Bud Newman. At those times, his distaste of wearing female clothes wasn't the only reason he took them off the moment it was safe to do so. They were uncomfortable. However, even when recognizing Hannah's reasons, he still frowned in disapproval at his wife and eldest daughter looking like men. So they compromised. Since Hank Johnston's existence perished with Murdock and Newman, Hannah wore trousers only when necessary for outdoor work. They compromised on this major difference between them.

The family made no additional trips to Fort Scott. Their only visitor was Walking Owl who dropped by soon after the duel at the stone barn.

"Thank you, Walker, for not telling the major my part in locating Newman," Hannah had said.

"Lieutenant Knowles got the credit," Walking Owl said.

"Good. That's fine, but you deserved credit, too."

"I was the scout and I 'found' them, so to speak. That's what I do."

"Did my lieutenant know what Mama did?" Dolly asked. "You know, about the tonic in the honey and fixing it so the horses got away?"

Walking Owl hesitated. "After I left here on my last visit, I reported to Captain Murdock where the Newman band was camped and that he and his men all seemed to have the trots. That's all I told him." Everyone grinned for they knew what "the trots" meant—frequent trips to an outhouse, or the bushes, because of diarrhea. "Lieutenant Knowles guessed that your mother had a hand in it when I told him in private that Newman hid out for a time in your house."

"And my lieutenant couldn't tell that to the captain 'cause then he'd have to tell that the house wasn't burned down and we were back here," Dolly said.

"Right. Then lots of people would have gotten into trouble," Walking Owl said. He paused, looked at Hannah, and continued, "And the lieutenant knew for sure after the shooting when he glimpsed you riding away over the hill on your bay."

"I guess I'm not as skilled as you, yet," Hannah said.

"But you should have got the credit, Walker, not the lieutenant," Leah said.

"No, I don't want any attention paid to me," Walking Owl said. "I'm like a shadow. I'm there, but no one notices me."

"I do," Leah said.

"Because you're special. Most people don't and that's the way I want it. But Knowles deserved the full credit for what happened once we got there. He gave the orders to quietly surround the place and pick the men off in the bush one by one. The captain was in one of his rages. He couldn't think of anything except killing Newman. Even his loyal followers from his Kansas Redleg days before the war looked to the lieutenant when the captain was like that. Knowles had instructed the men not to fire until he gave the order. He was the one that contrived it so that instead of a massacre, it became a duel between the captain and Newman. Between two men blinded by power, revenge, and hate."

"Newman learned it as a boy when he was Murdock's victim," Paul said.

Walking Owl sighed. "I know his story." All at once he looked his age as worry lines creased his face. "Why can't men understand that defying the law and using force to get what they want only perpetuates greed, hatred, and murder. Since we can't change what's done, we must go forward from there, not compound the problem with equal brutality."

The Rockforts knew their friend was thinking about his tribe's policy of ceding their land and moving to Kansas, peacefully accepting the greater power of the United States and remaining friends in order for their culture to survive. Just over thirty years before, the land of Prairie Wood Ranch was part of the huge area controlled by the Osages before the arrival of American settlers, like Paul's and Hannah's parents. The Osages' main village used to be only twenty miles straight east of them.

But that was long ago. Just as Hannah switched easily from female to male roles, Walking Owl existed in both the white and Indian worlds. Shrugging off his philosophical thoughts, he turned to Dolly with a smile. "Because of what he did at the stone barn, your lieutenant is now Captain Knowles." Dolly clapped her hands in joy as Walking Owl continued with merriment in his eyes, "Even though he gets a lot of ribbing about winning the Battle of the Trots. The men respect him. They know that if they had made a frontal attack, had barged in on the Bushwhackers as was Murdock's practice, many of them would have been killed from Newman's sharpshooters barricaded behind the stone walls."

HANNAH AND Paul spent the mild February day riding over all parts of their thousand acres. For the first time since his forced conscription into the Confederate Army by young Newman, Paul rode over many parts of the ranch. Its emptiness overcame him. Instead of the herds of cattle, there was only an occasional deer. In the distance where Philip Newman's house once stood on a small mound surrounded by young trees, there was standing only the stone chimney. No other of their former neighbors' places were close enough to see, but he knew that those buildings were also destroyed. Even across the river that was not included in the Order, their neighbors had all fled from the armies months before Order No. 11 was issued. Hannah estimated that there was not another family living north, south or east within twenty miles of them. They were very much alone.

The land was empty and deserted, not the way is was when their parents settled here thirty years ago when the land was wild, open, and untouched except for the hunting and trapping of the Osages. But now raped and burned, the land lay empty with only remnants from the settlers such as half-burnt fence rails, broken wagon spokes, and sandstone slabs laid carefully in rectangular order without the upper structure they were intended to support.

Like! Walking Owl, they didn't dwell on the past. As their parents did, they would need to build again with nothing but the land. It was still theirs. When the war was over people would return. There would again be towns, and churches, and schools. Democratic law and order would return. There would again be neighborliness so that they could help a sick neighbor without witnessing a murder. With returning normality, they would build up their herd and raise hogs. Renewed health and the spring-like weather filled Paul with ambition and ideas. He chatted with Hannah, telling his ideas and asking for her thoughts and opinions.

Hannah smiled in satisfaction at this equal give and take. Before the war Paul did not consult her. He simply made the decisions and told her what they were. Her shorter hair and the trousers she was wearing were not the only physical marks of change. She sat upright and confident in her western saddle. A strand of brown hair fell into her face. Unconsciously she pushed it back into her bonnet. In the warm sunshine, she removed her heavy shawl, wound it up into a neat bundle, and tied it behind the saddle seat. Her linsey-woolsy blouse was enough protection. Together they planned the broad future of "beyond the war." And more immediate, they planned what they would do this spring.

Back at the house they dismounted to accessed the damage. They planned to build a log shed to start with to replace the barn, and later construct an even larger barn than the one that burned. They would plant as much corn this spring as they could prepare the land. With the extra horses from Newman's band, they might break a few more acres, but they wanted to keep most of the land in prairie for cattle. When they took their winter's catch of pelts to Fort Scott, they would trade for more seed, buy a couple of sows, and a few head of cattle to form the nucleus of the herd they wanted. They both laughed when the dominicker hen ran squawking ahead of them.

"And we'll get some more chickens, little Dominicker, so you won't be alone," Hannah said.

Paul hugged her. "Most definitely. And a new dog to replace little Poco Leah told me about."

Arm in arm they watched the little hen scurry out of sight in the rubble from the barn. A couple of male rabbits chased each other, fighting for a hidden doe Hannah and Paul couldn't see.

Hannah kissed Paul's cheek. "We aren't the only ones that have returned," she said, pointing to the yard where many robins were on the ground and in the maple tree in front.

Full of optimism, they returned to the shack. Walking Owl's horse was tied on the one dry spot near the door. Leah and Dolly opened the door and yelled out, "Walker's here. Order Number Eleven has been canceled!"

The Osage met them at the door nodding his head and smiling. "That's right," he said. "The Order was revoked February 18. The District of the Border is abolished. There's a new commander with headquarters at Independence, and General Ewing has been ordered to Pilot Knob over in southeastern Missouri."

"And Walker says we can live in our house again," Leah said.

"Yes, that's right," Walking Owl assured Hannah. "There's no restrictions to keep people from coming back."

Paul and Hannah hugged each other. The girls joined in, Leah pulling in Walking Owl so that the three adults and three children stood in the middle of the shack hugging one another and laughing. Paul picked up Mazie and danced around the room with her. Hannah did a doe-si-doe with Dolly, and Leah held both of Walking Owl's hands as they circled each other. In the crowded shack the people bumped into one another. After expressing their jubilation, the adults sat on the bench and chair while the girls sat on the floor.

Hannah said to their friend. "Walker, you are again the bearer of good news. We thank you for coming here to tell us."

"You would have heard it soon."

"People will come back again," Leah said, thinking of friends, school, and church.

"Beulah and Virgil can come home," Dolly said.

"I don't think they will, Dolly. They told me they would stay in Clinton."

Dolly frowned. She was looking forward to having friends to play with again.

Walking Owl said, "People already here, like you, can live openly again, but I doubt that many will come back for awhile."

"Why not?" Dolly asked, disappointed.

"Well, the war is not over. And now that winter is almost over, Bushwhackers will probably come back. Lieutenant, er, Captain Knowles has increased his patrols to watch for them. And there's always the possibility of renewed military action in this area."

The girls sat back down, no longer wanting to celebrate.

"What's the news of the war?" Paul asked. "We've been so isolated here we almost forgot about it."

"The news is mostly good. It's going our way now. After Grant's victory at Vicksburg, he's taking the offensive in eastern Tennessee. The Confederates are losing on all fronts."

"Then we won't have to worry about the Confederate Army around here anymore," Hannah signed in relief.

"We hope not, but I wouldn't discount it," Walking Owl said. "General Price hasn't forgotten that he wants Missouri. The talk at the post is that he may try another swing through the state, if nothing more than to force General Grant to divert some troops back here and relieve the pressure on Lee."

"And if Price does, he'll likely come this way?" Paul said.

Walking Owl nodded. "To the military arsenals either at Jefferson Barracks in eastern Missouri or at Kansas City and Lexington here in the west. They would be obvious targets for him. Maybe both."

"I think that is a possibility," Paul said. "When I was with Price he was keen on Missouri going with the South. I doubt that he's given that up."

"Yes, that's what the talk is at the post."

The group was silent for a few minutes. Hannah was thinking that the plans she and Paul just made may be premature. If the armies came through again and raided their place, she doubted that either she or Paul could spring back again. Maybe they should hold off longer on restocking the ranch.

"How much longer do you think the war will last?" she asked.

Walking Owl shook his head. "Hard to say. No one thought it would last this long. But we are getting stronger while Lee has nothing more to give and no hope of help from Europe. Another year, maybe."

"The South won't give up," Paul said. "It'll probably last more than a year."

Hannah sighed. "We can hold on that long. The girls and I know how to survive, don't we, children?" Sobered by the thought that they could not yet live normal lives, they nodded.

"But at least the Union Army is no longer after us and we can live in our house," Hannah said, cheerfully.

"That's right," Walking Owl said, "and the patrols will now be out to protect you from Bushwhackers. We'll warn you when we can." He pulled out some papers and handed them to Paul. "Captain Knowles and I encouraged the major to send word to Missouri military headquarters to get the record correct about Sergeant Paul Rockfort. He agreed because of Hank Johnston's inquiries and his subsequent information that you," he pointed to Paul, "were located and recovering. It is now on the official records that you were captured at Pea Ridge, participated in a prisoner exchange, but because of your wound and illness were left at Jefferson City. The doctor there signed a paper stating that this here-to-fore unknown soldier known only as Rocky, now identified as Paul Rockfort, left his barracks in the care of his wife and cousin Hank Johnston who then took him to Clinton to recover."

"How did you get him to sign that?" Hannah asked. "He seemed adamant that Paul couldn't leave until officially released."

"He's a doctor first. He was glad to learn that Paul recovered, so he didn't worry about army protocol."

"Once again I see your hand in this," Hannah said.

"Actually, Captain Knowles convinced the major. He has the rank." Walking Owl then pointed to one paper that Paul was holding. "That paper, dated February 6, 1864, is your official honorable discharge from the army because of injury and illness."

Paul looked from the papers to Walking Owl and to his wife. "I think that Hank and I should make a trip to Fort Scott to thank the major in person."

"No," Hannah said, "Hank is gone. He has no further business at the post now that his cousin has been found. Sergeant Rockfort's wife, Hannah, can join her husband in thanking him."

Leah took hold of Walking Owl's hand. She knew that the officers would not have acted without the Osage's suggestions. "Walker, why have you helped us so much? You didn't even know us."

"Well," he laughed, and then became serious, "as I said before, I admired you clever girls and your spunky mother. She reminded me of a woman I knew. I didn't want another good family deposed from this land. And when the war is over and people start flocking in to grab what they can of this rich land, I want someone here who remembers that this was first the land of the mighty Osages. I want someone here who will treasure their mother earth and care for it as my people did for winters without number."

"You sound like an Indian," Dolly said.

"Silly, he is an Indian," Leah scoffed.

"An Osage," Walking Owl said proudly.

"You can be sure that we love this land," Paul said. Everyone nodded agreement.

Hannah asked, "Who was the woman I reminded you of?"

"My mother. The way you marched away from your home was like I remember her taking my brothers and me when we relocated to Kansas."

"Only she knew she could never come back," Hannah said sadly.

"Yes, but she wasn't alone. She had her whole family with her, and it was the decision of the tribe to leave. She knew it meant our being able to continue our way of life, just as you knew when you left here that you were going to continue yours."

"But you don't follow the Osage way, being in the army and all," Leah said.

"Sometimes I do. Right now it seems more important to be a white man to help get this war over. Then we, Osages and Whites, can resume living. I concentrate on the best each culture has to offer and forget the bad."

Paul was listening intently to the conversation. "Walker, until now I didn't know of any way my family could repay you. Hannah and I were just today planning what we want to do with our ranch. I'm sure she will agree with me that we will keep the land in prairie grass and woods as much as possible in its natural state as a memorial to your people and you."

Walking Owl smiled.

Hannah said, "And we need to learn to put personal greed and hatred aside." She stood up. "Leah, let's fix Walker a meal in celebration of our friendship. One step toward this new world of ours is completed. Order Number Eleven is no more, and the burnt district is greening up for spring."

Historical Afterward

AFTER LEAVING the District of the Border, Union General Thomas Ewing was stationed at Fort Davidson, an earthen fort at Pilot Knob in southeastern Missouri. In September 1864, seven months after the end of events of this novel, Confederate General Sterling Price marched twelve thousand men into Missouri, intending to surprise and capture Jefferson Barracks at St. Louis. This was a last ditch attempt to regain Missouri and to divert some of Grant's forces from the East. Price came by Fort Davidson on his way.

Though overwhelmingly outnumbered, in one of the bloodiest battles of the Civil War, Ewing held the Confederates off until dark. Most of the casualties were to Price's poorly armed and clothed men. During the night, Ewing blew up his ammunition stores within the fort and in a daring move, escaped with all his men and portable equipment.

Instead of going to St. Louis as planned, Price cut across Missouri to Jefferson City and finally to Kansas City, where he was soundly defeated at the Battle of Westport. Once again Price's Confederate Army retreated south along the Missouri-Kansas border, pursued by the Union forces.

Ewing was a capable and brave soldier. His mistake was one of judgment in issuing Order No. 11. The noted artist and journalist, George Caleb Bingham, who was on his staff, had tried to dissuade Ewing from making the order. Bingham saw first hand the results of the Order and declared that he would ruin Ewing. His two widely published paintings of the forced evictions and killings of women and children, as well as the many articles he wrote, finally put enough pressure on the authorities to force Ewing to rescind the Order. But it was too late; the damage had been done to the Missouri inhabitants, the area, and to Ewing's future.

Ewing had political ambitions. After the war when he ran for governor from Ohio, his native state, Bingham used his journalistic influence against Ewing, retelling the horrors of what happened in Missouri. Ewing lost the race by a narrow margin. Had he won, with the governorship of Ohio behind him, he probably would have run for President of the United States.

Though Order No. 11 is little known in United States history, its results were far-reaching. In Missouri, even when the Order was revoked, people did not return to the area until the war's end. Many never returned. No one received any restitution for crops, stock, or property destroyed and taken.

The border disputes over Kansas statehood were a prelude to the Civil War. The Bushwhacker activities of southern soldiers and sympathizers and the equally brutal actions sanctioned by the Union Army kept the unrest alive for years, so that outlawry such as the Younger Gang and the James Brothers continued long after the war was over. All of those troubles occurred in the rich prairie lands of the western tier of counties in Missouri, which because of Order No. 11, became dubbed the Burnt District.

The End